CRITICS PRAISE ROSE LERNER'S DEBUT *IN FOR A PENNY*

"Georgette Heyer, watch out! Rose Lerner serves up a sprightly and splendid Regency romance."
—Lauren Willig, author of
The Secret History of the Pink Carnation

"The grit of Dickens and the true-to-life, breathing characters of Austen. Rose Lerner is a new star in the Regency firmament."
—Judith Laik, author of *The Lady Is Mine*

"As a debut Regency novel, *In for a Penny* really hits the mark. Unlike so many other Regency novels, this one really dealt with the grit of day-to-day life for a lord and lady. I was drawn into the story from page one . . . beautifully drawn characters in a richly painted setting."
—Book Binge

"Rich in subtle characterization, deftly seasoned with danger, and tempered with just the right dash of tart wit and historical grit, Lerner's historical romance is to be savored."
—*Booklist*

"Not infrequently, I find myself read: novels with heart. However, finding a br  s a first novel that not only has life, l   ng characters, and attention to the s   . *In for a Penny* is just such a book, a   ll About Romance

"Lerner's prose is ap   the era, yet updated enough to delight today's reader. Her debut's quick pace and smart dialogue are perfect as the adventure and passion unfold."
—*RT Book Reviews*

"*In for a Penny* is a wonderful, unusual, well-written Regency romance that is easily one of the best of the year so far. Leisure has a real gem in Rose Lerner and I can't wait for her next release."
—The Romance Reader

"*In for a Penny* is a charming and original Regency that will make you wish a man like Nev would stroll through your front door."
—Eloisa James, Barnes and Noble review columnist

Other books by Rose Lerner:

IN FOR A PENNY

ROSE LERNER

A Lily Among Thorns

Dorchester
Publishing

For Masha, the first to be enthusiastic about this book, and the best friend I could have asked for during the worst time in my life.

DORCHESTER PUBLISHING

Published by

Dorchester Publishing Co., Inc.
200 Madison Avenue
New York, NY 10016

ISBN 13: 978-1-4285-1176-7
E-ISBN: 978-1-4285-0989-4

First Dorchester Publishing, Co., Inc. edition: September 2011

The "DP" logo is the property of Dorchester Publishing Co., Inc.

Printed in the United States of America.

Visit us online at www.dorchesterpub.com.

ACKNOWLEDGMENTS

This book had two editors. I'd like to thank the first, Leah Hultenschmidt, for caring so much about this book's success and for spotting exactly what it was missing, and the second, Chris Keeslar, for being kind and welcoming to an author nervous about change. I'd like to thank Tanya at Dorchester's marketing department for making things much less scary for a newbie author, and Renee in production for making my books so pretty. I'd also like to thank my fabulous copyeditor, Kim Runciman, for asking good questions and saving me from many embarrassing errors and anachronisms.

Thank you, of course, to my agent, Kevan Lyon, for being unfailingly even-keeled and good at your job, and just all-around awesome.

Thank you to this book's first readers and cheerleaders: Matti Klock, Dina Aronzon, Greg Holt, Steve Holt, and my mother, who all provided key pieces and made me believe the story had a future. Thank you to more recent ones: Gwen Mitchell for helping get the first three chapters in shape, Sonia Portnoy-Leemon for getting me through that nerve-racking time between submission and the revision letter, and Kate Addison for helpful feedback, helpful squee, and explaining why Serena couldn't be eating a hot cross bun.

Thank you to my fellow members of the Greater Seattle RWA for your advice, support, and friendship, and for putting on an amazing conference every year. I can't even begin to list the ways you've helped me. Thank you to all my friends and family for believing in me, for being fabulous, funny, and generous, and for making my heart grow three sizes on a regular basis.

And, finally and always, thanks to the Demimondaines: Alyssa Everett, Karen Dobbins, Vonnie Hughes, and especially Susanna Fraser, for seeing this book through several drafts and more than one identity crisis. I am so lucky to belong to a group of not just talented writers and wonderful friends, but also talented critiquers, who understand how a book fits together under its skin, and week after week tell me the hard truth kindly and tactfully.

Prologue

September 29, 1809

Solomon Hathaway was drunk. He was drunk, and he didn't want to go to a brothel. On the other hand, Mme Deveraux's front steps were cold and windy. "'The mouth of strange women is a deep pit: he that is abhorred of the Lord shall fall therein,'" he said, and clung to the wrought-iron railing.

Ashton and Braithwaite shared a disbelieving look. "Is the parson's son quoting Scripture again?" said Ashton.

"Don't—don't call me that."

"D'you prefer 'tailor's nephew'?" Braithwaite asked. Drink always made him cruel.

Ashton snickered. "Leave off. It's normal for a virgin to be nervous."

Solomon straightened. The motion made his head whirl. "I'm going back to the hotel."

Ashton grabbed his sleeve. "Oh, don't take it like that, Hathaway. Come along, this is the best house in London! This is why we came up to town on quarter day, isn't it? To spend our blunt on things we can't get in Cambridge?"

"Yes . . ." Solomon was already regretting it. He should have gone home and let Elijah lecture him on obscure French poetry instead. "I was going to buy a cal—calor—calorimeter."

"A what?"

"It measures heat. Lavoisier disproved the existence of phlogiston with it. No, wait—I'm getting my experiments confused—"

Braithwaite pushed open the door of the brothel. "He's just

making up words now. I'm going in. If Hathaway wants to turn twenty-one without ever knowing the touch of a woman, let him." Heat gusted out in his wake, and after a moment his two friends followed him.

Inside, Solomon took a deep breath into his cold lungs—and choked on an attar-of-roses fog. Scalding tears sprang to his eyes, refracting the room into red and gilt and skin. A great deal of skin, multiplied by dozens of elegant mirrors. He averted his eyes, but not before a flash of petticoat revealed raised red welts on a smooth thigh.

A girl touched his arm, startling him. She was pale and dark and hit him like a fever, hot and cold at once. But even that chill grounded him, blocking out the heat of the salon. Were the fires kept too high, or had the brandy affected his senses? It would be an interesting experiment, the exact effects of alcohol on the blood—

"Come upstairs," she said.

Solomon blinked, focused his eyes on her again. She was looking at him, but her eyes were empty. Nothing there. No human connection at all. He swallowed, trying to keep the bile down. "I think I should go."

"You'll like it."

He followed her up a red-carpeted stair; she never once looked back, even when he stumbled. She wore a thin lavender percale, inexpertly embroidered with seed pearls. Its single muslin petticoat revealed every angle of her legs—or would have if he could have taken his eyes off the stairs long enough to see much above her ankles. They were neat ankles.

The gown was stylish and becoming, but second-rate, he decided as they went down a dimly lit corridor. The muslin was not quite of the best quality. It wasn't well-fitted either, but maybe she'd lost weight. She was very thin. His mother would want to feed her, give her bread with extra cheese and bowls of clotted cream the way she'd done to Solomon and Elijah when they were younger, "to put meat on their bones"—oh Lord, why was he thinking about his mother *now*?

She went through an open door into an unoccupied room. The fire lit an enormous bed with hangings the color of red lead. He pressed his hand against the door frame, trying to stop his head from spinning. "It's very warm downstairs." It was warmer here. Only the girl's cold face and the cool of the corridor against his back steadied him. There was a tiny round birthmark above her left eyebrow. He wanted to touch it.

"It's nearly October. Gentlemen don't like gooseflesh. Just take off your coat."

He nodded. "Of course." She met his eyes then. Hers were gray, gray and still empty. He was fairly sure she hated him. "We really needn't—"

There was a flash of scorn in her face. "Come in." She wrapped her pale fingers around his arm and pulled him into the room. Her breasts pressed against the front of his coat as she reached behind him to pull the door shut.

A tremor ran through him, a tremor that was all heat. This wasn't how he'd imagined his first time with a woman, but maybe—

She went backward, and he followed—but the bed took up most of the room, and he didn't notice when she stopped moving. Suddenly he was pressed up hard against her, the busk of her stays jabbing into his stomach and her legs trapped between his own and the bed. They both grabbed at the bedpost for balance; his fingers meshed accidentally with hers and she kissed him. Her lips were warm and soft. She smelled like almonds and cheap perfume.

She leaned back. Dazed, he tried to follow, but she'd brought her arm up between them to pop the buttons at her shoulders. Her bodice fell away entirely, revealing bare shoulders and arms and the tops of her breasts swelling above her stays. There was a little round birthmark there, too.

The curtains were imperfectly drawn; a beam of moonlight fell starkly across her skin. That strip of moonlit flesh stood out like the mark of a whip. It shone with the faint bluish-white sheen of arsenic.

Everything came to a head—the brandy and the sickening stench of roses, her distaste and his nerves, and most of all his uneasy guilt at trafficking in human flesh. He was in hell, and she was a damned soul sent to tempt him. Solomon stumbled back, his gorge rising. Hardly knowing what he did, he tugged his purse out of his greatcoat pocket. His entire quarterly allowance was in it, one hundred and twenty-five pounds lovingly counted out that morning at his uncle's solicitor's, and he held it out like a beggar with his alms cup.

"Take it. Please, I'm sorry, take it." He'd regret it in the morning, he knew that, but at the moment there didn't seem to be much choice. Maybe if she took it, she'd forgive him. Forgive him for coming here, for whatever sins Ashton and Braithwaite were even now visiting upon some poor girl—and most of all, for wanting to push her back onto the bed and stare into her gray eyes and fuck her.

He groped behind him for the doorknob. It was difficult, because his hands were shaking.

She didn't take the money, only watched him with her unreadable eyes. He dropped it on the floor and fled the room, covering his mouth with one hand.

Chapter 1

June 7, 1815

"There's a man to see you," Sophy said, sticking her head through Serena's office door. "He says he needs your help locating a missing object. What should I tell him?"

Serena, up to her eyeballs in ledgers, opened her mouth to say no. Right now it was hard enough looking after her own people. She didn't need to take on a stranger's problem.

On the other hand, he would probably pay her for her help. God knew she could use the money; the Ravenshaw Arms' profits were down by four percent from this time last year. Because of the damned war, no doubt. Everyone had flitted off to Belgium to gawk at the young men about to be brutally slaughtered by Napoleon. As always, one person's tragedy was someone else's entertainment.

Four percent wasn't too bad, but she couldn't help worrying. She'd already put off buying new bed-hangings for some of the rooms for months, out of a reluctance to deplete her small reserve. She didn't like to risk compromising the inn's wealthy, fashionable image, but it was better than letting some of the staff go.

Serena couldn't face that. She remembered what it was like to be penniless and on the street. "Show him in," she told Sophy.

Serena had found that it was a good idea to make visitors wait for her attention; it established that she was in charge, and gave them time to get nervous. So when the door opened again and the stranger came in, she finished her sum and double-checked it before looking up.

It was him.

She couldn't breathe. She couldn't believe she had almost sent him away. She'd been looking for him for years. The Hundred and Twenty-Five Pounds, she called him, and she remembered him as if it had been yesterday. Hair like ripe wheat, freckles in a pale face, dreamy hazel eyes, a flexible mouth, and that unexpectedly stubborn chin. He'd looked like an angel.

Either she'd embellished, or he'd grown up, or both. He didn't look like an angel now. He looked like a man, solid and broad and taller than she'd thought.

He looked tired, too, and worn. His hazel eyes were watchful now. It was idiotic how much it hurt her, that he hadn't stayed young and unbruised forever. *But he's still beautiful,* she thought. As if it made any difference what she thought.

It didn't, because on top of everything else he looked rich. Rich and stylish, in a well-cut coat and breeches, tasseled Hessians, an exquisitely tied cravat, and a fanciful crimson waistcoat, its enormous pocket flaps embroidered in orange and pale green. Everything brand-new and expensive, and cheerful in a way that jarred with his expression.

She'd known he was a gentleman, coming into Mme Deveraux's with his noble friends, but it still made her feel a little queasy. People like him didn't associate with whores like her.

"Good afternoon," he said. "I'm Solomon Hathaway." She hadn't remembered his voice at all beyond his educated accent; he'd barely spoken. Husky and a little rough around the edges, it wasn't what she'd expected. "And you must be Lady Serena."

She nodded, carefully keeping all expression from her face.

"I—" He took a deep breath. "I've been told you could help me. There's been a theft—a family heirloom—" He flushed a startling shade of red.

He couldn't even get the words out. No doubt he thought a man like him asking a woman like her for a favor went against the natural order of things. "Ashamed to ask for my help?"

He frowned. "Of course I'm ashamed," he said impatiently. "If Susannah weren't so superstitious, she'd just get married without the damned things. Sorry. The dashed things." He squinted at her. "Do I know you?"

He didn't recognize her. He was branded into her mind and he didn't recognize her?

He was getting *married?*

Who cared? She wasn't some daydreaming schoolgirl. She'd known the odds were slim that she'd ever see him again. She hadn't expected anything to come of it even if she did.

Yes, this was perfect. He didn't know who she was. She'd find his missing object and they would be even. She'd repay her debt, send him on his way, and be free of him.

Perfect.

"No, we've never met." She gave him a smooth smile. "Now tell me, why do you think I can help you?"

"My uncle Dewington says you know every rogue in London by his Christian name." There was a beat, and then he sighed, as if he'd just realized that was a strange thing to say but was resigned to it.

He'd heard part of her reputation, anyway. "His or her Christian name, yes," she said dryly. His uneasiness intrigued her. It seemed to be about a quarter self-consciousness and three-quarters not focusing on the conversation. What was he really thinking about?

It annoyed her that she wanted to know, and, annoyed, she gave in to the temptation of a little rudeness. Just to see if she could make him blush again. "Solomon Hathaway. And the Earl of Dewington's your uncle. Then—hmm. Your mother married beneath her, didn't she?"

He focused on the conversation then, his hazel eyes going green and piercing. "No one with Lord Dewington in her family could *possibly* marry beneath her," he snapped. Well, she agreed with him there.

Usually she liked to keep her desk between herself and visitors, but on impulse she came around and leaned back against the front edge. From up close, he looked even more tired, and thinner than she remembered. What had happened? Did it have anything to do with the help he wanted from her? "So, what is this heirloom you're looking to recover?"

He gazed out the window behind her. "It's the Stuart earrings. My grandfather's great-grandfather, John Hathaway, let Charles the Second spend a couple of nights in his printing house when the king was fleeing one of Cromwell's victories. Charles gave him the earrings as a reward. If you ask me, it's a blot on the family escutcheon—not that we have one. I'd prefer a 'death to tyrants!' sort of forebear. But last week the earrings were being sent up to Shropshire by special courier for the wedding, and a highwayman robbed the coach. Susannah won't get married without them."

Ah yes, Susannah. If he was engaged, why was he running on as if he'd barely spoken to anyone in who knew how long? The amount of words convinced her that she was right and he wasn't shy, only distracted or unhappy. Clearly Susannah wasn't taking proper care of him.

Not taking proper care of him? she mocked herself. *Who are you and what have you done with Serena? Next you'll be making him calf's-foot jelly.* "The earrings are valuable, I take it?"

He shrugged. "The workmanship is excellent. Two good-sized rubies set in gold filigree with four tiny diamonds—very grand for a Hathaway, but nothing out of the common way for a Ravenshaw."

Serena didn't wear jewelry. Possibly he was realizing that, because he glanced up at her hands and neckline and then launched back into speech without ever meeting her eyes.

"But that isn't it. It's the family superstition. The king told John that they would bring him good fortune. There's even a verse saying to give them to one's wife for luck. And sure enough, the woman John loved was widowed in a tragic oven accident and they were able to marry. Since then all the Hathaway brides have worn the earrings. By now, that means that if one doesn't wear them—"

"Bad luck, yes. But surely you, Solomon, are not so—unwise— as to be swayed by such things."

He looked at her then. "A pun on my name, how original." But he was smiling a little, which threw her off. "Susannah lacks the scientific temperament."

She couldn't help it: she leaned forward. "And yet you're marrying her."

He blinked. "What? Oh—Lord, no. Susannah's my sister. It's not *my* wedding."

Relief flooded her throat; she swallowed it and took refuge in sarcasm. "My apologies. Susannah is lucky to have such a scientific gentleman for a brother."

He stiffened. At first she thought he was taking exception to her tone, but then he said, sounding affronted, "I'm not a *gentleman*. I work for my living. My lady."

She raised her eyebrows, startled. "I apologize if I've accidentally dampened your pretensions to being a member of the lower orders." Of course, *she* worked for a living, and she had an aristocratic accent and dressed to the nines. But she was a special case. Wasn't she?

He looked down at his clothes, and went faintly pink. "Oh. I—I borrowed these clothes from the shop. My uncle Dewington hates it when I visit him looking like a tradesman." He gave her the edge of a crooked smile, as if waiting to see if she'd smile back. "You can't see it, but there's a hole in my stockings. Here." He circled a spot on his breeches just above the knee. His kid-gloved index finger rubbed against the buckskin, only inches above the row of buttons stretching the leather tight around his calves, and Serena felt her temperature rising. She didn't smile back. "And I gilded the watch-chain myself."

"You did?" The chain looked brand-new and perfect. Why would he know how to do that?

"I'm a chemist," he said proudly. "Well, I do some design and pitch in with the tailoring when Uncle Hathaway needs the help, but mostly I make all our dyes. We match any shade, and we're famed for the brilliancy of our colors."

And then the whole story came back to her. Hathaway's Fine Tailoring, the men's shop on Bond Street that was all the rage these days. It had been opened almost thirty years ago, before Serena was born, by a pair of brothers fresh up from the country. But one of the brothers, having more of a taste for religion than business, had soon left the shop to be ordained. During his studies, he'd supported himself as a Latin tutor—in the Earl of Dewington's household, among others. Lady Lydia had run off with him, and not been acknowledged by the family again until her father's death. Her brother, the present earl, had been generous enough to send her son to Cambridge, only to be neverendingly mortified when the boy chose to work at Hathaway's Fine Tailoring after all. And that was Solomon, apparently.

There was something else, though, something Dewington had told her about his nephew. What was it?

"So will you help me?" he asked.

It was such a tiny favor, tracking down a stolen piece of jewelry. Would it really even the scales? She didn't want to be in his debt anymore. *Maybe you just want to keep him around*, she suggested scornfully, and then told herself to shut up. "Certainly. I'd also like to order some cloth from you. Some of our beds need new hangings, and the wallpaper would have to be matched." She tilted her head. "Are you sure you can do it?"

He straightened. Ha! She'd thought that would get him. "Yes," he said curtly. "I could match the color of your eyes better than your current modiste, too."

She glanced down at her gray bombazine in surprise. "Could you?" Didn't it match? And—he'd noticed her eyes?

For the first time since he'd got there, he looked into her eyes for longer than a few seconds. Stared into them, and she couldn't look away. Couldn't help breathing faster.

He frowned, a tiny line between his brows. They arched so perfectly. She was drawn to him, and she didn't want to be. "Solomon?" she said coolly, or meant to. Her voice was rough and hot.

He might not have noticed. That deep, deep flush swept over him again, and she smiled involuntarily. "Now I understand why you dyed your waistcoat that enchanting shade of red."

"Wh—?" He cleared his throat. "What?" he asked, his husky voice dropping even further.

"It matches the tips of your ears to perfection."

He rolled his eyes, but he smiled sheepishly back.

Christ, she was *flirting* with him. She had to get him out of here before she completely lost her dignity. "As charming as this interview has been, I'm sure you have business to attend to. Have supper with me tonight, and we'll discuss the details of your little robbery."

"Then you'll help me?"

She nodded.

He looked relieved. "We can pay you, of course—"

There. Now she didn't feel like flirting. "*No*," she interrupted. *You will never pay me for anything, ever again.* She swallowed the feeling of claustrophobia. Maybe if she paid back this one great debt, she would feel free for once in her life. "Let Sophy show you to your room. You'll be staying here. Gratis."

His jaw dropped. "I couldn't dream of it! This is much too elegant an establishment for me—I have rooms—"

"I daresay you do—in Cheapside," she said, naming a neighborhood in the City filled with warehouses, butchers' shops, and tradesmen's lodgings.

He glared at her. "I'm not ashamed of my address."

He was so *prickly*. She tried not to smile again. "As worthy and respectable as Cheapside no doubt is, it's some little distance from me, and I want you on hand to consult with."

"I don't see why that's necessary."

It wasn't necessary. In fact, it was probably a terrible idea. Too late. "You want my help, don't you? Susannah and her betrothed are waiting . . ."

"You won't help me unless I stay here?" He sounded as if he didn't know whether to be annoyed, or just puzzled.

"Believe me, you won't be arguing with me once you've had supper. My chef is the best in the business." *You just think he hasn't been eating enough. You're acting like somebody's* mother. She crossed her arms. "That's my offer. Take it or leave it."

He spread his hands in a frustrated, resigned gesture. "If I'm going to stay here, I'll have to bring all my equipment from my rooms," he warned her.

"Then do so at once." She rang the bell on the wall behind her desk. When she was done with him, he'd be so far in her debt he'd never get out. She just had to do it before he realized who she was and headed for the hills.

How had he agreed to this? Lady Serena was strange and confusing and quite possibly mad, even if she *was* the most beautiful woman he'd ever seen. But Uncle Dewington had said she could help find the earrings, and his mother was at her wit's end. It was his duty to obtain Lady Serena's help by any means necessary, and if that meant free lodgings and fine dining, well—

Put that way, why had he ever demurred? He really had turned into a hermit this last year and a half.

When the young black woman in spectacles who'd shown him in reappeared, Lady Serena instructed her, without looking at him and without any more sarcasm than seemed present in everything she said, to show him to the Stuart bedroom.

"The Stuart bedroom?" he asked, following the girl down a narrow, low hallway back to the public part of the inn.

"King Charles stayed here a lot, the one who was beheaded," Sophy said. "Legend has it the future James the Second hid himself here for a spot, too, when he fled London before his father's execution. That was long before her ladyship and monseigneur du Sacreval had anything to do with the place, obviously. It had a different name then."

"Monseigneur du Sacreval?"

"Yes, sir. He came over during the Terror—his parents were slaughtered by their tenants." She shrugged. "Likely deserved it. He went back to France to try to reclaim the title after Boney went to Elba, and we haven't heard from him since, so the inn is Lady Serena's now. It's only fair. Most of the money was monseigneur's, but all the head for trade was hers."

"Why didn't they call it the Sacreval Arms?"

"Why, sir, who cares about Frog noblemen? Half the people who come here have French chefs higher born than monseigneur. But anybody would like to be served by a marquess's daughter, and that's a fact. Cits and nobles alike." She frowned. "They don't see what it does to her. She didn't always look like that."

Solomon thought he knew what she meant. Lady Serena looked—well, she looked perfect. Her face was a perfect oval, her nose razor-straight and patrician. Her mouth looked as if it had come out of a Greek anatomy textbook, and so did her figure. Solomon had almost been tempted to get out his tape measure and start looking for instances of the Golden Mean. Her coloring only added to the impression—pale skin, pale gray eyes and black lashes, and hair as black and heavy as Ethiops mineral. The only impurity was a small birthmark over her left brow, like a circle of brown velvet.

But there had been something about the look on her face— something about the way she smiled without her eyes that said she wanted him to notice it; something that was polite and challenging, blank and vital all at once. She reminded him of a bead of mercury: bright and shining and gray, spellbinding and utterly impenetrable to the eye. No one got that way without a lot of practice.

So yes, he thought he knew what Sophy meant by *she didn't always look like that*, but he'd frequently found that playing dumb got better information. "What did she look like before? She could hardly have been more beautiful."

Sophy caught her breath. "Men are all alike! But even you would—you didn't see her before. She used to have the most expressive eyes."

Solomon would have liked to see that. *You didn't see her before*—before what? He was surprised by how much he wanted to know. But maybe if he knew, he'd understand how she could be so damn striking and yet he couldn't remember where he'd seen her.

Perhaps feeling she had said too much, Sophy pressed her lips together. "Here we are, sir. The Stuart bedroom."

A huge oak bed with far too many claret-colored hangings made the room look smaller than it was. A large portrait of King Charles I, "the one who was beheaded," hung over the mantel.

The sun blazed in through a wide leaded-glass window to the right of the bed; it illuminated gleaming oak paneling, claret-colored paper, a thick claret-colored carpet (probably Aubusson, Solomon thought glumly), and a carved oak fireplace. Diana took aim across the hearth at Orion, and between them a clock, set in Apollo's sun chariot, showed the time and the phases of the moon. Midsized rubies twinkled at him from half a dozen places in the carving, though one or two had fallen out over the years—or maybe been prised out by enterprising tenants.

On the wall to his right, a sturdy oak door was set in an ornate door frame. "Is that a dressing room?"

"No, sir, that leads to Lady Serena's room," she answered without expression.

He glanced at her in surprise.

She shrugged. "This used to be monseigneur's own room. It locks from her side, so don't try to take advantage." Solomon tried to look innocent. Since he'd instantly begun to speculate as to whether monseigneur had taken advantage, he probably wasn't succeeding.

All in all, the room was far grander than anything he'd ever not wanted to touch in case he got fingerprints on it. Charles's headless body must be turning over in its grave at the idea of a Hathaway sleeping in its bed, and all because Lady Serena thought it was funny that he wasn't a Jacobite.

But he didn't appear to have a choice, so after muttering, "At least no one will be able to tell if I spill claret on anything," he resigned himself to the inevitable. If he got started right away, he could borrow Uncle Dewington's coach and driver and have his laboratory transported here before dinner, maybe start work on a new dye. A gray, quicksilver sort of dye.

Solomon stopped short in the doorway to the dining room. Surely that wasn't—but yes, it was. Of course it was. Lord Smollett. The bane of his Cambridge career.

"Welcome to the Ravenshaw Arms, my lord," Lady Serena said graciously. "Your usual table is waiting for you."

"Thank you, m'dear," said the all-too-familiar drawl. "You are an excellent hostess. Although I much preferred your other career." Smollett guffawed. Solomon, gritting his teeth, considered going back to his room and locking the door.

Lady Serena smiled blandly, but a tenseness in her jaw suggested her teeth were gritted, too. "As flattering as that is, I can't say the same for myself."

"Now that's not very flattering to *me*!" said Smollett. What did he mean by that? What had Lady Serena's other career been? She didn't so much as lift an eyebrow, but Solomon could almost hear her say, *Exactly*. He tried surreptitiously to attract her attention.

But Smollett spotted him before she did. "Well, if it isn't the Hatherdasher!" He strode purposefully toward his new prey. "Matching the upholstery, are you?"

Solomon sighed. Some things never changed. "Why yes, I am, as a matter of fact. May I congratulate you on the cut of your coat, my lord? Weston's, isn't it? We have a new piqué jonquil waistcoat in the window that would go perfectly."

"Dash it all, Hathaway, you talk like a damn tradesman!" He paused to consider this. "Course, you are one. I might have known you wouldn't be anyplace so dashing on your own account. A fellow like you hardly has hopes of slipping into the Siren's bed." He laughed again.

Solomon leaned hopelessly against the door frame and gazed over the top of Smollett's head. Hadn't he had enough of this at school? Now he couldn't even write to Elijah about it later and laugh.

Luckily, Lady Serena apparently *had* had enough. "Oh, Solomon!" she called carelessly. "What the devil were you about, keeping me waiting all this time? I'd nearly given up on you. I saved that little table in the corner for us. Oh, pardon me, my lord." She brushed past Lord Smollett and, taking Solomon's arm in a proprietary grip, tugged him in the direction she'd indicated.

Solomon tried not to smile smugly at the expression on Smollett's face. "Thank you," he said when they were out of range. "Lord Smollett has a somewhat paralyzing effect on me."

"I believe he has that effect generally," Lady Serena said, surprising him. She let go of his arm, rather to his regret, and sat down in the chair that faced the room without waiting for him to pull it out for her.

"Yes, well, he gave me my Cambridge nickname. The—" He stopped.

Her eyes crinkled. "The Hatherdasher, yes, I heard."

"You and everyone else in the room."

"Smollett came up with that? He must be cleverer than I gave him credit for."

"I mean, it's a bit rich, coming from someone whose name originally meant 'small head'!"

Something very like a snort escaped Lady Serena. She'd seemed so intimidating at their first meeting, but maybe he'd just been nervous. Maybe she was an ordinary woman after all. "It did?" she asked.

"Yes, I came across it once in an etymological text. I told him, but he and his friends just looked at each other and laughed. It was an utter rout."

"You can't fight the Smolletts of this world on their own terms. But I find utter indifference works wonders."

"'Forsake the foolish, and live.' Yes, I know." He ducked his head at her quizzical expression. "Proverbs Nine: Six. Sorry, I—the Proverbs were written by Solomon, you know, so I liked them when I was a boy."

"And you were the sort of boy who memorized things."

There was a smile in her dry voice, so he laughed instead of taking offense. "How did you guess? But forsaking the foolish—it's easier said than done. You seemed rather nettled yourself when I came in."

She stiffened. "It takes a deal more than Lord Smollett to nettle *me*."

Solomon was skeptical, but he turned the subject. "Where did you get the nickname of Siren?"

"It sounds like my name," she said shortly, and so coldly that he flushed. She signaled to a waiter, and in a very few minutes of awkward silence, their places were laid with gleaming silver and spotless china. Wine and water were poured, a basket of fresh hot rolls was placed with a flourish in the center of the table, and two attractive bowls of cucumber soup were set before them.

Solomon's mouth watered. He'd been living on bread and cheese and mince pies from the corner shop for a long time.

He'd often thanked Heaven for sending him to Cambridge (much oftener than he'd thanked Uncle Dewington for the same favor), but it was generally for the excellent education in chemistry he'd received there. Now he was grateful that Cambridge had taught him a more arcane science, one his republican mother had scorned and his father had never known: which spoon to use and the correct manner of unfolding his napkin.

When Lady Serena had tasted her wine, selected a roll, and picked up her spoon, he finally dared to try the soup. *Ohhh.* It was all worth it—Lady Serena's mockery and Charles I's portrait and Lord Smollett—just for this. "It's ambrosial!"

Her face lit with a startlingly genuine smile—Solomon felt a tug, somewhere in his chest—and then she looked away, as if she didn't want him to see it. "Good. Have a roll, they're baked fresh."

He hesitated. But he couldn't say no, so he stripped his gloves off and laid them on the table. She could see his hands, now, the stains and blotches and calluses. The tiny round acid scars that dotted his skin. He'd got used to this over the years. The prick of anxiety and self-consciousness had grown dull and distant, especially since Elijah died. He'd outgrown it, he'd thought; he'd realized how trivial it was. And yet here he was, afraid to look at Lady Serena's expression. He took a roll, instead, and broke it apart. Steam rose from the center. It smelled delicious.

He glanced up at Lady Serena. She was staring at his hands. He put the roll down on his plate and pushed it away.

She blinked and raised her luminous gray eyes to his face. "No, I was only—" She sighed. "These earrings of yours, you said there was a verse about them?"

He cringed. "Do you really want to hear it? It doesn't even scan."

"You never know what may prove important."

Solomon gave in to the inevitable.

"'Wouldst thou have the rose of fortune fair?
Place these jewels among Phoebe's sweet hair.
By the thistle of ill fate wouldst be undone?
Then let the jewels languish, nor shine in the sun.'

"You must imagine, of course, that 'sun' is spelled s-o-n-n-e," he concluded.

"Hmm. It certainly lacks artistic merit."

He laughed. "Maybe, but it incorporates the Royalist mania for the English rose and Scottish thistle, which is in its favor."

She nodded. "They certainly seem to have left enough inns with that name. 'The Rose and Thistle' was even the name of the Arms when René and I bought it."

"Oh yes, the Stuart bedroom. Why did Charles have need of an inn in his own capital?"

"He'd taken a fancy to his clockmaker's daughter. That mantel clock is one of the man's creations. Charles brought her here so he could derive a delicious satisfaction from ruining the girl under her father's nose, so to speak." The depth of bitterness in her voice surprised him.

"I told you the Stuarts were a bad lot," he said, trying to make light of it.

She gave him that icy, heated look of hers. "You're not as wise as you seem if you think most men are any different."

There was silence. They regarded each other across the table, and Solomon could see this was a fight he couldn't win. He didn't even know why they were fighting. He hunched his shoulders and picked up his roll. "Maybe not."

Lady Serena gave him a surprised frown. For a moment he thought she was going to say something, but there was a sound of breaking china and raucous laughter behind him. She rose from her chair to see what had happened and went pale with anger. Paler, anyway.

Solomon turned; a chubby serving girl was loading broken china onto a tray, to the great amusement of a party of young bloods at a nearby table. Cucumber soup spattered her apron and spread across the floor. He had a very clear memory of one of those men "accidentally" bumping into him as he carried an expensive set of glass pipes across the quad.

Solomon got down on the parquet—carefully, so as not to stain his breeches. "Give me your apron," he said quietly. "I'll mop up the soup."

The girl fumbled at her apron strings, tugging it off and pressing it into his hands. "I'll get my things as soon as I'm cleared up here, my lady."

Lady Serena's eyebrows rose. "Don't be a fool, Charlotte. There's a reason I don't put carpets in the dining room. I'm very pleased with your work so far." She turned to the group of young men, who tried unsuccessfully to hide their grins. Solomon felt the old knot of useless anger in his throat, watching them. "These—gentlemen— didn't have anything to do with your little mishap, did they?"

The girl went very still. "No, my lady."

"Are you sure? I dislike being lied to. And if you imagine I'd allow any of them to exact any sort of retribution from you, you're an even greater fool than I took you for."

Charlotte's lips tightened. "One of them pinched me."

Lady Serena's mouth set dangerously. "Did he now? I find that interesting. I thought I'd made it very clear to everyone that I would not tolerate anything of that sort in my establishment." One of the young men began an insincere apology, but she cut him off. "You gentlemen will kindly take your leave."

Amusement turned to shocked indignation; Lady Serena's voice sliced through the angry babble. "Get out. Next time I will bar you from the premises permanently."

Solomon mentally shifted her from *ordinary woman* back to *intimidating*. Very, very intimidating. She was like an ice storm, a whirlwind of glittering frozen shards. And, like the first breath of icy air after sitting dully in a warm house, she made his blood run faster. He wanted to breathe her in.

Maybe you ought to stick to chemistry and leave the overwrought poetry to Elijah, he told himself, concentrating on wiping the last of the soup from the wooden floor's shining wax coat. But he wasn't surprised when, grumbling but evidently mortified, the young men hastened to depart.

Lady Serena sat back down, and Solomon put the sodden apron on Charlotte's tray. "Thank you," the girl said quietly. He smiled at her and returned to his chair. The hushed silence in the room quickly gave way to pleasantly scandalized murmurings. Only Lady Serena was silent, her eyes fixed on the empty table behind Solomon.

Once, she picked up her spoon, but it rattled slightly against the lip of her bowl. Her eyes flew apprehensively to his, and then she looked away and set the spoon down again with an angry click. It took him a moment to believe the evidence of his own eyes. Her hands were shaking.

He felt a sudden rush of sympathy, remembering more vividly than he had in a long time how badly he'd wanted to seem cool and collected in front of those boys at Cambridge, how he'd tried for a bored drawl and could never, ever manage it. How much he'd hated them for that.

Don't take it so hard, he wanted to tell her. *You were amazing.* But he didn't need to be an empirical scientist to guess that she would hate that. She hadn't even wanted to admit to being nettled by Lord Smollett. So he waited until the soup plates were removed and two lovely fillets of sole *à la Lyonnaise* were brought out to venture a "Lady Serena?"

She started like a sleepwalker. "Yes, what is it?" She picked up her first fork and began to push the sole around her plate.

"Are you—?" Her eyebrows drew together, and he gave up. "We were speaking of my robbery."

"Yes, of course. Your robbery," she said mechanically. "Tell me about it."

Solomon didn't want to discuss it either. He wanted to talk about something else, something that had nothing to do with business or family. He wanted to see if he could make her laugh. He wanted to tell her, even though he knew she would sneer (no, *because* he knew she would sneer; he liked her sneer) how much he'd like to be able to silence a party of young bucks with just a lifted brow and an icy tone of command. He'd always been able to manage chemical reactions, but people frequently eluded him.

But his mother was at her wits' end. Besides, just because he liked her and they both hated Lord Smollett, it didn't mean anything. It certainly didn't mean they had a connection or that she wanted to talk to *him*. He only felt as if it did because he missed his brother so much he would have talked to a rock if it stayed still long enough. *Only you wouldn't, would you?* he thought. *You haven't wanted to talk to anyone in a year and a half.* "It happened Monday last," he said. "On the road not far from London, just before High Wycombe. I assumed the earrings would be sold immediately, but I've had no luck tracking them down. I've circulated their description to as many jewelers as I could find, but I'm sure I missed dozens. The earrings aren't in any catalog and they aren't valuable enough to be recognized on sight."

Lady Serena shook her head impatiently. "Jewelers won't help you. You need to seek out receivers."

"I don't know any receivers."

Bullying him seemed to restore her good humor. She gave him a small, superior smile. "Naturally you don't, Solomon. Why would a fine, upstanding citizen like you be acquainted with anyone who traffics in stolen goods? That is why you have engaged someone who knows every rogue in London by their Christian name to act for you in the matter."

So calling him by his Christian name hadn't just been for Smollett's benefit. She was teasing him about Uncle Dewington's comment. Well, two could play that game. He smiled back. "Then what's our first step, Serena?"

She ignored the "our" and the "Serena" equally. "I'll put out some initial inquiries, but anything more will have to wait. The greater part of the Carlton House set is coming here for dinner on Saturday and I won't have time for anything else until after that."

Solomon felt ashamed of his awe, but he couldn't help it. "The Carlton House set? You mean, the Prince Regent?"

On anyone else, it would have been a grin. On her, it was an amused smile. "Surely you aren't impressed? A good republican like you?"

Solomon spent most of the next day collecting wallpaper samples for Lady Serena's bed-hangings and attempting to match the saffron color of one of the most dilapidated rooms. At first it felt strange working in an unfamiliar room, but before long he'd forgotten everything but the three feet of table in front of him, clear and clean and brilliantly lit by his clockwork Carcel oil lamp, scrimped for and ordered from Paris. He loved working; it made everything else go away. Since Elijah's death, it was the only thing that could.

When someone knocked on his door, he started as if awakening from a drug-induced stupor. When had it gone dark out? He looked at the mantel clock and saw that it was nine o'clock. Hours ago, then. "Come."

Lady Serena swung the door open. Her eyebrows rose at the disarray of the room, lifting that little birthmark of hers with them. The elegant rug was rolled up to where it met the bed; a jumble of glass, brass, and iron occupied the remaining space, some of it loaded onto a large table Solomon had talked Sophy into having brought up.

He wasn't spared a sweeping look, either, and he realized he was wearing his oldest shirt with the sleeves rolled up and a pair of awful mud-colored breeches someone had returned to his uncle's shop. He'd lay odds there was a grimy smudge all across his forehead, too, where he'd wiped away the sweat. She was as alluring and perfect as ever, and he looked like a chimney sweep.

Lady Serena wrinkled her nose and crossed to the window. "I make it a practice to keep all my rooms well-aired," she said just as the wick in his lamp began to smoke.

He flushed and took the glass chimney off to trim the wick. "You don't smell it after a while. I can't have varying temperatures and wind while I'm working." Sure enough, the moment she opened the window, a damp gust of wind extinguished the lamp. Solomon felt at once vindicated and even more embarrassed. Fumbling for his tinder among the jars and crucibles, he glanced up at Lady Serena. In the moonlight her skin seemed to glint bluish-white, that distinctive birthmark thrown into sharp relief—

"Serena!" came Sophy's worried voice from the corridor just as Solomon's fingers closed on the tinderbox. "Lord Blackthorne's here!"

Lady Serena froze. "What did you say?" Her voice sounded strangled.

"Your father. He's here!"

Chapter 2

A tall, imperious man strode into the dark room. "Thank you, girl, that will be all." Solomon thought Sophy would have liked to stay, but after a moment's hesitation she bobbed a curtsey and whisked herself out the door.

Lady Serena turned to face her father. Solomon realized with a jolt that she was several inches shorter than Lord Blackthorne, and wished, irrationally, that it were not so. He hurried to strike a spark, but the flint and steel refused to cooperate.

"So this is where I find you. In his room, in the dark!"

"Why are you here, Father? This is my property and you're not welcome."

The lamp finally, blessedly, flared into light, and Solomon replaced the chimney before looking up at Lord Blackthorne. He blinked at the family resemblance: the razor-straight, patrician nose and hawklike gray eyes. It was impossible to guess if they'd shared the raven hair, as Lord Blackthorne's thick locks were completely gray. And his attire, while expensive, was not as tasteful or well-tailored as his daughter's. Solomon repressed a professional shudder at the combination of black and brown.

"I've stayed away too long as it is. Even you must admit that I have been patient with you, Reenie."

"You certainly left me to myself," she said lightly. A little too lightly, and it occurred to Solomon for the first time that she was probably younger than he was. She made it look easy, her self-reliance and her air of command, but it wasn't, not really. And she had had to learn it, somewhere along the way. *You didn't see her before*, Sophy had said.

"It wasn't enough that you dragged the Ravenshaw name

through the mud, not enough that you gave it to a common inn, not enough that every day I hear your name bandied about by men I would never allow in my home, but now you take up with a Cit?" Lord Blackthorne's eyes swept Solomon and his chiseled mouth curled into a sneer—less polished than his daughter's, but still effective. "Hell, Cit is too good a name for him! You've allied yourself with a *tradesman*. You have low tastes, girl. But surely you didn't expect me to stand by."

Solomon swallowed his affront and waited for her to deny the implication. But her birthmark lifted as she raised an eyebrow and smiled. "What do you intend to do about it? The Ravenshaw Arms is mine. I'm of age. I'll ally myself with whomever I please."

"No, you won't. You're correct: I can't take the inn from you. But a father has some rights, even in these degenerate times." He paused, grimly satisfied. "For example, I could have you put in Bedlam. Self-destructive promiscuity."

Solomon clenched his fist. It wasn't his business. He turned to Lady Serena, waiting for her to put her father in his place, as she had Lord Smollett and the table of young men at dinner. But she didn't. She just stood there.

Her eyes reminded Solomon of an experiment he'd done with frozen mercury. He'd put a tiny chip in a glass of water, and in an instant had been left with a block of ice, and at the center a living drop of quicksilver.

He was abruptly and blindly angry. Only it wasn't abrupt; it wasn't new. He'd been filled with blind anger for a year and a half, he realized. And he'd ignored it and shoved it down, because there was no one to blame for Elijah's death, except God and perhaps Napoleon. There was no point railing at beings who were so far away and so utterly unaffected by his resentment. Lord Blackthorne was right here, and he was going to pay for that look on Lady Serena's face. "How dare you, my lord? You—you—" He could hear his voice going Shropshire until his words rolled and lilted in his mouth. "She owes you no more loyalty than she owes the Corsican monster! Have you never read that 'he that troubleth his own house shall inherit the wind?'"

"Keep your nose out of what don't concern you, boy, or you may lose it. This is between myself and my daughter." Lord Blackthorne's snarl would ordinarily have had Solomon hurrying to shut his mouth. But Lord Blackthorne wasn't a customer and Solomon wasn't backing down. It was all he could do to keep his voice from swelling until it could have filled every corner of his father's church. *Everybody fights the way they're trained*, Elijah used to say.

"You call her your daughter, but 'a friend loveth at all times, and a brother is born for adversity'! How much more so a father, bound to his child by the most unbreakable and sacred ties of responsibility and natural affection? To suggest what you have suggested—to threaten one who should rely on you for protection—" He gulped for breath and plunged on. "Your daughter has done what none of your blood has done since the Conquest—kept an honest roof over her head with the fruits of her own honest labor! And you come here and insult her under it. Are you not *ashamed?*"

Lord Blackthorne's lips were white. "If you were a gentleman I would call you out for that. As it is, you are fit only for horsewhipping."

"That's just as well, for I should certainly not meet you," Solomon bit out. "Dueling is an outmoded and barbaric custom, fit only for killing off the stupider members of a thoroughly useless class."

Lord Blackthorne had been angry. Now, he was simply astonished. "Is he this prosy between the sheets?" he asked his daughter.

Her smile was cold, but her eyes were dancing now. "Oh no, Father. *There* he is pure poetry."

That pulled Solomon up short. Lord Blackthorne wasn't going

to believe *that*, was he? Solomon could barely believe she'd said it. He blinked again to dispel the images called up by her suggestive tone of voice. *Definitely lacking in verisimilitude*, he told himself.

But Lord Blackthorne's jaw dropped, and Lady Serena's smile widened. "Now get out before I have you tossed out."

Lord Blackthorne gave them the look of a cornered wolf. "I want him gone or I shall take steps. I give you two weeks. Good night." With that Parthian shot he stormed out.

They stood staring at each other for a moment. Lady Serena's smile was gone, but there was something warm and tired in her expression that he'd never seen before. "Has anyone ever told you you're beautiful when you're angry?"

He gave an unsteady, surprised laugh, trying to slow the exhilarated pounding of his heart. He felt clean, like a lanced wound. "I don't know what came over me. That is—it's my best impression of my father giving a sermon. That's his accent. My brother Elijah used to fall out of his chair laughing."

She met his gaze and shook her head regretfully. "You show such a touching faith in my character that I'm almost loath to destroy it. You called me an honest woman. I'm not. I'm one of the most notorious ex-whores in London." Her face showed perfect unconcern, but she didn't appear to be breathing. He couldn't believe that *that* was what she was worrying about, now, after her father's threats. Did she care that much what he thought?

He grinned at her. "I know."

She blinked. "You know?"

"I recognized you as soon as I saw you in the dark."

Serena couldn't believe it. He knew, and still he'd defended her.

Once, when she was eighteen and had done something new with her protector, and not liked it, she had lain in bed after he'd gone home and shivered in the dark and thought, *No honest man will ever want me now.*

She didn't, generally, let herself dwell on things like that; there was no use moping over facts, and honest men could go hang. But that night she hadn't been able to help herself. For days afterward, despite her best efforts, she had felt cold and miserable and damaged, somehow, inside—*ruined.*

Solomon wasn't looking at her as if he thought she was ruined.

He'd done the same thing six years ago; he'd come into that awful place and looked at her as if he saw her, as if he *wanted* to see her. And that forced her to see him, and she didn't want to. She couldn't afford to, not when she needed all the energy she had for herself, simply to get through each moment.

"Why did you do it?" she asked. "Why did you give me the money?" She'd wanted to know for years; she focused on that. If she let herself think of Bedlam—she couldn't think of it. She couldn't.

He chewed on his lip. "Because you needed it?"

"Didn't you?"

He laughed. "Yes, I did. It was my entire allowance for the quarter. But is it not written, 'He that loveth wine and oil shall not be rich'?"

He said it as if it could be as simple as it seemed. He was a kind young man, and he'd been drunk, and she had needed it. Try as she might, she could not twist it into selfishness or lust, into something she understood; it unsettled her. "Did you regret it?"

"Of course." He shrugged. "But not—I regretted it, but I didn't want to change it." He gave her a rueful half smile. She didn't say anything, and the smile faded; his eyes dropped and he rubbed his thumb along the edge of his table of equipment. "I do wish I'd borrowed the money to buy my brother Elijah a birthday gift."

She shrugged. "I've never understood the great fuss about birthdays."

"He only had two more of them after that," he said, and she felt abruptly cold. "And he gave me just the thing I wanted."

"On his own birthday—" Halfway through the sentence she understood, but it was too late.

"Sorry, I—we were born on the same day," he explained. "We were twins."

She stood, frozen. She should say something. She had to say something. But she couldn't think of anything. So this was why he'd lost weight, and why his freckles stood out starkly against his pale skin, and why he had that drawn, defeated look she'd steadfastly refused to be concerned about from the moment she'd seen him again.

"And now I've got to go on having birthday after birthday without him." He looked up; the sweetness of his smile was foreign and incomprehensible, but she felt a piercing kinship at the self-derision in his eyes. "I always thought—I'd know if anything happened to him. I'd feel it. But that was rot. I had no idea. I was laughing or eating and he was dead. He bled in the dirt all alone."

Serena had no idea what to do. *I'm very sorry for your loss*, she thought, dredging the polite courtesy up from God knew where. But she couldn't say it, didn't know how to make her tongue form the words. She was more helpless before his simple, ordinary need than she would have been before any display of mastery. For long, painful moments, the only sound was the rain on the roof and the cobblestones.

"How on earth did you end up at Mme Deveraux's?" he asked, finally.

"I slept with the footman," she told him, angrily conscious of her own failure.

"And your father kicked you out?" He shot a sharp, frowning glance at the door Lord Blackthorne had just walked out of.

There, he was doing it already. Trying to make her an abused innocent, searching for the heart of gold among her brass. "No, I left," she said with a false, brilliant smile. "I became a whore to spite him." It was about half true. She had left to go after Harry, the footman; she'd intended to marry him. Harry, however, had had no such intention. When she'd gone to the address he'd given her, he hadn't been there, and his friends had refused to give her any information about his whereabouts at all.

She'd been starving by the time Mme Deveraux's procurer approached her in the street. But it hadn't only been desperation; she had signed her contract with a flourish, feeling hot and triumphant at the thought of what her father would say. She'd been an idiot.

Solomon didn't say anything; he looked as if he saw through the smile. He was doing it again, *seeing* her, and she hated it. She was afraid of what he would see—and worse, that he wouldn't like it. "I bought back my contract with your money," she told him. "But I didn't stop. I was the most expensive whore in London for a year, and no matter how high my rates were, there was always someone willing to offer more. I couldn't have done it without you. How do you feel about that?"

He swallowed. "Lady—" He stopped, evidently realizing how stupid it was to speak formally after the conversation they'd just had. "Serena, I don't know what you want me to say."

She didn't either. "I suppose I want you to know what to say." Stupid, but true. "Fit for Bedlam, aren't I?"

Black fear rose, then, from where it had been waiting. Her father could do it. He could really do it, and no sweet drunk boy would save her from that. Why now? He'd left her alone for years. She'd thought she was free of him, and instead he was like some deus ex machina who could walk in and out of her life whenever he pleased, handing down ultimatums and commands with no forewarning and no hope of escape.

She pressed her fist to her mouth. "I—I'll see you tomorrow," she said, quite calmly, and left the room.

Solomon woke at eight o'clock, not at all refreshed. Serena, he knew, must be already awake and dealing with business, and he wanted to see how she was. He wanted to see *her*. Within twenty minutes he was dressed and hurrying down the back corridor to her office.

In his haste, he ran straight into a tall man in obviously Parisian tailoring. Annoyed at his own gracelessness—but making a mental note to experiment further with gilt thread and pocket-flap shapes—he apologized and tried to move past.

To his surprise, the stranger's dark eyes lit up and he embraced Solomon enthusiastically, talking in rapid French. "*Thierry! Comme ça me fait plaisir de te revoir! Mais où est-ce que t'es parti, hein? Je m'inquiétais tant quand t'as disparu—*"

Solomon disengaged himself and stood stock-still. Once, he'd been used to this—being approached by people he didn't know and called by a name that wasn't his. When Elijah was alive, it had usually annoyed him and sometimes entertained him enormously. Now it did neither.

Shortly after Elijah died, someone who hadn't known yet had mistaken Solomon for his twin, and he'd gone along with it for a joke the way he sometimes had before, thinking—God, he'd been stupid—thinking that it might make him feel better. After five sentences he'd gone outside and been sick.

"*Mais pourquoi tu ne réponds pas? T'es pas heureux de me voir?*"

"I—I'm sorry, I don't speak French."

The man frowned, laughed, and ran his fingers through his dark hair, making it stand straight up. "You do not speak French!" he said in lightly accented English. "Thierry, you are teasing me! And me, I did not even know you speak English! *Tiens*, do not pretend not to know me any longer. I am not so sure I can bear it."

He wanted to snap at the man, to tell him to go away and stop making Solomon feel like this. "I'm sorry, but it's true," he said gently. "You must have been a friend of my brother's."

The man stilled in a way that reminded Solomon a little of Serena. "Your brother?"

"Yes, my brother Elijah. He spoke French very well."

The man's dark eyes examined Solomon, suspicious at first and then merely disappointed. "No, I see you are not he. But it is his face, his voice: yes, his brother. I—did not know he was English." He shook himself a little, and asked more cheerfully, "But Thierry—Elijah"—he pronounced it carefully—"you are his brother, you know where he is—how I can find him?"

Solomon looked away. "Elijah's dead."

"Pardon?" But from the tremor in his voice, Solomon thought the man had understood.

"He's dead. I'm sorry."

"Dead. As, he lives no more?"

Solomon nodded. How many more times would he have to say it?

All the blood drained from the man's face. "I see. How did he die, if you please?"

"He was killed by—" Solomon was about to say *the French*, but thought better of it. "He was shot."

The man's lips parted, as if he himself had taken a bullet. "I see. Please, accept my condolences on the loss of your brother."

"Thank you. How—how did you know him? Please, I'd like to hear—" Actually, he could imagine it easily. It would have been very like Elijah to meet the Frenchman by chance and see if he could pass himself off as French, and very like Elijah—who had always been announcing he would build a six—no, an eight—no, a twelve-story house of cards, and who had always laughed when it came tumbling down—to see how far he could take it. Apparently rather far.

"Well, after all, I did not know him very well."

"But—"

"*Mais non*, I assure you, we did not meet but once or twice."

"René!" Lady Serena's voice, behind them, was more unabashedly happy than he'd ever heard it. Solomon felt a small, irrational pang of jealousy. "How charming to see you again. But what is the matter? You look queer as Dick's hatband."

"Nothing, *ma petite sirène*," he said as she ushered the two of them into her office. "It will pass. I—only I knew this gentleman's brother, a little, and he is dead, it appears."

Serena stole a glance at Solomon. "Yes," she said quietly. "He is." They stood in silence for a few moments. "But I must introduce to you the gentleman who has taken your room. René, allow me to present Solomon Hathaway. Solomon, this is René, marquis du Sacreval and my erstwhile business partner." She still sounded so damn happy and trying to hide it, like a child who thought she was too old to make a fuss about Christmas.

The marquis and Solomon evinced equal surprise—Solomon would have almost said the Frenchman looked unsettled. "Did you say Hattaway?" he asked, nose wrinkling. "How very English. And are you from Stratford?"

"Yes, Hathaway," Solomon said. "Sorry about the t-h. No, it's no relation to Shakespeare's wife that I know. We're from Shropshire."

The marquis frowned and turned cajolingly to Serena. "You have given him my room, *ma sirène*? But I will be needing it."

She shrugged. "If you'd sent me word you were coming I could have saved it for you, but as it is, I'll hardly ask Solomon to move. You can have the apricot room if you like; it's just across the hall."

"He can have the room," Solomon said, trying not to think of that connecting door. "It's his, after all."

Her eyes narrowed. "No, the room is mine. I'm happy to put René up free of charge at any time, but, as I'm sure he will acknowledge, I bought out his share in the Arms when he left for France."

The marquis pressed his lips together, looking cornered. "It is that which I must speak to you about, *ma sirène*. I have not been able to recover my lands in France, Napoleon is back, *alors*, I am forced to return to your green island."

Serena's birthmark lifted hopefully. "You must be disappointed, but of course I'll be delighted to sell you back any share of the Arms you care to buy, up to fifty percent, or to hire you on as my assistant for a fixed salary if you'd prefer."

"I would be prepared to buy you out."

The birthmark hunkered down. "Buy me out, René?" she asked. "You know I won't leave the Arms."

His gaze held hers unwaveringly. "You are sure that you do not want to consider it? I can give you double what we paid for it."

Her happiness was snuffed out now like a candle, and as jealous as Solomon had been, he felt a pang at its loss. "René, what is this about? If you're in trouble, you know I'll help you, but as for leaving the Arms, it's out of the question."

He took a deep breath, then gave a slight Gallic shrug. "Is that any way to treat your husband, *sirène?*"

Chapter 3

Surely René hadn't just said what Serena thought he'd said. "Doing it a bit too brown, René. My husband? Come, what is all this nonsense?" Surely it was a joke. Surely in a moment René would laugh and hold out his hands for her to clasp, and there was no need for her heart to stutter in her chest like that. No need at all.

René didn't smile as he drew a paper from inside his coat. "It is not nonsense, *sirène*. Under your English law everything you have is legally mine. Even the Arms. Particularly the Arms."

She had missed him so much, wanted him to come back for so long. She had been so happy to see him. She had been worried by his stricken look, and he wanted to take the Arms away from her.

She said, with a calm that frightened her, "Let me see that." René handed her the paper without a word. The marriage lines looked undeniably genuine. Her signature was perfect.

Five years, she thought.

For five years she had lived at the Arms, had got up every morning at dawn to consult with Antoine on the menus and gone to bed late every night after doing the books. For five years she had worked to make the Arms a success, and more, a fixture of the London scene. And all of it meant nothing, because some forger had written *Serena Ravenshaw married René du Sacreval* on a piece of paper.

For five years she had been an independent woman with a reliable income. And she owed that, at the heart of it, to the two men standing in this room. Men had saved her, and men could destroy her. A woman couldn't be independent, not really.

She'd been staring at the paper for far longer than the most careful examination required. She had to say something, but she very simply could not move. She couldn't speak. She couldn't think.

Solomon came to her side and pried the piece of paper from her fingers, squeezing one of her hands as he did so. "Are you really married?" he murmured. She shook her head dumbly.

Solomon turned to René. "And if I should put it in the fire?"

"Then what of the parish register?"

She had always loved René's voice; it had meant safety to her to hear it ringing out from the other side of the taproom. Now it sounded diabolical.

"How much does one have to pay the vicar of"—Solomon glanced at the paper—"Saint Andrew of the Cross to put false names in the register?" He was buying her time, hiding her weakness. It was the second time he'd had to do it.

René tsked. "Do not be foolish, dear boy. If those were false— which I do not admit, mind you—would I take a vicar into my confidence? In England they can have scruples, these men of the cloth."

Serena spoke with an effort. "I thought I was inured to betrayal, but I must confess this somewhat surprises me. Where do you expect me to go, René?" Too late, she saw she'd made a play for his sympathy; she was a woman, bargaining from a position of weakness, and he and Solomon could both see it.

"Go home to your father, *sirène*," René said gently. "Or take the money I am offering you."

She laughed a little hysterically. "My father came here yesterday and threatened to lock me up in Bedlam."

René closed his eyes. "I am sorry." He really did sound sorry, very sorry; that made her angrier. "But—there is nothing I can do about that, *chérie*."

Was that all he could say? Serena looked at René, at her oldest, dearest friend, and was possessed by a white-hot fury. As if from very far away, her voice said, "It hardly matters in any case, because I won't be leaving. You have no next of kin, so as your widow, the Arms will revert to me. I shan't like to see you hang, but one does what one must. Good day, René."

His familiar lively features seemed carved out of harsh white stone. "It is not like you to make empty threats, *sirène*. *Écoute*, I will give you two weeks to reflect. If you decide to sell to me, you will be still an independent woman, and rich. I hope you will. But if you are not *raisonnable*, I will be forced to take this paper into a court of law. I will move my things into the apricot room while you decide."

After he had gone, silence reigned in the office. Serena, still sizzling with furious energy, began creating and discarding ever more elaborate plots to destroy René. There was no point thinking of anything else, because she wasn't going to lose the Arms.

"Can you really get him hanged?" Solomon asked.

"Nothing simpler." Serena would never have imagined the words could be so easy to say. "He's a French spy."

Solomon gaped. "Wh—what?"

"This inn was only a front for him. I'm not sure why he thought I wouldn't realize what was going on."

Solomon stared at her in horror. "You knew he was a spy, and you did nothing?"

She shrugged. He didn't need to know how she had agonized, weighing up the evidence of René's guilt again and again, and the consequences if she were right. How she had imagined heroically informing on him, giving up the Arms, taking another protector. And how she couldn't do it. "I needed the Arms," she said flatly. "Besides, I didn't *know*. It could all have been completely innocent."

"But—" He looked in the direction René had gone. She had never seen his face so cold. "He could have passed the information that killed Elijah."

Serena swallowed. He was right. Had she done that to him? Did she have that to answer for, too? She couldn't think about it now. "Does that mean you'll help me?"

"What? Serena—"

She gripped the underside of her desk tightly, where he couldn't see, and tried not to raise her voice. "I'm sorry, Solomon, but I didn't feel as if I owed it to English men to save them, after—at that point in my life, I didn't feel I owed them anything. Besides . . ." She drew in a deep breath. "René was my friend." It hurt to say it; if she went on, if she said enough to make him really understand, if she told him how René had taken care of her when she was nineteen and scared, she would vomit. So she didn't go on, and the skepticism in Solomon's eyes hurt almost as much.

She didn't really expect him to let it go, but he did. "If you had no proof, then how are you going to have him hanged now?"

She wanted to sit down, but that would be one more show of weakness. "He's right, that was an empty threat. If he's hanged for treason, his property is forfeit to the Crown. He would have nothing more to lose; he'd produce those documents and I'd lose the Arms. I have to prove the marriage is a forgery first. Vengeance can come later."

He looked disappointed. She wondered if he wanted to tell her that vengeance was unchristian, or if he simply didn't want to wait for his own. "Yes," he said. "Yes, I'll help you."

His voice sounded like safety. She had been stupid once; she couldn't do it again. No matter how much she wanted to. "Thank you." *Pull yourself together.* "If you don't mind, I'd like to be alone."

He frowned, giving her that piercing hazel look. "Are you sure you'll be all right?"

She nodded. For a moment she thought he wouldn't listen to her, that he would refuse to go; the panicky, powerless feeling in her chest started to take up space she needed for her lungs. But he just looked at her for another moment, and then he nodded and left the room.

She let out her breath, shakily, and sat behind her desk. She ran her hand over the smooth mahogany. She loved that desk. It had been René's, before Serena discovered that he had no head for money. Gradually she'd taken over nearly all the management of the inn, but it had still been René's idea. It was René who had come to her bijou residence that she hated, and sat in her dressing room amid French lingerie and perfume bottles and vaginal sponges—he hadn't even lifted an eyebrow—and offered her, not carte blanche, but a business proposition. He would put up three-quarters of the money, and she would put up the rest, plus her father's name.

Serena pulled one of the heavy ledgers toward her and opened it. *Candles, 15l.*, she read, written in her own neat script. *Firewood, 26l. 6s. New register, 8s. 2p.* This was her life now. How could she abandon it?

She had been staring blankly at the ledger for nearly a quarter of an hour when Sophy came in with a tea tray. "Mr. Hathaway said you wanted this."

Serena looked up at Sophy. Familiar Sophy, who had been there from the beginning. "René wants to take the Arms away from me." She hated how lost her voice sounded.

"What?" Sophy set the tea tray down on the edge of the desk and sat down.

"He's forged marriage lines that say he's my husband."

Sophy's eyes went grim behind her spectacles. "I never liked him."

Serena could not decide whether to laugh or mourn at the patent untruth. "Of course you liked him. I did too. Everybody liked him. But it doesn't matter. He won't get the Arms. Do you know if Antoine's prepared the menus yet for Saturday?"

Sophy accepted the change in topic without a flicker of an eyelid. "I have them right here. He was occupied with tonight's ragout, but he asked me to have you look them over and bring them back when you were through with them."

Serena spread the menus in front of her like a fan, her mind turning to sauces, wine selections, and table arrangements.

This was her life. And she would see René hanged, drawn, and quartered before she would lose it.

Solomon was awakened by muffled voices coming from Serena's room.

"René, he's the hundred and twenty-five pounds. I'm not asking him to move and that's final."

"Is he *really?*" The marquis sounded appreciative, even through several inches of oak. "I always imagined him more sickly looking."

Serena snorted with quickly bitten-off laughter. Solomon cringed. She had told Sacreval about him? What had she said?

"Why do you need him in *my* room, however? I see the door between is locked, which defeats my first guess."

"Oh, I would only leave that door unlocked for someone I *really* trusted, like you," Serena said poisonously. "Solomon is here on business. I'm recovering a family heirloom for him."

"What sort of heirloom?"

"A pair of ruby earrings. A bit of doggerel has made them indispensable to family weddings and they're needed rather urgently."

Solomon flushed at her dismissive tone. Admittedly, that was just how he had described it to her, but it still stung.

"What sort of doggerel?"

Solomon's embarrassment increased as she recited it.

"And they have gone missing?" the marquis said through his laughter. "How convenient for you—Monsieur Hundred-and-Twenty-Five-Pounds' wedding is delayed, and he stays here with you while you search. Where have you hidden them, I should like to know?"

To Solomon's surprise, Serena didn't seem to take offense. "It's his sister's wedding, you clunch. They were stolen by a highwayman on the road to Shropshire last week."

"Then once again I ask, why is he in *my* room? I know you have always had a romantic fancy about that boy, but—" The marquis broke off with a laugh. Solomon could imagine Serena's glare. "My apologies. *Bien sûr*, you have never had a romantic fancy in your life. But I thought our friendship was stronger than that."

"I was stupid enough to think so, too, before you threatened to confiscate my rightful property," she said bitterly. "You of all people ought to be ashamed, using the law's injustice to further yourself. Lord knows you've committed hanging offenses enough, even setting aside your activities for the French crown."

There was a brief silence. "You would not have me hanged for that."

"No, I wouldn't. But you would forge marriage lines to take away my right to own property. Now I find that ironic, don't you?"

"I am truly sorry, *sirène*. It is vile. You ought to take my offer to buy you out."

"Get out of my room, René," Serena said wearily. A few seconds later, the hall door shut quietly.

So. Apparently the ties of old friendship were too strong to be all loosed at once. Solomon sighed. He had been a little shocked at her ruthlessness, earlier, though her shock and misery had been plain enough beneath it. But now he had heard them talking familiarly together—even if it was about *him*—he understood how well they had known each other, and how hard the betrayal must have hit.

Solomon felt abruptly guilty. In the midst of her first furious hurt, he had experienced nothing but relief. Relief that she wasn't really married, as he'd believed for one brief but surprisingly awful moment. He was glad Serena didn't know that.

He knocked on the connecting door. "Yes?" she called.

"Let me in."

After a few moments of silence, she turned the key and opened the door. She was still fully dressed, though it was past midnight; there were ink stains on her fingers. A woman of business, indeed. Solomon felt inexplicably pleased. "Are you all right?"

She stared at him. "You knocked on my door after midnight to ask after my health?"

They both knew he hadn't meant her health. "Well," he said mildly, "I was awakened by people talking about me loudly in the next room."

She froze. "René doesn't know what he's talking about. You know how the French are."

He blinked. "I do?"

"Full of romantic notions about everything."

God, she was impossible. He came to see how she did, even after she'd laughed at him behind his back, and still her first priority was to show she'd never once thought fondly of him. His eyes narrowed. "Since finding my family heirloom is apparently so trivial, perhaps I ought to ask for something extra in return for my help with Sacreval."

Serena's brows drew together. She had the most adorable frown. And she'd kill him if she knew he was thinking that. "Don't think that just because René said I used to have a fancy for you, I'd be willing to—"

Did she really expect him to ask her to sleep with him? He sagged, making a face of theatrical disappointment. "But, Serena—"

She looked murderous. Solomon couldn't help it: he laughed. Her frown softened at the edges.

Solomon flushed without quite knowing why. *Had* she had a romantic fancy about him? She'd thought about him apparently.

He had thought about her, too, at first. For those wretched, penniless four months at Cambridge, he'd thought about her every time he had to borrow a half-crown from his friends. He'd spun himself tales about her triumphant return home to lead a happy and virtuous life, trying to convince himself it had been worth it, even though he'd known it was likelier her madam had stolen every penny. He was ashamed to realize that once his penury ended and the next quarter's allowance appeared, and Ashton and Braithwaite stopped needling him about it, he hadn't thought about her much at all.

He had certainly never imagined *this*. He smiled at her. "When the Prince Regent brings his friends here for dinner on Saturday, you have to wear a gown made with fabric from my uncle's shop."

She looked at him, and sighed. "Solomon, this isn't a joke."

He almost gave in. After all, she'd had a large shock that day. But—he ran his gaze up and down her figure appraisingly, and dress patterns and color combinations started to turn ecstatic somersaults his head. It was improbable, how beautiful she was. "I'm not joking."

"I suppose I hardly have a choice. But no red. I'm not in the mood for scarlet woman gibes."

"Pink?" he asked hopefully, and snickered when she glared.

Serena had barely any fault to find with the gown as she tried it on early Saturday morning. The severe cut of the thin wool gave her height, and the deep apricot color made her hair and skin glow; yet neither the cloth nor the color seemed too rich for a hard-working woman of business. The long, full sleeves were gathered in three places by white ribbon covered with delicate gilt flourishes.

"Raizh your armzh," Solomon said around a mouthful of pins. She obeyed. "Doezh it feel tight?"

"No. I think it's a trifle loose on the left, actually." Under pretense of eying her reflection, she watched Solomon in the full-length mirror she'd had carried into her office for the purpose. He was kneeling beside her in his shirtsleeves (which were rolled up above the elbow), a tape measure draped about his neck. There was something very charming about it.

She watched his strong hands and forearms as he pulled a few pins from between his lips. His light skin, with its downy blond hair and smattering of bright freckles, made her think of orchids dipped in honey. As he pulled the left-hand seam of the bodice tighter, one dye-stained thumb slid over the soft edge of her breast. Not quite to Serena's surprise, her skin began to tingle pleasantly. Damn. She had been a fool to agree to this, even if her own dressmaker *was* too busy to do the final fitting. She shifted slightly, and to her relief he pricked her. "Ow!"

He looked up at her reprovingly over a pair of severe half-glasses that seemed at odds with his untidy yellow hair.

"And why the devil are you wearing spectacles?" she demanded. "I've seen you read without them."

"Zhey make me look professional." Serena raised a mocking eyebrow for form's sake, but his next words echoed her thoughts eerily. "Don't look at me like zhat. You of all people undershtand about looking professional."

She didn't like that. He was supposed to think she *was* professional. He wasn't supposed to know it was a struggle. "It was much less expensive when looking professional meant wearing almost nothing."

Solomon made a choking noise and a shower of pins hit the floor. She expected him to turn red with embarrassment, but then his shoulders shook and when his eyes met hers in the mirror she saw he was laughing. He didn't do it enough. "Don't make me laugh!" he said, picking the pins up, wiping them on his breeches, and putting them back in his mouth. "Besides, everybody knows that 'almost nothing' is more expensive than a lot where clothes are concerned."

Serena glanced down at the top of his head with a mixture of exasperation and something else she didn't want to examine too closely—and fortunately for her peace of mind was instantly distracted. From this angle it became very clear that there *was* something wrong with the gown.

"While we're on the subject of almost nothing, don't you think this is a trifle décolleté for my present line of work?" Of course she had had to speak up—she couldn't go into the dining room like this—but she almost wished she hadn't when his brief glance at her bodice had her nipples all but standing up on their hind legs and begging.

He raised his eyebrows. Damnation, that was *her* supercilious facial expression and it wasn't fair of him to do it so well. "Don't you trust me?" he asked. "The chemisette has to be fitted, too."

Turning to the bandbox in which the gown had been packed, he pulled out two triangular pieces of fine linen, piped with the same white-and-gold ribbon as the sleeves. When sewn into the dress, they would transform the extremely revealing square neckline into a modest V, and hide the birthmark on the slope of her left breast.

He stood and reached for her neckline, but that was going too far. She held out her hand imperiously. "I'll do it."

He looked at her in exasperation. "You don't know how to do it, and anyway you can't see it. Are you this missish with your modiste?"

"My modiste is—" *not you.* "A woman."

His mouth set in a hard line. "Serena, have I been in any way unprofessional?"

"I'm afraid I don't see—" she began in her most calmly patronizing tone.

"Have I?"

"No, Solomon, you've been quite the gentleman, but—"

"Then quit acting as if the only thought in my thimble-sized brain is to get my hands on you. I'm not Lord Smollett!"

Thank God. He was completely unaware of her actual motive. (Also thank God he wasn't Lord Smollett.) She didn't know what to say; she was half-afraid that if she said anything further, he would point out that he'd been a lot closer to her and seen a lot more, six years ago. If she weren't a ruined woman, she thought, he wouldn't have dared to suggest fitting the dress himself at all.

But that was only half the story, wasn't it? He'd suggested it—and she had agreed. She'd wanted his hands on her and now she had them, and she had better pretend it wasn't affecting her in the slightest. "Go ahead," she muttered.

"*Thank* you."

She set her jaw and hoped he couldn't feel the absurdly fast beating of her heart as she imagined his hands moving lower, cupping her breasts and roaming over her belly, her hips, her—

"There," he said. He stepped back and nodded with satisfaction. "You look like Lucretia Borgia."

Serena would have sighed with relief if her breathing hadn't already been nearly out of her control. "Lucretia Borgia was blond." But she didn't dare essay a superior smile.

Besides, she saw what he meant. The gown made her look mysterious and alluring, and at the same time commanding and even a little dangerous—all the things she had striven to be. All the things she had made herself. It was perfect.

And Solomon had designed it for her. He had given her a spangled domino to match her mask—when no one else had ever suspected she was wearing one. It frightened her, made her feel naked and cold. She drew herself up. "Charming, nevertheless. Your talents are wasted on waistcoats." But light irony had deserted her. Her words sounded sarcastic and ill-humored.

He sighed. "You don't like it."

Her twinge of guilt irritated her. "Don't be a fool," she said awkwardly. "You don't need me to tell you you're talented."

He relaxed, grinning sheepishly at her. "It looks as if I do. Sorry."

She made a dismissive gesture as he reached for the hem of

her sleeve. Their fingers brushed; electricity tore through her. Solomon's hazel eyes sharpened over the ridiculous spectacles, and the air between them shimmered and changed—

The door to her office swung open so hard it thunked against the wall.

Chapter 4

"I cannot be doing zis!" said a ringing Cockney voice with a French accent so fake even the Prince Regent could probably have seen through it. "Ze pastry cook's boys, zey are not being here! My reputation, it will be in shreds. It is ze end, ze end. I am putting a period to my existence!"

Serena turned around and looked at her head chef, trying not to be annoyed at the interruption. "Please don't do it in my kitchen."

Antoine really did look distraught, his chef's hat askew on his carroty locks and a towel half-falling from his shoulders. "You laugh but it is serious I am. By ze way, you look like a goddess. And if I do not have ze finest dessert to set before ze Prince Regent tonight, I will throw myself off of a bridge! I do not jest. It is a tradition among us chefs. Vatel stabbed himself eight times when ze fish he was to prepare for ze king did not arrive!"

"But the fish came in the end," Solomon said. "He should have waited. Are you sure the pastry cook's boys aren't coming?"

Serena stared at him. "How do you know the fish came?"

"The same way your cook does, I'd imagine. I read the new translation of Mme de Sevigné's letters that was published last month."

The cook nodded. "A brilliant woman—so typical of my beloved France!" The closest Antoine had ever come to France was when Serena sent him to the spice market in Horsham, two hours south of London. "But ze boys—zey are not coming. One of zem has ze influenza; we cannot risk spreading the contagion to our beloved future monarch."

Serena cursed. "Can't Ying whip up something?"

"It will take her all day to make the bread."

"Is it too late to send to Gunter's?"

"Yes, and besides, we will not impress His Royal Highness with the culinary excellence of ze house in zis manner! I am sure he knows every dessert in Gunter's *ménu* like the back of his royal hand."

"How many people do you expect?" Solomon asked.

"Fifty at least!"

He smiled. "Your worries are over. I can make the dessert if I start now."

Serena's jaw dropped. Had everyone gone mad? "You? *You* can make dessert for the Carlton House set?"

"Would you prefer burnt cream or almond-pear tartlets? Those are the most elegant selections in my repertoire." His smile turned self-deprecating and conspiratorial. "Actually, those are the only selections in my repertoire. But they're both good."

"Is there no end to your womanly talents?"

"Baking is just like chemistry!" he protested.

Her lips twitched. "Let's have the almond-pear tartlets."

An hour later, Solomon stared in awe at the gigantic kitchen. Spits turned on their own power in the huge fireplace, shining copperware filled the shelves, and bundles of dried herbs hung from the wall. In one corner dangled a great hook whose purpose he could only guess at. The center of the room was occupied by an enormous steam table, on which a number of covered dishes already rested. On a low stove in the corner, Antoine stirred a huge pot of something that smelled delicious.

When he saw his employer, the chef made his way across the room toward them, unslinging a towel from around his neck and wiping the sweat from his face. He had to stop several times along the way to critique the actions of undercooks and kitchen maids, in one case taking a knife away from a boy and showing him the proper way to cut carrots into fine, long strips.

"He's not French," Solomon said.

"Of course not," Serena agreed. "But he thought it was funny to copy René's accent and pretend he was a snooty French chef. René used to—used to give him pointers on Gallicisms." She was quiet for a moment. "Antoine was cook in a gin shop before this."

"And how, precisely, did he learn to cook like a French chef?"

She gave him an amused, sidelong glance. "Don't be snide. The Blue Ruin was famous for its food."

Antoine reached them. "Oh, you will make me blush! But it is true. *Hélas*, it was hard to reconcile myself to working in zat sordid pit of vice after my youth among ze lavender fields of Provence. But a true chef takes his satisfaction in staying faithful to his vocation, even when ze creations of his genius go to feed English criminals wis no appreciation of ze finer zings in life!"

"Now, Antoine, you know your patrons at the Blue Ruin appreciated you enormously. I thought they would riot when I hired you to work here."

Antoine seized Serena's hand and kissed it. She only looked mildly discomfited. That surprised Solomon; she'd hated the fitting.

He'd hated the fitting. Or he'd loved it, he wasn't sure which. It had been a stupid thing to suggest, but her modiste was busy and—he'd wanted to touch her. Then he'd had to try desperately to touch her as little as possible. He'd pretended he was at the shop, told himself that he was a tradesman, that he had no feelings or thoughts, that he was an automaton built only for tailoring and laughing at customers' jokes. It was no use. If it had gone on one moment longer he would have made a fool of himself, and she would have never spoken to him again. It was lucky that hardly any adjustments had been necessary—Serena's modiste was talented and knew Serena's measurements well. They were nice measurements.

"I owe everyzing to you, my beloved mistress," Antoine said. "Thanks to your farsighted decision to hire me, I have attained ze pinnacle of my art, and even now I prepare a meal for ze regent!"

"It was a sensible business decision, that's all." But her smile reminded Solomon of how his mother used to look when he'd singed off Elijah's hair or scorched sugar onto the bottom of all the pots in the kitchen in one of his childish experiments. There was that same reluctant, affectionate pride in it, trying to hide under sternness.

He realized, as he'd failed to do before, that Serena felt about the inn the way he felt about Hathaway's Fine Tailoring. And Sacreval wanted to take it away from her. *Never*, he vowed silently. "Did you buy what I asked for?" he asked Antoine.

"But of course! It is in ze pastry kitchen right now. Do you wish me to show you?"

"The pastry kitchen? How many kitchens do you have?"

"Zere is ze pastry kitchen, ze ice room, ze larder, and ze bakehouse. I have asked and asked for a confectioner's room, but again and again I am refused." He said this last with a meaningful glance at Serena.

"We don't have a confectioner," Serena pointed out.

"We ought to hire one. Zen we would not be in zis position."

"Make do."

Antoine gave a long-suffering sigh. "And zese are ze conditions under which I must create my masterpieces!"

"And yet somehow you always manage," Serena said. Antoine smiled at her.

Footmen paraded by, carrying crates of fine china with a coat of arms emblazoned in the center: two ravens pecking at the visor of a helmet, on a scarlet shield topped with a marquess's coronet. Solomon recognized the design from the swinging wooden sign outside the inn.

Two of the footmen were dark-haired boys with a striking resemblance to each other. The elder hunched to one side with his crate to whisper something in the younger's ear. Solomon felt a familiar rush of gnawing, resentful envy, and then a familiar rush of shame at feeling anything so petty.

Laughing and distracted, the younger boy jostled Serena as he passed. "Have a care with our best china!" she chided the unfortunate young man, who stammered apologetically and hurried to rejoin the train.

"Are they brothers?" Solomon asked, and then wished he hadn't when Serena gave him a sorry, awkward look.

She nodded. "The young one's new. Their mother took in laundry, and he used to help her, but she died this spring, so Jem needed new work."

Solomon felt doubly ashamed of his moment of envy. "And were those really the Ravenshaw arms?" he said to turn the subject.

She smirked. "It wouldn't be any fun if they weren't. I only wish I could justify the expense of putting them on *all* our china."

"It's a pretty morbid coat of arms."

"I always liked it."

She would. He smiled. "I suppose morbidity can be glamorous, in its way."

Serena raised an eyebrow. "Never tell me you were one of those young men who lurks about in graveyards, drooping languidly and wearing black."

Solomon grinned. "No, I wasn't. But Elijah was for about two months. Being the parson's sons, we had unlimited access to the churchyard. He even penned a few verses on the brevity of life." He had been marvelously good at drooping languidly, but his verses, which he had read to Solomon with great enthusiasm, had been uniformly bad.

Serena moved a step closer in silent acknowledgment. He

found it unexpectedly comforting. "Did it drive the young ladies wild?" she asked.

"Naturally. Who doesn't wish to be kissed behind a tombstone?"

"Who indeed?" She sighed. "I'd better go see if the flowers have arrived. Let me know if you need anything." She disappeared out the door. He watched her go, trying not to remember the way she'd curved under his hands when he'd pinned her dress.

"She takes such a childlike pleasure in spiting her fazzer," Antoine said. "And never once has he come here to appreciate it, until zis week."

Solomon stared. "*Never?*" He had known he was undesirable, but so undesirable that Lord Blackthorne had broken a five-year pattern to get rid of him? His social standing had reached a new low, and Blackthorne was an even viler snob than he'd thought.

"Not once. It is a subject of much conversation among ze staff." He turned calculating eyes on Solomon. "You were zere. What did he want?"

"Er. I don't think I ought to tell you."

"No, you oughtn't. But Sophy was worried, and she told me to ask. Are you sure you will not reveal your secrets?"

"Yes, I'm sure."

"All right zen," Antoine said with a Gallic shrug that was the image of Sacreval's. "Let me show you what we have bought you. Ze finest pears in London, zat is what!"

The dining room was scrubbed, the good china laid out, and all the waiters and waitresses dressed in their finest livery. Serena resisted the urge to go and look at herself in the mirror again. The gown would look as perfect this time as it had the previous twenty-seven, and she would look just as pale and cold. It was how she wanted to look, and yet thinking of Solomon—with his grins and flushes and expressive hazel eyes, and the way the set of his shoulders could tell you exactly how he was feeling at all times—she couldn't help wondering if she repelled him. She tried not to regret her tongue-tied schoolgirl self. That self could never have survived the past six years.

That self couldn't have curtsied politely to the Prince Regent and ten of his closest friends. She couldn't have smoothly ignored the men's ogling, knowing she'd slept with at least half of them, or brushed off their wives' avid stares, as if she were some outlandish creature in a menagerie.

That self *certainly* couldn't have hidden her boundless contempt for Sir Percy Blakeney and his inane little wife. She didn't care how many French aristocrats the former Scarlet Pimpernel had saved from the Terror, he was insufferable. It was only five minutes into the meal, and he was *already* telling that story about escaping through the gates of Paris in '93 dressed as an old hag, with the de Tourneys hidden under the cabbages.

"Wherever did you get that stunning gown?" Lady Blakeney asked Serena in her charmingly accented English. "The clarity of the color is remarkable. It is as bright as those waistcoats my husband ordered from Hathaway's Fine Tailoring!"

"As a matter of fact," Serena said, "it *is* from Hathaway's. It was designed for me by Mr. Solomon Hathaway himself." She wondered what they would say if she told them he had fitted it, too.

Lord Alvanley, celebrated wit and dandy, smiled maliciously. "I say, Dewington, I believe she's speaking of your nephew!"

"You've boasted often enough of having designed a gown for the Siren yourself," Dewington snapped. Lady Dewington elbowed him.

Alvanley had the grace to look abashed. He threw Serena an apprehensive glance. She gritted her teeth. She remembered that gown. It hadn't been very comfortable, but the dandy had offered her fifty pounds to wear it. He still owed her the money.

"He makes up the dyes, don't he?" asked Sir Percy. "Talented fellow, for a shopkeeper—oh, sorry, your nevvy, of course, Dewington."

"Well, a young man must sow his wild oats somehow," Dewington said without conviction.

"There!" said Lady Blakeney. "Did I not say it was from Hathaway's?"

Sir Percy beamed proudly. "So you did, m'dear. Demmed clever woman, my wife. Cleverest woman in Europe, don't you know. Star of the *Comédie Française*. I had to fight my way into her greenroom." No one had called Lady Blakeney the cleverest woman in Europe in at *least* fifteen years. Serena had her private suspicions that those who had, even then, had not been Europe's brightest lights.

Lady Blakeney gave a trilling laugh. "Oh, that was *years* ago! We are not so young as we were, Sir Percy."

Sir Percy glowered. "I'm still young enough to show those Frogs a thing or two about British ingenuity! I say, Your Highness, have you spoken to Varney about sending me to France as I asked? I speak French like a native, you know."

Serena did not stare. She didn't laugh. She didn't picture Sir Percy—all foppish, red-faced, middle-aged six feet of him, who got out of breath walking from the dining room to his carriage—as an agent of the Crown in Napoleon's Paris. She found, though—and it was an unsettling sensation—that she could not wait to tell Solomon all about it.

"Varney likes to hire his own agents," Prinny said placidly. "He has some excellent French speakers already. I told him you were a deuced clever fellow, but he said your exploits as the Scarlet Pimpernel were too celebrated to allow you the proper incognito."

"Indeed, Sir Percy," Lady Blakeney scolded, "I have told you! I spent my youth worrying you would lose your head, but now we are older I wish we might simply be comfortable."

"My wife worries too much," Sir Percy said jovially. "Why, once I was forced to feign my own death to throw off that little Chauvelin, and I vow she nearly—"

Lady Blakeney hit him smartly with her fan. "I do not find that story *amusant*, Sir Percy!"

"But you would not have made such a regal little widow if you had known, m'dear—" Sir Percy's eyes narrowed. "I say, who the devil is that?" He spoke in the same jovial tones, and gestured languidly in the direction of the kitchens, but Serena suddenly felt a little less sure that Sir Percy had never been a force to be reckoned with. She turned to look.

It was René, who had always managed to avoid Sir Percy in the past. Serena did not step protectively between them; she was bitterly ashamed that she still wanted to. "That is monseigneur du Sacreval, my former business partner. Do you know him, Sir Percy?"

But Sir Percy was shaking his head and leaning back in his chair. "Not in the least, m'dear. He is the spitting image of a baker I once knew, a member of the Committee of Public Safety. But that man would be at least thirty years older than your partner now, if he were still alive—and now I think of it, I saw him beheaded myself."

I'm only relieved because I'm afraid for the Arms, Serena told herself. *I don't care what happens to René. Not at all.* As she headed to the foot of the table to tell Joe to bring up more rolls, she happened to glance at the regent. He was watching René with narrowed, considering eyes. "The fellow's back, is he?" he asked.

Serena felt cold. "Indeed, Your Highness. He returned only a few days ago. He is waiting for the Bourbons to be restored once more so that he can return to France."

The regent nodded genially. Serena decided to see how things were progressing in the kitchens.

It was a mistake.

Solomon was leaning against the door frame of the pastry

kitchen, covered in flour to the elbows, listening to something Antoine was saying. He glanced up at her and smiled just as he licked a large dollop of almond-pear off his thumb.

Now she remembered why she disliked the kitchens during dinner. The ovens made everything so damned hot.

"Want a taste?" he yelled above the kitchen's racket.

Chapter 5

Well. She had to make sure he hadn't, oh, forgotten the sugar or something, didn't she? It was her responsibility. She pulled a spoon from a jar of them that sat on the counter and headed over.

"How are things upstairs?" he asked. He licked a last drop of sticky tart filling off his lip, and Serena swallowed.

"Good. I don't know how qualified our regent is to direct national politics, but he's an excellent gourmand. Probably one of my few former patrons who's wholeheartedly pleased with my change in professions." She dipped her spoon in his bowl. Somehow, it seemed like an incredibly intimate act. Her cheeks heated. *It's just the ovens.*

His eyes widened. "You mean you—you *slept* with the Prince Regent?"

The pleasant heat faded. Not this again. "I did."

He chewed at his lower lip. "Can I ask you something? I wouldn't, but I've always wanted to know—"

"Certainly," she said coolly. "But I shan't promise to answer it."

"Does he use French holes?"

She stared at him. She hated to admit that Solomon knew of a perversion of which *she* had never heard, but there was nothing for it. "French holes?"

"On his corset," Solomon said impatiently. "You know—most use ordinary buttonholes, but some use a sort of eyelet made of ivory or bone. You can lace them tighter that way."

She blinked. Then she bit the back of her hand, shaking with silent, helpless laughter. "I never noticed," she admitted, when she could speak again.

He sniffed scornfully, but his eyes were warm.

She realized she was still holding her spoon, full of almond-pear filling. She put it in her mouth, and her eyes widened. "Oh."

He smiled at her. "It's good, isn't it?" he said in a low, warm voice, and she immediately pictured him saying the same thing in quite another context.

She eyed him suspiciously. Had he *meant* that to sound indecent? He blinked innocently at her, and she decided that he had. "It'll do," she said. "Did you know that Sir Percy Blakeney is angling to be sent to France as a spy?"

"No!" Solomon's whole face lit up with glee.

The prince's eyes popped. "I say, Dewington, these are your Mrs. Jones's pear-almond tartlets! I've been trying to buy the recipe from her for decades! What did you pay, Lady Serena?"

The look of dawning horror on Dewington's face as he realized exactly how that recipe had made its way into Serena's kitchen would be forever precious to her. "Not a farthing, Your Highness," she said.

"Then how—no one knows the recipe but Dewington's cook!"

Serena met Dewington's eyes. The man was fidgeting in his seat and twitching slightly. She smiled slowly. "I think Mrs. Jones must have confided the recipe to Lord Dewington's sister." All eyes turned to Dewington, who gritted his teeth manfully. His wife looked ready to sink into the floor.

"Good Lord!" Sir Percy exclaimed. "Your nevvy's working in the kitchens!"

Lord Petersham shook his head. "There but for the grace of God go I. Will Hathaway was my Latin tutor too, and my sister would have run off with him in a trice if he'd asked her. Handsome devil. Heard the boy looks just like him."

"He has my sister's eyes," Dewington said. No one seemed to quite know what to say to that.

Ordinarily, Serena would have entered the day's earnings and expenses in the books before bed, but she was exhausted. Ordinarily, she would have taken the back stairs to the first floor to avoid running into guests in the hallway, but—"she was exhausted" wouldn't wash as a reason for that, would it?

She would have done the books before bed, and she would have taken the back stairs, only Solomon was heading for the public rooms and the main staircase right now (it didn't seem to have occurred to him that the back way was faster from the kitchens), and she had fallen into step with him without thinking about it—without wanting to think about it. She compromised by not speaking and going over the night's numbers in her head, instead. The silence felt oddly companionable, and yet oddly charged.

Outside his room, he stopped. She could have kept walking, but instead she stopped with him. "Thank you for your help today," she said, meaning to sound businesslike and sounding grateful instead.

He smiled and ducked his head. "You're welcome." Was it her imagination, or was his low, rough voice a little lower and rougher than usual? He raised his head and met her eyes, and she thought that yes, it must have been, because he was giving her a low, rough look.

That doesn't even make sense, she thought. *A look can't be low and rough.* And then it didn't matter, because he was leaning in to kiss her.

She took a step backward, and he missed. But instead of giving up, as she wanted—expected—feared—he gave her a reproachful look and tried again. His lips brushed against hers softly, gently, as if it were her first time. It wasn't her first time. It was her thousandth time, her millionth, and she had never, in her whole life, felt anything like this. She felt as if she were a neat page in a ledger and he'd spilled ink across her. She could feel it spreading over her skin, soaking in, making her messy and vivid and irrevocably destroyed.

He gasped against her mouth (when had they opened their mouths? the world tasted like almonds and pears) and put his hands on her hips, turning them so they fell against the door to his room. She could feel the carved wood against her back with more immediacy than she'd felt anything in ages. Someone could see them, a guest could walk by and see them. She cared about that. She should care about that.

But she was paralyzed by desire and the sudden bloom of color across her blankness; she could only tremble and kiss him back. When he leaned his weight on her it felt as if they were melting into each other like sugar and water caramelizing in a double boiler, slow and delicious. His chest was heaving against hers. Her breasts strained against her corset when she breathed, too. She wanted him to touch them, but he didn't. He just pressed against her, his hands resting on her hips, and kissed her as if that was all he wanted, as if he could do it forever. As if it were her first time.

But it *wasn't* her first time. He should know that. Why didn't he know that? She was a whore and she wanted more from him than kisses, and when he realized that—he wouldn't kiss her like this anymore. He was giving her this, and that meant he could take it away. He was in control, now. He nipped at her lower lip, and she made a needy, surprised little sound, like a damned *kitten*. She froze, mortified.

But if Serena had learned one thing in the last six years, it was that when you were threatened, usually the best thing to do was go on the attack. She wrenched herself away. "Someone will see us."

He blinked at her, his eyes dark in the dim corridor. His lips were wet and parted. "Oh." He cleared his throat. "Sorry."

She smiled, slow and full of promise. "Open your door."

He swallowed. "Y—yes. I—" He fumbled in his pocket for his key, and just like that, she was on top again. She could do this. She could kiss him and still be herself, still be in control. It took him three tries to get the key in the lock.

The door swung open, and bright light danced and leapt onto the hallway carpet. She smelled smoke even before she pushed past him into the room and saw. The great carved mantelpiece was on fire.

The flames had not yet reached very high. It wouldn't be a disaster if she acted quickly. But Solomon had made her soft and open, and terror swept right in. She was rooted to the spot. It was Solomon who rushed to the water jug and found it empty.

"I filled it this afternoon!" He glanced once around the room and then, muttering something that sounded suspiciously like "Sorry, Uncle Hathaway," he grabbed a stylish greatcoat off the bed, knelt down, and smothered the flames.

Now Serena could move again. She strode to the hearth and whisked away what remained of a very fine coat. She coughed helplessly, tears springing to her eyes at the smoke. An overturned candlestick, a puddle of hot wax, the ashes of some stray kindling from the fire that had been set for Solomon to light when he returned, and the charred underside of a carved crescent moon were all she could see through the afterimage of the flames. She turned a furious face on him. "You left a candle burning?" she rasped.

"Of course not. Someone set that up! I *never* leave a candle burning. A chemist learns soon enough to be very careful with fire or he finds his house in ashes!"

Her eyes turned to Solomon's worktable, covered with mysterious jars, beakers, and bags. He was dangerous. She had known it, and here was the proof. "You mean there are things there that could blow up the Arms?"

Getting to his feet, Solomon rolled his eyes. "Not in their

current state. Besides, I make dyes, not gunpowder. But when I was a student—"

She barely heard him. All she could see or hear was the Arms engulfed in flame. The Arms, gone. He had almost caused it, and it didn't even give him pause. Her life had been built so painstakingly; it was fragile, and he couldn't seem to realize it. He just went his merry way, charming her and kissing her and *almost burning her home to the ground*—"That's it," she told him. "Get out. Just—just go. First thing in the morning, you *and* your infernal chemicals!"

He gaped at her. "What?"

He sounded so incredulous, as if he knew how much she wanted him. As if he knew how much she already regretted her words. It goaded her on. "You heard me."

He frowned at her. "Serena, if this is about the kiss—I didn't expect that either, I didn't expect it to be so—"

"Boring?" she said cruelly, and went through the connecting door and slammed it.

Solomon stood there, trying to figure out what had just happened. He'd thought everything had been going so well.

Too well, maybe. He'd pushed her too far, thrown her off-balance with the kiss. Maybe he should have given up when she'd backed away, that first moment. But that was what he liked about her, how she fought everything. How she'd been crushed so many times and she just kept going, kept clawing her way forward.

He'd let so many things pass in his life, told himself they didn't matter, that it was useless to fight, and she treated everything as if it was a pitched battle—one she could *win*. She fought her father and Sacreval and still managed to find energy for Lord Smollett and a customer who pinched a waitress. He'd wanted to kiss her so badly, and when she'd backed away he'd thought, *Of course you're fighting this, too*, and something in him had refused to give up this time.

And he'd won—he'd felt like he'd won, anyway, felt such a thrill of victory and joy and wanted to make her feel it, too. He had made her feel it. He remembered how she'd kissed him back, how she'd let him hold her, and the little disbelieving yearning sound she'd made. She had sounded so surprised that she could feel good, and he'd felt such a startling, aching tenderness—he'd never felt *anything* like that before. Then she'd stiffened as if caught in a shameful weakness, and somehow that had only made the tenderness worse.

That was the problem, though. She fought her own pleasure just as she fought everything else; she didn't seem to know how to stop fighting. And then the fire had frightened her, and she'd panicked, and now it was too late for her to retreat from her ultimatum.

If he was going to talk her out of it, he was going to have to be very, very careful. He narrowed his eyes, thinking. A show of compliance would probably help. Kicking the remains of his coat out of the way, he headed down the stairs to ask Antoine to save him some crates to pack his belongings in.

He was awakened by muffled cries of pain from the room next door. He lay there for a moment, disoriented, and then Serena said, very distinctly, "No!"

He was at the door in seconds, uselessly rattling the knob. Locked. He dashed to his worktable. In too much of a hurry for finesse, he grabbed the beaker of hydrochloric acid and tipped a healthy amount down the keyhole, covering his nose and mouth with one hand to avoid breathing in noxious fumes. The lock mechanism and most of the face of the keyhole sizzled and dissolved. Hastily capping the beaker and setting it back on the table, he turned the now unresisting doorknob and burst through the door.

Chapter 6

To Solomon's surprise, the only occupant of the room was Serena—fast asleep. Her fists were clenched and her face was set in lines of determination and fear as she threw herself from side to side, straining against invisible bonds. "No! No, damn you!"

Solomon took hold of her shoulders and shook her. "Serena, wake up!" he said as loudly as he dared. "Wake up, you're all right!"

Serena jolted awake. It hadn't just been a dream, then—someone was holding her shoulders, restraining her. She bolted upright and punched him squarely in the stomach. "Let me go, you son of a bitch!" she hissed, and went for the pistol in her bedside drawer.

Solomon held up the hand that wasn't clutching his stomach and shook his head frantically. Oh. She was awake. That had been a dream. Right. She took a deep breath and abandoned the drawer. "Solomon? What the devil are you doing here?"

He pointed to his throat.

"Did I wind you? My humblest apologies. I imagine you have some perfectly innocent reason for having broken into my room in the dead of night?"

"You were yelling," he croaked. "I was worried."

Damn. "I'm fine. It was just a dream."

He sat down on the edge of her bed, massaging his stomach. "You don't look fine." Abruptly his eyes widened, riveted on her breasts, all too exposed in her thin cotton shift.

Serena shivered nervously under his gaze, then wished she hadn't. "It's chilly in here," she said shortly, although the room was very warm. "Hand me my robe." Ordinarily she would have died rather than let Solomon see her robe (an orange silk fringed thing covered in a riot of embroidered chrysanthemums, peacock feathers, pomegranates, and other bright designs), but right now she just wanted another layer between him and her breasts. She crossed her arms over her chest.

Solomon reddened and jerked his eyes away. "Er. Sorry."

When he handed her the robe, she shoved her arms into the fringed sleeves, wrapped the orange silk tight across her chest, and hugged herself. Solomon sighed, and said the last thing she would have expected. "Come on, I'll make you a cup of chocolate."

"You have chocolate in your room?"

"What kind of bachelor would I be if I didn't?"

Chocolate seemed like the absolute best thing that could happen just then, so she followed him without demur. Handing her a chipped earthenware mug with "A Present from Swansea" painted on the side, he rummaged through his equipment. After a short search he lined up a battered crucible, a glass bowl, and a small, crinkled paper sack on the edge of the table.

"You're making the chocolate in that? Have you washed it?"

Solomon gave her an exasperated look. "This is my chocolate-making equipment. I don't use it for experiments. It's safe." He soon had a merry flame lit under the crucible. Serena relaxed a little in the light—that is, until Solomon said, "What were you dreaming about?"

She stared at him.

"Talking about it will make you feel better."

Was he mad? "I assure you, I'm quite recovered already. Besides, there's nothing you can do."

"I can listen."

Serena didn't answer.

Solomon's broad back was to her as he poured water into the crucible and the glass bowl. "After Elijah died," he said in conversational tones, "I used to dream nearly every night that

I saw him die. Over and over, and I *felt* it. The bullet would hit him in the chest, and the pain—sometimes he would fall off his horse, and I could feel my neck snap." He paused. "In some ways that was better than the nights I dreamed he was back and it was all a mistake."

Good Lord. "And did telling someone that make you *feel* better?" she asked harshly. "Did it make it go away?"

He set the bowl into the crucible's mouth to make a small double boiler. "No, it didn't make it go away. It will never *go away*. But—I do feel better now, actually." He glanced over his shoulder with a rueful chuckle. *Now*. He believed that a trouble shared was a trouble halved and yet he hadn't told anyone either, hadn't had anyone to tell. He'd waited for nearly two years, only to tell *her*. Of all the people he could have chosen—people who might have known what to say, people who might not have kicked him out of their hotels the evening before for no good reason—he'd chosen her, and telling her had made him feel better.

She wanted to go to him—but he didn't want that. He had told her what he wanted: he wanted her nightmare. "All right." She sat down on the edge of his bed. He sat on his workbench and watched her. She fixed her eyes on the mug. "René came to take me off to Bedlam. Only I knew somehow that it wouldn't be Bedlam, it would be Mme Deveraux's house, but when I said so they all looked at me if I were raving. And then they dragged me out the front door, and they were turning everyone out into the street. All the staff, and it was cold, and they locked the front doors shut and put up a big 'Closed' placard. I couldn't stop them, they wouldn't listen to me and I couldn't—I couldn't do a damn thing."

She could barely get the words out, they felt so intimate and shameful.

He sat down on the bed beside her with a thump. "That isn't going to happen," he told her.

"Why?" she demanded. "Because you won't let it?"

He smiled at her. "No. Because you won't."

Which was stupid. She didn't have a damn clue how to stop René. But Solomon saying it made her feel better anyway. Her authority, her control—it was all smoke and mirrors, but it hadn't stopped working yet. He still believed in it.

He reached over and tugged one of her pigtails. "Maybe—" He got up and began measuring cocoa powder into the hot water with a spoon. "Maybe you should take Sacreval up on his offer to buy the place."

She had thought about that too, lying in bed staring at the ceiling in the cold cowardly early morning, but it wasn't just her blind panic at losing the Arms that stopped her. "Yes, and when I've used the money to buy a new establishment, perhaps he'll decide he wants that one, too. As long as he's alive and has a copy of those marriage lines, I'm beaten."

He stirred the chocolate slowly. "Serena, can I ask you a question?"

"All right," she said warily.

"Where did you get that robe? It's not anyone in London that I recognize."

Before she knew it she was smiling—a real, happy smile. It felt disturbingly unfamiliar on her face. "One thing I love about you, Solomon, is your predictability." He watched her inquiringly through his blush, and finally she looked at her mug and told him the truth. "I made it myself."

"*What?*"

"Well, you needn't look so shocked. I was a bored young lady once, you know."

"You did that yourself?"

"For the third time, *yes.*" Embroidery was a proper, ladylike occupation, and it didn't require talking to anyone. She could spend hours at it and no one would bother her. The robe was one of the few things she'd taken with her when she left Ravenscroft.

"Would you consider doing piecework for my uncle?"

She laughed. "Where's my chocolate?"

He held out his hand for her mug. She gave it to him reluctantly, not knowing what to do with her hands when it was gone. He set another mug beside it on the table—this one with Nelson's portrait on it—and tipped steaming chocolate into them. Then he rummaged some more. Serena would have to take a more careful look at his things one of these days, because she'd never noticed that jar of sugar cubes or the little bottle of—Madeira? He flashed her a wicked smile. "Want some?"

"Of course." He poured a healthy dollop into both cups. She took hers and sipped. It warmed her cold fingers, and warmth spread comfortably down her throat and into her stomach. Glancing up, she caught Solomon licking away chocolate from the corner of his mouth. A jolt of heat went through her that had nothing to do with chocolate or Madeira.

She looked at her mug. "Solomon?"

"Yes?"

"Why have you been so kind to me? I've been nothing but rude to you, and you—"

He looked at her silently for a moment, and suddenly she heard what he'd said when she asked him about the hundred and twenty-five pounds. *Because you needed it.* Was he going to say it again? It was true, of course, and she knew he knew it. She had needed his kindness, she needed it now, and she could already feel the resentment and gratitude twisting together in her chest—

Maybe it showed on her face. He turned away and picked up another sugar cube. It fell into his chocolate with a final little *plop.* "I was tired of dining on bread and cheese, that's all."

Her heart sank, but she hadn't earned a better answer, had she? He'd given her more honesty than she deserved already. She hadn't even managed to ask him to stay yet. She opened her mouth, then shut it and nodded.

He looked at her and sighed. "Serena, I put up with you because I liked you. That's why people put up with each other."

He *liked* her? What did that mean exactly?

He caught her wary look. "And I *don't* mean because I want to kiss you. After tonight we both know I do want to kiss you, but that isn't what I meant." He crushed the sugar cube against the side of his mug with a spoon. "'The full soul loatheth a honeycomb; but to the hungry soul every bitter thing is sweet.'"

Serena pressed her lips together. "Solomon, about that kiss— "

He smiled suddenly. "Yes?"

"I was perhaps more harsh than necessary."

He gave a choke of laughter. "You don't say?" He took the spoon out of his mug and sucked it clean, slowly. She kept her breath from hitching, but only by stopping breathing altogether for several seconds. He set the spoon down with a smirk. "You enjoyed it as much as I did."

Her lips twitched. "Well, maybe."

For a few minutes there was nothing but the sound of chocolate being drunk. Then Solomon collected their empty mugs to put on the worktable till morning.

Serena did not want to go back to her room. *You have to*, she told herself. *What, are you afraid of the dark now?* She stood. "Thank you."

"Any time," he said, although he still thought he was leaving in the morning.

She paused at the door, hesitating. *Go on, damn you!*

"Are you sure you're all right?"

"Of course I am." She marched smartly through the door and shut it behind her. But it took her hours to fall asleep, and when she did, she dozed fitfully.

To an outside observer, it might have looked as though Serena were entering yesterday's numbers in the ledger. Actually, she was composing her apology.

Perhaps I was a little hasty. I see no harm in your staying a little longer. No.

In the clear light of day, it is apparent to me that I may have overestimated—No.

I'm sorry. I was wrong. Please don't go. It was so easy a child could do it. But not Serena. She couldn't even say the words here, in the solitude of her own office.

Yes, you can. You've done plenty of more frightening things. She stood up. "I'm." She cleared her throat. "I'm sorry. I—I was—I was rash. No. I was *wrong*, and—"

The door opened and Sophy stuck her head in. She frowned. "Serena? Is everything all right?"

She felt her face heating. "Why do you ask?"

"No reason. Your father's here again, what should I do with him?"

Serena considered her options. She could have him thrown out, but he wouldn't take it kindly; he might be vindictive, later. She could go out to meet him, but who knew what he would say? In the ordinary course of things her business thrived on gossip, of course, but she couldn't afford to have people know how close she was to losing the Arms. Let them see blood in the water, and they'd be on her like sharks. "Show him in."

In daylight, she could see that Lord Blackthorne looked much more prosperous than he ever had when she was growing up. His changes in farming techniques at Ravenscroft must have succeeded beyond his dreams, and she was willing to wager the tenants were seeing none of the benefits.

Well, that would be Cousin Bernard's problem one day, not hers. She wished she hadn't let him into her office; she hated having him here, in a place that meant so much to her. His eyes on her pictures and bookcases, her pens and paper and ink stains, made her feel exposed and dirty. Even settling deeper into her well-worn chair and regarding him across the familiar, solid mahogany failed to reassure her. She steepled her fingers. "Well?"

His mouth twisted as he sat. "In that much of a hurry to get rid of me, are you? Very well, I won't mince words. I told you to get rid of that tradesman or I would take steps. And now instead of going away he is giving you gowns and baking for your customers." He said this last word as if it pained him. "Reenie, you—"

After all these years, she still hated it when he called her that. "You never cared what I did before. Why this sudden interest?"

His eyes slid away. "You have been an innkeeper for too long if you have to ask that question." He moved a hand restlessly. "I should have done something when you started this mad scheme."

"Why didn't you?" She leaned forward, more curious to hear his response than she wanted to be.

He blinked, startled, as if the answer were so obvious he didn't understand why she had to ask. "You made your bed."

She folded her hands tightly together. The stubborn old bastard would never change. She had known when she left Ravenscroft that from that day forward, he wouldn't lift a finger to help her if she were drowning before his eyes. Not unless she begged him—and with just the right degree of humility. "So I did. And I'll lie in it with whomever I please."

He stood up. "Clearly you don't take me seriously. I think it's time I told you what happened to your last ill-bred lover."

He was trying to tower over her, but standing herself wouldn't make her taller than him. It would only show that she noticed. She tilted her head and smiled, ignoring her sudden unease. "Who, Harry Jenkins? He threw me over, if that's what you mean. Why, did you bribe him to do it? I hope you're satisfied with the results."

His eyes glinted. "Don't be a fool. The boy probably would have married you if he hadn't died of a beating on the way to London."

Her smile didn't slip, but everything else did. The world was tipping sideways; at any moment the ledgers would start to slide off her desk, she was sure of it. Harry had had white-gold eyelashes, and a scar on his left hipbone that no one would ever again trace with her tongue. "You had a boy murdered just to prevent me from making a *mésalliance?*"

He shifted uncomfortably. "The idea was merely to beat some sense into him and warn him off, but my agents were regrettably—overenthusiastic."

"I see." Harry had been seventeen, a year younger than she. Too young to lie in his own blood on the highway. She'd hated him for abandoning her. Christ, how she wished now that he had! "I'm glad one of us had the presence of mind to preserve the family name from such an association."

He smiled. "I'm glad you're being so reasonable, my dear. Now for God's sake send the tailor packing."

It took a moment for her sluggish brain to catch his meaning, and then the slow sideways feeling was gone. Everything was very clear and easy. "I'm nothing if not reasonable, Father." She stood, putting her palms on her desk and leaning forward. Every muscle in her body screamed at her to lunge across it and get her hands round his throat.

Instead, she let her smile spread. "That's why I'm not going to have you killed outright. But I recommend you hire *bodyguards* for Solomon, because if he so much as nicks himself shaving, you'll find yourself in a gutter with your throat cut. You should know I have the means to do it. Don't think any foolish sentimentality will prevent me." She nodded toward the door. "Now get out and be grateful for my forbearance."

He was shaken, but he tried to bluster through. "What, you'd kill your own father? Surely—"

"If you'd ever bothered to inquire, you'd know I never make empty threats. I don't give a tinker's damn that you're my father. I only still call you that because I know how much the connection mortifies you."

"Does he really mean this much to you, then, this tradesman?"

She couldn't remember ever being this angry, which was saying a great deal. She laughed softly. "Oh no. I'm not doing this for him." It was a lie. But her father didn't seem to know it. She thanked God for that, though she didn't believe in Him. "No, it's the principle of the thing. It's time you learned not to meddle in my affairs. I hate you, you know." She wasn't sure if that was a lie or not. The bright sharp feeling that rose like bile in her throat at the sound of his voice—was that hatred? "I daresay I've been waiting for this excuse for a long time. I should have done it when you were here last week. But it's never too late. If I end in Bedlam, you're dead then too. I have friends who'll make sure of it. Now get out and leave me alone."

"Is there no end to your depravity, Reenie? I hear that Frenchman who was keeping you is back as well!" He gave her a sly look. "Maybe I ought to have a word with the fellow, tell him he's been cuckolded."

Serena blanched a little at the word "cuckolded." *There is no way he could know about those marriage lines*, she told herself. "I'm sure if he were here, René would be shocked to hear that I'm not as chaste a mistress as he thought, but he went to the British Museum." An odd choice, given that he'd never shown the slightest interest in antiquities before, but no doubt he found time hanging heavy on his hands while he waited to take possession of the Arms.

"Hmm, too bad," Lord Blackthorne said, sounding pleased. Serena felt sure he would head over to the museum the moment he was out the door. At any other time, she would have been amused at her father trying to play Iago to René's Othello. But the idea lost its piquancy now she knew that, like Iago, her father did not balk at murder.

There would be no apology to make, after all. There was that to be grateful for.

Serena didn't feel grateful. She took a deep breath, picked a piece of lint off her sleeve, and went to find Solomon.

Chapter 7

Solomon still didn't have a plan to make Serena let him stay. He was hoping that after last night, she would just give in and save him the trouble. In the meantime, he was packing very slowly. He put on his shirt very slowly and buttoned his waistcoat very slowly.

If he couldn't make her give in, he'd be back in Cheapside by dinnertime. The thought depressed his spirits unutterably.

Depression felt disturbingly normal, as if feeling alive and interested in the day, as he had for the past few mornings, was some sort of aberration. *Welcome back, blue-devils.*

Slowly shrugging into his coat, he looked out the window and saw Lord Blackthorne getting into his carriage. The old bastard must be delighted at this turn of events. A moment later Solomon felt guilty for his surge of resentment. If he left, the threat of Bedlam would be lifted. It would be a blessed relief for Serena, even if Sacreval remained to be dealt with.

But damn it, Solomon wanted to help her deal with him. He yanked open the wardrobe and started throwing things onto the bed.

A knock came at the door, and Serena walked in. She stopped short when she saw the pile of clothes, and his open valise. "Oh, good, you're going," she said flatly.

His heart sank. "What did your father want?"

She frowned. "How did you know—never mind. Nothing important. Be gone by lunchtime or I'll have you evicted for trespassing."

"Honestly, Serena, only you could add insult to injury with

such—" She put up a hand to rub at her temple, and he saw white dents where her nails had bit the palm. He turned sharp eyes on her and saw her face was bloodless. "Good God, Serena, you look—you look *bleached*! What did that bastard say to you? Did he threaten to have you locked up again?"

She looked at her hand and smiled crookedly. "You're too knowing by half. But—yes." She took a breath. "He says he'll let me alone if you just go. I'm sorry, but I can't risk it. You may not have seen Bedlam, but I have. One of my protectors was keen on that sort of thing." She actually shuddered.

A flood of stupid relief washed over him at the regret in her voice. Perhaps she'd meant to ask him to stay after all. That would have to be enough, because thinking of Serena in an asylum made him—actually, he preferred not to think of it. It didn't matter what he wanted; it mattered that she was safe. "I understand," he said, surprised at how calm he sounded. "I'll find the earrings another way." She was already turning to leave, not meeting his eyes, when he said, stumbling over the words now, "I . . . Good-bye, Serena. I—it's been . . ."

She turned and fixed her gray eyes on him. He straightened his shoulders and tried to look stoic. He must have been failing because she got that annoyed look she always got—Solomon was beginning to realize—when she felt guilty. Now there was something else in it, too: fear. That bastard Blackthorne should be strung up by his thumbs.

Her next words took him by surprise. "Solomon, don't go down any dark alleys for the next month or so, will you?"

His eyes narrowed. "What aren't you telling me?"

"Nothing," she said with absolute assurance and just the right undertone of amused impatience.

Two could play at that game. "All right. It looks to be a fine day, don't you think? Maybe I'll go for a walk along the river tonight."

She gazed at him for long moments. "My father says he'll have you killed if you stay here."

"What?" It was Solomon's turn to stare at his hands and, no doubt, look rather bleached. "R—really?"

She nodded.

"Do you think he would?"

She smiled unpleasantly. "I think he *would,* but I somehow suspect that he *won't.*"

"And I somehow suspect he didn't change his mind out of Christian charity."

"Ah, the wisdom of Solomon! No, you are quite right. I told him that if he harmed you I would have his throat cut."

"And he believed you?"

"I think so. But he may have thought it was an empty threat."

He frowned. "Wasn't it?"

She raised an eyebrow. "Of course not. One empty threat can damage a reputation more than twenty direct admissions of weakness. Now, will you be leaving? I think it the wiser course."

He thought it over. He thought about eating mince pie alone at night. He thought about leaving her to deal with Sacreval on her own. "No." He gave her a half smile. "I think I'll feel safer here where you can keep an eye on me."

She relaxed a little, and he felt warm. He'd lost all sense of proportion. Serena's shoulders moving an eighth of an inch shouldn't matter more than a direct threat to his life, but at the moment, it did. "Very well," she said. "If you will excuse me, I'd better go and spread the word that you're not to be touched, and put some arrangements in place. Watch your back, will you?"

He caught her wrist. "Don't do it."

She turned on him with a mocking smile. "And break my word? Have you no thought for my honor?"

"I mean it, Serena. I'm not worth becoming a murderer for."

She gently removed his hand. "I'm afraid our opinions are destined to differ on this point, as on so many others. I'm damned if he'll hurt you."

He sighed. "A year ago I wouldn't even have been afraid."

"What do you mean?" she asked sharply.

"A year ago I would have been tempted to go walking by the river anyway." He wouldn't have done it, of course, but he would have thought about it. Never again waking up thinking, *I dreamed Elijah was dead*, and then realizing it was true. Never again finding himself standing in the middle of the room crying and not remembering how he got there. And not even having to do it himself—it would have sounded rather appealing. The sharp stab of fear he'd felt a minute ago had surprised him. He had felt, for a moment, almost like a traitor.

"Don't even think about it," Serena said in a biting tone of command, and he looked up in surprise to see that her eyes were blazing. "Don't *ever* think about it. I wish your brother were here, too. He'd tell you not to be a fool. But I'm happy to do it for him. I meant what I said. If you're hurt I'm damned."

He rolled his eyes. For her, surely it was just one more tussle for dominance with her father.

She slammed her fist down on his worktable so hard Solomon had to leap forward to save his muriate of tin from an untimely end. He frowned at her, and she glared unrepentantly back.

"Serena, calm down. I'm not going to do anything rash. I was only saying—"

"Then don't say it," she said harshly, "because if I have to go collect your body from God knows where, I will be seriously displeased."

She was fighting for him now. He couldn't help it. He smiled at her.

She stood there a little longer, looking vaguely at a loss. Then she said, abruptly, "I'm sorry about last night. With the candle.

That was stupid of me." She spun on her heel and left the room, presumably to put arrangements in place. This time he didn't try to stop her.

René came in late, feeling very harassed. Supper was over, and the hall was abandoned except for Serena, waiting alone at the desk for any latecomers in need of a room and going over what looked like next week's grocery orders. "Well," she inquired maliciously, "did my father find you?"

René glared at her. "Yes, he did. Really, *sirène*. How could you set him on me like that? I was peacefully viewing the antiquities, and then, there I was, cornered by your father! It was not *amusant*, I assure you!" Seeing Lord Blackthorne was never *amusant*. And the way he was dealing with Serena was a fool's way. Of course, René had not been precisely clever himself.

Serena smiled. "What did he say?"

"He—er—he said that I must look to you closely, and that you are not faithful to me! I thanked him and tried to duck into the next room, but he had hold of my sleeve. My favorite coat, *sirène*! He *touched* it. I will have to have it washed and pressed!" He thrust the sleeve out for her inspection, but Serena was giggling and didn't look at it. "Perhaps I should send him the bill, what do you think?"

Not many people, he thought, had seen Serena laugh like that. He'd always been proud of that—how after the first few months of their partnership, when she was too stiff and cold and desperate not to appear a frivolous little girl, he could always make her laugh. She had been so young; she was still so young. The lost look on her face when he'd handed her those marriage documents was like a hole in his chest. But now, for a moment at least, he could pretend everything was all right between them.

He drew himself up theatrically. "It is not to laugh, *sirène*! I can scarcely believe my ears! My beloved, sneaking about with a rascally tailor who is not so handsome as I!" Serena laughed harder. "Where is he, this wretch who has brought shame to the Sacreval name? I will teach him to cuckold me!"

Serena stopped laughing abruptly, and the hole in his chest widened. "No one can cuckold you, René, because *we're not married!*" She went through the swinging door to the servants' corridors, shoving it hard. René stood where she had left him, watching the door sweep back and forth.

In a few minutes Sophy came out. Without a word she walked to the desk, taking care not to come within three feet of him. She wobbled a little. It was Sunday night, so Serena had probably pulled her away from cards and whisky with Antoine. She was wearing long sleeves. He wondered whether she still hid aces up her cuffs.

She had been dear to him, too. "Sophy, we are old friends. Do not—"

"You and Serena are old friends too and it didn't stop you stabbing her in the back first chance you got. So apparently old friendship permits me to tell you to get your ugly Frog mug out of our front hall. Good night to you, *my lord.*"

René bit his lip. "Good night, Sophy," he said quietly, and went upstairs.

He stopped before his door—that is, he still thought of it as his door, but it was Solomon Hathaway's door now. He cursed that damned *anglais* with all his heart. This was his fault. René had never wanted to use the marriage lines; when his superiors had pressed him to do it, he had told them no. He hadn't thought he would need to. His *sirène* would take him back, and everything would go forward as before.

He had heard that a man was living in his room, the Stuart Room. He knew that Lord Blackthorne had failed to oust him. But Blackthorne was a crude, vicious Englishman whom Serena hated. She would listen to René because he was her friend. Her friend—the irony of it made him clench his fist now.

He had come here, almost pleased to be back, and seen

Hathaway. He had thought it was Thierry and been so glad. And then . . . Thierry was dead—and an Englishman—and this Hathaway was living in René's room. Hathaway had stood there and looked at him with Thierry's eyes, and Serena wouldn't make him go away. She wouldn't even make him leave her office so René could think. All he had had were those papers. And the man was a Hathaway from Shropshire, so René had not been able to risk waiting.

He closed his eyes against Serena's look, but it stayed, her stricken face clear and perfect in the darkness. He hadn't seen her look like that since—he had *never* seen her look like that.

In the beginning, he had seen her will herself calm every time an old protector walked in the door; he had seen her tense whenever someone casually touched her arm. He remembered her white face when one of the kitchen maids had nearly been raped in the courtyard. She had looked even worse two weeks later when the two of them had been out walking and passed the bastard who did it in the street. The man had been using a cane, his face one mottled, fading bruise. René had known at once that it was Serena's doing, that she'd hired someone to do it; she had somehow looked miserable and terrifyingly fierce at the same time.

But that was just it. Before, she had always had that spark of ice in her eyes. She had always been *fighting*, daring the world to do its worst. There had never been that dazed, vulnerable look.

She had never felt betrayed because she had never expected better. But she had expected better of René. He'd worked so hard to win her trust, and he had, and now—

There must have been another way. He had cursed himself afterward for his stupidity. He had learned quickly enough that Solomon had no idea what the Hathaway legacy meant. But René hadn't been able to think what to do. He had barely been able to speak. All he could think was that Thierry was dead—that he would never speak again.

It was too late now, of course. If he changed his mind and tried to find another way, she would be suspicious, and then when he made his move she would know. She would guess that he had set that fire. She would realize that he hadn't threatened her until she refused him the room, and that would spell disaster—for him, for his informants, for the men in the French army who needed what he provided.

He thought about the years he had spent building his career, and about how they would be lost if he let his friendship for Serena rule him. He thought about his young cousin, serving in a regiment that was bound to come under heavy fire in the battles to come. It was no use; his mind kept coming back to his *sirène*, looking young and scared.

"Are you all right?" Thierry's voice asked, and René jumped, his heart pounding. Of course it was only Hathaway, wondering why René was staring at the door to his room.

He had better start thinking of Thierry as Elijah Hathaway. Even the name Thierry had been a lie; even that was gone. Nothing was his anymore. "I'm fine," he snapped, and went into the apricot room and slammed the door.

A knock came on the connecting door early the next morning. Solomon was already awake and dressed, gathering the things he needed for his trip to Hathaway's Fine Tailoring to drop off the week's commissions and get the following week's. "Come," he called, shoving a couple of hanks of dyed silk thread into his pocket.

Serena walked through the door. He glanced up—and stared. She was wearing a morning gown of cheap, pale orange cotton, a pretty linen ruffle tucked into the neckline. The lace shawl over her elbows looked to have been made on one of the new Leavers machines. A chinoiserie ivory fan and a beaded reticule dangled from her wrist. More surprising still, her dark hair was wrapped in an orange-and-gold-striped bandeau and gathered into an adorably careless bundle at the crown of her head. Solomon could have sworn he even caught a touch of rouge on her magnolia skin. She looked like an adorable young bourgeoise. It was only on a second, closer inspection that he saw the pinning of the bodice and her careful walk to hide that the dress wasn't hers. It had been made for someone larger in the bust, and maybe a little taller.

Her silver eyes glinted at his slack-jawed expression. "Oh, good, you're wearing something middle-class. Come along, we're going to St. Andrew of the Cross." She held out her left hand and Solomon saw a little pearl ring on the third finger. "You're my fiancé now. I hope you don't mind."

Chapter 8

The church was an old, drafty place with a few beautiful stained-glass windows and a large number of boarded-up holes that presumably had once been beautiful stained-glass windows. On the threshold, Solomon offered Serena his arm. He expected a rebuff, but she breathed in deep, whipped open her fan, and took it.

A man Solomon assumed to be the rector was replacing candle stubs in one corner. Serena headed straight for him, tugging Solomon along in her wake. "Oh, sir," she called prettily, "do you think you could do me a very great favor?" Her accent had gone South London and middle-class.

The rector looked up. He was a tall, thin man in his middle sixties, with an extremely incompetent tailor. "For a pretty young lady like yourself? Certainly." He gave an avuncular chuckle.

Serena giggled behind her fan. Solomon looked at her in surprise. She was dimpling and ducking her head, so he couldn't see her eyes. "Well, you see, sir, I want to get my sister an anniversary gift, but I can't remember what day she was married, and I do so want it to be a surprise. She was married here last year, so I thought if I could just see the register—"

The rector smiled. "Of course. I'm sure your sister will be very pleased."

"I hope so. Oh, but I'm being rude! My name is Elizabeth Jeeves, and this is my fiancé, David Burbank."

The rector bowed over her proffered hand. "Charles Waddell." He led them to a small back room, where an oak lectern held a slim leather book with "St. Andrew of the Cross Register" inked across the front. On the shelf below, older registers were stacked in an untidy pile.

"Oh, good!" Serena walked toward the lectern. Halfway there, she stopped and put a hand on her stomach. "Oh," she said in a very different tone of voice. "Mr. Burbank—" Her other hand fluttered toward him and she swayed.

"Miss Jeeves!" Solomon rushed forward and put his arm around her waist.

She leaned into him and gripped his lapel. She still smelled like almonds, just as she had all those years ago.

"Are you all right?" he asked, remembering at the last second to broaden the Shropshire in his own voice.

She smiled weakly up at him. "It's nothing. Not even as bad as yesterday. I don't think I shall"—she glanced down in embarrassment—"I don't think I shall be sick. I'd just like to sit down for a bit, if I may." She grimaced queasily.

Solomon turned to Mr. Waddell. "Is there a chair you could bring in here?"

"Yes, yes, of course." The rector bustled out. He was soon back again with a hard wooden bench.

Solomon helped Serena sit. She clung to his sleeve in a way that made him swallow rather hard. "Thank you," she said. "I'm so sorry. It's very silly of me to be always—"

"Not at all," Solomon said firmly. "I'll just stay here with you for a while, and when you feel better, we can look at the register and find your sister."

Serena threw him a look of adoration. "You're so good to me! But I won't hear of it. This is a lovely old church and there's no reason you can't see some more of it. I shall just rest here for a while and you shall come back and find me when you've taken a look at those delightful windows. You can show Mr. Burbank the stained glass, can't you, Mr. Waddell?"

The rector frowned. "Of course I can, Miss Jeeves. But are you sure you'll be all right alone?"

Serena nodded. "I just feel ill some days. It's nothing, really."

Mr. Waddell's eyes narrowed. Solomon wondered yet again why they hadn't simply pretended to be married. With considerably less enthusiasm than he had shown before, the rector gestured to Solomon to precede him out of the room.

"Oh, Mr. Burbank, won't you give me a kiss before you go?"

Solomon stared at Serena. She tilted up her head invitingly, and her gray eyes shimmered. It would serve her right if he shoved his tongue in her mouth. Instead he leaned down and gave her a quick peck on the cheek. "Don't forget to talk as loudly as possible," she whispered in his ear.

Solomon smiled insincerely. She hadn't needed to remind him yet again. He already had a plan. He had formed it the moment they walked through the door. "Here, my dear," he said solicitously, pulling a small Bible off a nearby shelf and handing it to her. "I wouldn't want you to be bored. Why don't you occupy yourself in reading Scripture while you wait for the reverend and me to return? May I recommend Proverbs Thirty-one to your attention? It speaks most eloquently of the duties of a virtuous wife."

Well, she needed *something* to pass the time until she was sure they were out of earshot. Idly, Serena opened the little Bible and turned to Proverbs. A number of them sounded familiar. She pictured Solomon as a little boy, memorizing the words of his namesake, and smiled.

From the front of the church, the organist began to practice. Good. That would nicely cover any sound she had to make.

Solomon had looked so put-upon when the rector decided they had been anticipating their vows. Pretending morning sickness had been the easiest way to convince him there was no need for a doctor. She knew it would have made more sense—and offended Solomon's sensibilities less—to simply pretend to be married, but somehow she hadn't been able to bring herself to do it. She was close enough to married as it was.

Serena told herself she ought to wait a minute or two more, to be certain the rector wouldn't return for something he had forgotten, or bring her a glass of water, or the like. But in truth, she was putting off looking for what she was afraid to find.

She glanced back down at Proverbs. She wondered if he liked the Song of Solomon, too. As a child she'd thought it rather peculiar, too many goats and odd metaphors, but when she flipped to it now and began reading, the words had a power she didn't expect.

As the lily among thorns, so is my love among the daughters. As the apple tree among the trees of the wood, so is my beloved among the sons.

She read it again. It was a perfect description of Solomon. An apple tree among the trees of the wood. She shut the book firmly. Enough maundering.

She rose from the hard bench and went to the lectern. Opening the register, she flipped backward until she came to Saturday, April 6, 1813. Surely she wouldn't find anything—

Christ, there it was. There it really was, neatly written in black ink.

René du Sacreval of Paris and Serena Ravenshaw of Ravenscroft both of this Parish were Married in this Church by Banns this sixth Day of April, one-thousand, eight hundreds and thirteen by me Charles Waddell Curate. This Marriage was Solemnized between us René du Sacreval and Serena Ravenshaw now du Sacreval, in the Presence of John Richardson & John Stephenson.

She gripped the edge of the lectern until her knuckles were white. How long had he been planning this, then? She looked at the preceding Sunday.

Sunday, March 31st. The Banns of Marriage were duly Published

the third time between René du Sacreval and Serena Ravenshaw,
both of this Parish by me Charles Waddell, Curate.

She turned the page feverishly.

Sunday, March 24th. The Banns of Marriage were duly
Published the second time between René du Sacreval and Serena
Ravenshaw, both of this Parish.

Sunday, March 17th. The Banns of Marriage were duly
Published the first time between René du Sacreval and Serena
Ravenshaw, both of this Parish.

Dear God. He had really done it. But how?

She looked closer. The handwriting didn't match, but the
signatures—the signatures were all perfect. She examined the
book more closely: it was loosely bound in groups of folded-in-
half sheets. If she ripped out both halves, she would leave no
telltale ragged edge. She looked at the page from the other side.
There was a note in the margin, half-hidden by her forefinger.
She took away her hand and read it.

Now she really did feel queasy. *Extracts made so far. April 21st,*
1813.

Bishop's transcripts. She had completely forgotten about
them. Maybe Mr. Waddell wasn't in on the plan—René had said
he wasn't—but his was the most unkindest cut of all. He had
copied out the false entries with the true and sent them all to
the bishop.

Serena closed the register quietly and sat down. Organ music
swelled in the background like a cheap melodrama. She couldn't
quite get enough air. She was married.

René could do anything he liked to her. And he owned the
Arms.

For the next ten minutes Serena sat on the hard wooden

bench, trying to breathe and wishing she could loosen her corset. Then she stood, waiting patiently for the dizzying rush to subside, and made her way back to the nave. She moved stiffly, like an old woman.

Solomon and the rector were nowhere in sight. She looked up at the windows that fronted the church. On the left was St. Margaret, stepping whole from inside a dragon—and if anyone believed a woman could do *that*, perhaps Serena could interest them in purchasing London Bridge. A woman could do exactly what men allowed her to do and no more.

Of course, God was a man. Perhaps it had pleased Him to let Margaret live to fight her dragon. But one day He might change His mind, and what then? Serena had escaped her dragon, too, and now first her father and then René waved their hands, and she could feel its throat tight around her and its teeth at her neck as if the intervening years had been a dream.

The organist played a complex harmony, and Serena glanced at him for a moment, impressed in spite of herself. She blinked, then looked again. It was Solomon.

All Serena could see was the back of his blond head, but she was sure. The rector stood at his elbow, nodding along to the music. She walked slowly down the nave, the music rising and falling around her, and thought about snapping all the panels of her charming little fan, one by one. She would have done it if it weren't Sophy's.

Step by careful step, she climbed the carved wooden stairs to the organ loft. Solomon came into view, his stained fingers moving over the keys, masterful and sure and tender like—like they would move over her body. He looked confident and happy. He made a few adjustments to the knobs, and it sounded as if a flute began to play.

The rector saw her coming. "Why, there you are, Miss Jeeves!"

Solomon's head snapped around to look at her. His playing

faltered; he looked like a boy caught with his hand in the cookie jar. Somehow that smote Serena nearly as hard as those few lines in the St. Andrew of the Cross register. Was she such an ogre?

He sprang to his feet, knocking the little bench backward with a clatter. "Miss Jeeves! You look—you look ill. Would you like me to escort you home?"

She didn't know what she would like, just that she didn't want to go home yet.

"Your fiancé is truly talented," the rector enthused. "You must be very proud."

"I am," Serena said softly. Solomon flushed and looked away, frowning in annoyance. Of course he thought she was shamming. She felt, if possible, worse. She wanted—suddenly she knew what she wanted.

"Play something for me." She sat down on the floor of the dusty organ loft, hugging her knees and leaning her head against the wooden paneling. From here she couldn't see over the wooden railing of the balcony. It made her feel small and invisible, and therefore safe.

Solomon sat. He laid his hand on her head for a brief moment, and then began playing something simple and elegiac that Serena soon recognized as "Angels We Have Heard on High."

Leaning against the vibrating wood, she felt the notes thrum through her and rise to fill the grimy arched ceiling that was all she could still see of the church. She closed her eyes and breathed deeply, dust tickling the back of her throat. The music shifted, soaring triumphantly. A tear slipped down her cheek; she hurriedly brushed it away.

Solomon squinted against the sunlight, stealing a glance at Serena as they stepped out of the church. When he had turned and seen her in the organ loft, she had looked positively woebegone, all the fight gone out of her for once. Now her eyes were unreadable again, and only a little subdued.

"I take it you found the record?" he asked gently.

She nodded. "It was sent to the bishop, too."

He swore under his breath. "I hadn't thought of that."

"Neither had I."

"Where does the bishop *keep* his records?"

Serena eyed him in faint amusement. "I feel a bad influence. But it's no use. I'd have to hire someone to replace the entire sheet in the register, and I'd have to have someone break in twice to the archives, once to steal the page and once to replace it with another, and even if they don't get caught, there's still the chance that someone will remember making the copy, or they'll have sent a copy to the archdeacon, or who knows what, and then it will look like *I'm* the forger."

"So what are you going to do next?"

"Right now?" she asked, with an undercurrent in her voice that he couldn't identify. "I'm going to do something more sensible with my hair."

"Oh, don't. I like it like that."

But Serena ruthlessly pulled out pin after pin. "Here, hold these for me." He held out his hand and a dozen pins fell into it. She unknotted the orange and gold bandeau. Her hair fell over her shoulders, black and untidy. The wind blew it into her eyes and she tried to blow it back as she shoved the bandeau into her reticule. He realized that this morning was the first time he'd seen her outside in daylight.

In the sun, her raven hair shone deep brown in places. He tried to imagine her at seventeen, wearing sprigged muslin and standing in the long rough grass of a Cornish cliff with the wind in her face—and found it was surprisingly easy.

She ran her fingers through her hair and twisted it expertly into its usual tight coil. Holding it in place with one hand, she stretched out the other for the pins. Solomon put his hand behind his back.

Serena rolled her eyes. "Oh, very amusing. Give them back."

"Mm-mm."

"This isn't funny, Solomon." Serena raised her eyebrows and shook her outstretched hand emphatically.

"Leave it down."

"I can't."

"Why not?"

"I just can't, all right?" she said with a sort of concentrated hopeless resentment. Too late he recognized the undercurrent in her voice—hysteria. "I know this is how you want me to be. I saw how you were looking at me in that church. You want that laughing flower of a girl who clings to your arm, but I can't *be* that. You think that if you just keep digging at me and trying to crack me open I'll giggle and say, 'Oh, la, Mr. Hathaway, what a tease you are!' You think it's somewhere underneath but it's not. I am what I am and—and you can go to the devil! Oh God, I can't breathe."

Solomon held out the pins at once, aghast. Instead of taking one at a time, she snatched them all, as if she didn't trust him not to change his mind.

"That's not true, I—" He stopped. He *had* been charmed by the act. It had been a relief, just for a few moments, to have a Serena who laughed and spoke freely and smiled up at him without a trace of irony. Who didn't see him as someone she needed to fight. "I'm sorry."

She shoved pins into her hair and didn't look at him.

He sighed. "Serena, let's take the day off, shall we? I have to go to Hathaway's Fine Tailoring to deliver a few things, but after that we can go on a picnic or something, visit the British Museum, I don't know—" He trailed off. "Sorry. I guess that must sound awfully childish."

The awkward silence was pierced by the shrill cry of the woman in the stall across the street. "Savoy cake and trifle, only tuppence! Naples biscuits, a farthing each!"

Serena smiled shakily. "I want a piece of tipsy cake."

Chapter 9

Serena noticed that Solomon's steps were getting slower and slower as they turned onto Savile Row. They were going at a crawl by the time Solomon stopped under a green-and-white striped awning. *Hathaway's Fine Tailoring* was emblazoned on the shop window in gold and black lettering. Underneath, in smaller letters, it read *Since 1786. Everything the Well-Dressed Gentleman Requires. We Match Any Colour.* A set each of fashionable morning, evening, and riding dress was prominently displayed, as well as a selection of waistcoats, ranging from brilliantly colored, heavily embroidered brocade to subtly tinted and unadorned piqué. Solomon was looking anywhere but at her now. "You needn't come in if you don't wish to."

Oh. Somehow she hadn't expected that. "I'll try not to be too vulgar in front of your relations."

His eyes flashed, and his mouth compressed into a thin, tight line. He slapped the flat of his hand against the door and pushed it open. A bell tinkled. Solomon bowed with a flourish. "After you," he said, adding something under his breath that sounded like, *Deserves what she gets.*

Perhaps the tipsy cake had been a mistake. She felt decidedly sticky. "Is there any custard on my face?" she asked in as dignified a way as possible, but it was hard to sound dignified asking something like that.

He gave her a wicked smile and nodded.

Serena narrowed her eyes. "Where, might I ask?"

Solomon brushed his thumb over the side of her mouth. "There," he said in his husky voice.

At once every nerve she had was tingling. The tears she knew were just below the surface threatened again. She hadn't cried in years, and now it seemed that it was all she felt like doing.

She pulled a handkerchief out of her reticule and looked at it for a moment. Then, knowing there was no help for it, she spit into the handkerchief and rubbed at her mouth. "Is it gone?"

His hazel eyes were almost blue with amusement. He nodded, and she swept ahead of him through the door.

The shop was very clean and very neat. Bolts of cloth stacked on shelves completely obscured the wall to their left. To the right was a table covered in copies of Ackermann's *Repository*, colored plates of French fashions, and diagrams on the proper method of tying a cravat. That was all, except for a door to the right of the counter that must lead to the fitting rooms. The walls were beautifully whitewashed, and the wooden floor shone. A boy in his late teens sprawled behind the counter, nose buried in a Minerva Press novel. His fair hair was flattened over his forehead and teased up farther back in an eager attempt at sophistication that only made him look impossibly youthful.

"Hullo, Arthur," Solomon said. "Is Uncle about?"

"He's in the back."

Serena was momentarily disconcerted by his voice. It was distinctly London, where Solomon's was Cambridge with a hint of Shropshire.

Arthur gave her the once-over and whistled appreciatively. "And you must be Lady Serena."

She inclined her head. Solomon shot his cousin a warning glance. "Sorry. Lady Serena, may I present my cousin Arthur?"

Arthur sketched a bow from his chair. "*Enchanté*," he said with a refreshing lack of concern for proper French pronunciation. "You're much more beautiful than I was expecting, seeing as you've been taking liberties with our Sol."

And yes, she had just been making a silent vow to be civil

if it killed her, but she couldn't be expected to let *that* slide. "That's funny, because you're *much* less mouthwatering than I was expecting, seeing as you're Solomon's cousin."

Solomon flushed, and it was her turn for his warning glance, but Arthur laughed good-naturedly. "Perhaps I'll just let you go and speak to Father."

Solomon offered her his arm. They went through several unoccupied fitting rooms before emerging in the true back of the shop: a low-ceilinged room furnished with two long tables, at which half a dozen men sat and sewed by the light from several enormous windows. At the near end of the right-hand table, a heavyset man in his mid-forties was cutting out a coat. His blond hair was darker than Solomon's and liberally streaked with gray, but his abstracted frown was very familiar. Serena assumed that *his* half-glasses were truly necessary. When he looked up, his eyes were brown, not hazel.

"Ah, Solomon," Mr. Hathaway said in a tone not calculated to reassure. "Just the man I've been wanting to see."

Solomon gulped. "Lady Serena, may I present my uncle, Mr. John Hathaway?"

Mr. Hathaway bowed very politely. "A privilege, my lady."

"The same, I'm sure."

He ushered them into a cramped office with only one tiny, high window. "Sol, I've had six ladies in since this morning wanting to buy our cloth. I thought I'd need a pair of shears to cut Lady Blakeney loose! You ought to realize that the margin of profit on a length of dyed cloth is much lower than on a finished garment. I was happy to contribute toward a new gown for Lady Serena since she is being so helpful to us, and the hangings for the Ravenshaw Arms are a large enough order to be profitable, but we aren't a wholesaler, you know."

Solomon looked hurt, but he stood his ground. "I was meaning to talk to you about that, Uncle. I hate to see a profitable market go to waste. Have you considered going into partnership with Mrs. Cook?"

A deep flush suffused the tailor's cheeks. Apparently Solomon had got that trait from his father's side of the family. "Mrs. Cook? Why should you ask? Simply because she comes to dinner occasionally and—and has been so good as to take Clara on as her assistant—"

Serena glanced at Solomon. He was trying to hide a smile. "Of course, Uncle. But surely you've noticed that she orders her material through Hyams. Mrs. Cook has a good eye for color and design, but she will never rise to the top of her profession so long as her draper uses such inferior dyes. I worry that Clara's formative years should be spent in anything less than a truly modish establishment."

Mr. Hathaway cleared his throat nervously. "Well, when you put it like that—and Mrs. Cook is a woman with a good head on her shoulders."

"Mrs. Cook is a fine woman," Solomon agreed gently. "And Arthur and Clara and Jack are very fond of her." He met his uncle's sharp eyes guilelessly. "It was just an idea."

"Mm, well, I'll think on it."

"Thank you, Uncle. But my real reason for coming by was to bring you this." Solomon dipped a hand in his pocket and came up with two hanks of brilliantly colored embroidery thread and a set of pale cream handkerchiefs. Each item had a scrap of like-colored cloth tied round it.

For the first time, Mr. Hathaway broke into a smile. "You matched them perfectly! Clever lad."

Solomon smiled proudly back. "We match any color. I'll send the new batches of pearl gray and bottle green round to the warehouse tomorrow. Have you any commissions for me?"

"Actually, we'll need a large quantity of your black. It looks like Lady M.'s going to stick her spoon in the wall any day now."

Solomon nodded. "Will do. Is that all?"

Mr. Hathaway's eyes flickered to Serena. "I'm not sure. Would you mind fetching my orders records from behind the counter?" Solomon hesitated, glancing at Serena. "Solomon?"

"Lady Serena, why don't you come with me?" Solomon suggested. "I can show you—"

She was tempted to escape, and that decided her. "I'm fine here, thank you."

Solomon's lips tightened, and he left the room. Mr. Hathaway regarded Serena over the top of his half-moon glasses. So this was the effect Solomon was going for with his own spectacles. He didn't come close to his uncle's mild, shrewd scrutiny. Perhaps in twenty years he'd have managed it. She realized with a pang that she would never know. They were unlikely to still know each other.

"I've heard a lot about you," Mr. Hathaway said.

She really didn't need this. "All true."

"I've also heard that you and my nephew were seen in a compromising position Saturday night."

So they *had* been seen kissing in the hallway; it was all over London. She had known she shouldn't, she had *known* it was stupid—but that was precisely the trouble. She had known, and she hadn't been able to stop herself. For a brief moment, she hadn't cared. Well, she would have to carry it off now. She would have to pretend that she was in control of this thing, that she had meant to do it.

Mr. Hathaway's desk was a mess, covered in paper and books and even a pair of scissors and a few spools of thread. *That's no way to run a business*, Serena thought. It didn't make sense—the shop was obviously doing splendidly—but that slight feeling of superiority gave her courage anyway. "Also true," she said calmly.

He harrumphed, his eyebrows rising in surprise. "What precisely is your interest in the boy?"

Serena raised her eyebrows back. "Your nephew is very charming."

"I won't stand by and see him made a May game of."

"As much as I admire your plain speaking, Mr. Hathaway, it's really none of your affair."

"That boy's welfare is very much my affair. Sol's a dear lad, but he needs looking after. I doubt he understands that the likes of you don't condescend to *care* for the likes of him. I'm sure you have your uses for him, and perhaps you even find him amusing. But when you're tired of him you'll toss him out on his ear and he won't be able to bear it. I don't know how far you are in his confidence, Lady Serena, but his brother was killed in Spain a year and a half ago."

She was having trouble breathing again. How *dare* he? As if that were something she should be tactfully informed of by relatives.

"There were times . . ." Mr. Hathaway faltered, and though his face closed completely after a moment, Serena knew what she had seen. She felt infinitesimally more charitable toward him. "It broke my heart to see him."

Serena would have laid odds that that wasn't what he had been about to say.

"Now he's finally back on his feet, and I've no desire to see all that undone by—I beg your pardon, my lady—a careless flirt. For the boy's sake, end it now."

She was silent for a moment. "So you are telling me you think your nephew is a milksop, Mr. Hathaway?"

Hathaway frowned. "Of course not, but he's a sensitive lad, and—"

"He's not a lad, Mr. Hathaway. He's a man grown." She paused. "I noticed your shop promises to match any color?"

He nodded stiffly.

"We both know it is Solomon who matches every color. Half the ladies in London are dying to have a gown colored by him, and you scolded him for it like a naughty schoolboy. I doubt you pay him a fraction of what he's worth. Furthermore, both you and your son have had the gall to be *puzzled* as to what I could possibly see in him."

Her nerves were buzzing as if she had just drunk eight cups of coffee, but it was a welcome change from the dead, dull feeling of a few minutes ago. "Solomon has decided he is willing to work for you under these conditions. Very well, it is none of my affair. But Solomon will also decide whether or not he is interested in a liaison with the Siren, and when I toss him out on his ear, I trust he will be man enough not to go into a decline." She couldn't resist a final scathing witticism. "Should he do so, however, I will be sure to have my chef send you an excellent recipe for a restorative broth. You can spoon-feed it to him while you read him the sermons of Hannah More."

Mr. Hathaway made a noise in the back of his throat that might almost have been amusement. "That's very generous of you." He chewed his lip thoughtfully. "I also heard you haven't taken a single lover since—well. In years."

The buzzing in her nerves died out, leaving her feeling worn and tender. Christ, not this. "Or perhaps I haven't taken any stupid enough to gossip about it."

"You haven't precisely been discreet about Solomon." Mr. Hathaway looked at her speculatively. Serena knew her face was blank, but—her actions spoke for themselves, didn't they? She'd been kissing Solomon in the hallway like an infatuated girl. Mr. Hathaway had to know how nearly impossible it would be for her to toss Solomon out on his ear. She had already tried, and failed.

This was exactly why she hadn't taken any lovers since she'd come to the Arms. She'd known it would make her weak. She'd known it would make people see her as a helpless girl again.

Sure enough, Mr. Hathaway smiled. "Well, perhaps I won't send to my brother for his copy of Hannah More just yet."

Serena felt suffocated.

"What's that about Hannah More?" Solomon walked back into the room with a wide, flat book under his arm.

"Lady Serena was merely offering me her opinion as to whether Clara would find her essays edifying."

Solomon blinked. "But when Father sent her a copy of *Practical Piety* for her birthday, you said you'd thank him to refrain from trying to turn Clara into a canting milk-and-water killjoy, and then you burned it!"

Mr. Hathaway laughed. "Mm, yes, well, hand me that book." He made a pretense of examining it. "No, it doesn't look as though I need anything specific at the moment. Lady Pursleigh is giving a masquerade next Sunday, though, and I'm bound to get some last-minute orders, so any simple costume designs you think of would be welcome."

Solomon smiled. "I'll keep it in mind. We'll be off, then."

Mr. Hathaway cleared his throat. "I heard—that is, I heard Lady Serena's gown was lovely. I should have liked to see it."

Solomon looked absurdly pleased. "Thank you."

Mr. Hathaway frowned. "Well, off you go."

Off they went, Serena feeling decidedly morose. No sooner had the door clanged shut behind them than Solomon asked, "What did my uncle say to you?"

"What makes you think I didn't start it?" she asked nastily.

"Because I know my uncle and I know you. Why do you think I didn't want to leave you alone with him?"

She blinked. "I naturally assumed you thought I'd say something cutting if you weren't there to restrain me."

Solomon smiled at her. "I wasn't worried. You're polite enough when you're not unduly provoked."

Her head started to ache. "What is wrong with all of you?"

Solomon chewed his lip. "Was it that bad? I was only gone a minute—"

"I am *not* polite," she said despairingly.

His smile returned, wider this time. "Is that all? It's not as if I said you were a sensible girl with a good head on her shoulders. You can be debonair, faintly sinister, *and* polite, you know."

Damn him, he was *laughing* at her. "Why must you always be so damned patient and reasonable?"

"Well, I could be unreasonable and accusatory if you prefer, but I don't think you'd find it entertaining after the first few minutes." When her scowl didn't lift, he said, "Cut line, Serena! You'd have been twice as annoyed if I'd assumed you'd started it, anyway."

"Don't act like you know me! You don't. None of you know me." She saw with dull satisfaction that he was beginning to lose his patience. Not surprising, of course. She could try the patience of a saint.

"I may not know you, Serena, but I've figured out by now that you never pass up the opportunity to enact a Cheltenham tragedy. If you don't want to tell me what my uncle said, well and good, but don't insult both our intelligences with this claptrap."

"Damnation, I don't enact Cheltenham tragedies!"

"Then what the hell is this? What are you so bloody upset about?"

"Your uncle thinks we—I don't even know what he thinks. I think he *likes* me."

"*That's* what this is about?" He stared at her. "Are you so determined to be universally detested?"

Frustration welled up inside her. She couldn't explain it; he would never understand.

He shrugged. "So you can enjoy dramatically disillusioning him when you toss me out on my ear."

She was a bit put out that he could sound so cavalier about it. "Before that, he as near as told me I was a dissolute lady, born with a silver spoon in my mouth, trifling with your naive affections for the sake of my own high-born amusement."

Solomon's jaw dropped. "But that's ridiculous. You work for a living, same as anyone! He might as well say *I*—" His face changed. He rubbed at his temple, looking defeated. "But he does think that, of course."

"He does?" she asked, startled.

He shrugged. She'd noticed that he always did that when he was angry with someone on his own account, as if it wasn't important. As if it didn't matter how he felt. "Oh, yes. When I started working there after Cambridge, he was always at me to weigh my options, not to let him hold me back. He never lets me sit behind the counter or do fittings, because that would be too menial for me—but he never lets me touch the books either, because I think he thinks anyone who's half a toff and went to university must have a wretched head for business. He thinks I'm just dabbling and when I get bored, I'll take Uncle Dewington's allowance and go. I've been working for him for four years now, and he just won't—"

"I haven't traded a poke for a fistful of the ready in five years, but no one's read *that* notice in the *Gazette*."

He sighed. "I'm awfully sorry."

"It's hardly your fault."

"I mean, I'm sorry about my uncle. I'll explain to him that you're not trifling with me—"

"Please don't," she said in heartfelt tones.

Solomon laughed. "Sorry, forgot about the horrors of being approved of. Damned if you do, damned if you don't, eh? I guess you'll just have to do what you want."

Tears pricked at her eyes. "What if I don't know what I want?"

"We'll have to wait and see then, won't we?" He stuck his hands in his pockets and looked at her as if that was nothing, as if he really was willing to wait as long as it took, as if he didn't mind waiting. As if he thought they might still know each other in twenty years.

"I told him that when I tossed you out on your ear you were unlikely to go into a fatal decline."

He smiled oddly. "Perhaps you give me too much credit."

"I generally find I don't give you enough," she said gruffly.

He reached out and laced his fingers with hers. "Come on. You'll feel better when you're eating a hot steak-and-kidney pie."

She had a thought. "How would you like it if we bought lunch and looked for your earrings at the same time?"

He tilted his head in a way that reminded her of his uncle. "How will we do that, pray?"

"You'll see."

Chapter 10

Solomon's stomach was starting to growl. They had already strolled past several mouthwatering pie stalls set up along the Strand. Finally a pieman wheeling an enormous barrow caught Serena's eye. "Hey there, Doyle!" she yelled.

He hurried over. "What'll it be, madam? Steak-and-kidney, mutton, pork, eel, or apple?"

"Two of whichever are least likely to contain rat and pigeon, please."

Doyle stared. "You want a pie?"

Serena snickered. "What, do they *all* contain rat?"

"Not on your life! My Bridget bakes these pies and they're all fine and fresh."

"In that case, I'll have a steak-and-kidney. What will you have, Solomon?"

"Eel, please."

Doyle bit his lip. "I shouldn't try the eel, sir."

Solomon laughed. "Steak-and-kidney for me, too, then."

"Very well, sir, milady, and would you like hot gravy with your pies?"

Serena nodded. Pies were handed over and gravy poured through the hole in the crust; tuppence changed hands. Then Serena said, "Pat, I need your professional opinion. I'm looking for a pair of stolen earrings. Rubies and gold, taken by a gentleman on the high toby Wednesday before last."

Solomon stared at her. "Serena—"

She smiled faintly at his puzzled expression. "Show him your wares, Pat."

Doyle grinned and turned back the gaudy checkered cloth in

which his pies nestled. Watches, billfolds, handkerchiefs, pocket knives, and dozens of other small items were revealed, crowding the bottom of the barrow.

He flicked back the cloth. "I haven't seen anything of that description, Thorn. But then, I'm not a baubles man and everyone knows it. You ought to try Dina Levy. I doubt anybody'd bring her something that fine, but she keeps her ears open. If she hasn't heard, you won't find it in Whitechapel, St. Giles, or Holborn."

"Dina's usually at her Lawrence Street house at this time of day, isn't she?"

"Not now, she'll be at her daughter's stall in the Fleet Market for elevenses. Make sure you try the apple fritters. My Bridget's been trying to get the recipe off Abigail Levy for years now, but Abby's a stubborn wench."

"I shall be sure to do so. Well, you've been very helpful. Will half a crown suffice?"

Doyle gestured expansively. "Wouldn't hear of it! You can be in my debt, if you like."

Serena raised her eyebrows. "I shall owe you a very *small* favor then. Now, if your young associate will return my friend's pocketbook, we'll be on our way."

Solomon started, feeling for his billfold. Sure enough, it was gone. He looked accusingly at Doyle, who sighed. "It's a devil of a job training new workers. I'm sure you find it the same at the Arms. Moreen!" he called. "Come here!"

A ragged little girl of perhaps six or seven detached herself from the crowd and came scuttling over. "Yes, sir?"

"Do you know who this lady is, Mo?"

The girl shook her head.

"Look at her face." Doyle tapped his brow meaningfully.

Mo's eyes went wide as platters. She stared at Serena's birthmark with something approaching worship. "You're the Black Thorn!"

Solomon saw that Serena was trying very hard to make her expression more forbidding and less charmed. She was such a soft touch. "Yes, I'm the Black Thorn. And you've stolen my friend Solomon's pocketbook."

The little girl's awe turned to horror. "*He's* Solomon Hathaway?" Solomon frowned. She'd heard of him?

Serena nodded.

"Are you going to have my—"

"Not if you give it back," Serena said very quickly. So she really had put it about that no one was to touch him, in terms so brutal she evidently didn't want him to hear what they were. And people were genuinely afraid of her. He tried to wrap his mind around that.

Mo fished his pocketbook out of a ragged pocket and handed it back to Solomon, who checked it for fleas under pretense of counting the bills. Sixpence was missing, but he didn't say anything. "I want to be just like you when I'm grown," Mo was telling Serena, who looked decidedly taken aback. "I want an inn and people under me, and if anyone touches me I'll have their—"

"I wish you luck," Serena interrupted. "Give Bridget my regards," she told Doyle, and tugged Solomon away.

As they walked away, he could hear Doyle saying, "I've told you a hundred times, you don't touch 'em till I give you the signal, like this—"

"The Black Thorn?" he asked.

She grimaced. She was so adorable when she was embarrassed. "It's a stupid nickname. I think it was a joke originally, because it sounded frightening and I was trying to be frightening and wasn't yet. The only thing intimidating about me was my father's title. By now it's just what people call me."

He wondered suddenly what it had been like for her when she was still learning how to be intimidating. What had she done then when someone pinched one of her waitresses or told her they'd liked her better as a whore? *She used to have the most expressive eyes,* Sophy had said. He hated the idea of everyone being able to see how scared she was. He hated the idea of her having to destroy that part of herself to become what she was. "What exactly did you tell people you would do to them if they hurt me?"

"You're too squeamish to know."

He looked back at Mo. "*I'm* too squeamish?"

Serena looked back at Mo, too. Her eyes were still expressive, when she wasn't thinking about it. That made him feel better. "I'm sure she's heard worse."

As they walked down to Fleet Market, occasionally stopping to talk to a strolling receiver, Solomon listened to the cries of the vendors with a new ear. "Fine silver eels!" and "Sweet china oranges! Scarlet strawberries!" and "Fresh hot!" How many of them had watches hidden in the bottom of their baskets? How many of them had grubby little apprentices? What could Mo really do if anyone touched her? He wished she'd stolen a shilling.

By the time they reached Fleet Street, he also wished he had four hands. Two pies, an orange, a pitcher of hot tea, and a twist of newspaper with oysters and butter bread inside was a lot to carry even for two people. Luckily, the next man Serena stopped was a basket man.

Dina Levy had heard of his earrings. "Decker has them, unless he is breaking them down already," she said in heavily accented English, pocketing the half-crown Doyle had refused. "He is a closemouthed old *courva*, but his client was down at the Blue Ruin last week. Everybody is a gossip with that much gin in them."

Serena smiled brilliantly. If anything could cheer her up, this would. She was in her element. Solomon tried not to think that if they found the earrings, he'd have no excuse to remain at the Arms. "Thank you, Dina," she said. "I can't tell you how much I appreciate your help."

"Anything I can do for you, Thorn."

Serena smiled wider. "I'm glad you say that. I owe Pat Doyle a favor, you see, and I know his wife would kill for Abby's apple fritter recipe."

Solomon looked at the basket of food with hopeless longing. "Do we have time to eat, do you think, or ought we to go and find Decker now?"

Serena cut her eyes at him. "*We* aren't going to Decker's. I'm going to Decker's. Alone."

He frowned. "Is it dangerous? Surely it's better if we go together."

"It's not dangerous. You just can't go."

"But he's got my earrings!"

"And he won't sell them between now and tomorrow morning. I'll send him a message directly to hold them for me. He owes me a favor."

"Why can't I go?"

She looked away, but he saw her eyes crinkle in amusement. "You're too squeamish to know."

When they were finally settled under the mulberry trees in St. James's Park with their lunch, Serena came out of a brown study to see that Solomon looked dejected, too. "I'll get the earrings."

He smiled at her. "I know."

She looked away.

"I really am sorry about my uncle."

"Why do you let him treat you like that?" She couldn't have borne it, but then, maybe that explained why he had a large family that were at least fond of him and she didn't. She took a bite of her pie.

Solomon looked surprised. "Isn't that how family is?"

"Endlessly belittling? That's certainly been my experience."

Solomon snorted. "It's different when it's Uncle Hathaway. When Uncle Dewington tells me it's time I put all this chemical dye nonsense behind me—deuced bad *ton*, don't you know—I just want his guts for garters. Uncle Hathaway has my best interests at heart, at least." He knotted his fingers and neatly cracked a walnut by snapping his palms together. It shouldn't have been erotic, but it was. It was getting to the point where nearly everything he did was erotic, simply because he did it.

"So has Hannah More."

Solomon smiled at the walnut in his hand, prying the meat out of its shell. "I'm fond of him, though. His family was awfully good to me when Elijah died."

"You mean they fell awkwardly silent at your approach and gazed at you pityingly over dinner, and occasionally your uncle would lay a supportive hand on your shoulder."

He laughed. "Well, yes. But—" He had eaten the walnut, but he kept his eyes on his hands. "Elijah was never interested in the shop. Uncle Hathaway was the only person I could be around without wondering if he would have rather I died instead."

"But—" she began, appalled. "Surely your parents didn't think that."

"Probably not. Probably I was the only one who did. But they were all so unhappy. Elijah was always the one who knew what to say, who made everyone laugh. If it had been me, he could have made them feel better. I—I could barely speak to them anymore. I could barely speak to anyone. How could they not wish it?"

"But—"

"You never met him," Solomon said with finality. "You don't understand. He may have looked like me, but he was special. When he walked into a room, everyone turned to look."

When Solomon walked into a room, every fiber of Serena's being swung toward him like a needle toward the pole. "You're special," she said stubbornly. "And your uncle still doesn't appreciate it enough."

He sighed. "Serena, I'm going to tell you something, but I don't necessarily want to discuss it."

She nodded.

"After Elijah died, I moved my laboratory into the back of the shop for a while."

"How kind of him, to allow you to use his space in your work for his business. I'll wager he doesn't pay you enough either."

"Did you tell him that?"

"Maybe."

The corner of his mouth quirked up. "Anyway, that's not what I meant. I moved it there because I—well, I caught myself eyeing the bottle of arsenic. And I didn't think I would, but I *knew* I wouldn't if my cousin Clara might find the body."

The oyster Serena had just eaten transformed itself into a brick in her stomach.

"I couldn't sleep and I'd show up there at all hours to work. Uncle Hathaway took to waking at three or four in the morning and coming downstairs. He'd bring in tea, and then he'd go into the other room and work. He didn't try to talk to me, but I could hear him through the door and it—it helped."

Serena leaned back against a tree. "I—"

"I said I didn't want to discuss it."

"I know. I just wish I could have been there."

Solomon looked at his hands. "So do I."

"Have some gingerbread. It's good."

He raised an eyebrow at her, but he reached for the gingerbread. She took the opportunity to brush their fingers together.

"Elijah would have liked you," he said. "I wish you could have met him."

She chewed her lip. "Are you sure he wouldn't have thought I was toying with your affections?"

"I'm sure you would have gone to a great deal of trouble to make him think so." He grinned at her. "You really oughtn't to think you're a heartless bitch just because people tell you so. 'Forsake the foolish, and live,' remember?"

"Because you haven't been affected at all by your family's

expectations that you're a dull-as-ditchwater milquetoast Quakerish idiot."

"I *am* a dull-as-ditchwater milquetoast Quakerish idiot," he said without heat. "Pass the orange."

"Precisely, and I'm a heartless bitch."

He stared at her with something approaching amazement. "Huh. You're right."

"I generally am."

He frowned. "So—does that mean I'm *not* a Quakerish idiot?"

She laughed weakly and threw the orange at him. "Well, you may be an idiot."

He pulled a knife from his pocket and sliced it into eighths. Juice ran over his fingers and he sucked it off, looking irked. Somehow that little frown made it even more seductive. "I was unforgivably foolish this morning. Miss Jeeves would bore me to tears, I know that. But—but she looked like you, except—"

"Except what?"

He hesitated. "Except she looked at me as if she—as if she didn't mind liking me."

Poor Solomon. He didn't even ask her to be pleasant. He just wanted her to be willing to like him, and show it. He had such low expectations, and she *still* couldn't meet them. What made it worse was that she liked him so damn much. But she couldn't show it like other women did. She couldn't be like other women. She didn't want to be. It was too frightening; it would make her too vulnerable. She sucked on a piece of orange and tried to think what to say.

He saved her the trouble. He probably thought she wouldn't have said anything anyway. "Isn't there anyone in your family you don't hate?" he asked.

"My mother, I suppose. I haven't seen her in six years."

Solomon's eyes widened. "Your mother is still alive? Where is she?"

"At Ravenscroft, I suppose." His jaw tightened. She said with as much conviction as she could, "It's not her fault. She can't control him, and she's not well, and she always tried to protect me." More or less. She could guess what he thought of her mother, anyway, and she didn't really want to hear it. To avoid looking at him, she untwisted the sheet of newspaper that had held their oysters and flattened it out.

DUCHESS OF RICHMOND PLANS BRUSSELS BALL FOR THE
17TH OF JUNE

LONDON, JUNE 11—FOREIGN OFFICE'S LORD VARNEY
ASKS PARLIAMENT FOR AN ADDITIONAL £20,000 TO
FIGHT FRENCH SPIES

Even here, she couldn't escape René for a moment.

"We'll get him," Solomon said, reading her thoughts as easily as if they were printed headlines. The coldness in his voice surprised her. But then, his brother had been killed by the French. He looked at René and he saw what he ought to see: the enemy. No matter how hard she tried, she could only see her friend. It didn't matter. She'd get him just the same.

"What I really miss is the sea," she said.

"I've never seen the sea."

Serena wished she could show it to him. "It's beautiful. Sometimes I miss it so badly I can almost smell it—except I can't." That tantalizing salty smell was forever out of her reach. All she had in London was soot and fog and almond soap. "Sometimes I go into the cellar and open the barrels of pickled cucumber, just to smell the brine."

Solomon's brow wrinkled. "The sea doesn't really smell like a gherkin barrel, does it?"

She laughed. "No." It struck her then, like a hammer blow, that she might never again after this week go down alone into the cool cellars of the Arms and open the gherkin barrels, or inventory the round smooth wheels of cheese, or inspect the long rows of wine. "Maybe I'll go to Brighton when I leave."

It wouldn't be Cornwall, but she'd rather die than crawl to Cornwall, alone and a failure. And Solomon, if he ever troubled to visit, would love the changes Nash was making to the Marine Pavilion. Prinny had shown her plans for the façade.

Serena hated Brighton already.

She looked up to find Solomon giving her that focused look of his. "Do you know what you need?" he asked.

"An annulment?"

"Later. Right now, you need to cartwheel."

"To cartwheel?"

He nodded decisively. "Elijah always said there was nothing like it for raising the spirits, and except for chocolate, he was right. Do you know how?"

"Yes, but—Solomon, I'm wearing skirts!"

He grinned wickedly at her. "There's no one about."

She was actually tempted. She used to turn cartwheels down the hill at Ravenscroft. And the idea of Solomon ogling her ankles wasn't precisely unpleasant. However, she didn't think turning cartwheels would be quite the same in stays and four layers of petticoat. "Perhaps later."

"I'll hold you to that."

Serena stared at her bed. Somehow, she couldn't quite get in and blow out the candle. Her nightmare of two days before, in the light of what she'd discovered at St. Andrew of the Cross, seemed all too plausible. *Go on, this is pathetic.* She took a resolute step toward the bed. But it was no use. She wasn't shaking with fright or weak in the knees, but she also wasn't going to get into the bed.

Like a spoiled child, she wanted light and warmth and comfort. She wanted chocolate. She wanted—why not admit it, since she wasn't fooling anyone?—to be held as she fell asleep.

All of that was there, on the other side of the door. But explaining to Solomon that she was afraid to sleep in her own room was every bit as unimaginable as getting into bed and pulling the curtains shut. He would know how weak she was, and he would be so gentlemanly about it, so good-natured, so sympathetic—the idea was appalling.

She had let her guard down with him too far already. In one short week, she had let herself feel safe with him. *To the hungry soul every bitter thing is sweet.* Small wonder that something as sweet and unexpected as Solomon had overwhelmed her. But she couldn't delude herself that because he made her feel safe, that he could really protect her, or even that he would really try. There was no such thing as safety. Even if people cared for you, in the end they put themselves first. René was proof of that.

As hard as she tried, she couldn't control how she felt about Solomon. But that didn't mean he had to *know*. He'd own her then.

Solomon had just finished making up the batch of black dye he'd promised Uncle Hathaway when the door beside the fireplace swung open. He looked up.

Serena was barefoot, her embroidered orange robe unfastened over her revealing shift. Her hair hung in a black curtain to the top of her breasts. His black dye was the best in the business, but even so it would streak and fade with time. It would never match the dark richness of her hair.

She leaned against the door frame, her face in shadow. "Hello, Solomon."

"Hello, Serena," he said warily.

She tilted her head and smiled oddly. Something was very wrong. "Now, Solomon, you sound so unfriendly. I thought you *liked* me."

"Yes, and I told you that I didn't mean I wanted to kiss you."

She moved forward until they stood barely two feet apart. Her eyes, fixed on his, glimmered strangely. "Oh, Solomon, so pure of heart. But as you also said, we both know that you *do* want to kiss me." And as much as he felt off balance, as much as he knew something was wrong—well, didn't he always feel off balance around her? She did it on purpose, and whether it was wrong or not, his body responded to her, to her low voice and her nearness and even the odd shine of her gray eyes.

She shrugged her shoulders, and the robe slithered to the floor with a fringed rustle. She stood before him in her shift, shoulders and arms bare, every curve plainly visible—and then she stepped closer and put her arms around his neck. Her breasts pressed against his waistcoat. He glanced down and there they were, there was the birthmark on the squashed curve of her left breast. He remembered the first time he had seen that swell of bosom, the horror it had evoked in him. Now everything had changed—now he knew her. He stifled a groan.

"'I have decked my bed with coverings of tapestry, with carved works, with fine linen of Egypt,'" she quoted. "'I have perfumed my bed with myrrh, aloes, and cinnamon.'" He knew the next line, just as she must have known he would. *Come, let us take our fill of love until the morning.* She had been reading Proverbs.

That brought him nearer to kissing her than any of the rest, but still he was checked by her odd half smile. He drew in a ragged breath. "Have you been drinking?"

Her smile widened, lazily. "Why don't you kiss me and find out?"

Self-control had its limits. "'She is loud and stubborn, her feet abide not in her house,'" he said, and kissed her hungrily.

Chapter 11

Her mouth opened readily beneath his. She didn't taste like liquor—she tasted, in fact, like strawberries. His last fractured thought, before everything was swallowed up by rising desire, was of the baskets of strawberries he had seen delivered to the kitchen that afternoon.

He ran his hands down her back, the softness of her flesh separated from him by nothing but a thin layer of cotton. Sliding one hand up between them to cover her breast, he squeezed lightly. Her nipple hardened against his palm and her breath shuddered against his mouth. She was close and he wanted her closer. Cupping the curve of her buttock, he pulled her to him, pressing the core of her against his erection.

He still couldn't shake the feeling that something was wrong, that this wasn't real, that she would melt away under his hands like fairy gold. But he couldn't think when she rolled her hips like that. His hands tightened on her, and she gasped and kissed him harder.

Finally she pulled away. "'The mouth of strange women is a deep pit; he that is abhorred of the Lord shall fall therein,'" she said. Solomon was still trying to make sense of that when she dropped to her knees and reached for the flap of his breeches.

Never mind the shocking heat that flooded him. Never mind how much he wanted her to. He leaped backward so fast he hit his head on the bedpost. "What the devil do you mean?"

She stayed on her knees. At first Solomon thought she looked as dazed and heated as he did, but when she looked up, her gray eyes were mocking. "Too squeamish for that, too?"

"I'm not interested in strange women."

Her head snapped back as if he'd punched her. "Oh no?" she said venomously, dropping her eyes to the unmistakable evidence of his interest. "What's that, then?"

"That's for *you*," he said fiercely. "I don't want you to be a strange woman, Serena."

She rocked back on her heels. "There's not much you can do about that at this late date."

"I mean that I don't want you to be a strange woman to *me*. Is that all I am to you? A—a *customer*?"

She rose to her feet, leaving her robe in a silken puddle around her ankles. She did it gracefully, but he still thought of an animal with its leg mangled in a trap. She looked as if she'd claw and spit at him if he came close.

"I don't care if you've slept with half the men in London," he said, too loudly. "That has nothing to do with how I feel. I said I liked you. And when I said that I meant I wasn't trying to *get* anything. Can't you understand that? Don't you like me too?"

She frowned.

He tried to ignore his hurt at her lack of an answer. He knew she liked him, damn it; but he wanted her to be able to *say* it. "Serena, all I want from you is you. If you don't want to give me that, fine, but get out of my room."

She looked at the ground. "I can't imagine why you would want that."

"Right now, I can't either." He strode to his lab table and pulled the bottle of Madeira out from behind a crucible in which he'd been trying to match the color of Serena's eyes. Bluish-gray liquid sloshed about in it, looking like dishwater. He took a shaky swig; wine burned away the taste of strawberries. "Listen, Serena. I find it equally difficult to imagine why you would want any part of me, so I can't be too critical. But don't do this again."

She pressed her eyes shut for a moment and ran a hand through her hair. When she opened her eyes, the act was gone; she just looked like herself. It was funny how much less graceful she was when she wasn't thinking about it. "Christ," she said. "Solomon, I—Christ, I'm such a harpy."

He held out the Madeira.

She took it and knocked it back expertly. "I really wasn't drinking before, you know." She rubbed the back of her hand across her mouth.

"I know."

"Would you like some strawberries?" she offered, uncertainly and intently.

He swallowed, almost choking on the desire that swamped him at the words. Would he ever be able to taste strawberries again and not think of Serena pressed against him? "Have you got some?"

"In the kitchen. Come on, we'll get some. If—if you want to." She didn't seem to have ever learned how to apologize, and yet she always tried, in her own way. She fought herself, too, when she had to. He nodded.

She smiled, transparently relieved. Solomon felt almost all right. "Just let me braid my hair."

He watched as she deftly wove her black hair into two plaits. Then she picked up her robe from the floor and wrapped it around her, fastening it securely. She picked up the candle from his bedside table and lit it at his lamp, the light briefly illuminating her face. When she walked past him to open the door, he saw that without a comb, her back part zigzagged crazily.

She opened the door and then, with her hand on the knob, she turned and said over her shoulder, "Oh, and Solomon—I never threaten to kill my father for people I don't like at least a *little*."

The kitchen felt strange without the blazing heat and light and the clamor of upraised voices and turning spits and, from outside, London. Moonlight streamed in through the now-closed sash windows along the high ceiling, silvering the long rows of copper pots.

To his surprise, Serena went, not toward the door to the ice room, but to the opposite corner of the kitchen. She bent and began tugging at something on the floor.

"What—" Then he saw. She pulled on a great hoop fixed into the floor, and a section of floor about four feet square swung up with a smooth gliding of gears and hinges. Serena pulled it back and fastened it open with the hook on the end of a chain that Solomon had wondered about when he first saw the kitchen.

"If you ever read in a history book that no one knows how young James escaped his pursuers when he went to ground here, then you know that that eminent historian has never spoken to anyone that actually works here," she said.

"A priest's hole?"

"Better. A secret passageway. I've no doubt he made his escape quite easily while they were guarding the doors."

"No popish treasure, then?"

"I'm afraid not. It isn't very secret either. It's a tunnel to the laundry, so we can bring the sheets and things back and forth in the rain without crossing the courtyard. It stays cool, so we have a little icebox here for our most delicate things. I'll be right back."

And she and the candle disappeared into the dark mouth of the tunnel. A minute passed, then another, and Solomon grew a little worried. He walked over and looked down the stairs. He couldn't see her. "Serena?"

"I'm fine, just a moment." Her cold tone was at such odds with her friendliness of a few minutes ago that Solomon knew at once something was wrong again. He went gingerly down the wooden steps, careful not to hit his head on the edge of the hole in the kitchen floor. The tunnel, its walls covered in neat blue-and-white tile, looked like the other servants' hallways in the inn. But it was wider and the floor was stone instead of wood, worn smooth by centuries of laundresses' feet.

There was a gap of about three feet between the staircase and the wall, and Solomon followed the glow of the candle under the stairs to a little icebox and Serena. She was leaning against the wall, her arms crossed tightly, huddled in on herself. When he neared, she turned her face away. "I'll be fine in a minute," she said indistinctly.

His first impulse was to go to her, but he tamped it down. He had learned she was a little like a wild bear—you had to tempt her to you with honey, or she would savage you.

Actually, now he thought about it, probably it wasn't a very good idea to tempt a wild bear to you with honey. What would they do when the honey was gone? Or what if you accidentally got some on your hands? But the principle was sound. "What's wrong, Serena?"

"I'll be fine in a minute," she repeated, and this time it sounded more like she was trying to convince herself than him. "Leave me alone."

"You know I'm not going to do that."

She nodded, huddling deeper into herself. "Sometimes I wish you would."

Only sometimes. Well, that was a victory of sorts. "You're not having a very good day, are you?"

She gestured at the icebox with one hand while the other stayed tightly clutching her upper arm. Her knuckles were white. "This is one more thing I'll never get to do again." She turned her face toward his at last, and the nakedness of her expression wrung something inside him. "How can I leave?" Her voice broke.

Thank you, Solomon said silently. *Thank you for letting me see this.* He did go to her then, gathering her into his arms. "You won't have to leave. We have another week. We'll figure something out. I promise."

She clung to him for long moments, as if she were still Miss Jeeves. He buried his face in her hair, breathing in the scent of almonds. She pressed into his embrace, reminding him all too clearly of what it had been like earlier, in his room.

Afraid that in her tangle of emotions she would try to stage an encore of the earlier scene—and that this time he wouldn't be able to resist—he moved away, holding her not quite at arm's length to examine her face. A little to his surprise, it wasn't tearstained, but it was lost and heartbroken and a number of other adjectives that Solomon didn't like at all.

"You know what you need?"

She shook her head, her eyes large and dark in the candlelight. "Do you?"

"Cartwheels."

She scoffed weakly, but didn't protest when he put an arm around her waist and drew her back into the main part of the tunnel.

"Come on, this is perfect! Here, I'll hold your robe for you—I don't want you to trip."

"But I'll be cold," she protested.

"You'll warm up fast." He held out his hand.

Obediently—and if anything could have told him how deeply miserable she was, it was that word, *obediently*, used in connection with Serena—she removed the robe and handed it to him. She stood there in her shift, shivering a little.

"Have you ever done one before?"

That spurred her into action. She spun away, took a few quick steps forward, and turned a long line of perfect cartwheels down the center of the tunnel.

He sat down on the steps and watched her spin back, bare feet and arms and long white legs flashing out of the darkness into the candlelight. She stopped a few yards from the stairs. Flushed with exertion, she pulled her shift quickly to rights—but not before he saw one dusky aureole. *Oh God.*

"Do—" He cleared his throat. "Do you feel better?"

She smiled at him, still panting. "I do, actually. I feel lighter."

"Good, I'll fetch the strawberries. Here's your robe." He shoved it quickly into her hands and fled back under the stairs.

They ate the strawberries sitting on the stairs. He was uncomfortably aware of her nearness, and tried not to watch her put the strawberries in her mouth, or to think about what else she would have put in her mouth if he hadn't had scruples.

When the strawberries were all gone Serena said with a sigh, "I suppose we should be getting back to bed."

"Just a little longer? I don't feel like sleeping just yet."

"It's late."

"I know." He looked down and rubbed at a strawberry stain on his finger. At least it didn't clash with the splotches of black. "Last night, I had one of those dreams about Elijah again. I—just stay a little longer."

He could hear the smile in her voice when she said, "Would you like me to stay all night?"

He looked askance at her.

"In an entirely platonic way, of course."

"You promise?"

"I promise. I'm not too keen on my own bed right now either."

He hesitated, as if there were any chance of his saying no. Serena in his bed. Waking up in the night and hearing her breathing, feeling her warmth. It would be torture, but he wanted it. Apparently, so did she. "Would you?"

"I never back out on a deal."

Serena was not amused when she woke early the next morning to find herself lying next to an angelically slumbering Solomon, her nose pressed into his side and her arm flung across his chest. She sat up. In the morning light, his freckles were sprinkled across his face like gold dust.

Lord, what a stupid thing to think. She rubbed at her eyes.

Last night had gone all wrong. She had merely planned to

seduce him, to get him to beg her to stay the night. True, she hadn't expected the experience to be unpleasant—quite the opposite. But she had planned to remain firmly in control.

Instead, the instant he gave in and kissed her, she'd forgotten all her skill and plans, lost in a wave of sensation, unable to do anything but pant and moan and—God, had she really?—*rub* herself against him like a cat in heat.

Her attempt to take back control had been disastrous. When he had recoiled, she'd thought she would die. When he'd said, *I'm not interested in strange women*, that awful ruined feeling from when she was eighteen had risen up and drowned her. *Whore*, she'd thought. *He's too good for you, and he knows it*. For a second she'd hated him with the same sullen contempt she'd felt the first time she'd seen him. And Solomon—bizarre, wonderful Solomon—had yet again only wanted something more honest from her.

He'd pulled back, stopped her from wrapping her mouth around him and showing him all the advantages of bedding the most notorious ex-whore in London, and somehow they'd ended up sleeping side by side like a couple of innocent babes. She'd *clung* to him. She had let him see her almost in tears. And his ridiculous cartwheels had actually made her feel better.

What was next? Frolicking through a field of daisies? Sweet, tender lovemaking? *That idea does* not *make me feel all warm and tingly*, she told herself firmly. Her mind ignored her, dwelling on the last few moments before Solomon had put a stop to things.

She'd pleasured plenty of men with her mouth and received more than her share of compliments on her technique. But last night it had been different—she'd really *wanted* to, wanted to feel Solomon trembling and hear him gasp with pleasure and know that it was her doing. She had wanted him to look at her the way he looked at his experiments, or at the organ in St. Andrew's—with utter concentration and joy. She had wanted to give him something wonderful.

She rolled over and looked at Solomon, stretched out in his bed with the morning sun caressing his limbs, and she felt it again. Her hands ached with the need to reach out and touch him. She could do it. He was right there. She could feel the heat from his body warming her legs.

It was seven o'clock. On an ordinary day she would have been up for two hours. She had all of yesterday's work to do, and Sophy's teasing to face. Sophy always came to her room in the mornings to help with her stays and buttons. Sophy would know she hadn't been there. Antoine probably already knew, just as he knew she hadn't looked at next week's menus yet. What was the point, when she was going to lose the Arms? She could stay here and touch Solomon, and not face it.

That was when Serena panicked. Solomon had to go. He was clouding her mind, keeping her from figuring out a solution to her problems. Keeping her from caring as much as she should. She was letting him make her feel safe, but the only person who could keep her safe was herself. She had to find his earrings so that he could go.

She would go to Decker's. She'd go right now. She slid out of bed as slowly as she could and tiptoed to the connecting door, which stood wide open. She shut the door quietly behind her and leaned against it, thinking. Decker required male attire.

Ten minutes later, Serena was tugging on a pair of gleaming Hessians that had stood hidden in her wardrobe behind a green wool evening gown. She shoved her hair inside an old beaver hat and inspected the result in the mirror. *I really must invest in a wig,* she thought distractedly, and left.

Fritz Decker's was one of the less reputable molly houses in London—that is to say, one of the less reputable establishments catering to men who preferred the company of other men, at least for certain very personal activities—but that didn't mean Decker was careless. Serena had to give her name, a sign, and a counter-

countersign to the burly, businesslike fellow at the door. At the conclusion of this formality, he ceremoniously showed her in to where the host was sitting in a corner of his taproom.

Decker was a red-nosed man, not many years past his prime. His green-and-gold-striped waistcoat had once been very fine, but was now several years further past its prime than its owner, and covered in grease and beer stains. "Morning, Thorn, it's good to see you again. What brings you to my humble establishment?"

"Good to see you too, Fritz. I daresay you got my message."

Decker shifted uneasily. "I warn you I can make no guarantees I'll tell you what you want to know."

She gave him a silky smile. "I'll just have to hope, won't I?"

Decker sighed lugubriously. "Come in the back and we'll discuss it."

Serena glanced about the taproom while he was heaving himself out of his chair. At half-past seven in the morning, there was almost no one about. A group of bleary-eyed men in one corner were glaring at two disgustingly cheery fellows in the opposite corner, who seemed to have just awoken from a good night's sleep, probably in each other's company. A few skinny, rouged boys sprawled across stools at the bar.

Serena didn't recognize more than a handful of the house's denizens, but she did note that Lord Hartleigh's coloring was better suited to his wife's peach sarsenet than Lady Hartleigh's, and that young Ravi Bhattacharya was thinner than ever and sporting a black eye. They could use a new kitchen boy at the Arms; she'd speak to him about it on her way out. Of course, Sophy had reminded her just last week when she'd hired Charlotte that the Arms wasn't a Home for Ruined Young Persons, but didn't she and Sophy give that the lie already?

And then Lord Hartleigh moved a little to the left and Serena's heart thudded and sank. Sitting just behind him, in close and *very* amiable conversation with Sir Nigel Anchridge, was Solomon.

Chapter 12

Serena headed straight for him, ignoring Decker's forceful sotto voce representations. "If you might give us a moment," she said to Sir Nigel in freezing accents, and stared at him until he shrugged, grinned, and wandered off. Turning her gaze on Solomon, she saw him give Sir Nigel a conspiratorial wink. "Solomon, what the devil is going on here?" she asked in a furious undertone.

His brow wrinkled. He was wearing fetchingly disheveled riding gear that Serena had never seen before. "I'm sorry to disappoint such a lovely young man, but my name's not Solomon." He gave her a friendly leer. "However, since you've driven off my friend, perhaps I might be of service to you instead?" He was affecting a different accent, a little more Shropshire and less Cambridge, but she'd already heard him use it at St. Andrew of the Cross.

"I don't give a damn how you choose to spend your spare time, but please have the courtesy not to lie to me to my face." It occurred to her, painfully, that this explained the hundred and twenty-five pounds. Not to mention last night. He'd been so kind, so respectful—because he *didn't want her.*

Solomon crossed a boot over his knee and tilted his head in just that way he had. "I'm very sorry, sir, but there's been a mistake." His right hand moved to rest lightly on his top-boot, and two things made Serena realize with a jolt that it was really not Solomon. For one thing, he evidently had a knife in his boot. For another, his hands were smooth and unstained. But they were unmistakably Solomon's hands—

Serena's eyes narrowed. "Elijah!" she hissed.

His left hand shot out and caught her by the wrist, and Elijah said pleasantly, "I'd be very much obliged to you if you didn't use my name here."

Her lips thinned. "Very well," she said quietly. "I'd be very much obliged to you if you'd come with me. Your brother has spent the past year and however long mourning you, and I don't plan to allow that to continue one moment longer than necessary. I have some business to conduct with our host, but I shall return shortly. I trust you'll still be here—but should you choose to go, I *can* find you."

His eyes narrowed. "I'm sorry, sir, but you have the advantage of me. Who are you, exactly?"

She laid her palm flat on the table and leaned forward. "I am Lady Serena Ravenshaw."

His brows rose, his eyes flickering to her bound breasts. "I see. Well, in that case I won't cross you. The Thorn's network of spies is legend." He flashed her an engaging grin eerily like Solomon's—and yet with rather more dash and conscious charm. She felt inexplicably unsettled.

"Flattery will get you nowhere," she said sharply, and gave him a last admonitory glare before returning to Decker, who stood watching her resignedly.

"I'm sure you wouldn't like it if I caused an upheaval at the Arms," he grumbled.

Serena shrugged. "Don't tell me your taproom has never seen a jealous lovers' spat before. That's all anyone thought it was."

Decker gave her a sideways grin. "A lovers' spat, Thorn? Is that the handsome tailor I hear you were kissing in a hallway a few nights ago?"

Serena raised an eyebrow. "Been listening to gossip, Fritz?"

"When do I listen to anything else? Can't say I wasn't pleased to hear it. You deserve some fun. I've a soft spot for tailors myself. Meticulous, that's what they are." He smiled reminiscently and blew his red nose into a cherry-striped handkerchief. "But if he's having a bit on the side, I say boot him out."

She was caught between Scylla and Charybdis. God only knew what Elijah was up to, lurking around pretending to be dead and seeming, for a corpse, rather dangerous. She could hardly reveal that he wasn't Solomon. Nor could she announce that she and Solomon weren't lovers, since, well, no one would believe it. Which meant Fritz Decker thought she was being cheated on, and there was nothing she could do about it. It was humiliating. "That's not what we were discussing," she said icily, and left it at that.

"Well, you always were one for keeping up a brave front," Decker said cheerily. If only she were a man, no one would say things like that to her.

He let them into a low unpainted room off the house's yard and latched the door behind them. A table covered in equipment stood in the center of the room. She'd seen it plenty of times before, but now it made her think of Solomon. In the corner was a large safe. As well as running one of London's less reputable molly houses, Decker was one of London's more discreet fences. "Now how can I help you?"

"I'm here to get those earrings. These *are* the same pair you bought off a highwayman last week, are they not?" She drew Solomon's sketch of the earrings from her pocket and handed it to Decker.

The look he gave her was really troubled. "These were the last things I ever expected *you* to ask about."

She frowned. "Why?"

He pursed his lips. "I'll tell you this much. I did have those earrings. They were here for almost five days. Then someone comes in yesterday morning, asking about them. I'm sorry, Thorn. They're gone. Were gone hours before I got your note."

"And who purchased them?"

His round mouth flattened out severely. "You know I won't tell you. My business relies on discretion."

"I'm discreet. And I would make it worth your while."

He looked affronted. "I wasn't asking for a bribe. I don't betray my customers. In either of my professions."

She leaned against the door frame, gave a long-suffering sigh, and fixed him with her blankest, mildest expression. "I need to know where those earrings went, Fritz. I should hate to have to resort to foolish violence." He quailed. Serena felt a shock of pure malicious satisfaction. That would teach him to tell her she put up a brave front.

"I can't, and I can't," he said pleadingly. "You've been accused of black things, Thorn, but violence to an undeserving man for pursuing his profession isn't one of them."

She grinned wolfishly. "You clearly haven't heard my latest orders."

He had. She saw it in his eyes. He took a hasty step backward. But he stuck obstinately to his guns. "Cutthroat ain't a profession, and your father deserves what he gets. This is different. But even if it wasn't, I'm between the devil and the deep sea. My life won't be worth a copper penny if one of my transactions becomes a source of unpleasantness because of me, and that's a fact."

Damn it, he was right. Serena just wanted this over with so she could go back out there and deal with Elijah. It filled her with angry frustration that the information she needed was so damn close and yet she wasn't going to get it.

On the other hand, she thought, *if I can't get the earrings, Solomon can't leave yet.* No, that was a *bad* thing. She glared at Decker.

"I owe you a debt, Thorn," Decker said unexpectedly, stepping forward again. "You didn't have to warn me about that police raid, and you did. And I like you, for all you could frighten our Lord himself. So let me warn you to be careful. I'm troubled in my mind that you should be asking about those earrings."

"Oh la," she drawled. "I'm ever so touched. I can make such practical use of *that* information. At least tell me one thing: were the earrings whole when you sold them?"

He nodded. His relieved smile that she was relenting just made her angrier. People weren't supposed to look at her like that. They weren't supposed to like her. Being *liked* didn't keep you safe. You couldn't predict it or rely on it. It was just something you had to keep earning, over and over.

"Thank you," she said. "But bear in mind that the *next* time I come across information that *you* need, I just may keep it to myself." But she didn't find Decker's hurt expression any more pleasant than his smile. It was an empty threat anyway, and he probably knew it.

Solomon was throwing her off her game, and now that the earrings were missing again, who knew when she could be rid of him?

To her surprise, Elijah was waiting patiently when she returned to the taproom. She motioned him to stay while she had a few words with Ravi Bhattacharya, who was still sitting at the bar with his head high and an empty glass of gin in his hand.

That business concluded, Serena jerked her head toward the door, and Elijah stood and followed her. They were waiting for a hackney on the pavement when Serena asked abruptly, "Is your brother—does he—" She gestured toward the pub behind them, frustrated that she couldn't seem to just come out and ask. But what would she say? *Does your brother like men? Because that would explain why he hasn't slept with me.*

A slow, pleased smile spread across Elijah's face, and Serena felt her temperature rising. Good God, was she blushing? "No," he said. "He isn't, and doesn't."

Serena concentrated very hard on watching the road for a hackney. Finally one came, and she hailed it. As Elijah was climbing in ahead of her, he flung back carelessly over his shoulder, "Oh, and Thorn, do me a favor, would you?"

"It depends on the favor."

He did not meet her eyes. "Don't tell Solomon where you found me?"

Her heart clenched. "It's no fun to have your family angry with you for sleeping with the wrong people, is it?"

He laughed. Then his brows drew together. "Surely *Solomon* isn't the wrong people."

"You Hathaways seem to have rather a lot of unjustified family pride," Serena said in some amusement. "Of course he is. But I'm not sleeping with him."

Elijah looked disappointed.

"I give you my word Solomon won't hear about your predilections from me. You should tell him, though. I think he'd take it very well, after the first few days."

"Maybe. What were *you* there for, if I may ask?"

"As you would know if you'd been at home, your family earrings have been stolen and Susannah refuses to get married without them. Solomon has engaged me to find them. Decker is a receiver."

Elijah's eyes widened. "Susannah is getting married?"

"So I'm told."

"Who's the bridegroom?"

She shrugged.

The carriage pulled into the Arms' courtyard. Serena won the ensuing argument about who would pay the hackney fare. "Come on upstairs. But let me go in first—I'd like to soften the shock a little."

"Don't be ridiculous," said Elijah, but he let her.

Solomon heard Elijah's step on the stair, but he ignored it. Hearing Elijah's step wasn't uncommon these days. At the beginning his heart had always jumped and begun to beat faster, but when he looked it was never Elijah. By now he'd got his heart's reaction down to an almost imperceptible tremor and he never looked—but the step was coming down the hall, and it really seemed to be Elijah's.

If you open that door, he told himself firmly, *you will see some young buck trying to break into Serena's room, and he will call you the Hatherdasher.* Then the connecting door opened and Serena came in.

Solomon was so shocked he forgot all about the step. "Serena, I can't believe you!" he said, standing. "*What* are you wearing?"

Serena looked down at her frock coat and Hessians in annoyance. "Solomon, I really don't have time for this right now—"

"You bought that from Fitzhugh! How *could* you be such a gull? Just look at that waistcoat. Not only is the color *streaky*, but if he had cut it differently and added some extra quilting toward the bottom, it would have hid your shape *much* better. And it's not as if his prices are cut-rate. Promise me you'll go to my uncle next time."

Serena smiled at him. "It was secondhand, but all right, I promise. Listen, I've got something to tell you. Maybe you should sit down. I—I met someone while I was out this morning, someone you thought—"

Solomon had already burst out of the room. "Elijah! Where are you? *Elijah!*"

When Serena followed Solomon into the hall, she had to jump back very nimbly to avoid being bowled over by a careening, shouting tangle of Hathaway limbs. It was several minutes before Solomon finally separated himself from Elijah, laughing and very pale and trying shakily to catch his breath. "I thought you were dead, you bastard! We all did."

Elijah looked down and scuffed the toe of his boot. "I'm sorry. It couldn't be helped, but I thought—I suppose I thought you would know I was all right."

Solomon's mouth twisted. Serena, remembering Solomon say *I didn't even know when he died,* wanted to rip Elijah's unexpectedly still-beating heart out of his chest.

"I *did!*" Solomon said. "But I couldn't let myself believe it. Men who've lost an arm can still feel their fingers itch, can't they? It's been a year and a half, Elijah! A year and a half of thinking you were gone, do you know what that feels like?" Elijah began to speak, but Solomon interrupted him. "No! No, you *don't*, because *I* never let you think I was *dead!*"

"I said I was sorry—"

But Solomon was only winding up. "And Mother! She lost a stone and didn't even alter her clothes! Father couldn't get into a proper rage for months! It was *painful* to hear him preach, and *Susannah*—why didn't you *write* to us? And now you're right here in London looking as debonair as ever, only *more* so because I would wager a hundred guineas that's Parisian tailoring, and I only know because Serena saw you in the *street?*"

"I was on my way here, you nodcock! As if I haven't been going mad wanting to see you all this time! I'll tell you all about it later, all right, only *not now*—"

They were too caught up in their argument to realize how loud they had become. So when the door across the hall opened and a tousled René in an elegant violet dressing gown stuck his head out, they jumped back with identical expressions of guilty chagrin. It was easy to picture them as caught-out little boys. It was adorable.

Then Elijah's expression changed. So did René's; he broke into a delighted grin. "*Thierry!*"

"René," Elijah acknowledged as he was seized in a warm embrace. René stepped back, beaming. Elijah looked less pleased. He shook René's hands off his shoulders with a glance at Solomon that said, *God spare me from emotional Frenchmen.* René did not stop beaming. Serena suddenly got a very unpleasant feeling in the pit of her stomach.

"Thierry! Your idiot of a brother told me you were dead!"

"He thought I was," Elijah said flatly. "Everyone did."

"But—but how is this possible?"

"I was in the army. They seconded me to a Spanish unit. We were on a reconnaissance mission behind enemy lines and a bullet killed my horse. I hit my head falling, and when I woke up my unit was gone." He glanced at Solomon. "I had no hope of getting back to the English army—I didn't even know where it was—and I spoke French well enough to pass, so I got rid of my uniform and decided to make my way back to England through France. I thought they could ship me out again from here if they wanted. But when Boney was sent to Elba, I decided to stay and see a little of Paris."

He looked at Solomon again and said, "I sent you a few letters. I suppose the reestablished mail lines weren't as reliable as they claimed. And then war broke out again and I couldn't get out. I had to go back to pretending to be French. That's when I met René." He looked at René and raised his chin a little.

"He was in a tavern brawl," René revealed. "He could barely walk. I took him in out of the goodness of my heart." Elijah glared.

"How lucky that you found such a selfless benefactor as our own marquis," Serena said when Solomon said nothing in response to this touching narrative.

Elijah smiled incredulously. "Marquis?"

"Yes," René said quickly. "It appears we were both incognito. I am the marquis du Sacreval. Or I will be, when Louis XVIII restores my titles."

Elijah started, frowning. "*You're* the marquis du Sacreval?"

"Yes."

"Oh Lord, I haven't time for this now. I've got to speak to my brother." And grabbing Solomon's arm, Elijah towed him into his room and slammed the door.

Serena and René were left standing in the hallway. They looked at each other and then at Solomon's door. "We are *not* going to listen in," Serena said. "And to make sure of it, you're going to come and have breakfast with me in the kitchen." He gave her a pleading glance, but she swept majestically past him down the corridor to the servants' stair.

Halfway down, Serena remembered what she was wearing. She could go back up and change, couldn't she? And if she overheard something, that wasn't her fault—

She hovered, undecided, and René said mischievously, "So now that you've seen Elijah, I imagine you won't have much use for his brother, *hein?*"

Let everyone stare. There was no way she was letting René near those boys if she could help it. She took off her hat and handed it to him. "Quite the opposite," she said coldly as she re-pinned her hair. "Elijah is a dear, but there's something *showy* about him, don't you think?" René laughed softly and Serena felt very irritated indeed.

In the Stuart room, the two brothers faced each other awkwardly. "I'm sorry," Elijah said again.

Solomon had been surprised to find that life went on without Elijah. Now he was surprised to find out that it went on *with* him. He wanted time to stop and let him figure out how he felt, accustom himself to this new world. But of course it didn't. He must carry on as if the dominant emotion of the past year and a half of his life hadn't been—unnecessary. Irrelevant. He sighed. "What really happened?"

Elijah looked down. "I explained that."

Solomon crossed his arms. "I know you've been gone a long time, Li, but I can still tell when you're lying."

Elijah nodded resignedly. "But it sounded plausible?"

Solomon frowned. "Yes, except for the part about your trying to write to us. That was an obvious fabrication."

"Good. Now loan me a pen and paper. I can't risk anyone overhearing what I'm about to tell you." In spite of his shock and anger, Solomon felt a deep thrill of anticipation. Elijah always made things exciting.

Elijah, gesturing to Solomon to stand by him, wrote, *I had to pretend to be dead because I'm a spy.*

"You, too!" Solomon exclaimed. Elijah glared at him and offered him the pen.

The marquis is a spy, too, Solomon wrote. *For the French. I assume you're a spy for the English?*

Elijah rolled his eyes. *Naturally. And I already know René is a spy, because.* Elijah stopped. He ran his fingers through his hair. Then he wrote, very firmly, *I'm in London to bring him and his informants to justice as soon as I can find concrete evidence.*

Solomon did not know quite what to write. Elijah looked so grim. He wrote *But* and paused. Then he continued, *you and Sacreval are friends. Aren't you?* Of course, Sacreval and Serena were friends, too.

Elijah glanced at Solomon. *We were. But he's a French spy. The best. He's passed lakes of information. We can't afford to have anything leak right now, or it'll be him hanging me.*

You didn't know it was him when you took the assignment, did you?

Elijah's shoulders sagged. He shook his head.

You can't though, yet. The marquis—

Elijah ripped the pen out of Solomon's hand and started writing very quickly. *He's no more a marquis than I am, damn it. He's got two little brothers and a sister and a mother, and they all live in a cramped apartment in the quartier Saint-Germain and keep a very small bakery that belonged to his father.* He stopped writing.

Solomon took the pen from his brother's unresisting hand. *I'm sorry, but you can't hang him just at the moment. He forged marriage lines to get the Arms from Serena, and if he's hanged, the inn will be forfeit to the Crown.*

And what am I going to tell the Foreign Office then? 'I'm sorry, but my brother says we can't hang an enemy—the nib caught and ink spattered across the paper. Solomon took the pen again.

Can you tell the others you're back?

Elijah nodded. *I have to. I'm supposed to stay here quite openly. That's why they were willing to sacrifice my connections in Paris, because they knew you were staying here and if I came suddenly back from the dead, I'd end up here too.*

If his connection to Serena hadn't suddenly proved useful to the Foreign Office, how long would he have had to wait to get his brother back? But there was no point asking that. *They'll pay your shot, won't they?*

Elijah laughed. "So, you and Lady Serena—"

"What about us?" Solomon asked.

"Sol."

"We're friends."

"You might as well tell me, because if you don't, I'll find out anyway."

"I forgot what a bully you are."

The two brothers looked at each other. Suddenly Solomon was smiling tremulously and Elijah's lashes were wet. They each looked firmly back at the paper, embarrassed. Then Elijah took the pen and wrote, *What the devil does he want with the inn anyway?*

I don't know, Solomon admitted, *but I'd swear he set a fire in my room two nights ago while we were out. Someone did, anyway. Tried to make it look like I left a candle burning on the mantel and it fell off.* He pointed at the damaged mantelpiece.

Elijah's eyes narrowed. *Destroy this paper,* he wrote. As Solomon reached for his tinderbox, Elijah went to the hearth. Getting on his knees, he examined the charred bottom of the carving. Solomon burned the paper in the bottom of a glass bowl and looked at his brother, who was really back.

"What's on the other side of the wall?" Elijah asked.

"Serena's room." Solomon flushed at his brother's raised brows. "She keeps the door locked."

Elijah glanced at the melted keyhole.

"Well, she did, before I dissolved the lock." Solomon flushed deeper. "She was having a nightmare."

Elijah, miraculously, decided to save the teasing for later. "Is it easier to break into this room than that one?"

"I'm not sure—oh. Yes, it is. Serena has a bar on her door. And I'm sure he wanted it to look to Serena as if I had done it."

"Can I take a look on the other side?"

Solomon hesitated. Serena would take a dim view of such proceedings, but maybe that was a good reason to get it over with while she wasn't around. Elijah didn't wait for his permission anyway. He just turned the doorknob and went in.

Solomon followed, trying not to get distracted by Serena's shift lying on the bed, or the three hairpins and a brush on her dressing table, or any of the countless other intimate things that said *Serena lives here.* "He's more likely to have been trying for my room anyway. It used to be his and he was very irritated that I'd got it."

Elijah rapped on the wall and listened carefully to the sound. "Maybe he was just annoyed at having to cross the hall to reach the Siren's bed," he suggested morosely.

This lowering thought had occurred to Solomon, too. "Don't call her that."

Elijah examined the floor near the wall. "I may have to take this flooring up. The fire makes me wonder if there's something important hidden in the Ravenshaw Arms. You're right, it's more likely to be on your side."

"Shall we search for it now?"

Elijah hesitated, then shook his head. "Later. Right now I want to know all about Susannah's engagement."

Serena expected Elijah to join her and Solomon for dinner that evening, naturally. And she was definitely unsurprised when Elijah and Solomon talked feverishly, their conversation heavily punctuated with ancient private jokes and obscure allusions, while she toyed with her food. After the first couple of courses she got up and left altogether. She wasn't sure Solomon noticed.

But that night she was awakened by knocking on the connecting door. "Come," she called.

Solomon opened the door. She couldn't quite see his face in the moonlight. "I'm sorry to bother you."

Serena sat up on her elbows. "What is it?"

"It's just—he's really back, isn't he? I didn't dream it?"

She shook her head. "No. You didn't dream it."

The tension eased out of his shoulders. "Thanks. And thank you for finding him."

She was angry with Elijah all over again, for tangling Solomon in whatever game he was playing. "Well," she said softly, "you did engage me to find things you lost, didn't you?"

The moon silvered his mouth as it curved, just a little. But she thought he was still staring at the floor.

"You must simply try to be a little less careless in future." When his chin jerked up, as she'd known it would, she pulled up the corner of the quilt and patted the sheets next to her.

The hopeful lifting of his brows made her bite her tongue to keep from showing—she wasn't sure what, but whatever it was she was feeling. He came to the side of the bed and stood there, looking down at her as if she were a puzzle he couldn't figure out. Her skin began to tingle pleasantly. After a few improbably long moments, he climbed into bed, the mattress shifting under his weight. Serena settled comfortably down with her nose pushed into his side.

"But don't think this is a permanent arrangement," she told him in a muffled voice.

"I know," he said. Then, "I was grieving for so long. I don't know how to make sense of myself anymore. I don't know how to feel."

"We'll just have to wait and see then, won't we?"

His hand settled, warm and heavy, on the back of her head. She could hear his smile in his voice. "I suppose we will."

Elijah had removed his coat and pried his boots off before he realized his cravat pin was missing. He didn't see it anywhere on the floor, so he went out into the hall with his candle to look. He was prowling past René's door when it swung open. Damn. This ought to be awkward.

"Thierry. You have lost something?"

Elijah was silent a moment, looking at René with his fashionably tousled hair and his brocade dressing gown. Marquis du Sacreval. Christ. "Yes, I rather think I have."

René opened the door a little further, and Elijah went in and put down his candle.

He tried to cast a professional eye over the room, looking for anything incriminating. But all he saw was René's burgundy coat hanging over a chair before René seized him by the shoulders and slammed him up against the wall. The door swung shut with a heavy clunk.

"Thierry—you—you—" René kissed him, hard.

Chapter 13

Elijah kissed him back, too numb to put up any resistance, or even to put his arms around René's neck. He leaned against the wall as René's hands roughly untied his cravat. René's hands—

Tears stung his eyes. He closed them. Despair and heat pooled in his chest, a surprisingly intoxicating mixture. Surely it wouldn't be wrong to allow himself this, one last time. One last time before—he failed to finish the thought as René began on his buttons.

Suddenly, from any number of long Palm Sunday services he'd daydreamed through in his father's church, a verse came back to him. *Now he that betrayed him gave them a sign, saying, Whomsoever I shall kiss, that same is he: hold him fast.*

Elijah opened his eyes and took René's familiar hands—which were on their last waistcoat button—in his. They were large and brown, with firm wrists and strong fingers. A baker's hands. "I never thought I'd see you again." If only he hadn't.

"*C'est la faute de qui, ça?*" René asked shakily.

Elijah raised his eyes to René's face. "It was my fault. But what would you have had me do? Leave you my address? *Stay* with you? The week before I left, Napoleon came back from exile, or don't you remember that? Every hour I spent with you was an hour I risked discovery—an hour I risked arrest. If any of you had noticed anything amiss with my accent—"

Of course, he'd already been living in Paris as a Frenchman for over a year then, as an under-clerk at the Ministry of Police. But with Napoleon back and seeing spies and assassins in every shadow, and the British Foreign Office desperate for anything he could give them, he hadn't been able to risk anyone getting to know him too closely. He hadn't been able to risk anyone asking what was in that locked trunk at the foot of his bed, or wanting to meet the fictitious sister he visited so often in Le Havre. But the lies flowed so naturally, so smoothly, that Elijah was almost surprised when a little bit of truth slipped in. "I only stayed so long because I couldn't—after I left, it was weeks before I learned how to fall asleep without you again."

"Me, I still have not learned," René said raggedly and dove in for another kiss. "What is this I taste? Salt? Ah, Thierry—"

René's mouth traced the tear tracks down his cheek. Elijah bit his tongue, hard, to keep from saying something else foolish. Soon René's hands began, more gently this time, to tug Elijah's shirt out of his breeches. "But now things will be as they were," he murmured.

Elijah pushed him away, at the same time propelling himself off of the wall. "René, they can't ever. *We* can't ever."

René stood still, breathing hard. "But why not?" He seemed almost menacing, standing so close in the darkness with an angry note in his voice. It sent shivers down Elijah's spine. The good sort.

Elijah struggled to think over the deafening pounding of his heart. "I—you can't possibly understand—"

René sighed and took a step back. "But I do understand. I know perfectly why you do not want us to be as we were."

Elijah stared. René knew he was a spy? He wished that he had his knife, but it was still in his boots down the hall. "You do?" he asked stupidly.

René's eyes gleamed. "Of course I do. Do you think that I am an idiot?"

Elijah thought of all the times he had seen candlelight reflected in René's eyes, and how different those times had been. Even the inn's fine beeswax gave a clearer, crueler light than the cheap tallow they'd used in Paris. He wished he could crawl back into that earlier, welcoming darkness and pull it over him. "No, I never thought that."

"It is because of your brother, *evidemment*. It is clear that he knows nothing."

Oh. Elijah hid his relief. "René, it would kill me if he found out. If any of them found out. It would kill my father. He's a clergyman." He took a deep breath to still the tremor in his voice. "I wish—I want—it's over. It has to be over." Saying no to René was harder than he had anticipated. Elijah reminded himself that this man worked for Bonaparte. That every day, Englishmen died because of him. "I'm sorry."

Unexpectedly, René nodded. He didn't even point out that in Paris, they had made love on the other side of a paper-thin wall from René's mother and sister—because after all there had been nowhere else—trying so hard not to make a sound and trying even harder not to laugh at their own efforts. Elijah wondered for the thousandth time if they had heard, if they had known. If they had cared. "Very well," René said. "But if you change your mind . . ."

Elijah tried to smile. *Traitor*, he thought viciously, and didn't know if he meant René or himself. "I know where to find you."

René didn't smile back. "I think that you should leave now."

Elijah nodded, ducked his head, and put his hand on the doorknob.

René did smile then. "You cannot go like this."

"What?"

René nodded his head in the general direction of Elijah's—oh. In the general direction of Elijah's open waistcoat and rumpled shirt. Elijah tucked in his shirt. He tried to fasten his first button and fumbled, twice. He swore under his breath.

"Let me." Gently, as one would for a child, René buttoned Elijah's waistcoat. "Now raise your chin." Elijah did, and René retied his cravat. He gave him a light push. "Now go."

Elijah went. He found his cravat pin under his bed the next morning.

Solomon was awakened by someone pounding on a door. He opened his eyes and blinked, startled to discover his bed curtains had changed color overnight. Then he remembered that he was in Serena's bed. Alone, it would appear. The pounding was coming from his own door in the other room.

"All right, I'm coming, possess thy soul in patience." Since they certainly couldn't hear his mutter, and he lacked the energy to yell, the pounding didn't stop. He got up and tiptoed back into his room, shutting the connecting door as softly as he could so the person knocking wouldn't realize he'd been anywhere but his own bed. Then he threw on his dressing gown and opened the door.

Elijah was in the hall, fully dressed. His presence didn't feel like any less of a miracle than it had yesterday.

"'He that blesseth his friend with a loud voice, rising early in the morning, it shall be counted a curse to him,'" Solomon said groggily.

Elijah ignored this. He pulled a note from his pocket, holding it in front of Solomon's as yet unfocused eyes.

I've considered, and I'll advise against arresting ~~Re~~ *Sacreval just yet if Lady S. can provide useful help in bringing down his network. We should discuss this in an open space.*

"A picnic?" Solomon said unenthusiastically. "What a lovely idea. I'm sure Serena would love to."

Elijah smiled, but he didn't look as if he'd slept well.

Serena really ought to be home supervising breakfast, not in the Green Park with Solomon and his brother. Especially with Ravi as their newest waiter. He might need her if any of his old customers showed up.

She had supervised breakfast every day for the past five years, and now she had failed to do so for three days running. Sophy was perfectly capable of dealing with most things, but if someone started trouble . . .

It was still early enough to be rather chilly, and they were almost the only people in the park. Serena wished she had brought gloves. Still, cold tongue, warm bread, and hard-boiled eggs made a satisfying meal, and none of them seemed to want to get round to business. If Serena was right about the nature of René and Elijah's relationship, no doubt Elijah was about as eager to see René hang as she was. But by the time she pulled Ying's strawberry tarts from the bottom of the basket, she was cold and guilty enough to want to get back to the Arms as soon as possible. "Well then," she said. "Solomon said you wanted to speak to me."

"Yes," Elijah said. "Sol tells me it would not be in your best interests right now to have Re—Sacreval arrested."

"Since he legally—well, illegally, really—owns the Arms, no. It would not be."

"So here's my bargain. You tell me what resources you and the Arms can offer me to bring in his people, and maybe I'll tell the Foreign Office it's best if Sacreval's not arrested just yet."

"Do you know who his people are?"

Elijah looked away in annoyance. "Actually, we only know Sir Nigel Anchridge. And Elbourn."

Serena gave him a superior smile. "Well, you've missed Lady Brendan and Lord Pursleigh. And a couple of clerks at the War Office and so on. Remind me to give you their names later. They aren't rich, so you won't need much proof to arrest them."

Elijah looked enlightened. "Of course! Brendan's in the War Office and Lady Brendan is French, isn't she? And Pursleigh is on the committee in charge of supplies for the army."

"Indeed," Serena said smugly.

"Well, if you're so clever, do you know how he gets the messages to France?"

"No, do you?"

Elijah shook his head. "We know his messengers sail from somewhere in Cornwall, but—"

"Cornwall's a big place," Serena commiserated. "And then, watching the entire coast would be *such* a threat to the lords' brandy, wouldn't it?"

Elijah sighed. "Just tell me how he contacts his informants."

Serena nodded. "Except for Sir Nigel, whom I expect he meets secretly some other way"—she shot Elijah a significant glance, and he nodded uncomfortably—"I think he ran it through the Arms' catering. Sacreval was always in charge of catering because I—well, I can't go to people's homes. The Elbourns, the Brendans, and the Pursleighs were always some of our best catering customers, but when Sacreval left, they stopped coming. And they used to spend the longest time closeted with him in his office, supposedly going over the menus. And—well, a host of reasons, really."

Elijah nodded. "But Sacreval isn't in charge of catering anymore, is he?"

"Of course not."

"All right, so we'll have to wait and see what they do."

"Mr. Elbourn," Solomon said. "Isn't he giving a ball for his wife's birthday on Friday? Uncle Dewington was trying to convince me to go last time I saw him."

Serena met Elijah's eyes. They both turned to look at Solomon, whose face fell comically. "I really don't want to go," he said. "Can't you just go and pretend to be me?"

"Don't be ridiculous," Elijah said.

"Don't be an arse," Serena snapped at him.

"Look, all he has to do is snoop around Elbourn's study, maybe pick a couple of locks—"

"I can't pick a lock," Solomon pointed out.

Elijah waved his hand. "I'll show you, it's not hard."

Serena didn't like the way he acted as if he had the whip-hand of Solomon. She didn't like how he took Solomon for granted. She didn't like a lot of things about him. "It took me months to learn," she said evenly. One of the other girls had taught her at Mme Deveraux's. Serena had spent hours at it until she could do it with her eyes closed. It was almost as good as embroidery for not thinking of anything else.

"Then you go."

She spread her hands in exasperation. "I was a whore! Don't you understand that? They don't want me there! Do it yourself."

"They don't want me either," Elijah said. "*I* didn't go to Cambridge."

"You didn't—you didn't go to *Cambridge?*" Serena sputtered, thinking of all the times her old acquaintances had cut her dead in the street, of the boys who had once merely ignored her at parties and now thought they could say anything they liked to her. "You can take your Foreign Office and shove them—"

"They aren't going to be happy I've taken you into my confidence anyway," Elijah said, looking almost glad to have picked a fight. "They don't trust you. This is your chance to prove you're on our side and that you can be useful. Besides, Sol and I will hardly be able to slip away without anyone noticing. If you and he wander off, no one will think twice."

Solomon, who had opened his mouth to speak, blushed bright, bright red. But he cleared his throat and said, "Don't talk to her that way. This isn't her job. She's doing you a favor."

"She isn't doing me a favor," Elijah said tightly. "She needs our help to break free of Sacreval as badly as we need hers to catch him."

Solomon cuffed his brother lightly on the back of the head. "Shut up. You aren't the only one this is hard for. He's her friend, too."

Serena felt suddenly much better. She tried to remember, before Solomon, the last time someone had stood up for her. The last time she had allowed someone to.

"Sorry," Elijah grumbled, ducking his head with the same abashed motion as Solomon.

"I know it's not pleasant for either of us," Serena said with an effort. It was worth it when she won a smile from Solomon. "All right. We'll go to the party. And tell the Foreign Office I can get the whole network within the week."

Elijah's brows rose. "A week? Are you sure?"

"It doesn't matter. A week from tomorrow, René will take the marriage lines to court." She tried not to think about her words. Court. She would find no sympathy in any court. And how was she to pay for lawyers? She had saved so little. She had put everything into the Arms. Why had she been so stupid?

"But I'll do my best," she finished. If she could get René's turncoats before then, surely he would leave. The Arms would be of no use to him then.

Elijah nodded. "I have one more condition. I need to search your room and Solomon's for whatever Sacreval has hidden there."

She frowned. "What makes you think he's hidden anything?"

"Solomon tells me he was awfully upset about Solomon getting his room. And that he set a fire there three days ago."

Serena swallowed. "Oh. Of course. How unforgivable of me not to have thought of it."

Elijah looked at her sharply. "Unless you can think of another motive for Sacreval to be furious at being denied his former room? Its peculiar placement, perhaps?"

Serena looked at him in puzzlement. Then she laughed. "Me and René? Never."

Solomon and Elijah, glancing away in opposite directions, both relaxed. Serena frowned. This was going to get complicated. And she'd better put a watch on Solomon's room. René wasn't going to cause a shilling's worth more of damage to the Arms.

Solomon had thought Serena's offer to bring in the entire network in a week was hopelessly grandiose, but when they returned to the Arms, Sophy told them that Lord Pursleigh had already stopped by to place a catering order for his wife's masquerade Sunday night. She also told them that the marquis had gone out for the afternoon. So Solomon and Elijah searched on both sides of the wall between Serena's bedchamber and the Stuart Room.

There weren't any suspiciously hollow panels or any knots that opened a secret passageway when pressed. There were no loose stones in the hearth, and no safe hidden behind the portrait of Charles I. They carefully pried up a couple of floorboards, but there were only old mice droppings and dust underneath. There were no loose bricks in the chimney.

While Solomon was taking a bath after confirming that, Elijah discovered that Diana's hand did twist halfway round in an odd fashion, but it didn't appear to do anything and they were forced to conclude that the hand had simply had to be replaced at some time since its creation. Serena was bringing someone in next week to do the same for the scorched foot.

Elijah ran his hand over the carving. "It's awfully Baroque. I wonder they don't just take it out and put in something modern and nonflammable."

"Charles the First's own clockmaker made it. This *is* the Stuart Room. Have some respect."

Elijah laughed. "You mean whoever pried these out was just a patriotic Roundhead, and not an enterprising chambermaid?" He ran his thumb over the holes where rubies had gone missing.

"Well, I wouldn't go that far," Solomon said.

Elijah slumped against the wall. "There's got to be something here! But where the devil is it?"

"Don't worry, Li. There'll be plenty of time to find it later."

"We don't know that," Elijah said grimly. "Things in Belgium are moving quickly. What if there's evidence in here that one of Bonaparte's generals is ripe for treason? We need to know *now*."

"Any information hidden here is a year old at least."

"I suppose you're right." Elijah sighed. "If I'm their best hope, then things don't look good for British intelligence. I just haven't been thinking clearly."

* * *

She came down the stairs, and even though Solomon had designed the dress himself, seeing her in it took his breath away. Its midnight blue folds took on a silver sheen when they caught the light (he'd worked through the night on that dye), and a wave of silver spangles rose from the hemline and crested halfway up her calves. More spangles edged a modest, square neckline and short unpuffed sleeves.

Serena had taken her hair out of its severe bun and made a complex coil at the crown of her head. She'd allowed a few tresses to escape—she'd even *curled* them, and scattered spangles and tiny blue silk flowers here and there in the blackness. She held long white kid gloves in one hand. Solomon felt suddenly unsure of himself.

"Well?" she said. "Behold your handiwork. Are you satisfied?"

He smiled ruefully. "You look like someone who wouldn't associate with me. I feel as if I ought to kiss your hand."

"Well, if you feel you must, don't let me stop you." She held out her hand.

He couldn't tell if she was joking or not. Slowly, he reached out his own gloved hand to grasp her bare one. She didn't pull away. His eyes closed involuntarily as his lips brushed her naked skin. The insides of his eyelids were awash with visions of kissing her arm, her shoulder, her breasts—

He dropped her hand abruptly and stepped back. "Sorry, I've never been good at doing the pretty."

"I thought you did that rather well."

The little sentence hung in the air between them, and then Solomon, already nervous at the prospect of an evening of hobnobbing with the Upper Ten Thousand—*spying*, he thought, *I'm nervous about* spying—said, "Those little flowers in your hair match splendidly. Where did you find them?"

He cursed inwardly. Of all the things he might have said, *why* did he pick that one? It was like at school, when he hadn't been able to talk about cards or racing or hounds or boxing, hadn't known a thing about any of the usual pursuits of the wealthy, so he'd tried to talk about clothes. It was an acceptable topic of conversation for gentlemen, but when *he* did it, it was because he was the Hatherdasher.

Serena grinned at him, though. "I got a patch of material from my dressmaker and sent one of the maids out shopping."

"You're going to make Uncle Hathaway rich," he said with awed sincerity. It was the nearest he could safely come to *You're beautiful.* He thought it would make her uncomfortable if he said that.

She raised her eyebrows. "I didn't do it for your uncle," she said, pulling on her gloves. "This is a mission." But there was a warm undercurrent in her voice that said she meant exactly the opposite. That she'd done it for him.

"I—I got you something to go with it." Not looking at her, he lifted a thin, wrapped parcel from the inlaid table next to them. "I know you never wear jewelry, but—"

Her face went cold, suddenly. "Jewelry is a bad investment. You can never sell it for what it cost."

He swallowed. This had seemed like such a good idea when he saw it in the window of the pawnshop. Of course jewelry was something men gave their mistresses, but they were going to a ball and she didn't *have* any. And it had cost only four shillings and he'd thought it would be all right. "I didn't mean—it wasn't very expensive. And if you hate it, I can probably take it back, so don't feel you have to, I just thought you might like it—" He tried to cut the string around the package, missed, and almost sliced his thumb open.

"Let me," she said, and he handed her the knife. She sliced the wrapping open and unrolled it with movements so precise they seemed angry. Then she tipped the bracelet into her palm and stared at it. It was made of gray-and-white cameos, ringed with glittering chips of faceted steel and linked together by tiny wrought-iron loops. On each cameo was a woman's face, contorted and howling with fury. Some had coiling snakes instead of hair.

"I'm a siren, not a gorgon, you know." But the warmth was back in her voice. She liked it.

Solomon let out the breath he'd been holding and grinned at her. "You'd like to turn people to stone with a look, though, wouldn't you? Hold out your wrist."

Chapter 14

The first person Serena saw in Mrs. Elbourn's ballroom was Lord Smollett. He took one look at the deep blue gown with its spangles and guffawed. "Must say, you never *used* to need that much fabric to dress as a lady of the evening!"

Serena met Solomon's eyes and sighed. "I can't win, can I?"

"No, so why try? You would look magnificent in scarlet."

Serena hastily turned her attention to the ballroom. Everyone in the room was watching them. The low murmur of conversation rose to an excited hum. At least Mrs. Elbourn looked pleasantly scandalized instead of horrified. This would make her party the talk of London. Perhaps that would be enough to keep them from being tossed out on their ears.

Solomon's shoulders slumped. "Shall we try the buffet table? Maybe there are lobster patties."

Serena felt warm. Was it because of all the eyes on her, or because Solomon had noticed she loved lobster patties when Antoine made them last week for supper? Before she could answer, a young matron in a towering purple-and-gold turban appeared and grabbed Serena's arm. With a small shock, she recognized Jenny Warrington, who had been so vivacious and pretty at school and had always made Serena feel like a colorless stick of a girl.

Serena hadn't thought about her in years and was vaguely surprised to find she still existed.

"Serena! It's been an age! How lovely to see you!"

"Good evening, Jenny," Serena said bemusedly.

Jenny, as vivacious and pretty as ever, was unabashed. "I daresay I should have come visit you at that inn, and I would have, for I was dreadfully curious, but well, you know, my dear Pursleigh wouldn't have liked it."

"Pursleigh?" Serena said, caught off guard. So Jenny was married to one of René's spies. And Serena hadn't known because Lord Pursleigh might be a turncoat, but he still didn't want his precious wife anywhere near the scandalous Lady Serena Ravenshaw.

"Oh yes, I'm Lady Pursleigh now. My husband won't like that I'm talking to you now either of course, and really I was planning to increase my consequence by cutting you dead, but that was before I saw what you were wearing! You never used to be so well-dressed. The way it changes color in the light—tell me who made it and I shall fire my modiste on the spot!" The clusters of blond curls at her temples bobbed with enthusiasm.

Serena gestured to a quietly beaming Solomon to take himself off while she advertised his wares. As Jenny monologued about Pursleigh and her sister Dora and her dear little nephew, Serena turned her bracelet round and round and thought.

It was true what she had said. Jewelry was a bad investment. But she hadn't said the rest, hadn't said how wearing jewelry was surrendering, how a necklace settled down around your throat like the yoke of servitude, so cunningly wrought that you were expected to be grateful for it. Already, just looking at that parcel, her throat had felt constricted.

She couldn't have told him that—she would have choked on the words. Wasn't she supposed to be indifferent to them all? Wasn't she supposed to have shed her pride along with her reputation? Let them think what they wanted, so long as it swelled her bank account, wasn't that her motto? And besides, if she'd said it, Solomon would have put the box away and tried to hide his disappointment and she couldn't, even though she'd been crawlingly aware that men at the ball would see her wearing it and think smugly, *So, the Siren's finally found a fisherman who can tame her!*

Then she'd seen the bracelet. It had cost ten shillings at the most. Not a mark of ownership at all—just a cheap trinket that had made Solomon think of her. And she *liked* it. Even when she'd heard the clasp click into place, like a tiny manacle, she had felt only—secure.

"Serena?" said Jenny impatiently. "Serena, are you listening to a word I'm saying?"

"No, Jenny, I'm not."

For a moment, Jenny's blue eyes narrowed in irritation.. Then she shrugged and smiled. "Well, you always *were* peculiar! I was just saying that I can't thank you enough for bringing Mr. Hathaway to liven up our evening. He's terribly handsome, and Dewington's bound to be mortified. Is it true the other one's been resurrected? And Mrs. Elbourn looks about to burst, though that's probably because of *you*. I shall certainly ask Pursleigh to stop by his shop next time he's in Savile Row. I don't care *what* he says, I *will* have a gown like that." It was like watching a partridge bob along, singing to itself, and knowing it was about to be shot. It felt so strange, to have the upper hand of Jenny. Serena wasn't entirely sure she liked it.

When Jenny finally abandoned her to spread whatever information she thought she had gleaned to the entire ballroom, Solomon was still at the buffet table with a plate of lobster patties in his hand, staring moodily at the dance floor.

"You really ought to look cheerier when news of your talent is about to become a nine days' wonder." She snagged a patty from his plate and popped it into her mouth. "Your matchmaking plans for your uncle and Mrs. Cook are proceeding apace."

He summoned a smile for her. "Thank you."

"I assure you, when we break into Elbourn's library you will repay me in full."

He looked at her hopefully. "Can we go and do that now?"

She laughed. "That eager to leave? Don't you want to ask anyone to dance? You strike me as the dancing sort."

He looked at the dance floor for a moment, wistfully. "Maybe. But I'm not about to place any girl in the embarrassing position of having to refuse me." He put down the plate and looked at his hands. Then, with a motion so angry it startled her, he yanked off his gloves and dropped them on the floor. "I don't know why I bother wearing these when everyone can see right through them."

"No, or when you have such nice hands," Serena said. He blinked at her, and she turned her face away. They'd been not-flirting all evening, but that had been a bit much. It was wrong of her to flirt, anyway, when she didn't know what was between them or what she wanted.

It was wrong and it was stupid, because in the end he might be hurt, but even so he could never have meant anything serious. He was the most respectable person she'd ever met. He was too kind to ask her to be his mistress, and anything else was impossible. She was the one who'd end up feeling ruined all over again, and she knew it. But she couldn't seem to help herself.

"Go on, ask someone," she said, wishing she sounded less sullen. "How about that bored-looking girl with glasses? She's very pretty." *And sweet and innocent, too, I'm sure. Perfect for you.*

Solomon didn't even glance at the girl. Instead, he rolled his eyes at Serena. "Do you honestly think there's one woman in this room who would be anything but aghast at an invitation to dance from an employee of Hathaway's Fine Tailoring?"

Serena could have told him that Jenny Pursleigh thought him terribly handsome. She could have told him that the way his black cutaway and dove-gray breeches fit him was a tailor's dream come true. She could have pointed out the interested looks he was getting from half the young ladies in the room.

"There's me," she said instead, and then hated how she must sound, like some blushing, hopeful debutante angling for an invitation. She had never used to hate every word that came out of her mouth. Before Solomon, she'd been comfortable with herself.

Well, that was a lie. She'd disliked herself for as long as she could remember. She'd just been used to it, before.

He gaped at her, then looked at the ground. "I'm not a very good dancer."

She bit her tongue, hard. "I see."

He looked up hurriedly. "It's not that! It's just—I'm not a very good dancer."

"You, Solomon?" she said with savage incredulity. "Surely you and your wholesome family thrived at country assemblies."

"Elijah danced. I usually played the piano." He shrugged. "You're the one who must have danced the night away."

"I was a wallflower," she said flatly.

He stared at her in shock.

Take that, Jenny Warrington, she thought, but at the same time she was startled that he hadn't guessed at the stubborn, awkward, silent girl she'd been. Sometimes it felt a lifetime away, but other times she didn't feel as if she'd changed that much.

"Well, all right, then," he said. "Let's dance." He took her hand and maneuvered them into a set that was forming.

At first, Serena was absorbed in watching Solomon's enthusiasm and enjoying the glittering swish of her skirts when she turned. He was right, he really wasn't a very good dancer. She smiled.

She was jerked unpleasantly from her thoughts when James Corbin, who had his arm round her waist and was turning her round, allowed his hand to slip too low. A glance told her that nearly every man in the set was leering unpleasantly at her. She couldn't believe she hadn't noticed. What was wrong with her?

Her next neighbor caressed her palm with his thumb, the next whispered filthy recollections of their dalliance in her ear, and so on down the line. She clenched her teeth together, fixed an icy smile on her face, and waited for the dance to be over. She didn't even turn her head to see what oaf was causing the steady progression of *oofs* and *ouches* that followed her down the set.

Lord Braithwaite held on to her arm for several seconds too long and she actually had to wrench away. She turned her back on him—and there was a heavy thud behind her. She turned round again to see Braithwaite sprawled on the floor. He rubbed at his elbow and glared at Solomon, who was standing over him looking very, very apologetic.

"Oh, I *am* sorry, Braithwaite," Solomon said earnestly, but there was a malicious note in his voice. "You know how clumsy I've always been. I hope I haven't mussed your coat, I worked so hard on it. Here, let me help you up." And he held out his hand. Braithwaite examined Solomon's dye-stained, scarred hand for a weighty moment—then curled his lip and got to his feet unaided.

A wash of red clouded Serena's vision. She lunged at Braithwaite, only to find herself cannoning solidly into Solomon's broad chest as he stepped between them.

"*Move*," she hissed, her gaze still fixed on Lord Braithwaite's smirk.

"Stop it," Solomon murmured. "It doesn't matter, I don't mind." Then, when she didn't step back, he added in an urgent undertone, "He's our *customer*, Serena, stop making a scene."

Her vision cleared, leaving her extremely conscious that she was pressed up against Solomon and that his hands were gripping her bare upper arms. She drew in a deep breath and stepped back. What had got into her?

Their entire set had stopped dancing and was staring at them. "This is precisely why people of their ilk should not be allowed in well-bred homes," someone whispered audibly.

Serena drew herself up. "It's getting stuffy in here," she said, with a disdainful, sweeping glance at the gawkers. "Let's find a withdrawing room." She took Solomon's arm and pulled him away.

Solomon followed Serena out of the ballroom into the hall. She looked left and right, then led the way unerringly to Mr. Elbourn's study. He looked a question at her. "A member of my staff bribed a member of his," she explained as the heavy wooden doors closed behind them.

Solomon wondered if he should say anything about the scene in the ballroom. But as nothing occurred to him, and as Serena began immediately to look behind the pictures over the mantel, he sat down in Mr. Elbourn's graceful chair and examined the drawers of his desk.

The first few drawers opened easily enough, but they merely contained stationery, old invitations, spare pen nibs, bottles of colored ink, and the like. The only thing that gave Solomon pause was the pistol in the shallow center drawer. The danger of their situation began to seem real.

The bottom left-hand drawer, which was deeper, was locked. "Serena."

She turned toward him from where she was turning over the cushions of the window seat, and the breath caught in his throat at the blank, bitter look in her quicksilver eyes. He had been almost satisfied earlier with his small revenge on the gentlemen who insulted her, but now he felt he could have disemboweled each and every one.

"Yes?" she asked impatiently. "Have you found something?"

"This drawer is locked." He pushed the chair back to give her room.

She knelt beside him, fishing in the neckline of her dress. He looked away hastily, and when he looked back she held a little roll of black velvet. With a flick of her wrist, the velvet unrolled to reveal a dozen curious steel implements. She laid her gloves on the desk and set to work on the locks. He watched her, watched her arms and hands in the moonlight, the way it silvered and shaded them, the tender back of her neck. He wondered if she knew he was watching.

One week, she had told Elijah. One week before either Sacreval tossed her into the street, or she broke him and his network. If she lost the Arms, where would she go? Would she let Solomon help her, or would sheer stubborn pride and shame and misery send her off to lick her wounds alone? What if she went back to whoring again? It would break her heart—and, he was beginning to suspect, his. Whatever happened, she wouldn't make it easy on either of them. It occurred to him that if they were successful and Sacreval was executed, she might not take that much better. And even if she did—

That thought, somehow, was even harder to face. When all the spying and the intrigue were over, what would be left? What did he want from her, and what would she give him? Could they really be happy together?

A week ago he had had nothing. He had looked forward to nothing. Now he had his brother again, and—and Serena, whatever she was to him. At some point in the last week, without his noticing, she had gone from an ice storm he wanted to breathe in to something as vital and familiar as the air in his lungs. Everything had changed in so short a time. He knew how easily it could change back. He was terribly, unbearably afraid that it would.

With an audible click, the drawer slid forward a fraction of an inch. Serena gave a satisfied smile and grasped the handle. Solomon shoved his thoughts aside and leaned forward.

At that moment there came the clear sound of footsteps in the corridor and the low murmur of well-bred masculine voices.

Solomon froze, but Serena never hesitated. Sweeping the lock picks out of sight under the desk, she straddled him. The rustle of her petticoats as they slid up to reveal a dazzling length of silk stocking was the loudest sound he had ever heard. A hand fell heavily on the doorknob, and she took his face in her hands and kissed him.

It was for the benefit of the men outside, he knew that. And yet it felt more genuine than either of their previous kisses. The first time, he'd kissed her, and she'd merely let him. The second time, she'd been playing some twisted game that made sense only to her.

Now she was kissing him with no pretense at all, as if she'd only been waiting for this excuse. As if she'd seen her chance and taken it. Her bare hands were chilly against his face, her mouth was hot, and both trembled.

He slid one hand up to cup the back of her head, tiny silk flowers and dark hair against his palm, and kissed her back fiercely. After a moment, her hands and lips gentled and steadied. She opened her mouth and pressed against him, unfurling under his touch like a lily blossoming among thorns, bright and unexpected and vulnerable. Her hands slid down to his shoulders and chest. He knew they were going to have to stop soon, but he couldn't remember why.

He ran his hand down over her thigh to where her petticoats pooled and slid it slowly up her leg under her skirts. Serena moaned against his mouth. He felt on the brink of being transmuted into something entirely new.

The door opened.

Chapter 15

It felt as good as Serena had known it would. It felt better. It was wonderful, and Solomon was kissing her back, and she wanted it to be just like this forever. She wanted it so badly. She should pull back now. She should look at Mr. Elbourn. Solomon's hand was warm and heavy on her thigh, and his other hand was tangled in her hair. His chest was rising and falling in great heaves under her palm; she could feel his breath on her skin in the tiny intervals between kisses.

Deep down she'd hoped all along she'd have to do this. It had been at the back of her mind all evening. She'd felt him watching her pick the lock, and she'd wanted his touch on the back of her neck the way a man wanted air when he was being smothered.

She wasn't going to stop until she had to.

She heard Mr. Elbourn's voice from the doorway. "I'll show you my First Folio another time, MacOwen." Footsteps retreated, and as the door closed behind them an undertone was carried back to them—"Get hold of yourself, man! It's nothing we haven't all seen before."

Serena surfaced with a gasp. Solomon's eyes were still closed, his chest still heaving under his purple silk waistcoat. She didn't know if he'd even heard.

It's nothing we haven't all seen before. But it was. True, they'd all seen her legs. They'd seen her naked body, but Solomon saw *her.* And she let him. None of them—not even Harry, her first, whom she'd thought she loved—had ever had the power over her that Solomon did after three kisses.

She climbed off him slowly, not meeting his eyes. Straightening her skirts, she leaned back against the desk, supporting herself with the heels of her hands on the rosewood. "I'm sorry. I shouldn't have done that." Her voice sounded exposed, too, raw and thready.

He blinked, stung. "Why *not?*"

With a swirl of skirts she knelt on the floor, yanking the drawer out onto the floor with a clatter. "Because it was stupid," she said savagely. She was so weak. Smollett and Elbourn and Braithwaite and all those men out there made her feel so awful and ashamed and angry with just their leers and their jibes, and she'd never given a damn about any of them. How would she feel when *Solomon* didn't think her worth a second glance anymore? Just the tiny frown now settling between his brows made the whole world seem wrong.

"Why was it stupid?" he demanded. "Dash it, Serena, are we going to have to do this *every* time we—?"

Every time: he was so sure of her already. Her mouth twisted. "We have work to do." She lifted out stacks of paper. Nothing interesting there that she could see, but the drawer looked shallower than it should. She felt around the edges of the bottom. Out of the corner of her eye she could see Solomon rolling up her lock-picking tools in their strip of black velvet and setting them next to her reticule. Then he waited.

With every movement she made, the gown he'd designed for her caught the light. The silk shifted against her legs. He'd had his hand on her thigh.

She could feel his presence even though she wasn't looking at him. She could feel his frown. She wanted to kiss him again. She wanted to apologize. She wanted to kiss him, then apologize, then kiss him again until he forgave her. She wanted to make him smile.

But she couldn't. She was a coward and she couldn't do anything but slide her fingers around the edges of Elbourn's desk drawer, pressing, pressing—

The bottom popped out of the drawer. "Aha!" She felt

ridiculous the next moment. *Aha?* But it was instantly clear that here were the incriminating documents they were looking for—the top one was in French, and under it was a map showing what looked to be troop movements.

It was working! It would work. She had bought herself and René a few more days. She selected a few sheets from the stack, replaced everything else in the drawer, and relocked it.

She turned her back to put the lock picks and the carefully folded documents into the bodice of her dress. "Solomon—" She paused for a long moment, drawing on her gloves.

He didn't wait for her to figure out what to say. "I'll go first. That way it will look like we're trying to hide our rendezvous. Meet me in the ballroom in ten minutes." And he left her there.

She had only managed to wait seven and a half minutes. She scanned the ballroom carefully. She couldn't see Solomon anywhere. He must be behind one of the great pillars or potted orange trees. She shifted to the right, by the buffet table.

Something caught her eye, peeking from under the tablecloth. The edge of a pair of gloves: Solomon's gloves. She bent down and picked them up. They were kid, butter-soft and expertly made with small mother-of-pearl buttons. They still retained, slightly, the shape of Solomon's hands. He'd taken them off, and his hand had been bare against her thigh. Hurriedly, she stuffed the gloves into her reticule.

Scanning the room again, she spotted him—he was indeed behind one of the pillars. She'd recognize that edge of shoulder anywhere.

As she got closer, she saw that he was in close conversation with Jack Ashton. She'd never much liked Ashton—he was always late paying his tab at the Arms and he'd had a reputation for doing the same at Mme Deveraux's. However, she supposed it stood to reason that Solomon would be happy to converse with a less taxing companion than herself. Succumbing to a base impulse, she kept the pillar between them and listened when she got close.

"Braithwaite's turned into a real ass since university, hasn't he?" said Ashton.

"He was always an ass," Solomon said.

Ashton made a noncommittal noise. "I still can't believe *you* managed to bag the Siren."

Serena couldn't hear Solomon's wince, but she could imagine it. "I wouldn't call it 'bagging,'" he said.

"So how many birthmarks have you seen?"

Had he seen the third in the library? Or had his eyes been closed by the time her skirts were pushed up high enough to reveal it?

There was a pause. Then Solomon asked, with an edge in his voice, "There's more than one?"

"Oho, a setdown! I daresay I deserved that. Naturally you've seen all three. But listen, Hathaway, be careful, will you?"

"What is that supposed to mean?"

"She isn't called the Siren for nothing."

Suddenly Serena couldn't quite catch her breath.

"Well, no, I assumed it was for her startling beauty and considerable personal charm," Solomon said bitterly.

"You've got it bad." Ashton sounded concerned.

Serena bit the inside of her cheek.

"That's not why," Ashton said. "Well, it is, but it's also because she lures men to their doom."

"She lures men to their *doom?* Ash—" Solomon sounded so intensely, incredulously exasperated that Serena's heart clenched with helpless affection. Oh God. She didn't want him to hear this story. It was private.

It was ridiculous to want something to be private when the whole *ton* knew about it—it was ridiculous to want *anything* to be private when she'd lived the life she had. But Solomon didn't know. Not yet. And she didn't want him to. She didn't want to be the Siren to him.

"There was this fellow," Ashton said. "Daubenay. Madly in love with her. He bought her so many extravagant presents he went under the hatches, but she tried to squeeze him for more, so he headed for the gaming dens. And when he had nothing left to give her, she gave him the cold shoulder and found a new protector. He blew his brains out. Left a note. In verse or some such rot. He made the pun on her name and it stuck."

I'm gone where Youth will cease to wither—
Oh, Love is a bloody tyrant;
"Serena," you who sent me thither
Were better named a "Siren."

Serena thought that she was probably the only person in London who still remembered that. Except, perhaps, for Daubenay's mother, who had made a scene in Serena's parlor. Serena could still picture the note, written in Daubenay's careless scrawl. The last thing those aristocratic hands would ever write. She had liked Daubenay, at first.

Solomon laughed. It was so incongruous with her own feelings that it shocked her. "I remember Alex Daubenay. My uncle cut his credit a few days before he died. I gave him the news myself and threatened to send for the constable when he made an unpleasant scene. Am I responsible for his death, too?"

"Of course not." Ashton sounded impatient. "But he *loved* her. He gave up everything for her and she turned him away."

"Ash, he was keeping her! It's a business relationship. I just hope *she* didn't allow him to buy on tick. My uncle was out two hundred pounds on his account, and we couldn't get a penny from the estate."

Serena was bitterly ashamed. She had dragged Solomon to this awful ball where he did not want to go, subjected him to the contempt of these people whom she hated, and been pointlessly nasty merely because she had enjoyed their kiss. Now she was even eavesdropping on him, and still he defended her. Serena had had enough. She rounded the potted plant.

"Mr. Hathaway," she said abruptly.

Solomon eyed her warily. "Lady Serena?"

"I'd like to go home. If—that is, if you—"

His eyebrows flew up, but he gave her his arm.

"Good night, Ash."

"Good night, Hathaway." Ashton shifted uncertainly. "You've been a stranger since we left school. Call on me, won't you? We'll dine together."

Solomon looked surprised. "I—of course," he said.

Serena didn't bother nodding to any of the people who stared at them on their way out.

She waited impatiently in the hall for Solomon and the footman to return with their things. She couldn't wait to be gone. At the sound of footsteps she started. It was Lord Braithwaite. Serena cursed inwardly and looked the other way.

"Lovely gown, Serena," he said with a familiarity that made her skin crawl.

"Thank you, my lord."

He smiled suggestively. "Call me Freddy. You used to when we were children."

"I don't work for you anymore," she said coldly. "I'm not obliged to do as you say."

"No, you're working for Hathaway now, aren't you? You used to aim higher, but then, you're not as young as you were."

"No." She looked him up and down. "I used to aim a lot lower. That coat his uncle made is the handsomest thing about you."

He shook his head. "You really like him, don't you?"

"Bugger your eyes," she said. It was probably foolish, but then, she'd found that backing down could be as unsafe as defiance in a situation like this. And defiance felt so much better.

Braithwaite's face went a shade of puce that clashed with his coat. He took an angry step toward her. Serena didn't give ground. He wouldn't hurt her in the Elbourns' front hall, and by now men of the *ton* generally knew that it was dangerous to push her too far. But inwardly she felt a small spark of fear, a kind that had once been all too familiar.

She'd almost forgotten what it was like. She'd felt safe at her inn these last few years. *René is never getting the Arms,* she resolved anew, feeling for the knife in her reticule.

He took another step forward and spat out, "If you were a gentleman, I'd call you out for that, you little wh—"

He never finished the word, because Solomon, who had returned without her noticing, stepped between them and landed a heavy blow solidly on Lord Braithwaite's chin. "Being a gentleman is looking less appealing all the time." Solomon's husky voice had gone deep and heavy with menace. "*Never* refer to the lady in such terms again, Braithwaite. In fact, don't come anywhere near her. Understand me?"

Lord Braithwaite glowered above the hand covering his rapidly bruising jaw. "Devil take it, Hathaway, you're overreacting," he said somewhat indistinctly, then hissed with pain and rubbed at his jaw. "She's not worth—"

"Don't make me hit you again."

Braithwaite's brows drew together. "That tears it!" He drew his other hand back and started forward.

Solomon pulled off his coat with an avid, angry gesture and dropped it on the floor. Serena couldn't see his face. What the hell was going on? Solomon didn't punch people. He didn't shrug out of his jacket at the least provocation and show off his broad shoulders, the muscles clearly outlined by the linen of his shirt. The linen back of his waistcoat stretched tight as he lifted his arms. Heat flared low in her belly at the knowledge that he was going to hit Braithwaite again.

Fortunately—since Serena seemed incapable of the most basic

common sense this evening—the Elbourns' footman intervened. "I'm dreadfully sorry, Lord Braithwaite. I shall eject these people immediately and have someone bring ice for your jaw." Then he picked up Solomon's coat and their other things from where Solomon had dropped them, took them by the arm, and marched them smartly to the door. Serena threw him a grateful glance, and he winked at her. She wished she had time to tip him. She would have to send someone over tomorrow.

Solomon put on his jacket and overcoat and gave her an uncertain look. "It's rather late. Shall I hail us a hackney?"

"Let's walk. I'd like some air."

"So would I."

They walked in silence. The weather had been warm for early June in London, but even so the night air was chilly. Solomon walked with his hands deep in the pockets of his fashionable carrick, not looking at her.

"You didn't have to do that," she said finally, unable to bear the silence. She had liked silence, once. "I know he's a customer."

He let out an impatient breath. "I was tired of the whole damned evening. It seemed the quickest way to shut his foul mouth."

Her stomach curled guiltily. "You have a punishing right."

Solomon glared at her. "Don't act so surprised. You can't get picked on as much as I did in school and not learn *something* about fighting."

"Did you hurt your hand?"

He pulled his hand out of his pocket to look. "Damn."

"What?"

"I forgot my gloves. They were worth two quid, and I just left them on the floor. I'm an idiot."

"Nothing wrong with a melodramatic gesture now and again." She pulled the gloves out of her reticule.

He stared at them for a moment, and then he beamed at her,

his frustration of a moment ago forgotten. She'd made him smile after all, without meaning to or trying, and her heart turned over. "Thank you," he said. "I—thank you."

His eyes sparkled at her; his coat was askew and it made her want to shove him up against the lamppost and kiss him again. When he reached for the gloves, she found herself turning over his hand and looking at his bloodied knuckles. He ducked his head.

She traced the bruises with a finger. "You engaged me to find things you lost, didn't you?"

"So I did," he said, watching her finger. "I'd better leave the gloves off. I don't want to get blood on them."

She could lean in, now, and kiss him. But she wasn't sure she'd deal with it any better this time, and Solomon *deserved* better. She let go of his hand and turned back toward the Arms. "I didn't know you were friends with Jack Ashton."

"I was friends with Braithwaite, too. I wanted to draw Braithwaite's cork half the time even then, but I never had the guts." Solomon shrugged. "We haven't seen each other much since Cambridge. I think we were friends more because I was lonely and Ash was softhearted than for any other reason. In the end, he was probably a better friend to me than I was to him. I liked him, but—he never paid his tradesmen's bills. There were always at least three duns hanging around his rooms. I hated it. And Lord, did he set my teeth on edge tonight."

She wanted to thank him for defending her to Ashton, but that would mean admitting she'd listened in. "Braithwaite was right," she said instead. It was hard to get the words out, but she knew they were true. "I'm not worth it."

He glanced at her, chewing his lip—apparently thinking about what to say. He was thinking about what she'd said, trying to understand her. Trying to find the right words. The way he listened was as dangerous and tempting as the way he looked at her. "Is that why it's stupid to kiss me?"

Damn him. She drew her cloak tighter around her and didn't answer.

He tried to wait her out, but she was better at silence than he was. After a few streets, he smiled and shrugged—not his annoyed shrug, just the shrug that meant he thought she was enacting a Cheltenham tragedy and he didn't intend to indulge her. It wasn't good, that she was starting to differentiate his shrugs. "I'm afraid our opinions are destined to differ on this point, as on so many others," he said. "I wish I'd thrashed him to a pulp."

She swallowed. *I wish you had, too* seemed like the wrong thing to say. "It would have been hell on your hands."

He laughed. "It was Ash and Braithwaite who brought me to Mme Deveraux's. We should thank them for that, at least."

Her throat felt tight, and she couldn't quite smile back. He could talk about Mme Deveraux's so easily. He was thankful to have met her. He thought she was worth it. She ducked her head and bumped her shoulder against his, and he shoved her back and laughed. London was beautiful at night.

As they came up to the front doors of the Arms, some tipsy young men spilled out into the street stumbling and laughing, and warmth and light spilled out with them. Even at that hour the taproom was bright and noisy and full. Charlotte bustled here and there, two tankards of ale held expertly in each hand. Only a week ago she'd been clumsy and scared to look customers in the eye. Now she belonged here. Serena had created a place where she could be safe, and happy. She felt such a rush of emotion, suddenly. Such a sense that everything was right, that Solomon was beside her and that she was home. She had to hang on to this—she had to.

Chapter 16

When they reached the Arms, it was eleven o'clock, hours before anyone would expect them back. Though he was usually in bed by now, tonight Solomon was wide awake.

Serena had gone to her office to do the day's books, and Elijah wasn't in his room, so Solomon headed to the taproom to wait for his brother. Nursing a mug of ale in the corner and trying to arrange what he would say, he became slightly less enthused about telling Elijah what had happened at the ball.

The whole thing was a little embarrassing, after all. A passionate kiss to cover up illicit spying followed by a fistfight ought to sound dashing and heroic, but Solomon thought it would probably sound a little pathetic instead. If it had been a story about Elijah, it would have sounded dashing and heroic; it would have *been* dashing and heroic, because Elijah would have done it all differently.

"Hullo," someone said. "Mind if I join you?"

He looked up. It was Sophy, her spectacles glinting in the yellow light from the taproom lamps and a cloak draped over her arm. He was a little surprised, but he said, "Please do. Would you like a pint?"

She smiled. "You paying?"

He nodded.

She waved at Charlotte, then slid into the booth across from him. She was wearing the orange dress Serena had worn to St. Andrew of the Cross. It disconcerted him how different it looked on her; even the color looked different against her dark skin. And she wasn't wearing any linen ruffles in the neckline. "How did it go?"

He glanced involuntarily to where Sacreval sat at the bar, surrounded, as he had been since his return, by patrons eager to hear details of life in Bonaparte's Paris.

"Don't look," Sophy said quietly. "He can't hear us from there, but he'll see if you look."

Solomon propped his cheek on his fist and watched her for a moment. "Why don't you ask Serena?"

"Because I want a straight answer," Sophy said promptly.

He snorted. "She's not very good at giving those, is she?"

She sucked her lower lip into her mouth. "No one is. But she's worse than most."

He spread his hands. "I don't understand it! I don't understand what is so dashed hard about admitting that you enjoyed a *kiss*, for heaven's sake. Everybody likes kissing, don't they?"

"I don't." Charlotte banged a small glass of dark liquor down in front of Sophy. Solomon blinked at her. "Well, I don't. Thanks for helping me clean up that cucumber soup last week, by the way."

"You're welcome."

"Thanks, Charlotte," Sophy said, picking up her glass. "It's on his tab." The waitress nodded and headed back to the bar, and Sophy tipped back her head and downed the liquor. "You sure you wouldn't like something stronger?"

"I'm not going to tell you what happened, so there's no need to ply me with liquor," he told her. "I know you're worried about Serena, but—"

Sophy's brows drew together. "I *am* worried about her," she agreed. "I'm also worried about my job and about everyone here. If Serena loses to Sacreval, the two of us are out in the cold sure as breathing. Who knows who else with us? Who knows what he'll do with the place?"

Solomon hadn't thought that far ahead. He hadn't thought about anything but Serena.

She sighed. "For your other question, the one about kissing, I stabbed a man once."

He eyed his tankard doubtfully. He should still be able to follow conversations after half a pint, shouldn't he? "Um. What?"

"It was years ago. He was drunk. I knew him"—she waved her hands vaguely before settling on—"before. He broke into my room here at the Arms. I had a knife. Serena had given it to me because of this man, because he'd been bothering me. I told him to leave. He didn't. He didn't believe a woman would really hurt him. He kept coming at me. He laughed. He saw the knife and he just didn't believe I would use it—"

"But you did."

She nodded. "I did. I stabbed him in the arm."

"That was generous of you."

Sophy snorted. "A black woman can't kill a gentleman and not pay for it. I knew that. But after Serena got up the stairs, he didn't half wish I *had* killed him. That's what I mean. He took one look at her, and he never doubted she'd gut him like a fish. She needs that. She couldn't run this place without it. And even so she has a bar across her door. You don't."

Serena couldn't have been much older than twenty when this happened. She'd already been responsible for all these people's safety.

"It's not something she can just open and shut like the tap in a beer keg. And it don't exactly go with melting into some man's arms and begging him to kiss you."

"Oi, Sophy, you coming?" someone called from the doorway. A group clustered there, talking and laughing and putting on greatcoats and pelisses. Solomon recognized some of them: two of the undercooks, the head laundress, a tapster, a young man who sometimes sat at the reception desk.

Sophy stood up. "If I can be of help, please tell me."

He nodded.

"Thanks for the whisky." She walked off, wrapping her cloak around her and pulling the hood up over her curly dark hair, and she and the others disappeared out the door. Where were they going? The theater? Another taproom? He didn't even know any of their names except for Sophy's.

He'd been so wrapped up in Serena that he'd forgotten to think about the inn beyond her. If she lost the Arms, all these people would lose. He had forgotten that—but Serena hadn't, had she? In her nightmare, she'd seen her staff being turned out into the chilly street. She knew exactly what was at stake. And she'd been carrying that burden alone since she was barely out of the schoolroom. So she'd snapped at him. So what?

Someone rapped the edge of his table with the silver head of a polished ebony cane. Solomon looked up at a dark-haired young man in a rakishly tilted beaver hat and a daring apricot waistcoat that Solomon recognized as his own work.

"Well, *hello*," the man said with a confidential smile. "I wasn't expecting to see *you* here."

Solomon flushed. "Our shop's matching the upholstery. I'm sorry—it's wretched of me, but I can't remember your name. I commend your taste, though." He nodded at the waistcoat and smiled his best customer-pleasing smile.

The man tilted his head and half-smiled back. "That *is* wretched of you. Besides, don't you think you're being a trifle smug?"

Solomon's eyes widened in mortification. "I—"

"Good evening, Sir Nigel," Elijah said from Solomon's elbow. His voice sounded rather peculiar.

Oh, the *spy*. Solomon looked for telltale signs of the moral bankruptcy that would allow a man to betray his country and his friends. He saw nothing but startled embarrassment. "Oh—*oh!*" Sir Nigel said. "I'm dreadfully sorry, I—"

"Allow me to introduce my brother, Mr. Solomon Hathaway."

"Charmed, I'm sure." Sir Nigel held out his gloved hand, attempting to compensate for his earlier familiarity with an exceedingly businesslike air. Then enlightenment struck. "Hathaway! Oh! The *waistcoat*. Oh Christ. Thank you, I'm—I'm very satisfied with it."

Solomon shook his hand and smiled, trying to be nonchalant and not suggest in any way that he knew Sir Nigel was a spy. Or that he was near to beaming at his first misidentification since Elijah's return.

Elijah's smile hit nonchalant dead in the center. "I'm glad you ran into Solomon. I've been wondering when I'd finally get a look at that perfectly balanced Spanish blade you were raving on about."

"Tonight, I hope. You're welcome to come by South Audley Street and try a few passes with it directly after I've dined with mine host."

"Lady Serena?" Elijah asked in surprise.

Sir Nigel laughed. "The Siren? Not likely. No, I mean Sacreval. I daresay he's got all kinds of stories about what's going on in Paris right now. Besides, once he's downed half a bottle of the cellar's finest, I can usually get a few pounds out of him at piquet."

Elijah snickered. "Poor Frog'll never know what hit him." Sir Nigel made his way over to Sacreval. He rapped the legs of the marquis's stool with his cane, and the marquis waved everyone off with a regal gesture and allowed Sir Nigel to invite him to a private table.

Solomon turned back to Elijah. "Well, *he* was rather odd. It's too bad we're to lose him as a customer, though. He looks very dashing in that waistcoat."

Elijah started and glanced over at Sir Nigel. "Do you think so?" He frowned. "I suppose he does. Shove over." Solomon did, and Elijah slid into the booth beside him. He said in a voice pitched low enough that no one else could hear him, "His closest boyhood friend died last year, raiding an enemy camp in Spain. We think he arranged it with Sacreval, leaked information about the raid, because his friend knew too many of his secrets."

"Oh." Sir Nigel did not look capable of it. Daring waistcoat or no, he looked ordinary and harmless. But he wasn't, and Elijah was going off with him. Alone. "How on earth will you manage to search his house without him catching you?"

Elijah gnawed at his lower lip. "I have my ways." He didn't look at Solomon. It was plain he did not mean to talk about it.

Solomon supposed liquor would be involved. "I think he's ordered a coat from us too. I hope it was paid in advance."

"Mmm," Elijah murmured, his eyes still fixed broodingly on Sir Nigel.

"Li, it's very conscientious of you, but Sir Nigel is hardly going to wander off."

Elijah started. "You're right," he said firmly. "Tell me about the Elbourn ball."

Solomon tried to ignore his mounting worry. "Here?"

"It's better than upstairs—less potential for eavesdroppers where I can't see them and more background noise to cover our voices. No one will think the two of us having a private conversation is the least suspicious."

But they hadn't had very many private conversations since Elijah had been back, had they? Oh, they'd talked about the family and Elijah's mission and probably every book they'd read in the last year and a half, but they'd left out everything important. "We got evidence," he said simply.

Elijah really looked at him for the first time, relief all over his face. "Oh, thank God. That buys us another few days at least. If I can pull this off tonight, I wager we'll get the whole week. Where's Lady Serena? Why aren't we celebrating?"

"She's doing the books."

He thought it a perfectly good reason, but Elijah frowned. "We'll celebrate just the two of us, then," he said. "Hey, Charlotte! A pigeon pie and two pints of cider, if you please!"

But Elijah didn't touch the pie when it came. He just drank the cider and watched Sir Nigel and the marquis. He didn't ask for any more details of the evening either, until Solomon reached for the knife to cut the pie. "What happened to your hand?"

"I punched someone," Solomon said.

Elijah frowned. "You *punched* someone? Did you get caught snooping? I thought you said—"

"It had nothing to do with that. Braithwaite called Serena a whore, so I punched him."

Elijah blinked. "Braithwaite? That little snob you were always hanging around with at Cambridge?"

He nodded uncomfortably.

Elijah smiled. "I didn't think you had it in you."

Solomon smothered his quick flash of resentment. "Neither did I," he said truthfully. "It felt magnificent, though."

"Well, good for you. Women like that sort of thing."

Solomon remembered Serena's hot stare as he helped her on with her cloak. "I think she did, actually."

But Elijah was looking at the card players again. Sir Nigel caught his eye and winked. Elijah gave an awkward nod. His earlier nonchalance appeared to have deserted him. He finished the last of his cider and started on Solomon's.

"Have you eaten?" Solomon asked. Damn. He sounded like their mother.

Elijah shrugged.

"If you're so nervous, maybe you oughtn't to go. Maybe— maybe it isn't safe."

"I'm not nervous! Of course it isn't *safe*, or—or pleasant, but"—Elijah drew a deep breath—"but it's my duty and I mean to do it. I managed myself for a year and a half without your advice and I think I can still do so now."

There was silence at the table for the next quarter of an hour. Elijah called defiantly for another pint.

"Li—" Solomon was beginning to remonstrate again, when Serena appeared at his elbow.

"I think I can arrange for some cake if the two of you—oh Lord, what are you fighting about now?"

She'd changed into one of her ordinary gray dresses and her hair was pulled back again. Solomon had a sudden, irrational sense of relief at the sight of her, as if she would be able to fix this, when there was no reason to think so. "Elijah is going to Sir Nigel's, and he's already on his third cider."

"I see," Serena said in a changed voice. She sat down at their table. "Drinking doesn't make things easier, you know. It just makes you less able to pretend."

"What do you know about it?" Elijah snapped.

Serena's eyebrows rose. "I'm the Siren, remember? I imagine I know a damn sight more about it than you." She leaned across the table and covered Elijah's restlessly fidgeting hand with her own. He raised his eyes to hers, and she gave him a rueful smile.

Solomon stared at their linked hands. Serena's words seemed to have some kind of hidden significance. How much experience did she have interrogating people and searching their houses, anyway? Was that even what she meant? Elijah certainly seemed to understand her.

Solomon looked at his brother. He hadn't changed for evening, so he was still wearing tight-fitting corduroy trousers, wrinkled boots, and that old bottle-green coat. They emphasized his more athletic figure and made him look appealingly careless. Solomon suddenly felt prim and overdressed in his evening clothes, and as if he should have tried harder to keep up with rowing after Cambridge.

He had forgotten what it was like to be Elijah's twin; these pangs of jealousy had once been familiar. Elijah was him, only cleverer, more charming, with a better hairstyle. Solomon, when Elijah was there, was always just last year's fashion plate.

Across the room, Sir Nigel and the marquis stood up from their card game, and Serena pulled her hand back. Sir Nigel came back to their table, dangling a couple of notes triumphantly from between his fingers. Five pounds and a tenner. "Can't hold their wine, the French." He turned to Elijah, who was holding his liquor quite well. "Care to take a look at that rapier?"

Elijah smiled. "Delighted." He stood and pulled his worn bottle-green jacket tighter around him. "I'll see you later, Sol, Thorn," he said, and followed Sir Nigel out.

Solomon looked at Serena. She was watching the door Elijah had just walked through. He thought she looked anxious.

"Oh, don't worry about him." Solomon knew he was being petty, but he couldn't seem to stop himself. "He's managed for a year and a half without advice, he'll be fine."

The anxious expression vanished, and Serena was instantly offended on his behalf. "Did he *say* that to you?"

Solomon felt better. "He was nervous, that's all."

Serena looked back at the door, anxious again, and Solomon couldn't shake the feeling that she knew something she wasn't saying.

Solomon tried to wait up for his brother. But at four o'clock he still hadn't heard the familiar step on the stair, and reluctantly went to sleep. When he awoke the next morning, Elijah was back. When Solomon asked what had happened in South Audley Street, Elijah just said, "Do I ask you what you put in your dyes?"

At this rate, a week to catch the spies might have been an overestimate.

Early that afternoon, while Serena was in her office with Solomon looking at fabric samples for the new hangings, Sophy announced Lady Brendan. The third traitor.

Serena had seen her many times over the years, of course, but she'd never really paid attention. Now she examined her carefully. The baroness was a stout, pretty woman, probably still two or three years on the right side of thirty, with a coil of dark brown hair and a splendid bust. Her eyes were of a pure, clear gray—very large, and very fine. She spoke with a faintly foreign intonation. And she looked near to fainting from nerves. "Lady Serena? I would like to speak to you alone, if I may."

Solomon rose hastily, but Serena grabbed his wrist and smiled politely. "Please have a seat, Lady Brendan. You're here for a catering order, aren't you?"

Lady Brendan sat down, her eyes shifting away and back. "I suppose so."

"This is Mr. Solomon Hathaway. He has offered our catering department his services as a baker, and I think you'll be glad of his advice in creating a menu."

"Are you the brother of a Mr. Elijah Hathaway?" she asked.

Solomon nodded, surprised. "Do you know my brother?"

"No—that is, I know *of* him—that is—I was sent here by his colleague Lord Varney at the Foreign Office. To help you—to help you arrest my husband."

Chapter 17

"Your *husband?*" Serena said.

"Yes, I—it appears that he's a traitor. He passes information to Bonaparte."

"But—" Solomon began.

Serena tightened her grip on his wrist. "Are you sure?" she asked calmly.

"Yes." Lady Brendan's voice shook, but she didn't look away. "I am sure. At first I could not believe it—his youngest son is with Wellington—but it is true."

"And what do you want us to do?" Serena thought she spoke perfectly politely, but the woman flinched back shamefully as if she were a servant Serena had slapped. Not that Serena had ever slapped a servant.

"My husband asked me to arrange for you to cater a Venetian breakfast we are giving Monday next," she said softly. "I believe he passes his information through monseigneur du Sacreval, who used to own this inn."

It was such a small point, but Serena couldn't let it pass. "Sacreval *never* owned this inn. He owned half of it."

Lady Brendan blinked. "Ah. Well, the man at the Foreign Office told me to obey my husband, and they would arrest him at the party. Red-handed, he said." She spoke the last few words so quietly Serena had to strain to hear them.

"Lady Brendan, may I point out that it was always you who placed catering orders here? You used to spend quite a long time closeted alone with Sacreval to do it. And"—Serena paused delicately—"you are French."

Lady Brendan's chin went up. "When I came here to confer

with that fraud of a marquis, it was because my husband asked it of me. My husband"—she faltered—"he likes to eat well. He had very specific instructions."

"In other words, he was using you to pass information," Serena said. "Are you sure you weren't in it together? Because I warn you, if you were, he'll turn on you the second he's taken."

"I am no spy," she said with quiet dignity. "I am loyal to my adopted country. My father was the vicomte de Tuyère. His blood and my brother's was spilt on the guillotine. We were driven out of France so that Corsican upstart and his vulgar brothers and sisters could call themselves emperors and princesses and dukes." Her lips trembled suddenly; she looked at her knotted hands. "And Lord Brendan's son—he was so small when his father married me. Not even nine. I used to kiss him good night—I do not wish him to be killed. I will do what I must."

"Very well," Serena said. "You may leave the matter in our hands. Now, what would you like served at your breakfast? As you know, our chef has a number of specialties. I have a printed menu here." She leaned over to get it out of her desk drawer.

"Lord Brendan always loved your *asperges à l'italienne*—" There was a choked noise, and when Serena looked up Lady Brendan's clear gray eyes were filled with tears. "I'm sorry—only—they will cut off his head, and he has been good to me."

Serena said nothing. What was there to say? If—*when* they arrested René, he would not even receive the peer's privilege of a quick beheading.

Luckily, Solomon was there to fill the breach. "How dreadful for you," he murmured, handing Lady Brendan his pocket-handkerchief.

She disappeared behind it for several seconds. "You must think I'm very weak and foolish," she said finally, looking up at him.

Serena did rather, unless it was all a lie and Lady Brendan the traitor after all, but Solomon replied warmly, "Not at all. I think it's very courageous and noble of you to risk everything for England this way."

Serena felt an unpleasant pang. She knew he thought she ought to have turned René in years ago.

"You're being a regular Trojan," he continued. "I am sure your stepson will look out for you, but if you find yourself in any financial difficulty—"

"Oh no, I couldn't," Lady Brendan broke in hurriedly. "I would prefer *anything* to accepting charity. I had enough of that when I was small." Her hands fluttered emphatically in her lap.

Was that a flash of annoyance in Solomon's eyes? No, it couldn't be, because he was reaching out to clasp her hand and smiling. "I wasn't speaking of charity. But I daresay I could find you a position as a seamstress if you wanted, or perhaps Lady Serena could find you a job, couldn't you, Lady Serena?"

Serena felt that she ought to be moved by all this, but she wasn't. The more sympathetic Solomon became, the less she felt anything at all—the colder, in fact, she found herself becoming. "Of course, if I find you have any useful talents."

Solomon glanced at her. *That* was definitely a flash of annoyance.

"Now I'm afraid I must go," Serena continued. "If you're going to cry any more, you'd better do it here where your husband can't see you, and wash your face before you go, too. I'll have some tea brought—"

"Free of charge," Solomon interjected.

"Free of charge, naturally," Serena agreed, "and I'm sure Mr. Hathaway would be delighted to bear you company."

"Thank you," Lady Brendan said with a sort of gracious, wounded misery, "but I don't like to trouble you."

"It's no trouble," Serena said, suddenly perversely determined to be troubled. "But let me show you to a private parlor." She was damned if she would leave a woman alone in her office whom only half an hour earlier she had believed a traitor.

Solomon offered Lady Brendan his arm, and when they had ensconced her in a private parlor, he pressed her hand before taking his leave. "If you need anything, just let us know."

When they were out the door and heading toward the kitchen, Solomon looked at Serena. "I can't believe you were so unfeeling to that young woman."

She had been, of course. "I am simply an unfeeling woman, I suppose. Perhaps that explains why I've never cried on anyone's shoulder or required free tea of utter strangers." She had cried on Solomon's shoulder, though, only a few nights ago in the laundry tunnel. She wished she hadn't.

"Very true," said Solomon. "Neither have you ever risked your all for the safety of English soldiers and the liberty of English citizens."

Serena clenched her jaw and said nothing.

"Not everyone can be such a Spartan as you. I think she's holding up remarkably well under the circumstances."

What circumstances? Being on the brink of seeing a man she cares about brutally executed and not knowing if she'll find herself on the streets? What would I know about that? It's not as if it were easy to be a Spartan, she wanted to yell. But she knew how these things worked. Lady Brendan, with her wet lashes and fluttering hands, would get nothing but sympathy, accolades, and male admiration for her courage. Serena, if the past were any indication of the future, would be termed a cold bitch.

Instead she said something nearly as ill judged. "You're right, of course. And then she is very pretty, isn't she?"

Solomon smiled suddenly. "I thought so," he agreed. "But then, I have an especial fondness for gray eyes."

Serena's mouth curved reluctantly. "Oh you have, have you?" They reached the kitchen before he could reply. "Antoine, can you have someone make up a tea tray, please?" She turned back to Solomon. "You'll take it in to her, won't you?"

"Not likely," he said with a grin. "She's unchaperoned, and

anyway, you're raving if you think I'll listen to more of that 'my father's blood was the bluest in France' drivel."

She looked at him in surprise.

"I say it to *you*," Solomon said, speaking very slowly, as if to a small child who was just learning English. "I don't say it to *her*. She's doing her best. Besides, if we don't calm her down and she breaks down at home, it's all our necks. Figuratively speaking."

And so it was Serena who carried in the tea tray, a small phial of rosewater perched on the edge. Lady Brendan was sitting where Serena had left her, staring out the window with swollen eyes. She started when Serena, both hands full of tray, let the door bang shut. "I brought your tea," Serena said, awkwardly.

"Thank you," Lady Brendan mumbled, and sniffled.

"You're welcome. I brought some rosewater too. Dab it around your eyes. It'll make them less red."

"Thank you." Lady Brendan essayed a weak smile. "I'm surprised you even know that. You don't seem as if you would ever cry."

Serena didn't know whether to be gratified or annoyed. "Concealing tears is only one of the many useful skills one learns in a brothel."

"Oh." Lady Brendan looked mortified.

Serena sat beside her on the sofa. "Did you marry him for love?"

"No. But after twelve years—I am fond of him."

Serena nodded. "It's hard. I'm rather fond of that fraud of a marquis, myself."

Lady Brendan's gray eyes darkened with sympathy. "Oh, were you two—"

"No!" Serena took a deep breath, and continued, "We were friends. Are friends. But he was using me for his own ends." She thought of the parish register, forged years ago against the day when it would be needed. "Always. And your husband used you. Remember that. Who do you think he intended to take the blame for his crimes? Why do you think he sent his foreign wife to pass along coded messages without her knowledge?"

For a moment Serena thought that that insight might be more than Lady Brendan could handle. Her hand flew to her mouth and her eyes widened. But then she straightened, and a martial light came into her face. "He *was* using me, wasn't he?"

"I'm afraid so." Serena sighed. "Here, have a ratafia cake. They were delivered this morning still hot." Both women looked at the airy, golden biscuits without appetite.

Lady Brendan gave her a forced smile. "No, thank you. I should be going."

"If you're sure you won't break down again."

"I'm sure." Standing reluctantly, Lady Brendan took up the rosewater and went to a small mirror that hung from the wall. She began dabbing it around her eyes with a perfectly clean handkerchief she pulled from her own reticule. She hadn't needed Solomon's at all.

"Just remember, lives could depend on how well you hold up when you go home."

Lady Brendan examined her eyes in the mirror. "I will."

"And let me give you a word of advice. If someone offers you charity, take it. Because 'anything' can be pretty dreadful."

Lady Brendan glanced at her and shuddered. Sometimes Serena felt like a walking morality play.

Lady M., for whose heirs Solomon had prepared two batches of black dye, had died the night before. Solomon was summoned to Hathaway's Fine Tailoring to help fill the massive order. The inevitable could be put off no longer, and that afternoon Elijah reluctantly followed Solomon to Savile Row to explain to his uncle why everyone had thought he was dead.

"And what you put your brother through—the poor lad was wasting away—" Uncle Hathaway was still saying twenty minutes later. Elijah and Solomon were flushing uncomfortably, Uncle Hathaway was gesticulating wildly, and a large group of interested seamsters had gathered.

"Uncle," Solomon interrupted firmly, "we don't need to go into all that."

Uncle Hathaway looked at Solomon, and his face softened. "Well, I suppose you look all right now. No thanks to this young scapegrace. Do you need a place to stay, Elijah? Arthur can sleep on the sofa."

"Thank you, but I think I'll be staying at the Ravenshaw Arms with Sol."

Mr. Hathaway frowned. "Thank God you're back, Elijah. Talk some sense into your brother, will you? That girl is bad news."

"Stop it, Uncle," Solomon said sharply. Elijah didn't appear to think Serena was such bad news, anyway.

At that point one of the younger seamsters, whom Arthur claimed wanted to be Solomon when he grew up, said, "That's enough, everyone," and began shepherding people out of the room.

"You created a scandal! You punched a *customer*, Sol! Braithwaite was a large account, and while I may not *like* him—"

"He called her a whore. What was I supposed to do?"

"She *is* a—" Uncle Hathaway stopped at the look on Solomon's face. "Do you know why she left home?" he demanded instead.

"Yes," Solomon said shortly. "She told me herself. May I ask where you got *your* information?"

"Our second seamster at the time had a cousin who worked at Ravenscroft." Hathaway's lips tightened. "He lost his job for her, and she hasn't even the grace to be ashamed of it."

Solomon's brows drew together. "I assume my own job isn't in danger?"

Hathaway looked taken aback. "Of course not."

"Not that it's any of your business, but she bitterly regrets what happened to H—her lover. And if I *ever* hear you've broached the subject with her, I—"

Hathaway waved his hand in a gesture of comprehension.

"Besides," Solomon went on, "*we* should be the last people to criticize a girl for dallying with the servants. After all, my father was Uncle Dewington's tutor."

"Yes, and your father never got another tutoring job, I promise you!" Hathaway said sharply.

Solomon knew that already. He knew that his father had lost his job. He knew that Uncle Hathaway had supported the young couple until his father finished divinity school and a small living was found for him back in Shropshire by a patron of the family—a much more modest living in a much smaller parish than William Hathaway's brilliant academic career had foreshadowed. He knew, too, that Uncle Hathaway did not quite approve of their mother. Uncle Hathaway had always tried to hide it, but over twenty-six years, things slipped out.

In the past, Solomon had always shrugged and ignored it. His mother had explained once that Uncle Hathaway just didn't like the gentry, because he dealt with them so much in his shop. Suddenly, Solomon wasn't sure that was the reason. And if it would make things easier for Serena, he wanted to know what the reason was.

"Father likes being a pastor," he said neutrally. It was true. His father had never seemed anything but content living on three-hundred pounds per annum in their little house—anything but completely happy with his titled wife and his three half-breed children.

"Your father could have done anything, Sol," Uncle Hathaway said wearily. "Everyone said he was brilliant, an orator, destined for great things. The whole family was sure he would make something of himself. I always knew I would be nothing but a tailor, but Will—there was talk of his one day going into

Parliament. And after he eloped with your mother and the Dewingtons wouldn't receive them, it was all over. His fine patrons dropped him like a hot potato."

"But—what does that have to do with Serena?"

"Don't be dense, Sol," Elijah said, an edge in his voice that Solomon didn't understand. "He means you're the family's hope for greatness now."

"Me?"

"You're just like him," Uncle Hathaway said. "Always such a clever boy. Your uncle gave you an education. You could invent great things, be a famous scientist, lecture all over the world to admiring crowds. But you never will if you attach yourself to a scandal like that."

Solomon's jaw dropped. After he got over how unlikely a portrait of himself it was, however, many things were suddenly very clear. He said the most important thing first. "My uncle did give me an education. *You* did, here at Hathaway's Fine Tailoring. You taught me everything. Uncle Dewington just paid for me to learn about chemistry."

Uncle Hathaway pressed his lips together. "You could do so much better."

"There is no better. Not for me. I always wanted to be just like you." He had always thought his uncle was the interesting brother. Uncle Hathaway lived in London and could add a row of figures in his head. He threw Hannah More in the fire.

But now it appeared that Solomon was more like Uncle Hathaway than he had supposed, and it made him rather uncomfortable. However touching it was that his uncle had somehow decided that he, and not Elijah, was the brilliant one, he hoped that in thirty years he would not be making an idiotic speech like this to Elijah's son.

"He did," Elijah confirmed. "He asked for half-spectacles for his seventh birthday."

Uncle Hathaway laughed at that.

"How long have I been working here, anyway?" Solomon asked.

"Sixteen years," Uncle Hathaway said promptly. "Every summer since you were ten, and full time for four years."

"With you fighting him every step of the way," Elijah said.

"Do you want me to leave?" Solomon knew the answer, but even so he held his breath.

"Oh, Sol, I don't know what we'd do without you," Uncle Hathaway said. "But you're throwing yourself away here."

"Don't you *like* being a tailor?" Solomon asked, exasperated.

"Of course I do," Uncle Hathaway said. "But the people who come through that door—they ought to look at *you* with respect."

Solomon laughed at the absurdity of it. "Well, I like it too. And I don't care about the respect of people like our customers. So go easy on Serena, all right? I don't know where things are going with her, but if we do—what's more natural than a tailor and an innkeeper?"

It probably wasn't over, but Uncle Hathaway looked like he'd think about it. Apparently standing your ground really worked. Solomon decided that next week, he'd ask for a few shifts behind the counter.

That night in Serena's office, Elijah told them that Elbourn and Sir Nigel had both been arrested. *Like lambs to the slaughter*, Solomon thought rather triumphantly. But Serena and Elijah both looked so bleak he held his tongue. He had thought they would be pleased at their success—but of course in the end it wouldn't make any difference. Things were moving so fast. The Pursleighs' masquerade was tomorrow, and the Brendan breakfast the morning after, and then there'd be no one between Sacreval and the gallows.

"Did you discover anything useful at Sir Nigel's house?" Serena asked.

"Nothing as useful as what my colleagues discovered when they interviewed the servants. Apparently the information was hidden in the pack of cards Sacreval and Sir Nigel played with. A parlormaid said she'd seen him marking a deck, very carefully and thoroughly. Since Sacreval hasn't been able to hold menu consultations with Brendan and Pursleigh as he used to, he may be using something similar with them."

There was silence for a moment.

"When we've got them all," Elijah said, "that will leave only Sacreval." He looked at Serena. "Are you sure you don't want to talk to any of my superiors about your marriage problem?"

Serena laughed bitterly. "I don't think any of your superiors will be particularly eager to help me."

"The regent is head of the Church of England, you know. I'm sure he has the influence to see the marriage annulled."

"I'm sure he does. I'm also sure he'll think the situation is a very great joke. I would prefer your superiors didn't know the problem even exists until it is absolutely necessary."

"You're hoping it won't become necessary, aren't you?"

"Aren't *you?*" Serena said sharply.

Elijah met Serena's eyes with perfect understanding for an instant, then looked away. "I will do my best to see the enemies of England brought to justice."

Solomon hoped for both their sakes that the marquis showed a little sense and fled the country. Maybe Solomon could suggest it if he proved reluctant. It certainly appeared the only way to make himself useful at present. Serena and Elijah did all the talking and planning, with their underworld experience and their cool demeanors and their dratted unspoken bond.

"Oh, and Elijah?" Serena said.

"Yes?"

"Do you have the schedule of payments René gave his contacts? I want to confirm that Brendan's our man and this isn't some ruse by his wife."

"I think Varney at the Foreign Office might have that, but how will you get hold of Brendan's financial information?"

Serena smiled enigmatically. "Leave that to me." She could be so theatrical sometimes. Solomon hid a grin.

A knock came at the door. "Yes?" Serena called.

"It is I, *sirène*."

The three looked at each other in momentary confusion. "Come," Serena called.

Sacreval entered but stopped short at the sight of the three of them sitting there.

"We were just discussing the final bill for Serena's order from Hathaway's Fine Tailoring," Solomon explained, "but if you need to speak to her, we can leave."

The marquis relaxed. "No, no, don't get up on my account. My request is this. *Sirène*, I am becoming extremely *ennuyé* merely lounging about waiting for you to make up your mind. I would like to make myself useful. Perhaps I might help you with the catering again."

Solomon tried to look uninterested.

Serena frowned. "You aren't part of this business anymore, René. I daresay you can wait another week to return to the delights of catering."

"Really, *sirène*, I would consider it a personal favor."

She stared at him. "Your gall is beyond anything, do you know that?" The marquis opened his mouth to respond, but she sighed and waved a hand wearily. "I suppose if you wish to work for free, I will hardly stop you. I just got a new order from Lady Brendan. I'll give you the details first thing tomorrow morning."

The marquis smiled in relief. "Thank you, *sirène*. I will be here to receive them."

When he was gone, the three conspirators looked at one another in silence.

"Like a lamb to the slaughter," Solomon said at last, and the other two flinched.

* * *

"Lady Serena and Uncle Hathaway," Elijah said over supper that evening. "I would have liked to see that. Who won?"

"It was a draw," Solomon said. "But he almost made her cry. He as good as said she was amusing herself among the lower orders and that I'd probably off myself when she jilted me."

"Cry? Lady Serena?"

"Well, it wasn't her best day."

"And—*off* yourself?" Elijah shook his head. "He didn't really say that, did he? It's insulting. You're not a damsel in a ballad."

Oh, hell, Solomon thought. He shrugged. "Who knows where the old man gets his ideas?" But he'd never been able to lie to Elijah.

There was a long silence. "Oh God," Elijah said in a changed voice. "You—you didn't—"

"No," Solomon said firmly. "I didn't. I don't think I would have. I thought about it desultorily, is all. Don't—don't mention it to anyone, all right? I'm not actually sure Uncle Hathaway knew—I may have extrapolated a trifle."

"I should never have taken this damn job," Elijah said bitterly. "They told me it was my patriotic duty, and I was so bloody proud of my French, and—"

To Solomon's complete astonishment, he began to cry—not all-out sobbing, but a sort of sniffling trickle that was somehow worse. "Oh God, Sol," he said again, messily. "I'm sorry, this is embarrassing, but—if you had—because of *me*—"

Solomon gave him a handkerchief and a crooked smile. "Now you begin to faintly imagine how *I* felt, sapskull."

Elijah blew his nose loudly. "And now—with René—I feel like such a Judas—"

Solomon sighed. "Serena does, too. Sometimes when she thinks no one's looking I catch her watching him with this unreadable expression—"

Elijah half-laughed, half-snorted. "Does she have any other kind?"

Chapter 18

They arrived two hours before the masquerade to take over the Pursleigh kitchens. There was to be a buffet table in the ballroom and a very light, very elegant supper served at half-past midnight. That was Lord Pursleigh's plan, at any rate. Presumably, news of his arrest would persuade Lady Pursleigh to call off the proceedings. Solomon felt sorry for the diminutive blonde. She had gone on with her party in defiance of the rumors flying about London that Wellington was defeated and that the French army was already looting Brussels. An expectant pall hung over the entire city, but Jenny Pursleigh had filled her townhouse with a blaze of light and celebration.

The viscountess was young—he had gathered at the Elbourn ball that she had been at school with Serena—and very flirtatious and very charming in her costume: winged Victory. A laurel wreath nestled in her curls and tiny wings of gold foil sprouted from her shoulders. Her yellow gown had barely any sleeves and fastened at the shoulders with vaguely Roman clasps. Gold sandals peeped from beneath the hem.

He wondered what Lord Pursleigh thought of his wife's patriotism. To drive the message home, she had amassed a small pile of papier-mâché broken Napoleonic eagles and a ripped and stained tricolor to stand in front of to receive her guests. It was all rather ridiculous and bound to be embarrassing when her husband was arrested for treason.

A sporting gentleman in his middle thirties, Lord Pursleigh was planning to dress as Richelieu in a combination of armor and red robes. Unfortunately, the possibilities for hiding a deck of cards in such an ensemble were nearly infinite, which boded ill for their plan to arrest Pursleigh quickly and quietly before the masquerade even started, so that the marquis wouldn't be sure enough of the connection to change his methods before Brendan could be taken the following morning.

But young Ravi Bhattacharya, whom Serena had hired the day after Elijah's return, proved to have nearly as many useful acquaintances as Serena. His particular friend Harry Spratt worked for the Pursleighs, and for the sum of five pounds had somehow contrived not only to sprain the ankle of Lord Pursleigh's trusted valet, but also to be appointed to dress Pursleigh in his place.

As soon as young Mr. Spratt identified the location of the infamous pack of cards, he was to alert Ravi, who would come straight to Elijah, who would ask Lord Pursleigh to step into the kitchens to confer about a problem. And when Lord Pursleigh stepped into the kitchen, he would be quietly arrested where only Serena's people could see it. She had assigned to the masquerade the staff she was most sure of, either as patriots or as personally loyal to her, and told a few of them what to expect.

That, at any rate, was the plan. In the meantime Solomon and Elijah, along with a few kitchen maids and kitchen boys and an undercook, were working in the kitchen under Sacreval's direction. Like Sacreval and the rest of the staff, the Hathaways were wearing the livery of the Arms—unrelieved white and black except for a pocket handkerchief lavishly embroidered with the Ravenshaw coat of arms in scarlet, black, and gold. Solomon thought he recognized the work as Serena's.

They had already heated wine for the syllabub, set pheasants to roasting, and put two small hams in the oven to warm. Ravi was bound to appear at any moment and the marquis showed no signs of going upstairs. Elijah was beginning to fidget, but at last Sacreval seized a carton full of fruit and flowers. "I am going *en haut* to make sure the buffet table is presentable. Jack, Emma, take those tubs and follow me." The pair hastened to obey, and Solomon heard Elijah breathe a sigh of relief.

But a quarter of an hour later, there was still no Ravi. Half an hour more passed. The first guests trickled in, and he had still not arrived. At five to nine he burst in, ran up to Elijah, and said urgently, "May I speak to you, sir?"

"Of course," Elijah said, leaving Solomon to finish the syllabub.

Elijah had not returned when Sacreval came in and said, "Is the syllabub ready?"

"Yes, monseigneur."

"*Merveilleux*. Where is that brother of yours? I need the pair of you to flank the buffet table. Twins at a masquerade, it is too perfect. We must show you off, *non?*"

"He stepped out. He'll be back any moment."

Just then, Elijah walked in, biting his lip.

"You," the marquis said imperiously. "Put on your mask, help your brother with that punch bowl there, and follow me."

"Yes, monseigneur," Elijah said ironically, and a dull flush crept across the marquis's face.

Carrying an enormous punch bowl up a flight of stairs was even harder than Solomon had expected. He was glad the punch itself was carried separately, by professionals.

At quarter past nine the marquis was still at the buffet table, so Solomon could not ask Elijah what had happened. Then Lord Pursleigh appeared.

"Fancy a game of piquet, old fellow?" he asked Sacreval jovially. "I heard an anecdote just the other day that I think you'll find hilarious." He winked.

Something had gone very wrong.

Solomon glanced at Elijah, who did not seem surprised, only intent on listening without appearing to. The marquis nodded, looking disgusted by his confederate's lack of subtlety, but before he could follow Pursleigh to one of the little tables set up along the side of the room, his arm was seized by the viscount's dainty wife.

"You can have him in a little while, Pursleigh," she said with a faint pout. "But first he must play with me. Last time he was here he trounced me thoroughly, and I want to show him I've grown up a bit since then."

"I hope not *too* much," Sacreval said. "You made *such* a charming girl."

Solomon gagged inwardly. Lady Pursleigh dimpled, and her husband frowned. "Jenny, wouldn't you rather dance with some of these besotted fellows?" He gestured at the cluster of costumed young men his wife had abandoned. "I let you muck up my house with laurel wreaths and broken scepters in honor of our *victory* over Napoleon,"—he said "victory" with an unpleasant sneer—"now you let me enjoy a game of piquet."

"Your husband asked me first," Sacreval told her. "But after our game, I am yours to command until I am needed for the laying out of the supper."

Lady Pursleigh's pout deepened. Her pretty blue eyes fixed appealingly on her husband. "Pursleigh, I only want him for half an hour and then you can talk boring old politics as much as you like. *I* want to hear what they're wearing in Paris!"

"If you insist," Lord Pursleigh said with ill grace.

The marquis gave him an apologetic shrug. "Half an hour, then," he said, and turned to kiss Lady Pursleigh's hand.

She slipped him a little pink note in a manner she evidently thought inconspicuous.

The marquis palmed it with a deal more grace, but his gaze shot apprehensively to Lord Pursleigh. The viscount, to Solomon's surprise, smiled maliciously. "All grown up, ain't she?"

When the pair was ensconced at a table at the far end of the room (playing with a fresh deck brought by a servant who carried a great stack of them), to all appearances flirting outrageously, Solomon made his way around the buffet table to Elijah. "Did you see that? She passed him a love note not two feet from her own husband! I thought I'd sink from embarrassment and I wasn't even involved."

Elijah was watching them with narrowed eyes. "I did see it. I can't help wondering if we've made the same mistake here we made with Brendan, only the other way round."

Solomon blinked. "Surely if she were passing state secrets, she wouldn't do it right under our noses."

"She doesn't know we're watching," Elijah pointed out. "And if she does, she may expect us to think exactly that. Dalliance is a splendid cover. If she's really bedding him, so much the better."

If Elijah was right, Solomon could only imagine what schoolgirl feuds must have been like at Serena's school, with Serena on one side and Jenny Pursleigh on the other. He sighed. "What did Ravi have to say?"

"Lord Pursleigh put nothing on his person but a small snuffbox, which Spratt vowed contained only snuff."

"So what do we do next?"

"Ravi is trailing Pursleigh to see if he picks anything up. Lady Serena said she'd be watching Sacreval. All we can do is wait." Elijah watched Sacreval and the viscountess. "I'm going to have to lift that note."

He tugged at his livery coat with suppressed irritation. "Where the devil is Lady Serena?"

Was that what was causing Elijah's fidgets? He was watching for Serena? "I haven't seen her," Solomon said shortly. He'd been looking. Whatever disguise she was affecting must be more effective than he'd thought possible. That was good, because she had no plausible reason to be here besides the real one of helping them keep watch on Sacreval. If the Frenchman spotted her, he'd know at once something was up.

"Oh, Lord," Elijah muttered. "Ravi is taking drinks to someone on the balcony. What does he think he's about?"

Solomon sighed. "Would you like me to go and follow Pursleigh myself?"

Elijah shook his head. "No, Sacreval would notice. Just go and fetch Ravi back, would you?"

Solomon made his way around the edge of the room to where French doors let in the summer evening. As he reached the doorway, he heard a drawling, well-bred voice say with some amusement, "Does the Siren *know* what sort of adder she's nursing in her bosom, Ravi? I swear, that inn gets more scandalous every year." Solomon peered out and saw that the voice belonged to a middle-aged Apollo whose toga looked more Roman than Greek.

Ravi raised his chin defiantly. "No, my lord, of course she does not."

But the boy took a step back when the Apollo said, "Bring me another glass of champagne, Ravi. Bring one for yourself, too."

"I can't. I am working, my lord."

Solomon had no idea what was going on, but it was clear in every line of Ravi's body that the boy was scared. Only Serena could turn half the work of innkeeping into preventing people from bullying her staff. Solomon obviously had to do something, but intimidating lords was exactly what he had always been worst at. He tried to think what Serena would do in this situation.

"I used to find you worked better after a glass or two," Apollo said slyly.

The look on Ravi's face galvanized Solomon into action. He stepped out onto the balcony so that his shoes rang on the stone. "Oh, there you are, Ravi. You're needed inside."

"I am very sorry, sir," Ravi said nervously. "I was only—his lordship asked me to—"

Solomon made a harried gesture and smiled at him. "You're not in any trouble, Ravi. Just get back inside. I'll help this gentleman."

"Yes, sir," Ravi gasped with a last pleading look at Apollo, and fled.

The Apollo turned to Solomon with a smile. "Thank you, I'd like another glass of champagne."

Solomon looked down his nose. It would have been more

effective with half-glasses instead of a half mask, but some things couldn't be helped. "You may get it yourself, my lord," he said pityingly. "And don't threaten a member of our staff again. Lady Serena frowns on it."

The gentleman chuckled incredulously. "My dear boy, I wasn't *threatening* anybody."

"Perhaps you don't care that Lady Serena frowns on it," Solomon suggested in a mild tone. "But I rather think you care to keep both your ears. Not to mention both of certain other appendages."

Apollo smiled uneasily, as if he wasn't sure whether that was a jest and hoped that if he pretended it was, Solomon would go along with it.

Solomon's borrowed livery jacket was a little too tight across the shoulders. When experimenting before the ball to see whether he could alter it successfully to fit (he couldn't, since there wasn't enough extra fabric on the inside seam), he'd discovered that it pulled uncomfortably taut when he brought his hands up to adjust his gloves. He did so now. "Do you understand me?"

Apollo eyed Solomon's broad shoulders nervously and did not respond.

"I believe I asked you a question."

He looked away. "Fine! Yes! I understand you!"

Solomon gave him an encouraging smile. "Good. Don't ever speak to that boy again." He turned and walked slowly inside. Once out of Apollo's line of sight, he leaned against the wall and tried to catch his breath. A little bubble of hilarity was lodged in the back of his throat.

I intimidated a lord, he thought incredulously. *I intimidated a lord! Soon I'll be a full-fledged member of the London underworld.* Now *that* called for cartwheels.

He looked up, and his victorious gaze fell on Lord Smollett, laying siege to an angel not a few feet distant. Her blond hair was piled high on her head and surmounted by a wire halo. Tiny, feathered wings sprouted from the back of her white muslin gown. Her entire face, with the exception of her eyes, was covered with a golden mask. Lord Smollett rumbled something, and the angel laughed, a husky, musical laugh that, although he had never heard it before, sent shivers down Solomon's spine.

Solomon knew at once that it must be her. Usually, of course, her severity was feigned, and her laughter was real. But only one woman had ever been able to make Solomon feel like this with just a laugh.

He looked closer, and sure enough, the angel had gray eyes. He grinned evilly and went off to fetch a champagne tray.

Chapter 19

When someone—say, Lord Smollett—was taking a full glass of champagne off a tray, Solomon discovered that it only took a very small jostle to make him spill it all down his front.

"I say, Smollett, I'm dashed sorry—haven't quite got the knack of these trays." Solomon dabbed at the spreading stain with the napkin he carried over one arm.

"Give me that!" Smollett snatched the napkin and tried to contain the champagne that now graced his waistcoat and breeches. He squinted at Solomon. "Why, if it isn't the Hatherdasher! No job too menial, eh? But I suppose when the Siren commands—"

Solomon winked conspiratorially. "Don't let's talk about Lady Serena just now," he said in a low voice perfectly calculated to reach Serena's ears. "Who is *this* diamond?"

She stiffened.

"Haven't the foggiest. An angel, isn't she?" Smollett said, and guffawed at his own wit. To Serena he said, "Sorry, m'dear, you'll have to excuse me for a moment. Have this fellow fetch you something, if you like." He squelched off toward the gentlemen's withdrawing room.

"Would you like a glass of champagne, madam?" Solomon asked.

"I would," she said in sultry tones. The effect was spoiled a little since her words were muffled by her mask, but Solomon's pulse sped up anyway. "But not on the front of my gown."

He smiled lazily at her. "I only spill champagne on gentlemen speaking to ladies I particularly wish to meet."

A Lily Among Thorns

She brought her feathered fan up in front of her face. "Naughty boy," she scolded huskily.

"Oh, I'm not a boy."

"I'm immortal, you all look like boys to me."

He stepped closer. "You're not an angel either."

"Don't you find my costume convincing?"

"Perhaps I would find it more convincing"—he took another step—"at closer quarters."

She rapped his knuckles with her fan—but very lightly, no doubt out of concern for the tray of champagne. "I ought to report you to your mistress."

Solomon couldn't keep a straight face anymore. "Please don't. She's a regular harpy."

Serena gave a little satisfied sigh and gestured to the champagne tray. Solomon held out a glass. She made no move to take it. "Thank you," she murmured, and he was about to nod, but she continued meaningfully, "for—" and tilted her head slightly to point toward the balcony. She trailed her feathered fan up his wrist. He shivered violently, sloshing the champagne, but thankfully it did not spill. "You were splendid."

Now she reached to take the glass, but he didn't quite release it, brushing their fingers together and stepping closer to whisper in her ear, "I'm sure you're dying to give me a frank critique of my methods."

She hummed low in her throat and tilted her head so that his lips almost brushed the magnolia line of her throat. "Cynical child! You were perfect."

He was bored suddenly. Bored and dying with impatience to hear Serena's real opinion, expressed in her ordinary voice. He wanted to see her face, see her birthmark creep upward and her lips curve sarcastically. He wanted to hear her laugh, her real laughter and not this husky kittenish purr. He could not quite credit that any man would prefer this. How could you be comfortable with a woman who told you only what you wanted to hear?

Well, she would tell him what she really thought later. He kissed her neck lightly—because who could resist?—let go of the glass, and stepped back. "I should get back to my duties. As for *that*—I assume you do know what kind of viper you're nursing in your bosom?"

"I always do."

He felt her quicksilver eyes on his back as he walked toward the buffet table, passing the marquis and Jenny Pursleigh on his way.

From the gestures Sacreval was making, he appeared to have just finished describing the latest Parisian sleeve as Solomon drew within hearing range. "—would look lovely in Paris styles. In France, you know, the women wear only one petticoat."

"*Really?*" She smiled mischievously. "I think Pursleigh would like that. It would be so much cheaper, and he is always complaining about how much I cost. His tenants are not at all industrious."

The marquis looked rather sardonic. If this was all a cover, it really was a good one. Solomon's money was still on the viscount.

Lady Pursleigh looked at her cards. "I think it is my trick again, René!"

The marquis sighed and passed over a sovereign. "At this rate you will have enough for a dozen petticoats, my dear. And that *would* be a shame."

She giggled. There was silence, and then Lady Pursleigh reached out and put a hand on Sacreval's arm. "You—you *do* think it's all a sham about Boney putting our troops to flight? You do think Wellington will thrash him, don't you?"

Sacreval covered her hand with his own, and she looked thrilled. "Of course, my dear. You must be brave."

After that, the evening dragged. Solomon and Elijah flanked

the buffet table, too far apart to carry on a conversation. Elijah watched Sacreval and Lady Pursleigh like a hawk, as if he suspected that at any moment Sacreval might bolt, or perhaps begin communicating with one or the other of the Pursleighs using secret hand gestures, Solomon wasn't sure.

Serena seemed to be having a good time, or else she feigned it beautifully. She didn't dance much. Solomon wondered if she had ever learned any of the newer dances. But she flirted madly with one enchanted gentleman after another, fluttering her fan and dipping her blond head and, if Solomon could judge from across the room, laughing that soft, husky little laugh. She sent them to fetch her things from the buffet table every so often— lobster patties and strawberries, mostly. It made him jealous as hell, but—it was nice, too. As herself, she would have been the subject of leers and snubs and speculations. As an anonymous angel, she could have fun—so long as she refrained from being herself. He wondered how she felt about that. Was she grateful for the reprieve, or did she feel stifled by it?

"Can you keep your eyes off her for five seconds?" Elijah hissed, under cover of restacking some rolls that had fallen out of their basket. "If Sacreval notices, he'll know it's her and we'll be rumbled."

"Well, maybe you should stop staring at Sacreval, then!" Solomon hissed back, stung. "He's bound to notice, and what reason can he possibly imagine?"

Elijah flushed a deep red and went back to his side of the table, leaving Solomon pleased that he had had the last word for once. Really, he hoped Elijah's surveillance was usually subtler than this, or his career as a spy would not be long.

It was nearly eleven before Pursleigh and Sacreval sat down to play. This deck, too, was brought by a servant.

"Damn," Elijah said. "Does he have a servant in his pay, too?"

Solomon looked at him. "They're *his* servants, Li. They're already in his pay."

Elijah was opening his mouth to retort when they saw it. They saw Pursleigh pull two sheets of paper from his pocket and rip them both in four pieces. They saw him have a pen brought to the table. They saw him write something on the first piece and pass it over to the marquis, who looked at it carefully under the candle and smiled. "*Where did he get that paper?*" Elijah hissed furiously.

Solomon couldn't believe it either. "He must have got it when Ravi was out on the balcony."

"This is a nightmare. Anything could be written on those papers in invisible ink. He could be writing anything on them right now and no one would think it was anything more than an IOU."

"Well, Sacreval is putting it in his pocket. We'll just have to steal it from him somehow, along with the little pink note."

Elijah blew his hair out of his eyes with a defeated sound. "We will, won't we?"

Elijah took off his coat and cravat. He left his waistcoat on, though, and tousled his hair just so. They had to have Lord Pursleigh's vowels and Lady Pursleigh's billet-doux. They had to get them now, before René destroyed them.

He had known that sooner or later it would come to this. Sooner or later he would have to walk into René's room and use what they had shared to move René one step closer to the gallows, simply because it was the worst thing that could happen and so it would. Now that it had, he couldn't tell whether the knot in the pit of his stomach was nausea or excitement.

He walked down the hall and knocked on René's door. René looked distinctly surprised to see him, but he opened the door wide.

The first thing Elijah saw when he stepped inside was the precious evidence, burning merrily on a silver salver.

"What's that?" he asked, even though he already knew. Lady

Pursleigh's stationery burned with a sickly sweet rose scent. The room smelled like dying summer.

René smiled maliciously. "Love letters."

Elijah's entire reason for being there was already gone, but he realized too late that it must not have been his entire reason after all. Instead of leaving, he said, "Your mistress isn't very subtle. People in France probably saw her pass you that note."

"She does have more hair than wit," René acknowledged. "But it is such delightful hair I am inclined to overlook the fault. One of those soft golden ringlets would make such a lovely keepsake, do you not think?"

Elijah said nothing.

René curled a lock of Elijah's own yellow hair around his finger. Elijah flinched away, and René sighed. "You cannot have it both ways, *chéri*. Why will you not admit that you love me? That we are meant to be together?"

"I don't love you!" Elijah strove to modulate his voice. "And we certainly aren't meant to be together. After all, you're a married man now, aren't you?"

René was the reason Lady Serena had been going around looking like death. Because of René, Elijah's brother might never be able to marry the woman he so obviously loved. Lady Serena was René's best friend, and he had done this to her.

Elijah wished he could hate René for it, but he understood. Elijah had betrayed people he loved in the service of his country, too. He could have driven his brother to suicide. He still meant to drive René to his death.

René's eyes darkened. For a long moment he was silent. "I am sorry that I am not the man you thought I was." He sounded genuinely regretful, but then he would have had training for that. "I would have liked to be such a man. But you are not the man I thought you were either."

It echoed Elijah's thoughts so closely that for a moment, he panicked. *Does he know?*

But René simply smiled and murmured, "Elijah." It was the first time he had used his real name. Elijah liked the way it sounded on his lips. "My little *anglais*. I would have sworn you were from the *quartier Saint-Michel*."

"I am not *your* anything."

"That is not what you told me when you first arrived. You told me you could not sleep without me, do you not remember?"

Elijah's fingers curled into a fist. "You must have misunderstood my English."

"So now it is my accent?" René said sharply. "I am sorry I am not such a linguist as you. *Mon Dieu*, I had forgotten how childish you could be."

"I suppose I might seem so to a man who'll never see forty again."

"I do not remember you telling me I was old when you were begging me to make love to you for the fourth time in one night."

Elijah's mouth curved ruefully. "Actually, I did. That was what convinced you." Their gazes caught, and suddenly Elijah could barely breathe. Very, very slowly, René reached out and pulled Elijah to him.

Serena crept up the servants' stair, her cloak wrapped around her to hide her wig and dress, and the wings and mask bundled under her left arm. René mustn't see her. She peered out into the hallway. The coast was clear. She moved softly to her door, unlocked it, and slipped inside. Dumping the mask, wings, and cloak on the bed, she knocked on Solomon's door to find out what had gone wrong with the plan. When were they supposed to get another opportunity this good to catch Pursleigh? Who knew when he would meet with René again?

"Come," Solomon called. She pushed the door open. He was in stocking feet and shirtsleeves, bent over something at his worktable. The lamp burned beside him. The Y of his braces defined his broad back and shoulders. His Arms livery had been made for someone slightly smaller, so the black breeches clung to his backside in an extremely impressive manner.

"What went wrong at the masquerade?"

He stood up and turned toward her. Serena sighed. "We don't know," he said. "Elijah thinks maybe we were wrong again, and Lady Pursleigh is the traitor. She passed Sacreval a note."

Serena blinked. Henwitted Jenny Warrington, a spy? "I'll check her banking records, too," she said. "But I can't imagine we'll find anything. More likely she has a *tendre* for René."

"Well, in that case Pursleigh decided to use IOUs, or maybe the paper they were written on, to communicate with Sacreval instead of cards. Either Spratt missed him hiding the paper in his costume, or he went and got them sometime in the five minutes we weren't watching him." He shook his head. "As if trying to blackmail poor Ravi weren't bad enough, that blackguard Apollo may be responsible for the escape of a traitor."

Serena's heart swelled when she remembered Solomon facing down Lord Teasdale with perfect politeness. She'd seen him hesitate just inside the French doors and thought she'd have to intervene herself; it might have proven difficult to do so unobtrusively. But she should have known Solomon wouldn't stand by and allow someone else to be bullied. "Do you really think I cut off their ears?" she asked.

Solomon smiled wickedly. "Don't you?"

She looked down her nose, as well as she could at someone half a head taller than her. "Of course not. I prefer not to leave a mark."

"So do you have any pointers for me?"

Serena frowned, thinking. "It wasn't my style at all, but very effective in its own right. I felt as if I were being scolded by my governess."

Solomon rolled his eyes. "Thanks."

"I lived in fear of my governess!" she protested. "I assure you, her memory invokes an almost primeval terror."

"My grandfather was a schoolmaster," Solomon admitted. "And then, of course, my father was a tutor for a while."

"Well, I'm grateful none of your family has ever shown any interest in a life of crime. The juxtaposition of your calm, almost professorial air with the brutal subject matter and the unspoken physical menace was really quite chilling."

"Take off the wig," he commanded suddenly.

She blinked. "I'm going to take it all off in a minute, but—"

"Please," he said a little desperately, "just take it off."

She did so, conscious that her hair must be flattened and disheveled underneath. He watched her with the quiet, perfect focus he could slip into so easily, as if he were content to observe indefinitely. She'd seen him give it to crucibles and organs and dress seams, but rarely to people. He gave it to her, though, sometimes. What did he see? She combed her hair ineffectually with her fingers. "I needed a costume no one would expect me to wear."

"You really did look like an angel."

"But if you had to choose a winged creature to represent me, it would be a harpy: yes, I know."

His eyes darkened. "Sometimes around you I have trouble remembering the difference."

She frowned in surprise, and then he was kissing her fiercely, his tongue in her mouth and his hands tangled in her hair.

Chapter 20

"I don't ever want you to be anything but what you are," he said raggedly. He kissed her jaw, her pulse, the curve of her neck; she tilted her head to let him, to silently beg for more. "You can be hateful sometimes, but you're *honest*."

"Is this about my rouge?" she inquired, concentrating so as not to sound breathless, and he laughed, his mouth opening against her collarbone.

"This evening, when I saw you—all I wanted—in the world—was for you to stand up straight—and say something"—his hands were on her waist, holding her steady as his mouth inched back up her neck to suck at a sensitive spot just above her racing pulse—"sardonic—and raise an eyebrow—"

"If I realized it would have this effect, I'd have stopped raising them days ago."

He pulled back for a moment to look at her. "That would have been a damned shame." He kissed her birthmark.

She shivered.

"Turn around," he said, and she did. He undid the buttons on the white gown—she knew he would never have tried to tear the cloth, but she could feel his impatience in every tiny, abrupt *pop*—tugging the sleeves down as he went and hungrily kissing her shoulders. Soon he had opened all the fastenings on her petticoats and she was standing in her shift and stays.

"I've always thought this part was far too complicated," he said.

"I've known men who just cut through the laces," she offered. There was silence.

She glanced over her shoulder. Solomon's eyes were narrow

with disapproval. For a moment she wondered if this reference to her past would destroy the mood, but he just said, "Good laces cost at least a shilling!" She laughed as he went to work on the knot.

When he had unlaced her stays and pulled them over her head, she turned once more to face him. For a moment he looked bewildered. "Serena, I—"

His voice was rough and throbbing and sad. She'd noticed from the moment they met how expressive his face and body were, how he smiled and frowned with all of him, how the way he leaned forward or scratched the back of his head could convey a world of meaning. Now he could smile and frown with *her* body, too. The want in his face and voice made her yank the shift over her head and toss it on the floor. He relaxed, his hands hovering for a moment above her skin before he touched her.

Serena closed her eyes. She made no sound, but she trembled and breathed hard as his hands and mouth moved on her breasts and down over her belly, his knees hitting the floor with an impact that jarred Serena from the soles of her feet to her fingertips.

He nuzzled her inner right thigh. "Third birthmark."

Her throat was tight. When his tongue dipped between her legs, she gave a wordless cry and clutched at him to keep from falling. *Oh God, Solomon.* When he groaned into her it was like—there were no words for what it was like. She could feel herself crumbling beneath his hands like badly fired clay. She wanted—she had never—she—it had been so long and even then—

He stopped, suddenly, letting go of her and getting to his feet. "Open your eyes," he said, but she couldn't. She reached out blindly, seizing his braces and burying her face in his chest. She mumbled something and didn't even know what—the only discernable words were *Solomon* and *please*.

"Serena, do you want this?"

She nodded hastily against his shirt.

"Say it out loud."

She waited until she was certain of her voice before answering him, even though each second he didn't touch her was torture. "What part of 'Solomon, please' do you find ambiguous?"

He broke away entirely, and she felt cold and naked. Of course, she *was* cold and naked. She kept her eyes tightly shut. "Not now, Serena," he said. "I need a straight answer. I need to know you won't hate me tomorrow."

She opened her eyes, crossing her arms over her chest instinctively. Did he know how much it would cost her to make that admission? She would regret it, of course, but he was watching her so earnestly, his heavy breathing loud in the silence. The lamplight turned his hair deep gold. It glinted at her from the open collar of his shirt. If he didn't take the shirt off soon she couldn't answer for the consequences. And there was something so implacable in his rough voice—he really did care more about how she would feel in the morning, about how she *felt*, than he did about anything else. He knew what he wanted from her and he refused to settle for anything less.

Something in her responded to his stubbornness, and yet for an instant she wished he were Lord Smollett or one of the others, who wouldn't ask her to say anything, who would just get on with it. And then she realized what she was thinking and disavowed it utterly and forever, because he was the only person in the world she wanted. Only him, and here he was. She couldn't quite help smiling. "I'll only hate you if you stop."

That seemed to be enough for him. He bounced a little on the balls of his feet, and his dazzling smile made her stomach do flip-flops. Exhilaration tried to climb out her throat as he laced his fingers through hers and yanked her to him.

Then she remembered something. "Solomon, wait."

"*What?*"

"I need something from my room."

He frowned. "You'll take a chill. Tell me where it is and I'll fetch it for you."

"I won't take a chill." She reached for her shift.

He caught her wrist. "Don't put it back on," he said intently, as if he thought she might not take it off again. "What do you need?"

She gave in. "It's in the drawer of my night table. It's a sponge."

"A sponge?"

She shoved at his shoulder. "Just fetch it. You'll see." She sat cross-legged on the bed to wait for him.

He was back in a few moments, staring at the little sponge with its trailing thread. "What's it for?"

"It's to keep me from finding myself in an interesting condition," she explained. "Have you got vinegar?"

Enlightenment dawned. "Of course." He pulled a small glass bottle from his worktable and, unstoppering it, poured some of its contents into a little dish.

"It *is* vinegar, and not deadly acid?"

He dipped a finger in the bowl. Before she knew what he was about he was sucking the vinegar off, slowly and teasingly, and heat flooded her even as she made an unconscious noise of protest. But he didn't scream or blister, so getting off the bed and taking the little sponge from him, she began methodically soaking it in vinegar.

"Why do you still have this?" he asked suspiciously.

She glanced at him out of the corner of her eyes. "I stole it from Sophy that time I tried to seduce you." She hadn't needed one since she left her last protector. She had vowed never to use one again. Never to be vulnerable again. Never to let anyone see her naked—never to let anyone see her at all. And now here she was. She tried not to think about it.

"Serena—"

"Yes?"

"Why *did* you try to seduce me?"

Serena eyed him warily, but he just looked curious. "I didn't want to sleep alone after my nightmare."

He stared at her. "But of course you couldn't just *ask* to sleep in my bed. No, that would be too easy."

"I hardly think doing it my way would have been such an ordeal," she snapped, and a little happy grin appeared on his face that made her want to—

"Can I put it in?"

"What?" she asked, startled.

"Can I put the sponge in?"

She looked at it, and at him. "Why?"

"Because it's interesting," he said as if it were obvious. "Does it kill the pox, too?"

"I doubt it. You haven't got the pox, have you?"

He shook his head. "Well, can I?" He looked so fascinated for an instant, before her better judgment reasserted itself, she was tempted to give in.

"Perhaps another time," she conceded, and didn't even realize what she'd said until she saw the glowing flush on Solomon's face, and then she could hardly regret it.

In her haste she fumbled with the sponge, and for a moment she was afraid that she wouldn't remember how to put it in properly, it had been so long—and then it was in and she couldn't wait any longer. "Take off your shirt."

She leaned back against a bedpost to watch as Solomon slid off his braces and pulled his shirt out of his breeches, not quite as deft with his own clothing as he had been with hers. She gave him a predatory smile and slid a hand under his shirt. His stomach was hot under her palm and his gasp sent shivers up her spine. She hummed in satisfaction and pulled the shirt over his head.

A quick tug, back and down, left his chest and shoulders bare and his arms trapped behind his back by the inside-out shirt. She ran her hands over his shoulders—they were pale and freckled and broad, and when she squeezed a little the muscles in them jumped and Solomon made a low growling sound in his throat.

Dear God, his upper arms. It was unfair that anyone should have arms like that. She pressed a hand against his chest. His lungs expanded and contracted, and his heart raced beneath her palm. He made no move to free his arms from their tangle of shirt, just watched her hands on his skin as if they were his hope of heaven. She let them wander lower, and finally set about unbuttoning his trousers. He stood very, very still until she slipped her hand inside and wrapped it around his cock. Then he bucked forward, once, as if he couldn't help it. He shut his eyes abruptly and made a sound that had no voice in it, only breath.

She put her other hand on the back of his neck and pulled him down to kiss her, hard, pressing against him, skin on skin, rubbing her nipples up and down on his chest. She stroked his cock, long, slow strokes, feeling a fierce, primitive satisfaction when he trembled against her.

"Serena," he gasped into her mouth.

"Take the shirt off," she said abruptly, letting go and stepping back. "I need you to touch me."

His eyes fluttered open, crinkling with laughter, and he fumbled to free his arms. Dropping the shirt on the floor and coming at her, he pushed her back onto the bed and dove on after her. They landed in a tangle of limbs, his hands holding her wrists captive above her head, one hard thigh between her legs. "Oh, you need me, do you? Maybe I should make you beg."

Serena stared at him. Would he really? And could she stop herself from doing it?

He snickered at her consternation and let go of her wrists, trailing his hands down over her arms and shoulders to cup her breasts. The sight of his stained hands on her naked breasts was the most erotic thing she had ever seen. One of his fingers was the exact same shade of blue as her third-best bedchamber. Why did that drive her wild? She arched up against him, unintentionally rubbing against his thigh.

She whimpered, and Solomon laughed softly and squeezed her breasts, catching her nipples between two of his fingers as he did so. She really might die, right here. All her experience, all her expertise, and she was as helpless and clumsy with desire as any green girl on her wedding night. "Do that again," she demanded.

He raised his eyebrows slightly, looking adorably pleased with himself, and obliged her.

Sliding down her body, he flicked at one nipple with his tongue before taking it in his mouth and sucking, hard. His hands swept down her sides and over her hips and back up again, his calluses catching lightly on her skin, his hands so hot that everywhere they touched felt cold when they were gone. She shivered again, and again, straining against his hands. "Solomon, I'm ready. I'm *ready*."

He pulled his mouth off her breast with a little nip that sent tingles of pleasure coursing all through her. His eyes suddenly solemn in the firelight, he raised himself back up to kiss her lightly on the lips. "Are you sure?" Guiding his cock with one hand, he rocked against her experimentally once, twice, three times.

Oh Christ yes now *I'm not a virgin what are you waiting for?* she thought, but she said, "I'm sure," and pulled him down for another kiss. And then in one stroke he was *in* her, Solomon was inside her, moving slow at first and then faster. She tilted her hips up and closed her eyes and met him thrust for thrust, strung so tight that it was hardly any time at all before she felt her release building.

She arched up against him, cursing, and opened her eyes. She met his darkened hazel gaze. He had been watching her face, and she *hated* when men did that but somehow, right here, right now, the shock of awareness that passed between them pushed her over the edge, her whole body racked with pleasure. She was melting, no, she was boiling. She was consumed like a snowflake falling into a bonfire.

"Solomon," she said softly. She continued to move against him, languorously, filled with a sense of well-being as the last tremors washed through her. He pressed his face into the curve of her neck then, moving faster. The edge of his shoulder was bright and haloed by the firelight, a sheen of sweat on him, and he too shuddered with release and collapsed on top of her.

"Oh God, Serena, I love you so much," he groaned.

Suddenly she couldn't breathe. *No.* His weight was crushing her. She couldn't get air into her lungs. "I—let me—" she said desperately, pushing at him with her hands until he moved off her. She rolled away from him, sitting up on her elbow and gasping for air.

"Serena, what is it? What's wrong?"

"Why do you have to make promises you can't keep?" she asked him, hating the plaintive note in her voice. "I gave you everything without that!"

When Elijah was sure René was asleep, he cautiously got up and moved to the heavy chest of drawers against the wall. He opened the top drawer and rummaged through it. Nothing. He opened the second one. Running his fingers along the back of the drawer, he found something solid. A tiny box. He didn't move it, just shoved aside some stockings and took off the lid. What he saw surprised him so much that he didn't even hear René sit up in bed.

But when René's feet hit the floor, Elijah had just enough time to return the lid and hide the box again before his wrists were seized from behind. "Just what do you think you're doing?" René asked in a dangerous voice.

"Trying to borrow a pair of stockings." Elijah twisted his head to look at him. "Is there something in your drawer you don't want me to see?" He reached for the drawer again and just managed to scrabble at some folded breeches before René spun him around.

"I want to see what's in your secret drawer," Elijah insisted, laughing, and tried to wrestle himself back around. "Let me go!" René started to tickle him, and he wriggled, and soon enough they were back on the bed.

Serena picked her shift up off the floor and pulled it back over her head.

"You don't have to say anything back," Solomon said behind her, sounding as if each word were an effort. "But—it's a promise I can keep. I didn't know I was going to say it. But it's true."

She turned to glare at him. It was a mistake. He was still naked. It was unnatural and improbable, how beautiful he was. He was perfect, and she was—not. "It's true today. But will it be true tomorrow? Will it be true in three months when you've seen me every day and I've snapped your head off half the time and you're tired of it? You think no one's loved me before?" She knew what love was. Love was belonging to someone else, it was letting yourself become what they wanted. And then when they were gone, because you weren't what they needed after all, you didn't even have yourself. All Serena *had* was herself.

"I'm not Daubenay," Solomon said sharply.

"Yes," she said wildly, "you're *exactly* like Daubenay. What I have to give isn't enough. You'll never be satisfied until you have it all, until I'm *yours* and I can't—I can't—because after all you *love* me and how could I—"

"I'm yours."

The feeling of not being able to breathe returned, like an enormous weight on her chest, the weight of a responsibility she would inevitably fail to live up to. "But I don't *want* you!" she said desperately.

He closed his eyes as if in pain, and she hadn't meant it like that, but what could she say?

Then his eyes snapped open. Serena stood stock-still, remembering how those eyes had watched her tumble headlong into orgasm. "You damn well do," he said furiously. "And not just for this either." He made a rude gesture toward his groin. "Last time—when you tried to seduce me—all you wanted that night was my friendship, but you were too much of a coward to *ask*. You'd rather pervert this into something cheap and dishonest and make this—what we have—even if it's *not* love, you shouldn't make it into a lie." He let out a short, frustrated breath. "I'd ask you what you were afraid of if you hadn't made it so damned obvious."

"I'm going to get Jenny's note and those vowels from René," she said. "Go back to sleep."

"Let Elijah do it."

"If you want something done right, do it yourself."

His eyebrow only moved a fraction of an inch, but she flushed all over. She'd liked it when he'd done it for her, and they both knew it.

"It's not safe," he said, getting up and pulling on his shirt and breeches. The loss of his bare skin felt like grief.

"René won't hurt me." It sounded stupid, when René *had* hurt her.

Solomon obviously thought so too. "I'm coming with you."

She sneered, but her hands were trembling, which spoiled the effect. "You would make a terrible spy. There are some jobs that are for one person."

"Some are for two."

She didn't feel like arguing. She had to get somewhere where she wasn't standing next to an empty bed. "Do as you like."

So he crept down the hall beside her. She slipped her master key from her pocket and slid it into the lock that Sophy had taken care to oil just that morning. It turned silently. The hinges had been oiled, too, and the door made no noise at all as Serena opened it.

Oh God, she thought in horror. How could she have been such a fool?

She tried desperately to back out, whispering, "We should come back later," but it was too late. Solomon had seen René's bed over her shoulder.

Sleeping on his stomach under tangled sheets, his head pillowed on René's shoulder and one arm thrown carelessly across René's waist, was Elijah.

Chapter 21

The brothers sat in Solomon's room without speaking. Elijah had dressed and was hugging his bottle-green coat around himself as if it were chilly. It wasn't. He and Serena had been naked and he'd never been cold. He couldn't think about that now. He looked back at his brother, and broke the silence with an effort. "How long—how long have you—"

"How long have I been a sodomite?" Elijah asked harshly. "About as long as you haven't been one, I daresay."

Solomon flinched. "How long have you and Sacreval been—"

"Lovers?"

They had always finished each other's sentences, so eager to move on to the next one. Now Solomon just didn't have the courage to finish them himself.

"Since I met him in Paris."

Solomon stared. "You mean, all this time—"

"I hadn't slept with him again until tonight, if that's what you're asking. For God's sake, I'm working to—" Elijah cut off with a glance at the door. *Hang him*, he mouthed, his face contorted with misery.

Solomon remembered Elijah staring as the marquis and Lady Pursleigh leaned toward each other in the candlelight, and the pen almost snapping in his hand when he wrote that he was here to hang the marquis du Sacreval. Suddenly Elijah's constant moody snappishness since his return resolved itself into perfect, gleaming sense. Part of Solomon thought with relief, *It wasn't my fault.* Then he thought of something else. "You slept with Sir Nigel."

Elijah bit his lip. "Sol, please—"

"You did, didn't you."

"Yes." So soft he wouldn't have heard it if it were anyone but Elijah.

"I don't know you anymore."

"You know me better than anyone!"

Solomon shook his head. "I always told you everything."

"I always hoped you weren't."

It took a moment for Solomon to catch his meaning. "You mean, you wished that I—" He couldn't keep the revulsion from his voice and Elijah didn't even flinch, just huddled deeper into his ratty old jacket.

"I just didn't want to be alone."

"You've *never* been alone." Solomon barely recognized his own voice. "Not like I was. For a year and a half. I had *no one*. You—have you ever done anything *but* lie to me?"

"I can't lie to you, you know that," Elijah snapped. "I just— didn't tell the truth."

Solomon snorted.

"When I started this job, they told me that the best lie is a half-truth. But I already knew that."

"I'm glad that our connection had *some* professional value to you!"

Before he could say anything else, Serena came in through the connecting door with a tea tray. It was late; she must have made it up herself, alone in the dark kitchen. "I thought you could use this," she said, her voice neutral. Even in the throes of passion she'd kept command of her voice. Only when he'd said he loved her had it risen, breaking like a snapped thread.

Her hair fell across her face and fringes rustled as she set the tray down on the table between them. She gathered her clothes off the floor. Her robe gaped a little as she bent over. Then she handed Solomon a note and walked out. He couldn't drag his eyes away from her until she'd shut the door.

He opened the torn-off strip of paper. In the same neat hand that filled her account books, it said, *A friend loveth at all times, and a brother is born for adversity.* He looked at Elijah, who obviously wanted to know what the note said and couldn't bring himself to ask for fear of a refusal. Silently Solomon pushed it across the table.

Elijah read it and passed it back. "Proverbs Seventeen: Seventeen," he said wryly. Their eyes met, and for a second Solomon could feel Elijah's terror beating against his own ribs like a trapped bird. Then Elijah looked away and said, "I wouldn't have thought Lady Serena even owned a Bible."

"I said it to her father, actually," Solomon said.

"Really?"

He nodded. "It was the best impression of Father I've ever done, you would have died—" He cut off abruptly. "I'll do an encore for you sometime."

Elijah raised his head hopefully. Solomon thought of the look in Elijah's eyes when he'd sat up in Sacreval's bed and seen Solomon. It was a look Solomon had seen in the mirror countless times over the last year and a half. The look of someone who has wakened into his own nightmare.

He watched Elijah now. His guilty air and the mutinous set of his mouth were familiar to Solomon from countless confrontations with their parents. The black despair in his eyes was not. If anyone else had brought that look to Elijah's face, Solomon would have wanted to rip his throat out.

He tore up the note. Elijah stared at the pieces as if they'd been his last breath of air. "For God's sake, Li, take that look off your face," Solomon said. "I don't need this note to remind me that you're my brother. You don't need to worry that you'll lose me. You never did. There is no wretched thing you could ever do that would make me want to be without you." It was true, and at that moment Solomon resented it furiously—resented that Elijah could have killed a man and Solomon would have burned him and dissolved his bones in vitriol to keep Elijah from the noose. And Elijah still didn't trust him. Had never trusted him. Solomon had paid a heavy price for that lack of trust, this past year and a half, and yet he'd let it go by the board, had welcomed his brother back without question—and *this* was his reward.

"'A brother offended is harder to be won than a strong city,'" Elijah whispered.

"I can't do without you and you know it," he said curtly. "You knew it a year and a half ago when you gallivanted off to France."

"I told you, I thought you would *know*."

"I didn't know *this*."

"I wanted you never to know. I tried so hard—I can't do without you either, Sol," Elijah said desperately. "I was so afraid I'd lose you. I'm losing you right now. That look on your face, like I'm some leper you've never seen before—"

Solomon tried to clear the anger from his expression. "We'll—we'll figure this thing out," he offered.

The blood rushed into Elijah's face. "There's nothing to figure out. I like men. I always have and I can't stop, not even for you. I'm not diseased, or mad, or wretched, and neither was what happened between me and René tonight. It was—" He looked at the mussed bed. "Well, I expect you know what it was like."

Solomon's eyes narrowed. How dare he make the comparison? "Sacreval is a—" Elijah shot a warning look at the door, and *spy* died in Solomon's throat. "Why did you go?" he asked instead.

Elijah sighed. "Remember Alan?"

"The blacksmith's apprentice? Of course. You lived in each other's pockets for—" He blinked. "Wait a minute, you and he—you—?"

"Yes," Elijah said defiantly. "We were. For years. And then he let his father marry him off, and he told me it wouldn't *change* anything."

Solomon scrubbed at his face. "He's a drunk now, you know."

Elijah stared at him. "*Really?*"

Solomon nodded. "His wife has to take in boarders because people don't want to go to the smithy."

Elijah's mouth twisted. "Poor girl."

"So—you're not interested in Serena, then?"

Elijah laughed incredulously. "Don't be ridiculous. Besides, it's plain as a pikestaff she's only got eyes for you."

Solomon swallowed and looked away. "I need to think about this," he said abruptly. He stood up. "I need to sleep."

Elijah nodded and went out silently. Solomon lifted the lid on Serena's pot and saw that it contained chocolate. It was rapidly cooling, but he poured himself a cup anyway, not bothering to add sugar. He'd just taken his first bitter sip when Sacreval walked in. His jaw was set and he was very pale.

"What in God's name are you doing here?"

"I came to talk to you about your brother."

"You ought to be ashamed to speak of him," Solomon said viciously. *Dissolute Frenchman.*

A muscle jumped in Sacreval's jaw. "You ought to be ashamed to say so," he said quietly. "You want your brother to repent of what he is? You want him to crawl through life apologizing for existing?"

"Why couldn't you leave him alone?" Solomon was embarrassed by the childishness of it the moment it left his mouth, but he couldn't help wanting to blame the whole mess on Sacreval. He turned everything he touched to ashes. Look what he had done to Serena—what would he take from Elijah when he was through with him? What had he already taken?

The marquis smiled crookedly, something sparking in his eyes that Solomon told himself was just lust. "Because he shone," Sacreval said. "From the first moment I saw him, there was a glow around him like our Savior in a painting."

"How dare you speak our Lord's name, you filthy—" The

marquis sucked in his breath sharply, and Solomon shut his lips on the slur.

"You English," Sacreval said furiously. "As if speaking it were the crime. You were happy for him to sin as much as he liked so long as he did not *speak* of it to you. So long as he felt properly *ashamed* and you did not have to hear it, you did not care."

Solomon surged to his feet. "That's not true," he bit out. "I didn't know! He never told me. He never told me *anything*."

"Because he knew that you would do exactly as you are doing. Last week he said to me, 'René, we cannot ever again, because it would kill me if he knew.' And his voice was shaking."

That was a lie, Solomon thought. *Because he couldn't say, 'You're a spy and I must kill you.'* But Elijah had said, not three minutes ago, *The best lie is a half-truth.*

"The other reason I did not leave him alone," the marquis continued, "is because if I had, they would have killed him."

Solomon's head snapped up. "Who?"

The marquis shrugged. "The police, who else? They raided the house we were in, in Paris. Your brother should have fled, but no, he is an Englishman, he faces three men down so that a fifteen-year-old whore can escape. By the time I reached him they were kicking in his ribs."

Bile rose in Solomon's throat, swamping his anger. "Christ," he said thickly.

Sacreval shrugged again. "They thought we ought to be ashamed. It was not a barroom brawl, but it was true what I said before. He could barely walk."

"Christ," Solomon repeated. He looked at the marquis almost pleadingly. "Is that going to be Elijah's life? Skulking around? Consorting with fifteen-year-old whores and their clients? Being beaten in disreputable houses? What kind of life is that?"

There was something wistful in the marquis's smile. "As odd as it may seem, an honest one."

Solomon laughed weakly.

"It is not all bad. I like disreputable houses. And the time I spent with your brother in Paris was the happiest of my life."

"You're not going to tell me you *love* him," Solomon said incredulously.

"Not if you don't wish me to. But that does not change the fact that it is true." He laughed softly at Solomon's expression. "What, did you think it was all unnatural lusts and depravity? Perhaps you should have read the sonnets of your Shakespeare more carefully." He stood there a moment longer, but when Solomon said nothing, he shrugged and walked out of the room.

Solomon thought about booted feet in Elijah's ribs. He thought about the tight knot of revulsion in his chest, and about anybody else looking at Elijah and feeling it.

Solomon vomited chocolate into his basin. He wanted more than anything else in the world to talk to Serena. But she'd looked so scared, so trapped. He'd told her he wasn't asking her for anything. He couldn't go running to her now.

Besides, even though he thought he understood, he was angry. Angry that he'd told her he loved her and she'd all but chewed off her own arm to get away. He gargled water until he could no longer taste the tainted acidic sweetness on his tongue.

Serena opened her eyes. Sunlight was streaming cheerily in through her window. She groaned and glanced at the clock. Quarter to eight. She sat bolt upright. How had she slept so late? Why had Sophy let her? She swung her legs over the side of the bed—and froze mid-stretch, paralyzed by the soft sound of water lapping against a metal hipbath.

Solomon was taking a bath.

Just a few inches of oak away.

Naked.

Hellfire and damnation. She had worked to avoid exactly this eventuality. It hadn't been difficult, precisely, because he usually

rose at seven, and she rose at five. But she had made sure to know
that when he had water brought up for his bath it was invariably
at half-past seven, and had taken pains never to be in her room
before the tub was carried back down the stairs and the water
thrown in the rear courtyard. It was bad enough that she herself
struggled to be perfectly silent as she took her own baths, so that
she would not wake him, so that he would not come through
the door that no longer locked and find her naked. It was bad
enough that every inch of her skin burned at the knowledge that
he could.

She did not want to listen to the faint lap of water against
a metal tub in the next room, or hear a splash and picture
Solomon pouring water over his shoulders and arms or, God
forbid, lathering his chest, or brushing wet hair back from his
forehead—

Memories flooded her, memories of Solomon's hands on her
breasts and Solomon's mouth on her skin, of his darkened hazel
eyes fixed on her face. Memories of him inside her. Memories of
feeling so intimately connected to Solomon that being separated
from him by the space of an inch would have killed her.

With the memories came the panic. Sheer, overpowering,
throat-closing fear at the strength of her own emotions. She was
drowning in him.

Moving in desperate haste and equally desperate silence,
Serena washed her face and neck and ran a comb through her
hair. She heard the rush of water when Solomon stood, and she
heard the creaking of the floor when he stepped out of the tub.
She dressed with trembling hands, putting on her short corset and
a gown that buttoned in the front so she wouldn't need help.

She slipped out of her room and hurried down the hallway, but
she was too late. As she passed Solomon's door, it opened.

Serena stopped and turned to look. She stood there, rooted to
the spot.

His pale hair was wet, and he was running one hand through

it. The indigo stain on his finger that she'd noticed the night before had faded to a faint powder blue.

He was back in the Arms livery. He looked as delicious as the Italian sweets they'd ordered for the Brendans' Venetian breakfast. And he was staring at her every bit as hungrily as she was staring at him.

He said he loved me. All I have to do is say I'm sorry, and he'd let me— She couldn't form a coherent thought. Her tongue was cloven to the roof of her mouth.

Solomon watched her, his eyes gold in the morning light. "Good morning," he said.

She didn't answer.

His eyes narrowed. "I still love you," he said evenly. Then he brushed past her and went down the hall. Her heart pounded in rhythm with his boot heels on the stairs.

Chapter 22

The beginning of the Brendans' party, René reflected, was hideously different from the beginning of the Pursleighs'. Not that he had been precisely at ease on that occasion, either, but now poor Elijah could not even look at him. The boy didn't look at his brother either, and Solomon was keeping his eyes studiously on the middle distance. René, seeing the circles under Elijah's eyes, would have liked to wring Solomon's puritanical little neck. The pair were both fidgeting like mad, and René didn't dare speak to either, even to give a simple order, for fear of provoking a confrontation.

It seemed like years, but was probably only twenty minutes, before he judged he might safely leave the kitchen to its own devices and supervise the arrangement of the tables in the courtyard. He escaped outside with a sense of profound relief.

So it was with a doubly sinking feeling that he realized they might have left the Italian pastries at the Arms. *There is no point going to see. Even if you find that you have, Hampstead is too far from London to retrieve them in time*, he told himself hopefully. But there was no help for it. He turned back to the house.

Of course, Lady Brendan chose that moment to become very concerned about the arrangement of the ice buckets for champagne and actually followed him to the kitchen demanding he return to give his opinion. He had forgotten how difficult *les aristos* could be about any service one provided them. At least the customers in his family's bakery were not quite so used to getting their own way every moment.

"Madame, I assure you there will be no trouble with the buckets," he said as patiently as he could, trying to meet her eyes deferentially without breaking his neck on the narrow back stairs. "We will arrange them together *l'instant même* that I assure myself we have not left your exquisite pastries behind at the Arms." On this last word René reached the kitchen.

Lord Brendan stood in the middle of the room, being gaped at by Arms staff and the Hathaway twins. His wrists were manacled behind his back, and extremely official-looking men stood on each side of him. One of them, René saw with a chill, held a deck of cards in one hand. France had so needed that information about the state of communications between the English and the Prussians.

Lady Brendan, several steps behind him, continued over the absolute silence in the kitchen, "I assure you, monsieur, it makes no odds. The crème brûlée will be quite—" She reached the door and stopped abruptly. "Ah, *merde*."

It would have greatly relieved René's feelings to say the same, and a deal more besides. It took all his will to merely glance at Lady Brendan in mild perplexity. "Why is your husband in irons in the middle of your kitchen, madame?"

"I—I—" she floundered.

Oh, *merde*. First Elbourn, then Sir Nigel, and now *this*?

Brendan figured it out a second after René did. "You *knew* about this?" he asked his wife in helpless disbelief.

"N—no—"

"Amélie?" The man looked suddenly defeated. Defeated and old.

"I'm sorry," she said. "It was my duty, but it was not easy."

Brendan's lips twisted unpleasantly. "And you always do your duty, don't you, Amélie?"

"Please, my lord," she whispered, trembling.

"Your duty is to *me*."

"My duty is to my king." Her voice was barely a thread. René thought she would be in hysterics before too long. She had always struck him as nervy as a thoroughbred—an *aristo* to the core. "And—how could you risk James, my lord?" she added, louder.

Brendan turned red as a lobster. "James! It's always James with you! You think I don't see? You married me for my money, you little slut, and now you want to get rid of me so you can be free to play the whore with my own son?"

Lady Brendan's eyes widened. "How dare you suggest such a thing?" she demanded, her voice high. "James is like a son to me, you filthy old lecher! Of course I married you for your money—why else would a sixteen-year-old girl marry an old man like you? But I was a wife to you for twelve years and I was fond of you. I cried when I knew you would be executed!" A couple of the kitchen boys gawked openly at her splendidly heaving bosom. If he stayed at the Arms long enough, he would have to talk to them about that later.

"I only turned to this to buy *you* the things you wanted. Where did you think the money was coming from to pay for all your damned hats?"

Since René happened to know that most of the money went to pay Brendan's gaming debts, this struck him as rather unfair.

"I hope you *drown* in your crocodile tears!" Brendan concluded with a flourish.

"Even if I did, I would outlive *you!*" She looked shocked by her own effrontery, but continued headlong, "You talk about doing my duty! You are only angry that I did not meekly take the blame as you've been setting me up to do for years! I was so blind—I didn't even see it until she told me how you'd been using me, always had been, just like he used her—" She stopped suddenly in horror, her hand flying to her mouth and her eyes flying to René.

He felt all the blood slowly drain from his face. Serena. His *sirène* had been talking to Lady Brendan, and now Lady Brendan had helped the Foreign Office arrest her husband. Serena was working against him. He had wondered, when she went to that party at the Elbourns', but he had dismissed the idea as impossible. He'd thought she was trying to please Elijah's idiot of a respectable brother.

Serena was closer to him than anyone. He knew she must have guessed who nearly all his people were, and he had let this happen. *Mon Dieu*, it was his fault, all of it, nearly all his people bound for the gallows because he was a fool.

His only excuse was that he hadn't understood until that moment just how Serena must have felt. How the years of friendship and intimacy and shared laughter must have been transformed in an instant into a humiliating mockery. He had felt guilty—of course he had—but it had never occurred to him to compare himself to Lord Brendan.

That it had occurred to Serena—that she thought he had used her like this *vieux traître méprisable* had used his pretty young French wife—how blind he had been, to think that the risk to the Arms would be enough to stay her hand! It was a miracle she hadn't already shot him.

He had never intended to use the marriage lines. They had been a sensible precaution, that was all. But she had forced his hand when she gave his room to that puling preacher's son.

He shot Solomon a venomous glance—and his gaze fell on his Thierry, who looked as if he were trying not to be sick. *Thierry*. Thierry knew. Thierry's name was Elijah and he was a loyal Englishman and René was *un sot, un con, un imbécile*. He had betrayed Serena and lost his lover and still not saved his men.

"Well," said one of the agents into the resulting silence. "We'll just be taking his lordship away now." And they did.

"Will you be going ahead with the entertainment?" René asked Lady Brendan. Merely as a courtesy; of course she would not.

Two spots of high color burned in her cheeks. "Yes. I rather feel like celebrating."

Everyone stared at her in horror as she swept from the room.

"You heard her," René said mechanically. "And that punch is about to boil over. Ravi, bring up the striped Sicilian cake and the nougats once you're done carving that chicken."

He went up the stairs and slipped out the front door.

"Fortunately, Lady Brendan burst into tears about half an hour later and fled the gardens, so we were able to gather everything up and escape back to the Arms," Elijah said. "Unfortunately, coaches full of caterers are not famous for their speed, but I told the agents who arrested Brendan that Sacreval likely knows he's been discovered." He glanced nervously at Solomon when he said René's name. Solomon was sitting on his workbench watching Serena, and didn't see.

Why were they in his room? Why had *that* become their usual meeting place and not some neutral spot like her office? She kept her eyes studiously off the bed, but she could sense its presence. She could sense Solomon sensing it. "'Regular Trojan' my arse," she said. "Lady Brendan as good as told René that I'm working against him."

"I know," Solomon said quietly.

"How did he take it?" She managed to keep her voice even, but Solomon's face softened anyway. How did he always know when she was struggling?

"He looked as if someone had kicked him in the stomach," he said.

Serena was torn between feeling triumphant, guilty, or pleased that René cared.

"There are agents stationed here in case he returns," Elijah said in a tight voice. "But very likely he won't."

Serena hoped he wouldn't. The Arms was worthless to him now. He could run, and live, and perhaps no one need ever know that those marriage lines existed. Maybe she could even suppress her newest discovery, delivered by messenger while the Hathaways were away. What right did the Foreign Office have to know? Who would it hurt? Hadn't she done enough for England? Restlessly she paced to the window. Sunlight fell on her face, making her blink.

There was a small, serviceable edition of Shakespeare lying on the window seat. Of course: Shakespeare's sonnets. René had told Solomon he hadn't read them carefully enough, so Solomon was reading them again, like a dutiful pupil. Serena's heart smote her. Poor Solomon. He tried so hard. He had only ever wanted the truth: from his brother, and from her.

"One of my contacts came by this morning while you were gone," she said quietly. "Jenny Pursleigh has an account at Rothschild's bank, and her deposits match René's payment schedule perfectly."

Elijah's head came up. Then he cursed. "It doesn't matter. I could send men to her house, but Sacreval's sure to have warned her by now. She's long gone."

"Don't be so sure," Solomon said, his face alight with suppressed excitement. "There's paperwork, when you close out an account at a bank. If we go to Rothschild's right away, I wager we can catch her."

Elijah shook his head. "If she's clever, and she is, she's abandoned the money. It's risking her neck to stay in London."

"I'll forgive you for saying that," Solomon said, "because you've never lived on your own earnings. But listen carefully. Serena, would you ever abandon a large sum of money you had accumulated over years of hard work?"

Serena shook her head. "I couldn't."

"No one alive could."

"In case, you'd better go to the Pursleigh townhouse," Serena said. "We'll go to Rothschild's."

Elijah nodded. "Why do you think she picked Rothschild's?" he asked abruptly. "Do you think he's disloyal?"

"No, I think he's expended a good deal of time and energy backing England and received precious little thanks. But

Rothschild's clerks are less likely than, say, Lloyd's to be starched-up old men who don't hold with young women having bank accounts."

"Nathan Rothschild came to us yesterday," Elijah said slowly. "Claimed he knew Wellington had won."

"Did the government believe him?" Serena asked.

Elijah bit his lip. "They want to. I want to. This war has gone on long enough."

She shrugged. "All I know is that he has always given me an excellent rate of interest on the Arms accounts."

Elijah rolled his eyes. "Bring her to Newgate if you get her. Then send me word care of Lord Varney. I'll have to go report to him on all this. When we get back here, we can go through Sacreval's things, see if—" His eyes went wide. "Oh Lord, I forgot! He's got our earrings, Sol!"

Chapter 23

But the matter of the earrings had to be put on hold until Jenny Pursleigh was captured. Serena and Solomon caught a hackney and bribed him to drive far too fast to Rothschild's bank. Awkward silence reigned in the carriage until Serena, frustrated, could not restrain herself. "Solomon, can't we—can't we just forget this love business and go on as we were?"

Solomon looked at her. Just that, just his eyes on her face, sent Serena's heart skittering madly in her chest. "So you'll sleep with me so long as I don't ask for anything else? I want more than that. I want *you*. I told you that ages ago."

And she wanted him. Oh, how she wanted him. But with the ache, last night's terror welled up again. The terror of what she felt, the terror of what she would give up for him if he asked her to, the terror that, give up what she would, it could never make her what he wanted, what he needed. "You don't want me," she told him, her voice strange in her own ears. "I can't *be* what you want." He deserved someone open and sweet, someone for whom love was easy, someone who would never bring that hurt, strained look to his face.

"Don't patronize me. I know what I want."

The hackney jolted to a stop in St. Swithin's Lane. Serena glanced out the window. Directly in front of the bank, another hackney waited. Could it be waiting for Jenny? If René didn't escape, keeping the Arms from being forfeit to the Crown might yet depend on getting in the regent's good graces, and that depended on catching Jenny. Yet Serena was tempted to waste precious time asking Solomon what, precisely, he wanted.

"Pay the driver," she said. "I'm going to talk to the driver of that hackney across the street."

He nodded. She trusted him to follow her, to protect her and listen to her instructions in a crisis. Why couldn't she trust him to love her? She hurried across the street. "Driver!"

He was a young black man—fresh-faced enough, but when he grinned down at her, half his teeth were rotted away. "Sorry, miss, I've been told to wait."

Miss. Hmmph. Serena tapped the birthmark above her eye. "Do you know who I am?"

The jarvey sat up straighter on his perch, and looked a little overawed. "Thorn, miss—m'lady—"

Oh, for Christ's sake. "Thorn will do nicely." She smiled reassuringly before she could catch herself. A few weeks ago—oh, she might as well face it, before she met Solomon—she would never have done that. And yet it seemed to be all right. He didn't look as if he were going to say, *Wait a minute, you're just a girl, why does everyone listen to you?* He simply looked a little less likely to freeze up in panic. Perhaps her position—if she could keep it past this week—wasn't entirely sleight of hand anymore. Perhaps she'd gained enough real clout that she could relax a little. "And your name is—"

"Tom," he said, ducking his head respectfully. "Tom Eaton."

"Tom, I need your help."

He frowned. "I've been asked to wait."

Jenny could walk out of that bank at any moment. But Solomon appeared at her elbow. It calmed her nerves and helped her keep frustration out of her voice. "Is your customer a pretty gentlewoman, blonde, about so tall?" She gestured.

He nodded, startled.

"Then I wish you to wait, just as you've been. I wish you only to allow my friend and myself inside your vehicle to wait for your customer as well. Of course I will pay you for this service—five guineas or I'll stand in your debt, as you choose."

He looked wary now. "To be sure, having the Black Thorn in his debt is what anybody couldn't help but like, but I'm an honest man, and—"

"Then you are just what I need." She paused, and then, mentally gagging, added, "Just what *England* needs. That young woman is a spy for Bonaparte."

He stared at her. "That tiny little gentry mort? You must be joking me!"

Serena gritted her teeth. Jenny was small and blonde, and that trumped everything else. The power of what men let themselves believe was staggering. But then, she herself hadn't really believed that Jenny could be guilty. She'd seen Jenny wrap the teachers around her little finger at school, seen her lie and manipulate and always come out smelling like roses. And yet she'd thought it was only feminine cunning, nothing dangerous or real. Jenny had always relied on people thinking that. Serena, of all people, should have known better. "I assure you, I am very serious. When she gets in, you may convey us to Newgate."

"Will I regret this?" Tom asked.

Serena met his eyes firmly. "Not if I can help it."

Tom nodded. "Well, get on in, then."

Serena glanced at Solomon, then abruptly climbed in without waiting for his arm. He climbed in after her and sat in the opposite seat. She sat very still, back against the squabs where she couldn't be seen from the street, and tried not to let any portion of herself touch any portion of Solomon. She didn't look at him.

After what seemed like hours, Jenny's voice rang out gaily, "Thank you, sir! Now if you could take me to where I may catch the stage to Dover, I would be ever so grateful."

"Yes, madam."

The door opened and Jenny got in. She straightened, letting go of her skirts—and Serena trained her pistol on her. Solomon reached past her and shut the door with a snap. "Sit down," Serena said.

Jenny's face was hidden by a heavy veil, so it was impossible to guess her expression. "S—Serena?" she said incredulously. "What on earth? If Pursleigh forgot to pay you for the catering, I'm sure we can find a better way to—"

Serena sighed. "There's no point to this, Jenny. We have evidence of your guilt. We'll probably find more when we search your house, although if you've been careful, perhaps not. And if you don't make an ill-judged escape attempt, you'll live to see if your blue eyes have more success with a jury of the House of Lords."

She gestured to Solomon to come sit beside her, which he did. "Solomon, I'm going to hand you the gun. I need you to keep it trained on Lady Pursleigh while I see if she's hiding any weapons." She had doubts about the wisdom of this plan, but since she had already considered and rejected the plan in which Solomon ran *his* hands all over Jenny, she had no choice.

When Solomon had the gun, Serena moved to the opposite seat and began systematically searching Jenny. This exposed far more of that lady to Solomon's view than she would have liked, but she did her best to move quickly and keep her eye on her job, even when Jenny squirmed under her hands and made little squeals of protest. Only once, as her hands ran up Jenny's legs to see if she had a knife in her garter, did she glance at Solomon. His eyes were glazed and his lips parted, but his hand seemed steady. Serena glanced away, feeling her temperature rising.

"Make her stop!" Jenny begged Solomon indignantly. "How can you just sit there? You wouldn't really shoot me, would you?"

Serena paused. She didn't look, but she could feel Solomon's eyes sharpen on her face for a moment.

"Care to wager?" he asked mildly.

Finally, she took off Jenny's bonnet and heavy veil and

confiscated her hatpins. Serena had found those to be useful weapons more than once herself.

Exposed to view, Jenny's cornflower blue eyes were wide. "What—what am I accused of?" she asked with a sort of plaintive dignity, trying modestly to put her clothing back to rights.

Serena glanced at Solomon and saw the pity in his eyes. Men.

She would have liked to take the gun back, but Jenny's best chance to escape was while they were switching. "Espionage and high treason."

Jenny laughed shakily. "But that—that's impossible!"

Serena didn't like Jenny; she never had. But she wanted this to be over. She wanted it desperately. "You're good," she said. "Maybe even good enough to get off. But I doubt it. Not after you attempted to flee the country with every penny you had the day Sacreval realized you were all compromised—as myself, Mr. Hathaway, and the hackney driver can all testify. Not after Mr. Rothschild gives the Crown your bank records, and they show that your deposits were made under an assumed name, stopped abruptly last April at the beginning of the Peace, and corresponded precisely with the schedule of payments from Sacreval to his informants."

Jenny, thinking this over, bit the inside of her lower lip in a way that made her mouth look full and pouty. "How much would I have to pay you to let me go?"

"There is no question of letting you go."

"I'll give you half of what I have here." She shifted in her seat, spreading her legs a little. "I'll give you anything you want." She looked between Serena and Solomon, searching for signs of softening.

Serena couldn't help but feel a twisted kinship with her. Enough to tell her the truth. "Sacreval has forged documents proving we are married. If he is condemned for treason, he'll certainly try to ensure that the Arms are forfeit to the Crown. I need the Crown in my debt just now. I can't let you go."

"Then you should understand why I did it," Jenny said fiercely. "I needed the money. I could save the pittance he gives me for pin money for a hundred years and not have enough to get away from Pursleigh."

Serena wanted very much to look away, but she kept her eyes firmly on Jenny's face, watching for sudden movements. "I do understand. But then *you* should understand why I won't help you." *I sold myself for money*, she wanted to say. *You sold other people.* But there was no point—Jenny was already beaten, and winning the argument too wouldn't make Serena feel any happier about it.

"We used to be friends," Jenny said—her last, pathetic weapon. They both knew they had never been friends.

"I'm sorry," Serena said, and wished Solomon weren't holding the gun so that she could lean on him.

After that they rode in silence. Jenny stared at the streets as they flashed by and picked absentmindedly at the unraveling edge of her veil.

As they were turning up onto the road to Newgate, she turned to Serena and said, with a tiny quaver in her voice, "Does it hurt very much to be beheaded?"

Serena swallowed. René had told her stories from the Terror of severed heads looking at their bodies, blinking, even trying to speak.

"No one knows for sure," Solomon said gently. "But my anatomy lecturer at Cambridge believed that a beheaded person loses consciousness after only a few seconds. Those tales about guillotined heads winking at the mob are probably tripe. And even in the worst of the stories, none of them looked to be in *pain*."

Jenny looked as abjectly grateful as Serena felt.

They pulled up in front of the prison. Jenny sat perfectly still, a greenish tinge to her cheeks. Serena wished she could think of something to say.

Solomon leaned forward a little, though he did not lower the pistol. "You look dreadful," he said gently. "Do you want them all to see you shamed and frightened?"

Their eyes met, and suddenly Jenny smiled. "Will you wait just a moment while I put on some rouge?"

Solomon nodded. "Serena will get it out of your reticule and hand it to you—and if you try to escape or injure her in any way, I'll shoot you."

Serena searched through the bag, retrieved a little pot of rouge, and handed it to Jenny.

She rubbed some color into each cheek and took a deep breath. "Shall we go, then?"

They gave her over into custody of the warden of the prison. Two hulking turnkeys appeared to escort her to her cell. Just before they rounded the corner, she blew Solomon and Serena a kiss, calling gaily, "*Vive l'empereur!*"

Only René was left now.

Solomon watched Serena, who was staring out the window of their hackney. It had been hard for her to turn over Lady Pursleigh; he could see that. And he thought he saw why.

He would have said that no two women could be more different, and yet—both women, forced to fend for themselves in a man's world, had been obliged to choose masks. Jenny Pursleigh, faced with men's expectations of what a pretty girl should be, fulfilled them all. Serena rejected them, every single one. Lady Pursleigh pretended to feelings she didn't in the least have. Serena pretended to feel absolutely nothing.

He'd resented that, all this time. But he was beginning to understand, finally, that the stubbornly blank lines of her face weren't a rejection. Not of him, anyway. They were an open challenge, a refusal to perform for the crowd.

I can't be what you want, she had said. What, exactly, did she think he wanted? He remembered Miss Jeeves, the happy, girlish role she'd played at St. Andrew of the Cross, and how angry she'd been when he enjoyed it. Did she think he wanted what Lord Pursleigh wanted? And how, living in the world they lived in, could he expect her to think anything else?

The afternoon stretched. Sacreval did not return. He must have really gone for good. There was nothing left to do. Serena retreated to her office, and Elijah was holed up in his own room with a couple of other agents. Solomon wondered what would happen between him and Serena now. They had found the earrings. She no longer needed his help against Sacreval. He was on the very last wallpaper sample for the Arms. Once he had matched it, he and Serena would have no external reason for further contact. He didn't know how matters stood between him and Elijah either, or how they would stand.

He tried to work on Serena's last dye, but his heart wasn't in it. In fact, his heart was dead set against it. Instead, he tried to read a poor translation of one of Chevreul's papers on indigo, ate an early supper alone in his room, and went to bed.

He dreamed he was thrashing Elijah. He was smashing Elijah's face with his fist and kicking him in the chest, and he could feel each blow in his own body, each sudden bright blossoming of pain. He could feel it when Elijah's ribs cracked.

He woke up. It was dark. Serena stood over him, having evidently shaken him awake. She looked so worried about him: her jaw tight and her hand firm on his shoulder, her perfect brows drawn together stubbornly as if she were doing a painful duty but would be damned before she'd let anyone, including Solomon, stop her. He wanted to bury his face in her shoulder and cry, and he thought she might let him. Instead he pulled her down on top of him and kissed her, smelling sweat and almonds.

Reluctantly, he pulled away.

"I'm sorry," he said hoarsely, passing the back of his hand across his eyes. "I shouldn't have done that."

"Why *not?*"

He sat up, giving her a rueful smile. "Because it was stupid."

She glared at him, not bothering to set her clothes to rights. He had to get out of this room.

"I'm going to get my earrings." Having a goal cleared his mind, a little. By dint of not looking at her, he managed to get out of bed and pull on his breeches—carefully—before changing his nightshirt for a shirt. "Can I have your key?"

She rolled her eyes, tugged her clothes into place, and went into her room to get it. She came back holding the key, but instead of giving it to him she went past him and out into the hall without a word. He followed her.

The earrings were not where Elijah had seen them. Serena watched him search tensely for a minute or two before suggesting, "Try the ledge inside the chimney. I sometimes hide things there in my room." He got soot all over his hands, but she was right.

Back in the Stuart room, he set the earrings on his worktable and went to wash his hands in the basin. When he turned around, Serena was turning the box from side to side, trying to see the earrings in the moonlight.

She saw him watching her. "We should examine them for damage," she said hastily.

He sighed and lit the lamp. Light glinted off the Hathaway rubies lying in her palm. What would they look like in her ears? He glanced at her face. She was gazing at the earrings with a kind of fascinated horror.

Then someone put a key into the lock and turned it, and before Serena could do more than take a step toward the fireplace poker, Sacreval was in the room with a gun pointed straight at them.

Neither of them moved as he shut and locked the door from the inside with his free hand. "Back away from that table, *sirène,*" he said calmly.

"You couldn't shoot me," Serena said with confidence.

He smiled a little sadly. "That is why I am not pointing the gun at you." And it was true, Solomon realized. The pistol was aimed straight and true for his own heart.

Chapter 24

Serena had a sudden vivid memory of pointing her pistol at the face of some drunk young tulip who'd broken into her room on a dare, back in the early days of the Arms. René had heard and come in. *As in all battles,* he'd said, *the heart makes a better target than the head. Even if you are a little off, you are likely to hit some vital organ or other.* She'd said she was never a little off, and he had smiled approvingly and shrugged and said, *Have it your own way then,* but he'd escorted the tulip off the premises himself and the next day the bar had appeared across her door—

Serena snapped herself back into the present.

"You can't shoot him either," she said calmly, still hoping against hope that she could somehow brazen this out. "He's Elijah's brother, or have you forgotten?"

"Back away from the table," René repeated.

The look on his face made her ill. "Oh, but you would, wouldn't you? And you would think you were doing a fine thing, a noble act, sacrificing your chance at happiness for—God, for what, René? Why the devil did you come back?"

"*Back away from the table,*" René said through gritted teeth, and he cocked the pistol.

Her back was against the wall and she couldn't remember moving. The sound of that pistol cocking was the loudest thing she had ever heard. There was still a roaring in her ears like a hundred people cheering.

"Let him go," she said, her voice sounding distant in her own ears. "Let him go, and I'll give you whatever you want."

"I don't think so," said René.

"I'll sign over the Arms to you."

René looked pitying. "I don't want the Arms, *sirène*."

Of course he didn't want the Arms anymore. She couldn't think. She had simply offered him the biggest thing she could think of, like poor Jenny Pursleigh trying to bribe her with sex and her carefully hoarded cash. René had ruined Jenny, too.

"It's all right, Serena," Solomon said. "Sacreval isn't going to shoot me if you just do as he says." He sounded calmer than she was. Her strength was just an act, had always been an act.

But it was an act she could still do. She drew in a deep breath and pulled herself up and away from the wall. "Very well, René. What is it you *do* want?"

René nodded at her approvingly, just as he had when she'd threatened the tulip, and she felt sick. "You are holding the Hathaway earrings, are you not?"

She unclenched her fist and held out her hand, palm up, so he could see the rubies in their box.

"Very good, *sirène*. I want you to examine them very carefully for any kind of catch or spring."

It was hard to see, even in the light from Solomon's newfangled clockwork lamp, but after an endless half minute or so she saw the tiny catch. She pressed it back, hard, and the central ruby and its gold backing popped out and lay in her hand.

René smiled in relief. "Excellent. Now, is there a piece of the backing that isn't attached?"

She looked, and sure enough, a thin strip of gold flipped out and extended from the back center of the gem. It looked almost like a key—she gasped.

"Good," he said, seeing that she understood. "Now do the same for the other and go and put them in their places."

"They'll go back together, won't they?" Solomon asked worriedly. "Susannah needs them."

"Hush, Solomon." Serena walked over to the mantelpiece. The left ruby fitted perfectly into the empty socket at the bottom of Diana's carved hair—she had always wondered why there was a tiny slit at the back. The other ruby fit equally perfectly into the empty socket in the sun's biggest right-hand ray. She looked at René, waiting for his signal.

He nodded. "Turn them, I think. It will need both of you. I couldn't reach, and between that and the guard you set on the room, I've had a devil of a time."

"So sorry to have inconvenienced you." Why had she posted the guard? If she hadn't, he would be gone now. He'd only come back for this. If he hurt Solomon—

"Don't try anything," René said as Solomon moved closer to her. She tried to calculate how much of Solomon's body she could shield with her own and decided that it was not enough to take the risk. Together they twisted the rubies, and the entire left-hand side of the mantel sprung forward slightly with an audible click. Serena felt oddly betrayed, as if the Arms had been conspiring with René against her.

"That royal bastard!" Solomon gave the portrait of Charles I a glare, as if that king were somehow to blame for his son's perfidy to the Hathaways. "He might have *told* us!"

Serena ignored him, looking at René.

"I want you to open it and take out all the papers that you see in there and burn them. I would like to blindfold you, but I do not have time, so let me warn you now: if you try to keep any back or leave any in there, I will see, and he will die. It is as simple as that."

She swung open the front of the carving. The back of the carving was covered in clockwork, and a shelf divided the interior into two compartments. The bottom compartment was empty. The top one held a mass of papers. She took them out, careful not to let any fall. "Why the devil would I try to keep any back—"

And then she saw the map. Even in the semi-dark she recognized that bit of Cornish coastline. Ravenscroft. "My *father*? My father was helping you?" She gaped. "I suppose that explains his sudden interest in me—"

There was a knock on the door. "Sol?" Elijah's voice asked. René turned white, but his hand did not shake. He raised his eyebrows meaningfully. Solomon didn't answer. In the listening silence Serena became aware that what she had thought was a roaring in her ears really *was* people cheering in the room below. She felt dimly that she ought to wonder why.

"Sol, I heard Lady Serena's voice, I know you're in there."

Solomon looked at René, who nodded, very slowly.

"That you, Elijah?"

Serena was amazed at how natural his voice sounded.

"Can I come in?" Elijah asked.

"The devil you can, Li. Serena and I are a trifle occupied at present and we wish you at Jericho."

When had he learned to lie so well?

Elijah laughed. "To Jericho I go, then." His footsteps retreated.

René let out his breath. "Now burn them, and I wouldn't recommend trying to throw acid at me or anything of that nature," he said softly. Serena was already moving to obey him when Solomon spoke.

"No, wait," he said.

Serena and René both stared at him.

"You might need those. If your father threatens to lock you up again. Sacreval said he couldn't shoot *you*."

Her heart almost stopped when she realized his meaning. He was offering his life in exchange for her freedom from her father's threats.

He gave her a crooked, shaky smile. He could make an offer like that, but he couldn't not look scared when he did it. Her heart swelled. "Don't be stupid," she said thickly, and opened his tinderbox.

As the last few papers crumbled into ash in Solomon's big crucible, there was a hush from downstairs and they heard, very clearly, a man yell, "—all the doors. Nobody do anything foolish. He won't escape." Booted feet strode down the corridor below them. Solomon breathed a sigh of relief. Elijah had come back with reinforcements, and sooner than Solomon had dared hope. If only he had come before Serena had burned that evidence!

He had wanted to help her against Sacreval. That was a joke. When had he done anything for Serena but be a convenient life to threaten when someone wanted to browbeat her into submission?

The marquis sagged like a puppet whose strings had been cut and let the gun fall to his side. "At least I saved *one* of my men." He reached into his jacket and pulled out a few sheets of paper. "*Sirène*, these are for you." He spoke quickly, racing against the booted feet that were starting up the stairs. "It's a marriage contract settling the Sacreval diamonds on you. Fraud is grounds for annulment in England. There is no such title as marquis du Sacreval and certainly no diamonds. There is also an affidavit swearing that the register is a forgery."

Serena's numb, blank look did not change.

"Oh, *ma petite sirène*, I would only have shot him in the leg."

Serena made a heaving sound, her shoulders relaxing with a shudder. She shut her eyes, and when she opened them her lashes were wet. "Oh, René."

"*Sirène*, it would be better if I were not taken," he said gently. She stilled.

"I won't if you don't want me to. But it will be easier this way."

"*Easier?*" She sniffled, and that little sound broke Solomon's heart.

"A trial would be painful for all of us. You would have to testify, your name would be in all the papers. And without a conviction you may not even need those documents to keep the Arms." His mouth twisted into something like a smile. "I'll try not to stain the wallpaper."

"You know I don't care about any of that," Serena said quietly. "Not even the wallpaper. Don't you?"

"I know."

"Then do it if you want to. I don't want to see you strung up and sliced open either."

"Don't look," Sacreval said, but Serena never turned her eyes away as he raised the gun to his own temple. Halfway there, he looked at Solomon.

"Elijah works for the Foreign Office, doesn't he?"

Solomon nodded.

"Tell him—" Sacreval stopped, and gave a glittering knifelike smile. "Tell him I knew all along. Tell him I was a heartless schemer who never loved him."

Solomon's eyes narrowed. "Give me that gun." René obeyed, frowning, but both he and Serena leaped forward when Solomon pointed it at his own arm.

"What the hell are you doing?" Serena hissed.

"How much are you willing to wager that Rothschild was right and Napoleon's been beaten?"

Her eyes widened, some life coming back into her face. "A great deal."

"Then England doesn't need Sacreval," Solomon said. "Enough people have died. You know damn well they aren't guarding *all* the doors. If I'm wounded, it'll distract Elijah long enough for you to get him out the laundry tunnel."

Serena stared at him, then picked up the knife from his worktable. "Is it clean?" She was so pale that he was reminded of their first meeting, how her skin had looked bluish-white, like arsenic. Only the lamplight gave her any color. But her hand was perfectly steady.

"Of course."

"Kneel down."

There was no time to ask why. He did it.

"Whatever you do, hold still."

He felt her slice lightly along the top of his head. Almost instantly blood began pouring down his forehead. He stood, and she hooked a finger of her left hand into his cravat, pulled him forward, and kissed him, hard. Absolutely without expression, she licked a drop of blood off her lip and handed him the knife. "Thank you," she said.

The booted feet were almost to the door. She picked up the gun and fired it straight into the wall. Solomon wiped the blood out of his eyes with his sleeve and by the time he looked up, the door to Serena's room was swinging shut. They'd have to wait in her room until Elijah and his men were out of the hallway, then get out without being heard and go down the back stairs to the kitchen.

Elijah's footsteps rang in the corridor. "We're coming in!"

"Wait!" Solomon called weakly. "I'm coming." Serena wouldn't be pleased if he let Elijah shoot her lock off.

"Solomon! Are you shot?"

"I'm fine," he mumbled. "I just—" Lying to Elijah was tricky, but it could be done. He concentrated very hard on his fear that the marquis would be caught and Serena accused of aiding him.

He knocked the bottle of Madeira onto the floor on his way to the door. Glass shattered across the floor—that might slow them down if they tried to go for the connecting door. "Sorry," he called. "Just a little woozy—" He did feel a little light-headed, actually. He turned the key in the lock and then, as Elijah pushed the door open, he collapsed onto the floor with an impressive thud. His elbow jarred painfully.

"Solomon!" Elijah cried wildly, rushing into the room followed by two of his fellow agents. They immediately made for the connecting door. One of them trod on Solomon's hand in his haste, and he gave a completely sincere groan of pain.

"Have a care, will you?" Elijah said sharply, heaving Solomon up.

"Wait, not that way," Solomon said weakly, and to his relief they stopped. He tried to sit up as noisily as possible, listening for Serena's door opening from the next room. Was that it? Elijah started to frantically feel Solomon's scalp. Solomon knocked his hand away under pretext of trying to wipe the blood away from his eyes with a supposedly shaky arm. "Which way did he go, Sol?" Elijah demanded. "He won't make it to the gallows, I swear. I'll kill him myself for this."

"'Vengeance is mine, sayeth the Lord.'" Solomon gave Elijah a small smile. "I'll be all right. It's Serena I'm worried about. He took her with him while you were—" He jerked his head in the direction of the door to the hallway. It really did hurt, and he winced. Elijah bit his lip, and with his brother thus distracted by murderous thoughts, Solomon said, "He said—there are a lot of people in the dining room who could get hurt." *The best lie is a half-truth.*

Elijah's lips thinned. "If he thinks he can take her out the public rooms and get away with it, he'll find his mistake. Be careful, gentlemen. If you let the lady get hurt, we'll all have to answer to his lordship her father. Tread carefully and don't hesitate to shoot if you see an opportunity." The agents nodded and disappeared out the door and, hopefully, down the main stairs.

Solomon closed his eyes in silent prayer.

"Steady on, Sol," Elijah said softly. "Scalp wounds always look worse than they are. Let me get you to the bed."

"Shouldn't you be chasing after Sacreval? He's got Serena."

"He's unlikely to get far. We're watching all the doors. I'll go as soon as I've seen to you. Now let me get you to the bed."

Solomon got to his feet, shaking his head. "I'll stain the sheets. Just get me some water. I'd say Madeira, but it's soaking into the floorboards as we speak." He hoped Serena wouldn't mind too much.

"Let's start with the water, shall we?"

"There are some clean rags on my worktable."

"Perfect. Sit on the bench by the lamp."

Elijah brought the pitcher over to the table, wet a rag, and gently dabbed at Solomon's cut. It stung, and Solomon drew in a hissing breath and jerked his head away.

"Solomon, you have to let me look at it."

"It's nothing." But he could only resist for so long, and finally he sat still and let Elijah lift the lamp to examine his head. Elijah froze. Solomon braced himself.

"This isn't a bullet wound," Elijah said in a hard voice.

They couldn't ask the kitchen to bear the burden of treason with them, so when they went through the kitchen door, Serena was in front of René like a shield. This was the part with the most likelihood of going wrong. His arm was around her throat and he had the cool butt of the pistol pressed against her temple. "Open the tunnel," René said.

There was absolute silence. This late, the only people working were Antoine, marinating meat for tomorrow's dinner, and two kitchen boys readying food for breakfast. Frozen in horror, they stared at the pair.

"Open the tunnel or she dies," René said. Antoine reached for his knife.

"Please, Antoine," Serena said. "Just let him go." It worked. Antoine hurried across the floor to the trapdoor and tugged on the iron ring. René pushed her gently across the kitchen.

"You son of a bitch," Antoine said viciously, all traces of his French accent gone. "You'll never get out of here alive."

"Then neither will she," René said, his voice strung taut. Serena shuddered. It was probably true, if not for the reasons Antoine thought.

The chef spat on the ground at their feet, but he stepped aside and left the way to the tunnel open. Hatred twisted his face. Serena, remembering the hours he and René had spent together, wanted to explain to him that it was all right, that it wasn't real. But that was impossible. She let René drag her down the stairs.

"If I hear anyone else come through this door, I will shoot her on the spot," René told them. "If you can hold them off long enough, though, I'll let her go safe and sound. Now close it and go about your business."

And the door closed over them, sealing the tunnel in darkness. René let her go, and they raced down the tunnel. When they got to the other end that came out at the laundry, they crouched down and listened.

Serena's heart sank. The laundry should have been empty at this hour, but the distinct sounds of sex came from above them: a faint rhythmic thumping and the occasional moan. Someone was using the laundry for illicit dalliance. She cursed.

"We'll give them two minutes to finish and go away," René said quietly. "Then we try to brazen it out, like we did back there. Once we get out, I can scale the fence behind the laundry." He sounded unnaturally calm.

Serena wondered how many times in the course of his career he had waited in darkness for the sounds of someone coming to arrest him. "Where will you go from there? What if they're watching the street?"

"I don't think I should tell you," René said. "It will be easier for you to lie that way. I don't think they'll be watching the street. They may be watching the courtyard. I shall have to take my chances. They are better than they were a few minutes ago, *sirène*. Thank you."

They settled down next to each other in the dark, counting the seconds and trying to ignore the sounds from above. Serena tried to think of what she would do if she were escaping over the back wall. She thought that if he could be quiet, René's chances of getting out of the courtyard unseen were good—the back door to the laundry came out in a narrow strip of yard enclosed on two sides by fence and shielded from view of most of the rest of the yard. There couldn't be many of the Foreign Office agents, and if they didn't know about the tunnel, there was no reason to put someone anywhere he might see René. In his place, once out, she would probably cross the alley, cut through some back gardens, come out in another street, and look for a hackney working late.

She shivered, wondering how many of the agents would know René by sight. If there weren't any watching the street—if they were watching the doors from the inside—it would probably be all right. But the thought of René walking across even that narrow strip of courtyard with nothing to hide or shield him was terrifying.

These were the last two minutes she might ever spend with him. She wanted suddenly to have one last ordinary, friendly conversation. "How did you know the earrings opened the fireplace?"

He chuckled. "The fireplace opens in two different ways. It *was* made by Charles the First's own clockmaker. You saw when we opened it—there's a clockwork timing mechanism of some sort with an unknown delay. You can open it once just by twisting Diana's hand halfway round, as I discovered. At that moment I happened to be in a hurry to hide those papers where you wouldn't find them. I was hasty. But once I'd hidden those papers in there and closed it, it refused to open that way again. I had given them up for lost when I saw some Stuart letters on display in an old *bibliothèque* in Paris. In one, Charles the Second wrote to his brother from Scotland, mysteriously assuring him that he had got the ruby earrings from their mother and would recapture his hidden treasure from the Rose and Thistle as soon as he reached London. In the other he said he'd given the earrings away to a fellow named Hathaway, in Shropshire."

"Was there a hidden treasure?" Serena asked.

"Not when I opened it. It had been two hundred years. Anyone could have found it in the meantime." He paused. "I am so sorry, *sirène*," he said, speaking fast. "I never wanted to use the marriage lines. But when I saw you had given my room to a Hathaway from Shropshire, I panicked. For all I knew, he had the earrings and the full secret of their use. If you had found those papers and turned your father in, my entire web of informants would have been useless. Everything went through Ravenscroft."

"It's all right." It wasn't, really. He had hurt her so much. He hadn't wanted to, but he had been willing to. And she would have been willing to kill him for the Arms. She didn't want to think about it.

She did have one question, though, that she had to know the answer to. "My father didn't—didn't send you to me, did he? When you came to me and asked me to be your partner?" She didn't know what she wanted to hear—yes, her father had wanted to save her and she owed him everything? Or no, the Arms was still hers and her father had never cared for a moment?

"*Non, ma petite sirène*," he said gently. "I found you all on my own. Your father never had a say in anything I did. He took the money he needed and we used his coastline and that was all."

Serena nodded. It was as good an answer as any, she decided. And it meant that her father's threat of Bedlam would disappear now the war was over. It meant she would probably never see him again. It was cold in the tunnel. She leaned her head on René's shoulder.

He went still for a moment, surprised, but then he put his arm around her shoulders. "You know how I finally figured out how the earrings worked?" he asked her, a teasing note in his voice.

She shook her head.

"When you recited that charming bit of verse to me, my first night back," he told her. "As soon as I heard 'place these jewels among Phoebe's sweet hair' and 'shine in the sun,' I remembered the missing rubies in the carving."

Serena could have kicked herself.

"If I don't get out of here, will you send some money to my mother? Elijah knows where."

"Of course," she promised. "But you'll get out. Do you want me to give Elijah a message?"

"No. If he wants me, he knows where to find me."

The thumping from above stopped abruptly. They both froze, listening. Serena thought about a minute and a half had passed. The couple had thirty seconds for pillow talk. Luckily, they didn't bother with it at all. Someone laughed, footsteps shifted, and a few seconds later the door banged shut. There was silence.

"It is time, *sirène*," René said. They stood. "How do you want to play your end of things?"

Serena had been thinking about this. "They can't suspect I was involved. You'll have to knock me out."

René cursed. "Take your stockings off. I'll bind and gag you. I should have been thinking of it all this time, instead of talking."

"I'm glad we talked, and there's no time." As she said it, they both heard yelling from the kitchen.

"Take off your stockings," René repeated.

Serena grabbed the lever that controlled the trapdoor from that end and pulled on it. Slowly, with a grinding of gears, the door swung open. Dim light and the scent of lye filled the tunnel.

Then she saw, as if in answer, a widening ray of light at the other end of the tunnel. The yelling was suddenly much louder.

"Don't go down there," Antoine shouted frantically. "Please! He'll kill her!"

Sophy appeared in the doorway of Solomon's room. "Is Serena all right—ohhh!" A hand flew up to cover her mouth when she saw the blood caked on Solomon's forehead. "What happened?"

"I'm fine, Sophy," he said reassuringly. "Here, why don't you come help me get cleaned up so my brother can go chasing after Sacreval?" He smiled at Elijah, ignoring the fury in his brother's eyes.

Elijah could hardly accuse him of treason in front of Sophy. His look promised a reckoning, however. "Yes, that would be very helpful, Sophy."

Sophy shut the door behind Elijah and hastened to Solomon's side. "Did Sacreval do that?" she asked bitterly, pointing to his wound.

"No," he whispered, gesturing her to come closer. "Listen, Sophy—Sacreval gave Serena papers that will give her the Arms back. She's taking him out the laundry tunnel right now. You've got to keep them from finding him."

Her eyes widened. She pushed her glasses up her nose decisively and was halfway to the door when a thought struck him.

"Sophy!"

She came back.

"My brother suspects what's going on. He may realize what I've told you and be waiting outside to follow you. If he is, you must lead him on a wild goose chase."

She nodded grimly. "Just leave it to me." She went and opened the door partway, poking her head out into the corridor and glancing about. Then she slipped out the door and shut it softly behind her.

After that, there wasn't really anything useful to do but wait. Solomon took up the rag and began washing the blood out of his hair. The ticking of the clock filled the room. They were still cheering downstairs. It must be for Wellington's victory; it must.

He should have let Sacreval blow his own brains out. He should never have let Serena out of his sight.

Solomon had never felt so helpless in his life. But there was nothing more he could do without risking making things much, much worse. He picked the broken pieces of his bottle of Madeira off the floor, piling them into a bowl.

Someone kicked the door open. Solomon sprang to his feet. The Foreign Office agents were entering the room, and one of them bore a lifeless Serena in his arms.

Chapter 25

Solomon leaned on his worktable for support as the world spun around him. He watched them lay Serena on the bed. There didn't seem to be any blood. Could he see her breathing, or was that just his light-headedness? No, she was definitely breathing, and Solomon could move his eyes again.

He seized one of the agents by his shirt and had him up against the wall before he knew what he was about. "What have you done to her? If you've hurt her, you bastard—"

Serena's voice came weakly from the bed. "Solomon?"

He turned. She was watching him, an amused light in her eyes. He didn't move. "I'm right here," he said. "What did they do to you?"

Her lips curved. "I imagine they carried me upstairs after René knocked me out."

"Oh." He let out a breath and let go of the agent's shirtfront. "Er, sorry. And did they catch him?"

Elijah raced into the room in time to hear this last question. He stood stock-still in the doorway and stared at his fellow agents. Serena swung herself into a sitting position on the edge of the bed.

"No," said the man Solomon had assaulted, brushing himself off with a dirty look in his direction. "Forced her ladyship to take him out a secret tunnel, and then he knocked her cold and took off just ahead of us, like. Went over the wall." The two agents were the only people in the room who were not secretly relieved, Solomon thought.

Elijah closed his eyes for a moment, then opened them. "It

doesn't matter. We can still send men after him to recover him before he ships for France."

"I must say I am not overly impressed with Foreign Office initiative," Serena commented dryly. A livid bruise was forming on her jaw and her lower lip was swelling. "You set up an elaborate operation to capture a man who lives in an inn with which he is intimately familiar, and you don't trouble to discover that there's a tunnel to the laundry? One of my employees might have been injured."

"Fortunate that no one was injured but the two of you, then," Elijah said blandly.

Serena smiled at him. "Very."

"Well," Solomon said, ignoring Elijah's gimlet eye, "all that terror has left me with a bit of an appetite. Do you think we might go down for a late supper?"

"Yes," Serena said. "If you have no further use for us, I should like to get dressed and verify that your men have not unduly terrified my guests."

"Don't think much could dampen the mood tonight," one of the agents said, grinning.

Solomon waited with bated breath. Had he and Serena won their gamble?

For the first time, Elijah smiled. "Bonaparte's been decisively defeated. Rothschild was right."

The cheering turned into a buzz of speculation when they walked into the taproom and everyone saw Serena's bruised jaw. She climbed onto a bench.

"Silence, everyone," she said in a carrying voice. "I am pleased to announce that my erstwhile business partner, the marquis du Sacreval, is no longer on the premises. No one but Mr. Hathaway and myself have been injured in his daring escape. It is to be hoped that the proper authorities can be relied upon to halt him in his headlong flight to the Continent. In celebration of the decisive victory of His Majesty's forces, champagne is on the house!"

Solomon and Serena were slumped on their stools, devouring a loaf of bread, when Lord Smollett walked in. "My, my," he roared. "It's a regular gin shop in here."

Serena tried to draw herself up coolly and smile. Solomon could see her face trying to fall into its accustomed sardonic lines for several moments before she gave up and laughed exhaustedly.

Smollett looked rather puzzled, but he quickly recovered himself and gave Solomon a conspiratorial wink. "Women, you know. Apt to be hysterical."

"Oh, go to hell," Solomon said.

Serena stood up. "Lord Smollett. Lovely to see you." She shook her head. "Christ. I can't believe I wasted so many years giving a damn what you thought of me. Do you want to know something? I don't regret having been your mistress. Know why?"

Lord Smollett patted his hair. "Don't think *any* of my lights-o'-love have had much to complain of."

"It was a small price to pay to be utterly ineligible ever to be your wife," she told him. "Now that *would* have been a fate worse than death."

Solomon thought he would treasure the look of stunned outrage on Smollett's face for the rest of his life. His lordship harrumphed, turned round, and marched straight to the bar. "A large ale, please, and make it snappy."

Serena sat down. "'Forsake the foolish and live,' right? What I don't understand is why I could never do it before."

"I think it's one of those things that works better with two people."

Solomon was trying to examine his cut in the mirror when a voice came from behind him. "Mr. Hathaway?"

Damn. He must have left the door open. He turned around

to see a small, middle-aged man with a nasty expression on his aquiline features.

"Yes?"

The man sneered. "Should have known I'd find you in front of a mirror. Man-milliner."

"I beg your pardon!"

"Oh, don't play the shocked parson's son with me, Hathaway. We don't pay you to have delicate sensibilities."

The penny dropped. Keeping a firm rein on his temper, Solomon began, "Perhaps you are seeking my—"

"I am seeking to know how you came to let Sacreval escape. You sodomites do stick together, don't you?"

Solomon, stunned into speechlessness, saw his brother standing in the doorway.

"Don't speak to my brother like that, Varney," Elijah said coldly.

"Don't you think that's my line, Li?" Solomon asked. His heart was racing with fury, but he managed to smile politely at his brother's Foreign Office superior. "Don't speak to my brother like that, Varney."

Varney looked from one to the other of them in fascination. "Oh yes, the twin brother. Does he take after you in that respect, too?"

"None of your damn business!" Solomon said hotly.

"Sol, stop," Elijah said harshly.

Solomon turned to him in surprise and almost missed Varney's gleaming, sharp-toothed smile.

"Public morality must be the concern of every citizen," Varney said. "I imagine that is why the pillory is such a popular spectacle."

Solomon had a sudden pleasing vision of his hands round Varney's neck while the man choked and turned purple.

"I am so glad to hear you say so," Serena said from the doorway, breaking through Solomon's anger. "Perhaps, as a concerned citizen, you can offer me some advice on a rather delicate matter."

Varney's sharklike grin widened. "At your service, Siren."

Solomon thought murderous thoughts, but he waited, because Serena could hold her own against this toad.

She smiled back and came to stand beside Solomon. "I've been thinking of publishing my memoirs."

Varney's grin disappeared.

"But you know," she continued blithely, "there are a few passages I hesitate to include, for fear they will corrupt the impressionable reader. You have sons. Tell me, do you think they would be overly influenced by the frank description of the perversions of certain men of rank?"

Varney flushed and turned away with an impotent snarl. "Tell me about Sacreval, Hathaway."

"Certainly, my lord," Elijah said politely. "He escaped through a secret tunnel that runs from the kitchen to the laundry. The intelligence I was given had not included mention of this tunnel, so I was unable to have it properly guarded. None of the livery stables in the area would admit to having provided Sacreval with a horse. I have posted scouts on all the major roads leading out of the city and sent men ahead to watch the Cornish coast. He did not get more than a quarter-hour's start of us. I still have hope of bringing him in before he sets sail."

Varney swore. "You know there's no hope of catching him. We can't blockade all of Cornwall. I take it you've had no luck discovering where his couriers land?"

Solomon tried not to look at Serena and not to catch Elijah's eye.

"None, I'm afraid," Elijah confirmed.

Varney gnawed on the inside of his cheek. "This was bungled badly."

Elijah drew himself up. "I assure you that all of us did our best, my lord. The fault was with our information. I had planned to speak to you as soon as possible about the matter. The slip could well have cost Lady Serena, who was Sacreval's unfortunate hostage, her life. We are all of us very lucky that she escaped with merely a bruise."

"Very lucky," Varney said with savage irony.

Serena's lips twitched.

"Well, keep me informed. I suppose with Boney finally whipped, the Frog can't do much harm at any rate." With another seething glance round the room, Varney saw himself out.

Solomon sighed in relief.

"I'm very sorry you had to be subjected to that," Elijah said stiffly.

Solomon stared at him. "*You're* apologizing to *me?*"

Elijah's lips tightened. "I know how unpleasant you must find such insinuations."

Solomon colored a little. "I only wish that our being twins could also convince people I was dashing and enigmatic."

Elijah looked away, and Solomon wondered what he had said wrong now. "I say, Lady Serena—if I ask you, will you tell me your dirt on Varney?"

Serena glanced sideways at Solomon. "I think your brother might be too squeamish to know."

He sighed. "I know you're fine and I'm being foolish, but when I think about you all alone finding out things about Varney that are too lurid to be published—"

"But I wasn't alone," Serena said innocently.

Solomon gave up. "Well, I do love watching you put the fear of God into someone."

"I never put the fear of God into anyone. I put the fear of me into them."

"Mmm," he agreed, lowering his voice. "And you do *such* a good job."

Elijah looked away. Solomon felt guilty, suddenly, flirting with Serena when Elijah's lover could already be captured or dead, for all they knew. "Sacreval will be all right," he said.

Elijah gave him a glance that could have sliced him in half. "None of us has the right to hope for that."

"That isn't stopping me."

"So I see. Interestingly neat pistol graze you've got there. Looks almost like it was made by a knife."

He couldn't lie to Elijah. "He was about to splatter his brains all over the wall"—Elijah sucked in his breath—"and he asked me to tell you not to feel guilty when he was dead. What was I supposed to do?"

Elijah's face contorted unpleasantly. "He was manipulating you, you idiot."

"He wasn't manipulating me. He said—"

"I don't want to hear what he said. I thought you didn't approve of our—connection."

Solomon flushed. "It's not that I don't approve, exactly—only I hate to see you exposing yourself to the insults of men like Varney." Serena drew in a sharp breath, but he couldn't take his eyes off Elijah. "When he said that about the pillory, Li—and that's not the worst of it. You could be—"

"Hanged," Elijah finished coldly.

Solomon shuddered.

"So I should arrange my life to please Varney now?" Elijah demanded. "I prefer to leave that sort of toadying to you. You've always been the dull, conventional one."

The blood drained from Solomon's face. "Elijah—"

"You just don't approve."

"How can you say that when I saved your lover's life?"

Elijah's eyes narrowed. "You want me to *thank* you for making me responsible for the escape of one of Napoleon's best agents?"

"The war is over, Elijah."

"You didn't know that. Sol, you let me think he *shot* you!"

"It was the only way I could think of to distract you."

"So much for all your wondering whether I really care about you. You damned hypocrite. I don't think I've ever hated anyone as much as I hated René in that moment."

Solomon stared at him.

"You abused my trust to make me betray my office," Elijah said coldly. "And before you chime in with 'you let me think you were dead for a year and a half'—I *know*. But I did it for my country—I did it so that *you*, so that our family would be safe from Napoleon. And you did this—why? To save Bonaparte's lackey because you thought I loved him?"

"Don't you?"

"You've made a mockery of both our sacrifices," Elijah told him. "What was it Varney said? That 'we sodomites stick together'? Do you expect me to thank you for proving him right?" He turned on his heel and stalked out.

Solomon ran out after him, but Elijah's door was already locked and he didn't answer when Solomon pounded on it.

Serena folded her arms and rested her cheek on the cool page of her account book, giving herself up to anxious thoughts. It was past two in the morning. She couldn't sleep, and she couldn't concentrate long enough to add a single set of figures.

She would have killed René for the Arms, but she had offered to trade it for Solomon. The crisis was over now: Solomon was safe, the Arms was hers, René would not be executed. But she could not feel relieved.

She would have traded anything to save Solomon—air and sunlight and freedom. She would have traded her life. Next time he told her he wouldn't touch her unless she begged, she would do it. And every time she thought that might be all right, something happened to remind her of who she was and who he was. There would always be something. What had he said? *I hate to see you exposing yourself to the insults of men like Varney.* She had exposed herself to so many insults.

Serena thought back to six years ago in her father's study, begging him on her knees not to fire Harry. She had been so afraid and so guilty. Harry's four-year-old sister might not have enough to eat without his wages. Her father had looked at her with contempt and reminded her what she owed her position. He had reminded her that she would have to marry soon and that no one wanted soiled goods, not even bought titles like the Braithwaites, so she had better stop whining and forget this ever happened.

Eventually she had got off her knees. Their voices had risen, Serena's getting more and more hysterical until she was nearly shrieking through her sobs. Her father had backed her against the wall, his pointing finger only an inch or two from her face. She had started to be really afraid when a maid had knocked on the door. Serena had been glad for the interruption, even though the maid had borne a message from Lady Blackthorne that all the shouting was making her ill.

Perhaps it had been foolish to leave. If she had known it would cost Harry his life, she certainly wouldn't have done it. But even after she had realized that there would be no virtuously poor married life with Harry, she hadn't been able to bring herself to go back.

She had never been sorry she'd chosen to become a whore instead. Because no matter how bad it got, she had known it could have been worse. She could have been at home. She could have been married to one of the men who bedded her.

She had never been sorry until now, when she wanted a parson's son more than anything in the world.

Perhaps at the moment he was truly willing to overlook her past for the sake of his lust—and, she would admit, genuine affection. Perhaps he thought—and there was nothing so naive

Solomon mightn't think it—that people would forget, in time. But Serena knew better.

He would tire of her. Hell, she was tired of herself half the time. He would wake up and find he wanted a sunny-tempered girl who had never threatened to have anyone killed. He would tire of hearing her name bandied about; he would wish her respectable; he would stop trying to talk her into wearing scarlet.

Serena had not worn a low-necked gown since she bought the Arms. But now, with trembling hands, she ripped the linen chemisette out of her dress before it smothered her. She stared down at the tops of her breasts, at the second birthmark no one had seen in years—no one but Solomon. He'd seen everything, it seemed, and yet he stubbornly refused to see how impossible it all was.

She heard his footsteps in the hall before he knocked. It had a kind of inevitability to it. "Come in, Solomon."

The door opened slowly. She remembered the first time he had come through that door, only two weeks ago, and how her heart had jumped in her chest at the sight of him. Now it pounded, rhythmically, like a headache.

"Serena, are you all right?"

"Yes," she said wearily. "What do you want?" *He'll tire of you if you keep treating him like this, he'll tire of you, he'll tire of you, he'll tire of you—*

"What's wrong?" He very carefully did not look at her torn neckline.

She clutched the arms of her chair so she wouldn't go to him. She wanted to press her ear against his naked chest and hear that his heart was still beating. "Nothing. I was just tired of all the carousing. I was just—tired."

His eyes searched her face, but after all, it was a plausible enough lie. He didn't push her. Instead, he came over and smoothed back her hair. She leaned into his touch like a dog. "It was a crazy night, wasn't it?" he said. "But thank God the war's over."

He sounded so happy about that. Serena supposed she was glad. She wished she were gladder, though. War was a brutish thing, but it had always seemed so far away, something that concerned other people. Perhaps if she hadn't been so selfish, so wrapped up in herself and her own safety, she would have turned in René years ago and Solomon wouldn't have almost been shot tonight.

"We're leaving Wednesday morning to take the earrings back to Shropshire," he said. "Will you come and meet my family?"

Serena's jaw dropped. "You do realize that's the worst idea you've ever had, don't you?"

He pursed his lips and crossed his arms, the picture of stubbornness. "I've had much worse."

"Solomon, you can't bring your mistress into your mother's house. You can't let her sit down to dinner with your sister."

"You're not my mistress."

"So soon they forget."

Solomon took a step closer and tilted her chin up so that she could not keep her eyes averted without seeming afraid. He knew her too damn well. His fingers were warm on her chin. She met his gaze defiantly. "You're not my mistress," he said with finality. "And my mother will like you. So will Susannah."

He didn't say anything about his father, she noticed. She wanted to beg him to change his mind, to spare her this final humiliation. But she couldn't. At this point she doubted she could refuse him anything.

So she would do this last thing for him. She would go to meet his family, and when he saw how they despised her, when he saw how he had tainted his pure, sweet sister and his respectable mother, when he realized at last how impossible it was for her to ever be anything *but* his mistress—then she would not refuse him his freedom.

Chapter 26

"You're going where?" Sophy asked.

Serena felt herself flushing. "Mr. Hathaway asked me to—he invited me to meet his family."

Sophy's eyebrows flew upward, but she only said, "I hope you have a lovely time."

Serena rubbed at her forehead. "Oh, don't be ridiculous, Sophy, it's going to be awful. But it's only for a few days, and I know you'll do a fine job of managing things while I'm gone."

"Thank you." But Sophy looked a little uncertain.

Serena felt suddenly selfish. "I'm sorry, I know it's a lot to ask—I'll pay you extra, of course."

Sophy's dark eyes lit with amusement. "So I'd assumed."

"And—Mr. Hathaway told me you kept his brother away from the tunnel today. I—thank you."

Sophy nodded. "This is my home, too. Of course I wanted to do my part."

She didn't sound resentful, but guilt smote Serena anyway—guilt, and regret. "I—I'm sorry," she said. "You've been here from the beginning. I don't know why we—that is—I wish we were better friends."

Sophy shrugged. "You don't have to be sorry. You came back and got me from Mme Deveraux's when you started the place up. You protected me here. You protect us all. That's enough."

"Yes, but—" She did not know how to say the truth, one she had forgotten until now; that she had wanted to be friends at first and hadn't known how. She had been afraid Sophy wouldn't like her. "I might have made more of an effort."

"You were busy. You and monseigneur were thick as thieves. It didn't bother me."

"I suppose we were," Serena said slowly. "It was easy to be friends with René. He never demanded confidences." She'd shown him what she wanted him to see, too: a girl who was frightened but game, who needed his help but could pull her own weight. He'd probably seen more than that, but he'd kept his mouth shut about it. No one had ever demanded confidences of her until Solomon.

Sophy laughed. "Are you saying I'm nosy?" she teased.

Serena smiled with an effort. "I only meant I was afraid." Christ, this was difficult, like wading through treacle filled with shoals of stinging jellyfish. But it had been too long coming already. And Sophy was listening. She was being friendly.

The Arms was going to be Serena's forever now. She had to begin as she meant to go on. "I meant that I've never—women don't like me. I don't know how to—I. Damn."

Sophy frowned, her face suddenly suffused with pity. *No,* Serena decided, *I won't call it pity.* With compassion, then. "I like you fine, Serena."

Tears pricked at Serena's eyes. She blinked, embarrassed. "Perhaps in future—"

Sophy's eyes crinkled warmly. "It's never too late. At least, not if you come back from Shropshire."

"Of course I'm coming back," she said, startled.

Sophy looked unconvinced.

"I'm coming back," Serena repeated. It was Solomon who likely wouldn't be coming back. She swallowed. Then a thought struck her, such an obvious one that she was ashamed she'd never thought of it before. "Would you be interested in part ownership?"

Sophy's mouth dropped open. "Part—*ownership?*"

"Of the Arms. René's gone, and it's too much work for one person to manage this place."

Sophy blinked. "I—" She tilted her head and thought. "Antoine ought to have a share, too," she said tentatively.

Serena considered it. It felt frightening. It meant she wouldn't be in absolute control anymore. But it meant shared risk, too. It meant, maybe, friends. "That seems fair."

A smile split Sophy's face. "I'd love to. I've got some money put by. Not much, but—"

Serena grinned and held out her hand. "We'll discuss terms when I get back." Sophy shook it, and then, impulsively, hugged her. Serena stiffened.

Sophy let go. "If we're going to be friends, you'll have to get used to it," she said heartlessly, and shut the door behind her with a cheerful bang.

No matter what happened in Shropshire, Serena would have this. It made her feel a little less sick.

I really am going to be sick, Serena thought as the coach jolted and swayed to a stop in the center of town.

"Corfield!" the driver announced.

Serena leaned back against the squabs, closed her eyes, and fought down her nausea and panic as the other passengers clambered out of the coach.

"Are you all right, m'lady?" Becky, the maid she'd chosen to play propriety, asked for the hundredth time. Serena didn't answer for fear of snapping at her.

Abruptly a flood of cursing met her ears. "Some rum son of a bitch has cut away the luggage!"

She allowed herself a small smile of satisfaction. Solomon's head poked back into the coach. "However did you contrive to keep our luggage from being taken with everyone else's?"

She felt her smile spread a little. "Why do you think I tied Ravenshaw Arms handkerchiefs so tightly to the handles? This coach is Tiny Jack Harris's favorite target."

Solomon shook his head admiringly. "You'd better come along before the rest of the passengers stone us."

The rest of the passengers were grumbling suspiciously as

Serena stepped out of the coach and blinked in the low evening sun. But she quickly saw that that wasn't the only reason they were the focus of attention. From every shop, people were running out the door to point at them. A girl of perhaps fourteen rushed out of the milliner's shop and threw herself on Solomon.

"You're alive!" she shrieked.

Solomon disentangled himself and laughed. "I'm Solomon, Peg."

Peg flushed furiously, turned, and primly held out her hand to Elijah, who shook it.

"I'm glad to see you, too, brat," he said with a grin. "Is choir practice still on Thursday evenings?"

She nodded vigorously. "*Nothing* ever changes around here. Are you going to the church then?"

Elijah nodded.

"I'll tell them you're coming," she said, and raced off, pigtails flying.

They were only halfway to the church when they met a small whirlwind of Hathaways coming in the other direction.

Elijah dropped his trunk just in time to catch a tall, plump young lady with honey-colored hair who ran toward him screaming "Elijah Elijah Elijah!" But not far behind were Solomon's parents, both red-faced but not slacking their pace in the slightest.

"Susannah Susannah Susannah," Elijah said, kissing the girl and setting her aside. Lady Lydia looked into his face for a moment, mouth trembling, before she buried her face in his waistcoat and squeezed him tightly. His arms went around her, too, and his face dropped to her shoulder. They stood like that for a minute, and then Lady Lydia pulled away.

"Here, let me take a look at you. Oh!" she scolded, "as if that coat wasn't bad enough when you left! People will think you were raised in a barn!" and she started sobbing.

"Now, now, Lydia," Mr. Hathaway said in a rather choked

voice, throwing an arm around his wife's shoulders and shaking Elijah's hand manfully. "Don't embarrass the boy."

Indeed, Elijah was flushing deeply and fumbling at the handkerchief on the handle of his trunk. It was nice to know that when the occasion required it, he could blush like a true Hathaway.

Elijah handed his mother the handkerchief. "I'm so sorry, Mama. But I'm back now, and I'll make it up to you."

Tears pricked at Serena's own eyes. What would it be like to see her mother again?

"What a morbid handkerchief," Lady Lydia said, looking at Serena's painstakingly embroidered ravens. "Wherever did you get it?"

"It's part of the Ravenshaw Arms livery," Solomon said. "Here, everybody, let me introduce you to Lady Serena."

Five blond heads and five pairs of reddened Hathaway eyes turned toward Serena. She swallowed and straightened.

"Lady Serena, may I present my mother, Mrs. Hathaway; my father, Mr. Hathaway; and my sister, Susannah." So Lady Lydia didn't use her title. What would she think of Serena's? "Lady Serena was instrumental in finding the Hathaway earrings and she's saved my life on at least two separate occasions, so I'd like all of you to be very kind to her and make her feel at home."

They all stared at her. How could they not, after an introduction like that? She was painfully conscious that there was a still a fading yellowish bruise on her jaw.

And yes, she had vowed to be unfriendly and shocking and end this farce as soon as possible, but of course she was quite incapable of doing it. "How do you do, Mrs. Hathaway," she said awkwardly. Damn. She shook herself, gave a brilliant smile, and held out a hand in a charmingly frank manner that faltered only a little when she met Mrs. Hathaway's eyes. Lord Dewington had been right; this was where Solomon had got his sharp hazel gaze.

"Very well, thank you," Mrs. Hathaway said with a smile, and shook her hand firmly. "What a lovely bracelet!"

It was the gorgon bracelet Solomon had given her. She had worn it—might as well admit it—for reassurance. But she had hoped Solomon wouldn't notice. Not looking at him, she hurried into speech. "Mr. Hathaway picked it out. Isn't it darling? He's so thoughtful!" Oh Lord, she sounded like an idiot.

Mrs. Hathaway gave Solomon a sharp look, but she said, "All my children have been blessed with a great deal more taste than their mother."

Then Serena was forgotten totally as the Hathaways once again crowded around Elijah. "We told the choristers to go home," Susannah said. "Let's go to the vicarage directly. Jonas is coming for a late supper! We are all dying to hear about your shocking exploits as an agent of the Crown."

"Later, brat," Elijah said, laughing. "For now I want to hear all about how you snared such a fine catch as the shopkeeper! After his stores of peppermint candy, weren't you?" With his mother hanging on to his arm, his father's arm around his shoulder, and his sister dancing backward in front of him, Elijah proceeded to the vicarage.

Solomon was left to walk with Serena. "You needn't act like Miss Jeeves, you know. This isn't St. Andrew of the Cross. I told you, they'll like you. And they would hate Miss Jeeves." He looked ahead, his eyes shining as he watched his family.

"If I'd known you were coming, I'd have put flowers in the spare room," Mrs. Hathaway apologized. "But fortunately I aired out the sheets only Monday. I'll fetch you some water and you can freshen up before supper."

"Thank you," Serena said, and gratefully shut the door behind Mrs. Hathaway.

The spare room was airy and bright. Serena found herself longing with a dreadful homesickness for her dark, stately room at the Arms. She sank down on the quilted counterpane for a moment. The sheets smelled of lavender.

"Do you want to change for supper, m'lady?" Becky asked. Resolutely, Serena got up and let Becky help her take off her dusty traveling gown and shake out her petticoats. She donned her severest gown, and while Becky buttoned it up, she brushed out and repinned her hair. She examined herself in the mirror. Except for the bruise on her jaw, she looked prim and proper enough in her forest-green cotton and trim linen fichu. Was it only two days ago she had vowed never to wear another fichu?

Serena sighed. She could face down a pistol-wielding spy, she could banter coolly with the regent—but these people paralyzed her, with their goodness and their respectability. She could not possibly go down to supper in a low-necked gown.

She hated that she was willing to crawl for their approval, that she was trying to pretend to be something she was not. But what *was* she? A whore?

That was the problem: she didn't know what she was. She had been the owner of the Arms; she had shared her bed with no one, and been proud of it; she had been defiant and acid-tongued and fiercely alone. None of those things felt permanent anymore. She wanted to be herself—not the embittered Siren; not Lady Serena, the consummate woman of business; not the silver-eyed Thorn with her web of favors and connections. They were all part of her, but she had never really believed, until she met Solomon, that she was capable of being something more.

Everything had been stripped away until all that really seemed to belong to her was the cheap trinket around her wrist—and why was Solomon's gift the one thing about her that did not seem created by someone else?

Mrs. Hathaway brought in the water. "There's food in the kitchen if you're hungry," she told Becky. Becky, knowing a dismissal when she heard it, looked at Serena. She nodded and the maid ran off. "I brought a fresh towel, too."

Serena washed the dust off her face and hands, sharply conscious of Solomon's mother behind her.

"If you're nervous, don't be. We're all very glad to meet you."

"Thank you."

"Did you really save Solomon's life twice?"

Serena turned around and looked at her. For the first time she noticed the deep lines in Mrs. Hathaway's round face, the way they fell into place when she frowned, as if they were carved there. Had Elijah's "death" done that? Would Solomon look like that, when he was older? Would he be happy without her? "Don't worry," she said. "No one will ever dare touch him again. I promise."

Mrs. Hathaway blinked. "I, er—all right, then."

It had been a very strange thing to say. Serena gritted her teeth.

"I hope you'll be comfortable here," Solomon's mother said, and folded her in a warm embrace that smelled like lavender and kitchens. Serena had been hugged more in the last few days than she had been in the previous ten years. This time she managed not to stiffen, but before she could contemplate raising her arms, Mrs. Hathaway released her.

"And if you don't care for the books in here, there are plenty more downstairs," she said, as if that was the most important thing for a guest to know. Serena almost laughed. There were two bursting bookshelves in her room already, more than most families owned in total. She looked at the titles: the Bible (in English, Latin, Hebrew, and Greek), Hannah More, and old novels jostled for space with a host of radicals and bluestockings: Wollstonecraft, Locke, Barbauld, Montagu, Godwin, Rousseau, Bentham. Perhaps supper would not be so bad after all.

Chapter 27

The folly of hoping for a smooth meal was evident before supper even began. The young people were waiting in the parlor while Mrs. Hathaway put the finishing touches on the roast and Mr. Hathaway set the table. Jonas, Susannah's betrothed, was struggling through his first conversation with Elijah, who didn't sound particularly keen on talking about the religious habits of the French but was trying.

Susannah flopped down next to Serena on the settee. "Is it true you were Lord Byron's mistress?"

Serena stared at Susannah in dismay. How could she talk to Solomon's innocent little sister about her past? But the girl's brown eyes were shining with admiration and pleasantly scandalized curiosity. It reminded her a little of Solomon, asking about the Prince Regent's corset.

"Susannah, Lady Serena doesn't have to answer any of your questions unless she wants to," Solomon said firmly. But he had paused just long enough that, although no trace of it showed in his voice, Serena knew he was curious. She glanced at Elijah. He was leaning forward in his chair with a dare in his smile. Well, what was the harm? Serena nodded.

Susannah sighed dreamily. "Did he ever write you any poems?"

Serena couldn't help it. She smiled. "Yes."

Susannah gasped. "Do you still have them?"

Serena did, but they were utterly unfit for the girl's perusal. "I'm afraid not." Her smile widened at Susannah's melancholy sigh—and she caught Jonas's shocked, angry gaze. She froze. *That* was the harm. How had she been so stupid?

"And is it true that you beat him in a shooting match wearing nothing but—"

"Susannah, that is *enough*!" Jonas burst out, rather red in the face. "You shouldn't know of such things!"

"Lady Serena knows of such things," Susannah pointed out.

"Lady Serena is—" Jonas began hotly, but he broke off as both Solomon and Elijah half-rose from their chairs. "Whatever Lady Serena's conduct may or may not have been, I do not wish my future wife to know of such matters, and if she knows of them, she can jolly well refrain from discussing them in company."

Susannah's mouth set in a hard line. "I apologize for Jonas, Lady Serena. And certainly I did not mean to pry."

"It's quite all right," Serena said hastily. "I suppose it is not a fit story for your ears."

Susannah looked daggers at her beloved. "Jonas is not my father."

"I think you know what your father would say about your behavior," Jonas snapped, and Susannah turned bright red.

Serena tried to remember why she had agreed to come here.

"Jonas, I am very warm," Susannah said in freezing accents. "Will you take a turn with me in the garden?"

"Certainly, my dear," Jonas said, equally coldly. He offered her his arm with a stiff bow.

Soon everyone in the room could hear the shouts (Jonas's) and low angry murmurs (Susannah's) coming from outside. Elijah got up and shut the window, but Serena still heard, at intervals, "most notorious courtesan in England," "your hoydenish behavior," "bringing his mistress home," "Lord Byron is a profligate rake and a scoundrel," "dashed insipid verse," and "can damn well marry *him* then!"

"He's a little prig, isn't he?" said Elijah. Solomon nodded resignedly.

It had already begun, just as she had known it would, as she had *warned* Solomon that it would. Her presence, like the apple of discord, was blighting Susannah's future and tainting Solomon's happy home. Why had he insisted she come?

Abruptly, Solomon stood and went to the small harpsichord by the hearth. He began banging out some old folk tune, unnecessarily loudly, and singing the words in a light baritone.

The shouts from the garden became indistinct and almost inaudible. Serena glanced at Elijah, who had picked up a book and was studiously reading. She went to the piano to turn Solomon's pages.

His stained fingers—fading violet and green, today—rattled expertly over the keys. He looked up at her again as she turned his page, his eyes bright, and she couldn't help but smile and lean toward him. This was why she had come.

"Come on, sing," he urged her.

"I don't know the words," she lied. But he raised his eyebrows at her and she was almost considering coming in on the chorus when Susannah and Jonas reappeared, both flushed and with glittering eyes. Serena looked from one to the other, trying to determine if all was over.

"Lady Serena," Susannah said awkwardly, "I owe you an apology."

Serena stared.

"I never considered that my questions might make you uncomfortable," the girl forged on. "I let my curiosity get the better of me. I ought to have thought before I spoke."

"Don't worry about it," Serena said uncomfortably. "I didn't really mind."

Susannah shot a rather triumphant look at Jonas, but said only, "I hope you won't think too ill of me. We all want you to be happy here, so that you'll come back."

Serena, speechless, glanced at Solomon. He was smiling at his sister, and Susannah, seeing it, smiled back.

"I hope we may become very good friends, almost like—like sisters," the girl said daringly, and Serena felt herself flush. She didn't dare look at Jonas. Susannah, though, turned expectant eyes on her betrothed.

"May I have a word with you, Lady Serena?" Jonas asked stiffly. "I would be delighted to show you the garden."

"C—certainly," Serena said, surprised.

Solomon frowned. "Susannah, I don't know what you're planning—" he began warningly.

Serena did not think she could bear another quarrel. "I'm *going.*"

"You don't have to."

"Mr. Hathaway, *please.*"

He looked at her and sighed. "All right, but if he says anything offensive, don't hesitate to darken his daylights."

It was lovely in the vicarage garden, moonlit and sweet-smelling and warm. Nevertheless, Serena wished she had a shawl. It would give her something to do with her hands. When had she last been at such a loss?

"I owe you an apology as well, Lady Serena."

She blinked.

"I have failed in my love toward my neighbor—have been, in a word, uncharitable. Whatever your past may be, that does not excuse my behavior."

She had at least four acerbic remarks on the tip of her tongue, but she found she had no desire to say any of them. He was so young and stilted and determined. And he was Solomon's sister's betrothed. And he was *apologizing* to her. "It's quite all right," she said awkwardly. "You mustn't blame Susannah—anyone can see how innocent she is—"

Jonas laughed incredulously. "Innocent? You clearly haven't known her long. That girl is the most hoydenish, knowing, impossible—"

Serena's heart sank. "I *told* Solomon he ought not to bring me here. I told him he couldn't bring a woman with my reputation into a house with his sister. He wouldn't listen to me."

"Hathaways never do when they've got a notion in their heads," Jonas said ruefully. He paused. "I—I hope you couldn't hear our argument."

She coughed. "Very little of it."

"I owe you a double apology then. The Hathaways might be unconventional, but even Solomon wouldn't really bring his mistress home to meet his family. I should be aiding you in putting your past behind you, not judging you on the strength of it."

Serena gulped. What would he do if he knew it was true? "Don't be angry with Susannah. If you'd rather I left, I—"

He looked at her incredulously. "If *I'd* rather? I assure you, Susannah would never forgive me."

"Of course she would. I meant to say—she's your betrothed—there might be gossip—"

Jonas drew himself up. "A true Christian does not act in deference to vulgar tongues."

"Then there are very few true Christians in England."

"Alas, that is true," Jonas said, with almost a smile. "But fortunately, you are among them now."

"The last thing I ever wanted was to cause trouble between you and Susannah."

Jonas snorted. "We don't need you to do that. Tonight was nothing. At any rate, I have no desire for a wife who would allow me to persist in folly without making me aware of it. Woman is man's helpmeet, not his slave," he concluded a trifle pompously.

Tonight was—nothing? She hadn't ruined Susannah's marriage? "A very enlightened view."

His face softened. "Honestly, I couldn't live without her, even if she can be absolutely daft. So I owe you not only an apology, but my eternal gratitude for finding those cursed earrings, because without them I would have been a bachelor until Kingdom come."

"It was nothing," Serena said, embarrassed.

"I wish she would agree to become a Methodist, though."

Serena blinked.

"You wouldn't be interested in Methodism, would you?" he asked eagerly. "We have among our number sisters from your former profession. You could serve our Lord like Mary Magdalene."

"Er, no, thank you. I don't think I have much in common with Mary Magdalene, my former profession notwithstanding."

He sighed. "I suppose not. Thank you. You've been very gracious about my atrocious behavior. Surely *everything* they say about you cannot be true."

"Well," Serena conceded for very likely the first time in her life, "perhaps not."

Mrs. Hathaway poked her head into the parlor almost the moment they were back inside. "Supper! I hope you like roast beef. I'm afraid I couldn't get a fatted calf on such short notice."

Dessert was almond-pear tartlets. "These are lovely, Mrs. Hathaway," Serena told her. "And I'm not the only one who thinks so. The Prince Regent ate six when Solomon made them."

Mrs. Hathaway waved her hand dismissively. "Oh, the Prince Regent."

"He said he'd been trying to buy the recipe from Mrs. Jones for years," Serena said. Happening to glance at Solomon, she surprised an expression of sudden enlightenment on his face. What had she said?

"Well, I hope you didn't sell it to him," Mrs. Hathaway said with a sniff.

"I did not." When she looked back, the expression was gone from Solomon's face, and she was left wondering if she had imagined it.

"You know who else liked your tartlets, Mama?" Solomon asked.

"Who, dear?"

"Sir Percy Blakeney."

The effect was electric. Susannah groaned, Elijah laughed, Mr. Hathaway threw his napkin on the table in disgust, and Mrs. Hathaway sat straighter in her seat and said, "Really? You aren't bamming me, are you, Sol?"

"Would I lie about something like that?"

"The Scarlet Pimpernel," Susannah explained to Jonas. "*You* know, he saved all those French aristocrats. Mama used to have the most enormous *tendre* for him."

"Oh, I did not. I was a married woman with more important things to think about, like keeping track of a naughty set of twins."

"I seem to remember you following his exploits pretty closely in the papers," Elijah said teasingly.

"I never saw what all the fuss was about," Mr. Hathaway grumbled. "A show of aristocratic solidarity, that's all. Afraid for their own necks if the peasants in England showed a bit of sense."

"But you must admit it was dreadfully romantic! Remember when he dressed as an old hag to smuggle out the *ci-devant* comtesse de Tourney and her children?"

"Yes," the entire family chorused.

"That's one of his favorites, too," Serena said. "He tells it at least once every time I see him. And he doesn't tip."

"So my brother-in-law tells me," Mrs. Hathaway said sadly, and Mr. Hathaway looked at Serena with something almost like approval.

Solomon and Elijah had barely spoken to each other since the night of Sacreval's escape. Solomon couldn't bear to go back to their room and face Elijah's stony silence, and if he lingered in one of the downstairs rooms, his mother was bound to hear him and want to know why. The only logical alternative was knocking on Serena's door.

It was good to have a logical reason to do what he wanted to do anyway, even if the reason was that his brother wasn't speaking to him. He knocked softly.

She opened the door in her shift and wrap. It occurred to him that he'd seen her in those maybe more than he'd seen her clothed. The bruise on her jaw had mostly faded already, the skin just faintly yellowed. He reached out to run his finger along it, and she flinched back. "Solomon!" she hissed. "We're in your parents' house, for God's sake!"

"Nothing will happen," he said softly, although he wanted it to. He wondered if she would let him. He thought they could be quiet.

She saw it in his face, he could tell; her lips parted and her eyes darkened, and then she said, "Go away!" and started to shut the door.

"I'll sit on the floor," he said quickly. "Please."

"No," she said, and held the door open for him. He sat on the floor under the window, and she sat on the edge of the bed. The candlelight made her look rich and rounded, darkness between her breasts and caressing her legs where the fringe of her wrap shivered and shook when she moved.

She cleared her throat. "So, the prodigal son returns," she said, in a husky voice that told him she was looking at him, too.

He half-laughed and tried to keep his eyes on her face. "You noticed Mother made a fatted calf joke before we'd been here half a day." Of course, if Elijah was the prodigal son, then he was the dutiful, bitter one. There was a truth to that that disturbed him. "Do you mean that I envy him?"

She shook her head. Probably she hadn't, but he found he wanted to talk to her about it anyway. Even here, in the bosom of his family, it was her he turned to. "I'm ashamed of it," he said. "Nothing's ever made me happier than knowing he's back. But mixed with the joy—I'm right back to envying him for *dressing* better than me, for heaven's sake. I want to have outgrown that."

"Do you want to know a secret? I think the way he does his hair looks rather silly."

He gave her a quick, pleased smile, then looked away. "Mother will be so upset when she finds he's going back to France."

"René can never come back to England now, can he?" She sounded sad.

Solomon couldn't help feeling that Sacreval didn't deserve all this devotion. "No, and Elijah won't come back either. He'll run off to France, and I'll never see him again." He was going to be alone all over again. And this time, he would *know* that it was because Elijah chose it.

Serena made a restless, abrupt gesture. "You can't blame him for being angry with you." She sounded angry, too. She thought he was whining, probably. And he was.

"I know he's right," he said steadily. "I *am* the dull, conventional one. But I'm trying to—I'm doing my best. I don't know what more I can do."

Serena wrapped the end of one of her braids around her finger, her mouth twisting. "Solomon, you aren't the dull, conventional one."

"Aren't I?"

"No. I agree it might look that way—"

He snorted.

"—to people who aren't very bright," she finished. "You've got to stop thinking he's just the calf-bound, gilt-edged edition of you. It isn't fair to either of you. You're two different people."

"Then why—Serena, he *said* it. And that's why you don't believe I love you, isn't it? Because you think I'm just a narrow-minded parson's son who can't possibly really want you. No matter how many times I tell you I don't care—"

"It's easy for you not to care!" she snapped. "It's easy for you not to consider it—for the moment, anyway, because no one's making you. Solomon, this isn't *about* you!"

He blinked. "What's it about, then?"

She closed her eyes for a moment. "Solomon, do you remember what I said to you after we kissed in the hallway, that first time?"

His lips tightened. "You said it was boring."

"But was it boring?"

He swallowed, remembering the way she'd trembled, the way the wool of her gown and the curve of her hips had felt under his hands. How shy and sweet her lips had been under his. "No."

"I was afraid," she said, a weight and a quiver in her voice that told him she meant, *I am afraid.* "I was afraid and I said what I knew would hurt you. Elijah—when he said that to you, he wasn't angry with you. He was just angry, because he was sick of being afraid. Because now you knew his deepest, dirtiest secret, and you could do whatever you liked with it. And why shouldn't he be afraid? You didn't react well when you found out about René. And then—do you think he liked you to see the way Varney treated him? He didn't want to make even scum like that angry enough at him to want revenge. Do you think that's the figure he wanted to cut in front of his brother?"

"I don't think any the worse of him for it," Solomon protested, but he was starting to feel sick.

"Don't you?" she demanded intently. "You blamed him for it. 'I hate to see you exposing yourself to the insults of men like Varney,'" she mimicked. "As if he did it on purpose!"

Was that how it had sounded to Elijah? It wasn't what he'd meant—was it? He just wanted his brother to be safe. "Sacreval told me that in Paris, the police beat Elijah so badly he could not walk. How am I supposed to approve of something that—that—"

"My father could have me locked up on a word," Serena said flatly. "Lord Braithwaite threatened and insulted me at a *ton* party. René could pretend to be my husband and take everything I owned, and no one would stop him. Because I'm a woman and because of the life I've lived, I sleep with a bar across my door and a loaded pistol in my night table. And I'm not asking for your *approval* for any of it."

In a sudden, blinding flash everything was clear. It was as she said: Elijah and Serena weren't angry with him. They were just sick of being afraid. But they couldn't stop, because it was dangerous simply to be themselves, simply for them to live honest lives. And what he had said to Elijah was, *If you stopped being yourself, you would be safe.* No one had ever said that to Solomon, because it was already safe to be him. No wonder Elijah was angry.

And no wonder Serena was angry. He remembered what she'd said outside St. Andrew of the Cross: *You think that if you just keep digging at me and trying to crack me open I'll giggle and say, 'Oh, la, Mr. Hathaway, what a tease you are!'* It wasn't really true; he had never wanted her to be sweeter or kinder. But he had wanted to crack her open. He still did. He wanted her to show herself to him, all the thoughts and feelings she'd been hiding for years.

He'd thought he could make her happy, that everything would be all right if she would just understand that he didn't care about her past—but she was right, it was easy for him not to care. It was Serena who cared, who cared deeply because she'd been deeply hurt. She was still being hurt every day, every time some blackguard like Smollett made a crass joke and every time a party of young bloods bullied a waitress.

This wasn't about him. It was about Serena, and about his brother. They were sick of being afraid—and hell, so was he. He was sick of being afraid that he wasn't good enough, when it had never been about that to begin with. He was sick of dragging things out because he was afraid to put them to the test.

"You're right," he said.

She blinked, her face going from "ready for battle" to "speechless" in about five seconds. He couldn't help laughing, even as his heart ached. How was he going to live, knowing that Serena was across town making a face and he couldn't see it?

"You're right," he said again. "I haven't been fair. I was afraid, too. Afraid of being alone, I suppose. Afraid of being without you. But—you know, I—" His voice cracked. Damn.

"Solomon—" she said, and he loved the way she said his name so much that he had to keep talking or he might do something selfish like tell her that.

"I never believed, before I met you, that I could go my own way," he said. "That I could deserve more than someone was willing to give me. That love might not be worth the sacrifices we have to make for it. You've taught me that. What I mean is—I *do* understand, if you decide you don't want—" He waved a hand between them, as if in a moment the word that would describe all that lay between them would pop into his head. As if such a word existed. He shook his head. "This."

She stared at him, the shadows making her eyes look huge. "You're giving up?"

He stood up. "That's exactly the problem. This has turned into some kind of tug-of-war. I'm not giving up. I'm just saying that I won't push you anymore. I won't ask for anything. I've been torturing you, and it's not fair. If nothing's changed when we go back to London on Sunday, I'll leave. Just please—make a decision that will make you happy. Take good care of yourself."

She looked as lost as he felt. He went to the bed and stood looking down at her: at her perfect face and her perfect body that suddenly, for the first time, looked ordinary.

She wasn't a goddess, or an angel, or a harpy. She was a woman, a frightened, unhappy, determined, beautiful woman, and he loved her so badly that just leaning down and brushing his lips across her left temple, where her birthmark was, brought tears to his eyes. "Thank you for everything," he said, and left.

Chapter 28

Solomon made his way back to the room he shared with Elijah—the room he had shared with his brother since they were born. The candle was out, and Elijah was lying on his side facing the wall, but Solomon could tell that he wasn't sleeping. Last night at the posting inn, it had been the same; but then he had let Elijah pretend and gone directly to his own bed. Not tonight. He lit the candle. "Li?"

After a moment, Elijah turned over and sat up. Except for his boots, he was still fully dressed, wearing his old bottle-green coat. For a jolting moment Solomon thought maybe it was all a dream, that Elijah was dead and not sitting here a few feet away. *It couldn't be a dream,* he told himself. *I would never dream that new darned place in the corner of Elijah's pocket.*

Then he remembered Serena saying that very first night, *You didn't just dream it,* and holding up the corner of her quilt, and the strange sense of vertigo receded. It was all real, and he had been ready to let it slip away without trying.

"Li," he began, "I've been a fool. I ought never to have said what I did—any of it."

Elijah's eyes shot up to meet his. "*What?*"

"Don't look so surprised. I know I've failed you—and if you don't want to speak to me again, at least this time I'll know you're all right—"

To his surprise, Elijah exploded. "Damn it, Sol, what the hell is wrong with you? Of course I want to speak to you again!"

Solomon sat down on the edge of his bed with a thump. "Thank God."

"How could you ever think I wouldn't?"

Solomon rubbed at his temple. "Well—you did without me before, didn't you? I didn't know it, but in a way you've been doing without me all our lives. I thought I knew you like the back of my hand, and now—I don't know what to think. I remember being jealous of you when we were boys because you'd wink at pretty girls in the street when I was afraid to, and I feel as if I must have been blind—"

Elijah said a French word Solomon was sure couldn't be translated in front of their mother. "Afraid—you were *afraid?* It was easy to wink at girls in the street because I didn't *want* them! When it came to what I did want, I was so terrified I could barely see straight. After I kissed Alan the first time, I was sick in the bushes on my way home. I was sure he'd never speak to me again, and he'd tell everyone, and *you'd* never speak to me again either because there was something wrong with me, something twisted and diseased."

"There's nothing wrong with you," Solomon said fiercely.

"Thank you," Elijah said with a rueful smile.

"God, how did I miss this? All those years—was I not paying attention? Didn't I care? How could I have failed you this badly?"

"Oh, for God's sake!" Elijah broke in. "We failed *each other*— you didn't know anything was wrong, but I did, and I didn't fix it. God, I was always so jealous of you, too."

Solomon stared. "Jealous of *me?*"

"Yes, you! You always knew where you belonged. You wanted to work for Uncle Hathaway and you wanted to be a chemist and you were *good* at it. You always knew exactly what you wanted and you always seemed to know what was right. Father approved of you. You didn't while away your hours tinkering in the blacksmith's shop and reading immoral French poetry. And he had no notion of the sick, shameful things I was *really* doing there. When I found out you were all going to think I was dead, I thought, 'At least it's me and not Solomon. None of them would know what to do without him.'" Elijah stopped for a moment. "You had no idea how lucky you were."

So Serena had been right; Elijah didn't think he was the dull, conventional one at all. His brother thought *he* was the lucky one, the one who had always known what to do. They had both been such blundering idiots. "I wish you had told me," he said at last. "You didn't have to do this alone."

"I know that now. But I was afraid. I'm not the dashing, enigmatic one," Elijah said desperately. "I'm just *me*, Sol, and you're ready to let me go because you think I'll be all right, but I *need* you."

"You did all right without me in France," he said, still struggling to accept this new vision of the world.

"You did all right, too."

And as awful as the last year and a half had been, Solomon realized abruptly that Elijah was right. Even if his brother had never come back—life would have gone on, somehow. He could even have been happy. Serena had shown him that it was possible.

Elijah was still speaking. "In books they always say, 'Without you it was as if someone had cut off my arm.' Sol, without you I felt like someone had sawed open my skull and ripped out half my brain. But I had to get the hell out of here. I had to stop being afraid all the time. I had to be alone. Paris was so different from Shropshire—there were clubs full of people like me, and I was helping England, and I was *good* at it. All that careful acting, all those years, had just been *practice*. I felt right, suddenly. But I missed you."

He pressed the heels of his hands into his eyes. "I should have told you I was alive. I told myself you would know so I wouldn't have to admit I was taking the coward's way out."

"We failed each other," Solomon said, and it felt like absolution. He smiled. "So we're all right now?"

Elijah smiled back. "We're all right now."

After a moment, Solomon asked, "When are you leaving for France?"

Elijah looked up guiltily. "As soon as I can. And—I never thanked you—"

"You don't have to."

"I think I do. You shouldn't have done it, but if I had walked into that room and seen his brains all over the wall—" Elijah swallowed.

"I know."

"I may be back very soon. He may not want me anymore."

Solomon snorted. "Doing it a little too brown, Li. When a man's final thought before he blows his brains out is to say what will make you feel best about driving him to it, he wants you."

Elijah looked up quickly. "It wasn't *really* his final thought, was it?"

Solomon assumed a romantic attitude. "'Please, tell him I'"—he sniffled and wiped away an imaginary tear with a dramatic forefinger—"'tell him I never loved him. Tell him I knew all along. Tell him I was a blackhearted rogue. Oh, Elijah, Elijah!'"

Elijah reached over and punched him in the shoulder, but he was beaming. "So—you think he'll take me back?"

"He'd better, or I'll be facing him at twenty paces for trifling with my brother."

"I thought you didn't approve of dueling."

"Well, no sense being slavish about it," Solomon replied airily.

Elijah laughed. "Thanks, Sol." He flashed a wicked grin. "So, you and Serena?"

Solomon swallowed hard and looked away, his relief fading. "I don't know." And finally, he began to tell his brother the whole story.

"I'm glad Solomon brought you," Mrs. Hathaway told Serena as they were in the kitchen preparing for dinner on Saturday.

Serena set down the spoons with a clatter. "How can you be? He oughtn't to have done it."

Mrs. Hathaway's eyebrows rose. "Well, perhaps it was a little thoughtless of him. It hasn't been a very comfortable visit for you, has it?" She sighed. "I hope we haven't given you a disgust of us."

No, it hadn't been a comfortable visit. True to his word, in the day and a half since their arrival Solomon had—not ignored her, never that, but there had been no more intimate conversations. He hadn't flirted. He'd watched her, that was all. His private communications and whispered asides had been saved for Elijah, and while she was glad matters were mended between them, she missed him dreadfully already. And even the new distance between them didn't spare her from Mr. Hathaway's evident skepticism or his attempts to keep Susannah from spending too much time in her company.

The worst of it was that she couldn't even long for the visit to be over, because when it was, they would go back to London and Solomon would leave—unless she asked him to stay. And how could she do that?

"Of course you haven't," she said. "That wasn't what I meant at all. Solomon loves you and I don't want—he'll quarrel with his father and I *told* him he couldn't bring me here even if you're all being very kind ignoring my awful reputation—" Her voice was rising alarmingly; she snapped her mouth shut and stood very still.

"Oh, you poor dear!" Mrs. Hathaway put an arm around Serena's shoulders. "Here, sit down, I see we need to talk. Would you like some tea?"

"No, thank you. Won't they be expecting their dinner?"

Mrs. Hathaway's eyes glinted brown like Solomon's when he was particularly determined about something. "They can wait." So they sat. Serena focused all her energy on not twisting her handkerchief in her lap.

"Allow me to apologize for my husband. I've spoken to him about his behavior, I promise you."

"Oh, I wish you hadn't—"

"I certainly did. But really, you mustn't take it to heart. Mr. Hathaway was much ruder to Jonas, I assure you."

"He was?" Serena wondered what Mr. Hathaway would think of René. Nothing good, probably.

"Jonas won't even come to church anymore."

"Isn't he a Methodist?"

"Yes, but he used to come every week when he was first courting Susannah. That was before some rather sharp words passed between them on the subject of the church's organ."

"The organ?"

Mrs. Hathaway smiled. "My husband is emphatically low church, but he loves that organ, and Solomon plays it. When Jonas intimated that perhaps incense would be next, Mr. Hathaway was very intemperate in his response."

Serena was surprised into a smile. "Oh, dear."

Mrs. Hathaway sighed. "You can't blame Solomon for wanting to show you off."

"What do you mean?"

Mrs. Hathaway smiled fondly. "It's obvious how proud he is of you, and well, he's always been so shy. Elijah was the one who was more popular with girls, you know, and—"

"But Solomon and I aren't—we're not—you didn't really think—" She had never lied so badly in her life.

But Mrs. Hathaway believed her. Her face fell. "Don't you care for Solomon?"

When had she ever cared for anything more? "You thought that Solomon and I—You wouldn't mind Solomon bringing home his—his—"

"Solomon wouldn't bring anyone here that he wasn't in deadly earnest about," Mrs. Hathaway said flatly. "Oh, dear. Are you sure you can't feel anything for him?"

Serena had not the slightest notion what to say. "He'll get over me," she said at last.

"I don't know," Mrs. Hathaway said worriedly. "He doesn't get over things easily. And I've never seen him look at anyone the way he looks at you."

"How—how does he look at me?"

"Don't tell me you haven't noticed! As if—as if he doesn't quite believe he's not dreaming. As if someone had lit a candle behind his eyes. Mr. Hathaway and I—we just assumed—"

Serena got that feeling again, as if everything was tilting sideways, the spoons about to slip off the table and crash onto the floor. "You really *want* me and Solomon to—"

Mrs. Hathaway sighed. "I just want my children to be happy."

"And you think I can make him happy?" An edge of skepticism made its way into Serena's voice despite her best efforts.

Mrs. Hathaway gave her a sharp look. "You don't?"

"I'm not—I'm not the sort of woman who makes people happy," she said, but it was starting to sound unconvincing even to her, as if the idea were a dress she had outgrown.

Mrs. Hathaway pursed her lips. "You don't seem to have made yourself very happy, certainly." She watched Serena, then said, "You know, I ran away from home too when I was a girl."

"Yes, to get married."

"True. I don't say I approve of the choice you made. If Mr. Hathaway hadn't married me, I would have gone back home. But—well, perhaps it's rude of me to tell you this, but I never thought your father would be very easy to live with."

Of course Mrs. Hathaway had known her father. They were all the same age. "Did you—did you know my mother?" she asked, her heart beating faster. She didn't know what she wanted to hear.

Mrs. Hathaway hesitated. "Yes. I—well, she was a very pretty, charming girl. You reminded me of her when we first met. But I don't suppose she could have stood up to him."

Serena blinked back tears, suddenly, for the pretty, charming girl her mother had been—even if Mrs. Hathaway obviously hadn't liked her. Of course Serena's girlish airs and graces, when she used them, were clumsily copied from her mother, who had thought they would protect her and had found out her mistake.

"But what I meant to say is that I do understand what made you do it," Mrs. Hathaway said. "I know what it's like to be raised as a gently bred girl and to feel as if your family is smothering you with a pillow and telling you it's for your own good. I told them to go hang, too, and then I cried myself to sleep when my parents wouldn't speak to me anymore." She laughed. "I was a great trial to him, but Mr. Hathaway was very patient." She reached across the table and put her hand on Serena's arm. "Can you not bring yourself to confide in me?"

To her surprise, Serena wanted to. That *was* how she'd felt, at home. It had been such a relief to break the rules. She'd never heard anyone say it out loud before. But she looked at Mrs. Hathaway, comfortable and motherly with the late afternoon sun streaming through the kitchen windows and turning her butter-colored hair to honey and her hazel eyes a warm gray, and the words dried up in her throat. "No, ma'am," she said with some difficulty. "I'd like to, but—"

"All right, then." Mrs. Hathaway squeezed her arm. "I've been awfully selfish, thinking only of my son, but of course you must follow your own heart. Don't let him wear you down—Solomon can be awfully persistent when he wants something. When he was seven and wanted his first chemistry set, he talked about it for six weeks straight until we sent away to London for it. And then when he decided nothing would do but Cambridge, we heard of nothing else for a good half a year until I gave in and asked my brother if he would send him when he was ready. My brother-in-law didn't want to hire him either. Thought he was born for better things, I suppose." Mrs. Hathaway pressed her lips together for a moment. "But Solomon talked him round. He's always known what he wanted, that boy."

Serena stared at the heap of spoons. Did Solomon really know what he wanted? Because if he did, then—

Serena had believed that she would make Solomon and herself miserable, and that he would let her. But—he wasn't letting her, was he? He was breaking it off. All this time, she had called him naive and deluded for loving her. But maybe Mrs. Hathaway was right—he merely saw things as they were and knew what he wanted.

She had thought of herself as different from other women; she had thought of Mrs. Hathaway as practically another species. But they were the same, really. Or they could be. The difference between them was that, like Solomon, Mrs. Hathaway dared to try to be happy.

That wasn't naiveté, it was confidence and courage, and Serena had refused to see it because then she would have to face her own fear and self-doubt, her own inability to believe she could have what she wanted—or having it, that she could be worthy of it.

What had Solomon said? That sometimes love wasn't worth what one had to sacrifice for it? Serena was suddenly afraid that all the things she had refused to sacrifice might not be worth what she had lost, what she still stood to lose. She had moped all this time about being ruined, but here she was, ruining herself. Turning herself into a hermit and a coward.

"I—would you be very angry if I asked Solomon to take a walk with me instead of going to dinner?" she asked. It was rude, but she didn't want to wait.

Mrs. Hathaway gave her a beaming smile. "Not at all."

Chapter 29

The sky was gray, but it was warm and the country lanes were picturesque. The path they were on led to an apple wood half a mile off, and when they wandered off onto the grass it was uneven and soft underfoot. Everything was so different from London. She had forgotten how clear the air was in the country.

"Solomon, I—" Now that the moment was here, she didn't know how to begin. "I—I want to talk to you."

"I thought you might." His face, for once, gave nothing away.

"I don't—I don't know how to say it." Her tongue felt clumsy in her mouth.

"You never do," he said with a touch of bitterness.

"Don't be an ass," she said. "I'm trying."

"You don't have to."

"Don't patronize me. I know I don't. But I am, because I want to."

"You look like you'd rather have your teeth pulled with red-hot pincers," he said. "When I tell you I love you, you look at me as if I'm holding your head underwater. I can't—I don't want to hurt you. I don't want to be like Daubenay. I don't want to make demands and beg until you hate me." But he waited, listening. He'd always believed she could do this, if she wanted to.

A few drops of summer rain splashed onto her hand and she shook them off. "I could never hate you," she got out. And yes, she *would* rather have her teeth pulled with red-hot pincers, but pulling out her teeth would never bring that wild, wary hope into Solomon's eyes.

And surely nothing, not even this, could be more terrifying

than losing him. Serena was tired of putting a brave face on things. She plunged forward.

"I'm no good at hating people, can't you see that? I try and I try and—oh, Lord Smollett is easy, I hate him right enough, but just look what happened with René. I thought he'd turned on me, I thought he didn't care what became of me, and I still couldn't hate him. I gossiped with him, I laughed at his jokes, I persuaded Elijah not to turn him in to the Foreign Office, and it wasn't because of those marriage lines. It was because the thought of him with a noose around his neck and a knife in his gut made me ill. And what I feel for you—it's so much more." It was raining a little harder now, but Serena didn't move, didn't even raise a hand to shield her face. Neither did Solomon.

"It's easy for you to say 'I love you.' Plenty of people have loved you and stood by you and told you you were worth the trouble. I—it isn't easy for me. I don't know how to say it, I don't know how to do it. I don't even know if this is love. It's deeper than I thought it would be—if I tried to uproot it, it would pull my heart out of my chest. I need you so desperately. I need you to make demands, I need you to hurt me. I need you to love me, and you could *stop*. You could decide I'm not what you wanted after all, that I'm not worth the trouble, and I won't be able to stop feeling this way, I won't be able to hate you, I won't be able to *live*—"

Tears stood in her eyes and Solomon, Solomon was looking at her like she was the Holy Grail, like she was the sacred thing he'd been seeking all his life.

"Oh, God, Serena, I—" he began incoherently. Then he stopped himself, smiling shakily. "I'll try to save the transports and the fevered kisses for a few minutes from now, shall I?"

She stared at her interlocked hands. They were white at the knuckles. A drop of water fell from her hair into her eyes. "I would appreciate that."

"You've never made any particular effort to be pleasant to me, have you?"

She shook her head.

"You've been quite a lot of trouble, haven't you?"

"Yes," she said in a low voice.

"I think you're worth it. And I always will."

"Why?"

"There isn't—there isn't a *reason*. I just love you." She opened her mouth to protest and he said, "All of you. Even the wretched parts. Even your nasty streak and your boring gray gowns."

She didn't know what to say. She didn't know what more she needed to hear.

"Now you're just fishing for compliments," he said.

"I am not," she said indignantly, and he stopped trying to hide his smile. He pulled her to him, turning her so her back was to his front, and wrapped his arms around her. "I love you because you understand me," he whispered in her ear. "I love you because you never give up. I love you because we both hate that Jack Ashton doesn't pay his bills on time, and because there is no dye that can match the color of your eyes." He nipped her ear. "Besides, have you ever looked in a mirror?"

She hit him, laughing, and then they were tussling and swatting at each other, giggling and dizzy and light-headed. They fetched up against an apple tree, shaking water down on themselves, and a small red-and-gold apple fell from the tree past Solomon's shoulder. Solomon reached out and caught it with unwonted grace.

"'As the apple tree among the trees of the wood, so is my beloved among the sons,'" she quoted, as he dried the fruit on his sleeve. "And what am I? A Thorn among the lilies."

He stilled in his polishing, and met her gaze. "'Thou art all fair, my love, there is no spot in thee,'" he promised softly, "no spot save this"—he brushed a thumb over the birthmark on her brow, and she shivered—"and this"—he made a small circle with his finger on her chemisette, over where the second birthmark lay, and desire unfurled inside her like a flowering tree—"and this—"

"Solomon!" she snapped in a small, pleased tone, and his eyes gleamed.

"I wouldn't trade one of those spots for all the muslin in India," he told her. "And is there any difference, really, between a thorn among lilies and a lily among thorns?"

But Serena did not give this philosophical speculation the attention it deserved, because Solomon held out the apple in his scarred hand and the world ground to a halt. Slowly, she reached out and took it. Slowly she brought it to her lips, and just as her teeth broke the skin with a crunch, he said, "Marry me."

Serena choked and spat out apple onto the ground. She stared at him in stunned disbelief. "You can't be serious."

He laughed. "So you're willing to accept my pledges of undying devotion, but you can't believe that I want to marry you?"

"But—but—" she sputtered, "have you run mad? You don't *marry* a woman like me. You *can't*. It just—it isn't *done*."

"Funny, I never thought that would be *your* objection. Not quite as unconventional as you like to appear, are you, my straitlaced sweetheart?"

There was a challenge in his eyes, and something in Serena rose joyfully to meet it. After all, she had never refused a dare in her life. "All right," she said, and found to her surprise that it was easy. She took another bite of apple. It was sweet and tart and tasted like happiness. "Let's get married."

He beamed. "If my father starts reading the banns next Sunday, we can be married in a month."

There was a problem with that, but Serena wanted to let him smile a little while longer. "Will your father mind?" she asked instead.

"Are you joking? This is exactly what he wants. It's us living in sin that he'd hate."

Serena blinked. Then she gave up; nothing made sense when Hathaways were involved. And she couldn't put off reminding him any longer. "It may not be for some time, though," she cautioned.

"What do you mean?"

"I'm still legally married to René."

He caught her hands. "Poor Serena. This isn't the best month of your life, is it? And here I am asking you to give me more—"

And now it was her turn to reach up and gently place a hand over his mouth. He bit her palm lightly, and she felt a lazy warmth settle in her belly. "It *is* the best month of my life," she told him. "And if René's papers don't get me an annulment, we can save up for a divorce, and perhaps in five or ten years—" It still seemed unreal, to think *in five or ten years*, and to believe that Solomon would be there.

Unexpectedly, he grinned behind her hand. "You'll get an annulment. Just leave it to me."

She raised her eyebrows. "Suffering delusions of grandeur?"

"Don't you trust me?" he asked with a teasing grin.

And the funny thing was, she did. He wouldn't say it if he didn't know it was true. "With my life."

He grinned wider. "I'm going to trade the Prince Regent Mother's tartlet recipe."

Oh God, that would really work. It would, and they would be married—she lunged at him and kissed him. It hurt her jaw, but she didn't care.

A short time later, she said rather unsteadily, "But don't think this means I'm not going to insist on very stringent marriage settlements."

"I never for a moment thought you wouldn't." He laughed. "I feel faint with happiness. If I swoon, don't tell my uncle, all right?"

She smiled suggestively. "Do you know what would make you even more light-headed?"

His eyes lit with anticipation.

"Cartwheels," she said cruelly.

His eyes narrowed. "It's raining."

"Not very hard."

"I'd rather stay here, where it's nice and dry." He began nuzzling her neck. It was actually fairly wet under the tree, but Serena didn't say so.

"How—how often do people walk this way?" she gasped.

"Not very often," he said, and kept going.

When they walked back to the house, sometime later, they were both dripping wet and muddy in patches. "I think you ruined my dress," Serena grumbled happily.

"I'll make you another."

Serena looked about her at the misty, sparkling countryside. Everything looked clean and new and full of possibilities. She lifted the muddy hem of her skirt away from her toes with one hand, and reached out for Solomon's hand with the other. "I want a red one."